PRAISE FOR JOHN SHIRLEY

"Shirley writes at the neon-lit frontier of sensory experience."
—*Publisher's Weekly*

"Snapping, snarling, vigorously wrought drama . . . Shirley writes splendid stuff."—*Kirkus Reviews*

"John Shirley has a reporter's eye and a demon's attitude. His stories will have you laughing one minute and curling into a sweaty fetal knot the next. If Jon Stewart was possessed by the devil these tales are what he'd sound like." —Richard Kadrey

"John Shirley serves up the bloody heart of a sick and rotting society with the aplomb of an Aztec surgeon on dexadrine . . ." —*Booklist*

". . . all his stories . . . give off the chill of top-grade horror. It's a moral chill, because Shirley's great subject is the terrible ease with which we modern Americans have learned to look away from pain and suffering . . . And while the matter of his stories is often shocking, his manner is calm, restrained. The prose is attitude-free and precise, its characteristic sound a minor chord of sorrow and banked anger. He writes about sensation un-sensationally, with a particular tenderness toward those who manage, against the odds and by whatever means, to feel something . . ." —*New York Times Review of Books*

". . . one of the darkest, edgiest, boldest writers around . . . [Shirley writes with] adrenalized, jivey, yet extremely artful prose that fairly skids across the page, dragging the reader along with it into shadowed corners of terror and desire. Yet while it's thrilling, there's psychological depth in it, too, as Shirley bores into the brains of his characters, revealing the motivations of those who walk on the wild side." —*Publishers Weekly*

IN EXTREMIS

THE MOST EXTREME SHORT STORIES OF
JOHN SHIRLEY

underland
U
press
UNDERLANDPRESS.COM

IN EXTREMIS:
THE MOST EXTREME SHORT STORIES OF JOHN
SHIRLEY
© 2011 John Shirley. All rights reserved.

Underland Press
www.underlandpress.com
Portland, Oregon

Cover design by Heidi Whitcomb
Book design by Heidi Whitcomb

ISBN13: 978-0-9826639-4-3

Printed in the United States of America
Distributed by PGW

First Underland Press Edition: August 2011

1 3 5 7 9 10 8 6 4 2

Printed in USA

CONTENTS

For Harlan Ellison

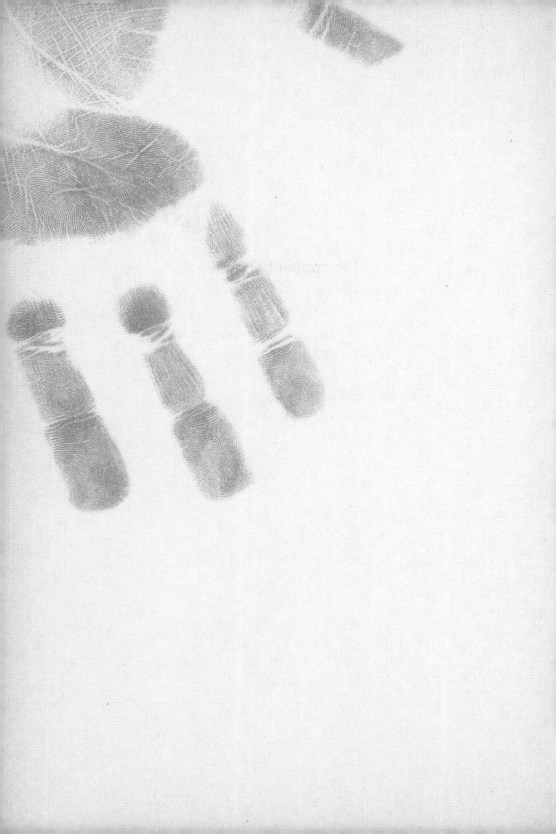

*Special thanks to Paula Guran,
who did a lot of work on this.*

*And thanks to Victoria Blake for her
visionary publishing and editorial help.*

*Also: a special thanks to Robert Curry.
Additional thanks to Micky Shirley.*

AN INTRODUCTION BY THE AUTHOR

in ex·tre·mis (ĭn ĕk-strē'mĭs) adv.
1. At the point of death.
2. In grave or extreme circumstances.

[Latin *in extrēmīs*: in, *in* + *ēxtrēmīs*, ablative pl. of *ēxtremus*, *extreme*.]
—*The American Heritage Dictionary of the English Language, Fourth Edition*.

Extremes are revealing. People under high duress show their dark sides and their heroism, their fears and their deepest secrets. Immediacy, urgency, rage, fear, degradation, wild disorientation, despair, perverse heights of joy—these are like lenses lined up in a microscope exposing the inner reality of the human condition.

The subtitle of this book is a risk—it could sound like pop debris. To some it might evoke "extreme sports" or "extreme video." There's a bowling alley near my home that has an "extreme bowling" night. Still, "the most extreme stories of" seemed the best way to say it. Why should we allow the word *extreme* to be hijacked by low commerce?

Much "extreme" writing is insignificant—it's the worst of pulp or it's mere porn, or self- indulgence—as in brutality for the sake of it. But other sorts of extreme writing have historically been quite significant. There were the novels by de Sade—I'm not a fan, but they were his honest attempt at art. There was "The Tell-Tale Heart" by Poe, its narrator in an extreme psychological state. Remember also the very dark late-career work of Mark Twain. There were heart-piercing stories by Ambrose Bierce; there were prose poems by Baudelaire eloquently extolling excess; there was Mirbeau's *The Torture Garden*;

there was Celine; there was Artaud's "Theatre of Cruelty" (its plays were not about sadism, but about confrontation with reality). We might think of the novels of Hubert Selby; or *The Killer Inside Me* by Jim Thompson—or *The Painted Bird* by Jerzy Kosinki. There were extreme works by Charles Bukowski and William Burroughs and Dennis Cooper, of course. There was J.G. Ballard's *The Atrocity Exhibition*; there were several particularly edgy works by Harlan Ellison (e.g., "A Boy and His Dog"); there were certain works by Samuel Delany. And one could compare it to extreme forms of music, like Penderecki, and the more powerful punk rock.

Some of the stories in this volume are *fleurs du mal* sprouting in the outer fringes of the American demimonde: they dramatize the extreme effects the worst drugs can have on people, the sick desperation that underlies prostitution, the instinctual power of violence; they explore sexual madness. Some characters and situations in this collection are based on my own lapses into that society, years ago. I had a window on some very extreme scenes. I met murderers, crack whores, and a good many "straight" men and women dragged down by that world. I've left those scenes behind—but much of what I saw stays with me.

I don't see those people as monsters—though they can be monstrous—I see them as people caught up by powerful impulses they don't understand. They are, in fact, human beings blindly trying to fumble their way out of their own special mazes.

A kind of bizarre, damaged sexual imagery crops up in this collection, with some regularity, though not in every story. Sexual extremes are instructive; they delve into the unconscious. Those passages are certainly not intended to be sexually arousing. If they are, consult your physician. (Of course, if it happens you're an eighteen-year-old boy, almost anything sexual is sexually arousing).

Other stories, here, are about social extremes. Some explore the surreal. Some are more intense than others, but they all explore some form of extremity. Some of them—like the first story in the book, or "Just Like Suzie"—evoke dark comedy, or absurdity, even "absurdism." They mingle horror and humor, liquefy them, stir them into one cocktail. Others are more frankly nightmarish.

In search of extreme effects, I broke some standard writing rules in a few of these tales—for example, occasional lines written IN ALL CAPS, in certain of the more absurdist works. I experimented. But I was in control of each story in this book.

I should mention that I've re-edited some of the older stories, and even updated them a little. I've arranged the stories in the collection to contrast with one another in tone, where possible; there is a certain rhythm in the levels of intensity as the book goes on.

Also, *In Extremis* is framed by shattered worlds: the first and last stories involve apocalypse. We start with the ultimate extreme and we end on it.

Finally, as I've written a good many extreme stories, this collection could have been 150,000 words instead of 100,000. But that would have made it unwieldy. Stories like "Jody and Annie on TV," "Six Kinds of Darkness," "Barbara" and "Equilibrium," to name a few, are conspicuously absent. But I had to make choices, and I was biased toward including more recent works. I wrote "The Gun as an Aid to Poetry" specifically for *In Extremis: The Most Extreme Stories of John Shirley.*

John Shirley
September 2010

YOU BLUNDERING IDIOT
YOU FUCKING FAILED TO KILL ME AGAIN

The Macrobeing had heard about the planet—it had heard terrible, appalling stories of conditions there. Out of curiosity and some awesome, unimaginable, cosmic variation of pity, the Macrobeing descended through many levels, through layers of laws, through dimension after dimension, down to a mere three dimensions, to see this world for itself. To see if the story was true . . .

Other members of the Macrobeings macroscopic race speculated that there must be some good and sufficient reason this planet was so polluted, so verminous, so pestilential, so dominated by brutality and predation—but the Macrobeing wasn't convinced. It wasn't so sure at all that this horror, the planet Earth, should be allowed to continue. The problem wasn't merely the dominant race: the lower animals, too, lived mostly by preying on one another—actually eating one another!—or by trying to avoid being eaten.

It seemed cruel to allow it to go on.

Samuel Masterson Helleck figured that Stubs Grunauer was the man for the job. Grunauer was bulky and strong and indifferent to the feelings of others out of an innate, happy-go-lucky stupidity, like a rhino stepping heedlessly on a bird, and he'd do anything for money that didn't require real sweat-breaking work, or thinking, and he never thought about consequences so he wouldn't worry about legality. Grunauer had been quite surprised the time he was arrested for breaking into a supermarket at night and cooking a steak on the concrete floor in the back room—he'd piled up barbecue charcoal. When the cops came in, alerted by several alarms, Grunauer was just sitting there drinking cheap vodka from a bottle—though he could just as easily have taken the good stuff off the shelves—and watching his steak sizzle directly on the coals . . .

"What? I was fucking *hungry,* dude!" he told them.

So Helleck figured that two hundred dollars would be enough to induce Grunauer to kill him—to effectuate his suicide—even though Grunauer was only three days out of jail.

A big man with a slack mouth and perpetual halitosis, his dishwater-hair cut in the shape of a bowl around his pimply forehead, Grunauer was wearing a black and silver Oakland Raiders shirt, a size too small for him, so that his gut slopped out under it, that drizzly July day in Fremont, California.

"Supposed to be sun out, in July," Grunauer observed as Helleck came into the weedy, junked-up backyard of Grunauer's white crackerbox house. Actually it was the house of Grunauer's long-suffering mother.

Grunauer was standing there in the drizzle, in his sagging jeans and rotting tennis shoes, gaping up at the sky, a forty of Olde English in his right hand.

"You keep standing like that, Grunauer," Helleck said, "eventually you're going to drown."

Grunauer blinked away rain, drank some beer, and looked at Helleck. He didn't seem surprised to see Helleck here, in his backyard, though they hadn't seen each other for seventeen years. Helleck's straw-like hair had receded to just above his ears, marking the passage of years, but Grunauer behaved as if they'd just seen each other at high school that day. "I mean, this fucking rain, man," Grunauer said. "You bring any beer, Helleck? I'm about out."

Grunauer had been a linebacker on the school team, Helleck had played tight end. Helleck had left the team because the coach wouldn't consider him when quarterback opened up—typical, in Helleck's view, of the unfair hands dealt to him by life. The coach was prejudiced against him because of his obvious artistic gifts—jocks always resented a genius—and then girls turned from him because, in all probability, they were intimidated by his spontaneous brilliance. Bosses fired him because his wit was too acerbic, his insight into their foibles too shatteringly incisive.

Helleck could take no more of the world's persecution. He would punish all humanity by withdrawing from it, and afterwards, after his death, his poetry, his lyrics, the acoustic songs he'd put up online, would shine out, would take the world by storm, and he would be appreciated like Van Gogh, like Poe, like Fred Smargenbarger. Well, not many knew about Fred Smargenbarger, but Helleck would never forget his immortal lines:

I turn to survey the fruit of my squatting—
How my crap shines in the moonlight!

Smargenbarger was a fellow unsung genius, in Helleck's view.

Helleck looked around the tatty backyard with distaste; saw a dead cat half hidden by a tarp in one corner; also a rusting oil barrel, an old soft-plastic kiddy pool, a rusting tire rim, a rusting wheel barrow, several overgrown piles of bricks.

"Your bricks are missing their brac," said Helleck.

Grunauer just stared at him. What had he expected? Wit was lost on the witless. But that made Grunauer perfect for the job: too stupid to think he might get arrested later if the cops came on him doing the deed.

"Grunauer," Helleck said. "I want to hire you for two hundred dollars."

"To do what?"

"To kill me. And I'll pay you for it."

"Uhhhh . . . 'kay," Grunauer said. "My ma's been getting on me, I don't earn no money. I remember when I forgot to go to school that year, she said, 'You ain't gonna earn no money if you don't go to school.' Only, I never figured out where they paid you at school—"

"Grunauer? Shut up. If you want the two hundred dollars, shut up. Now—here's one hundred dollars of the money."

He handed Grunauer five twenties, half of what remained of his final unemployment check. "Here's the first half. You get the second hundred after . . ."

Grunauer blinked at him. "You give it to me after I kill you?"

"What? No, no, no . . . after I'm dead, look in my wallet, there's an address where the rest is, under my bed."

"Wait—who'd you say you wanted me to kill?"

"Me."

"You? No, but . . . who?"

"Me, you idiot, me! It's a suicide! I want to be dead! The world doesn't fucking deserve me! And I don't think I could bring myself to jump off a building or something—I'd lose my nerve. Someone's got to *do it to me*."

Grunauer nodded seven or eight times. Then he nodded three times more. Then twice more. "'Kay. You bring, um, a gun?"

"No. I looked into that, and it's really hard to buy a gun legally, takes weeks. I've got to get this done while I'm psyched to do it. And I already sent the letters to the papers and editors and everyone with samples of my poetry and tapes of my songs and stuff. So it's gotta be done. I tried to buy a gun on the street but I couldn't find anybody I trusted not to pretend they were gonna sell me a gun and just take the money and not come across with the gun—since, after all, they'd have a gun and I wouldn't. So we're gonna do it some other way."

"How you want me to kill you?"

"Well . . . is that an old kiddy pool, there? One of those little inflatable swimming pools?"

"Yuh. My mum found it on some free stuff heap somewheres." Grunauer took another long pull of his beer.

"It's already half full of water—just fill it with the hose there and hold my head down in it."

"Uh-kay . . . No."

"What?"

"I don't mind doin' the job of killing you but fillin' it up is *work*, dude."

"I . . . fuck it, I'll do it." Helleck found a hose, turned the water on, filled the blue and yellow plastic kiddy pool. There were pictures of SpongeBob mixed with some kind of dancing grinning starfish around the side. SpongeBob and that starfish would witness his death and rejoice with him. There was a poem in that, somewhere. But the time for all that was past—except for the final poetic statement; his death.

Helleck tossed the hose aside, knelt, and waved Grunauer over. "Okay, come on, hold my head down in here till I drown."

"Uh-kay, yuh sure. The money's in your wallet?"

"No, the rest of it's at my house, the address is in my wallet. Come on, let's get it done!"

Grunauer finished the Olde English, tossed the bottle aside with a clunk, and sat on Helleck so that his face was smashed down into the water.

Helleck immediately tried to cry out in protest—somehow being crushed by Grunauer's ass lacked dignity as a way to die—but water filled his mouth and nose and rushed down into his lungs and SpongeBob seemed to dance in front of him, wavering through the lens of the water as he drowned, and he reflected that, after all, drowning is drowning. Fuck, but this really hurt, it hurt in his lungs, he hoped it would be over soon. It really, really hurt. It was too much, it hurt too much, and he started flailing around to break free and—

That moron Grunauer stood up.

Helleck sat up, spewing water, coughing, and heard a woman talking, the bent little white-haired toothless woman in the stained shift who'd let him into the backyard, Grunauer's mother. "I don't care what he is paying you, you sure as hell can't do that here," she was saying. "Now Stubs git out of here with that, I don't want to know about it! And leave the money here for me to take care of!"

"Uh-kay Ma."

"Grunauer," Helleck managed to say, between gasps, "you idiot! You could have ignored her and finished the job!"

"Naw, she hides the TV remote if I don't do what she says."

"Oh for Christ's—alright, come on, let's go somewhere else."

Helleck's lungs still burned as they walked out through the gate, past the yammering old lady, neither one of them taking in what she was saying, then down the street two blocks to the railroad tracks that ran through a district of mostly abandoned warehouses. They crossed the gravel strip to the tracks and then Grunauer got an inspired look on his face and pointed. "Huh look, there's a big piece-a metal like a crowbar kinda thing—them railroad guys musta lost it there. I could use that to bash you in! Put your head on the railroad tracks!"

Helleck grimaced—but then shrugged and said, "Why not—it sounds quick. Just get it done fast, okay?"

"Yuh."

Helleck lay down on the gravel, head on the railing, right side down, and began singing one of his songs.

I don't care If you don't know it
I know I'm a genius and the world doesn't deserve me
I know it because the rats tell it to the cockroaches who told it to me
So fuck you all, fuck you all, fuck you all, fuck you all . . ."

He broke off and looked sidelong up at Grunauer who was towering over him, a smelly silhouette. "Grunauer—what are you waiting for?"

"I was listening to your song!"

"Just tell people you heard it at the end and how great you thought it was—now do it! Break my skull!"

"Uh-kay."

Helleck closed his eyes, half inclined to run—but it was too late, he heard a whipping sound of something coming through the air, and then—*crack*. Tremendous pain in his left ear. This is it! The end!

Tremendous pain, waves of pain, on the left side of his head . . .

That didn't stop. Just . . . that one crack and then . . .

He opened his eyes. "Grunauer—shit that hurts!—why'd you stop?"

Grunauer's voice sounded distorted through all the blood pooling in his ear. "Yuh ain't dead yet?"

"No!"

"My arm hurts—that thing's heavy!"

"So?" Helleck felt dizzy, removed, dreamlike. "You only hit me once! Now bust my fuckin' skull!"

"Uh-kay."

Crack. Another blazing pain this time on the side of his head above his ear.

"Shit! Ow! Can't you hit straight! Kill me!"

"I want some more beer, dude!"

"Get it later! Come on, I paid you—make like Nike and just fucking do it! "

"I just . . . it's fucked up Helleck . . . I don't like breaking open heads . . . it makes my stomach hurt! I like *stabbing* okay . . . couldn't I stab you some?"

"What? With what? Ow, my fucking head . . ."

"There's a big old rusty nail lying over here . . . on this wood thing . . . useta be old Gunky's shack . . ."

"Whatever, just get it fucking done! I can't stand this! End it! Stab me—here, I'm turning on my back, stab me in the chest, stab me now, stab me in the fucking chest RIGHT FUCKING NOW!"

"I didn't pick up the nail yet."

"You . . . moron!"

"Wait, I got it now . . . I got it . . . Oh, let me put down this other thing . . . okay . . . hey, there's old Gunky down there, waving! Maybe he's got some wine! When I was a kid he gave me wine if I let him play with my peter! Do you think he's got some wine, Helleck?"

"WILL YOU FUCKING KILL ME YOU CRETIN?"

"I don't like to be called names. But, whatever, dude. Uh-kay. I'm kneeling down here . . . Ow—kneeling here on these rocks hurts my knees, dude!"

"My fucking skull is cracked! You don't think that hurts? Just do the job! FUUUUUUUCK! NOW! STAB ME IN THE HEART RIGHT FUCKING NOW!"

"Uh-kay."

Grunauer took the long rusty nail in his hand the way a man holds an ice pick, and stabbed down—right into Helleck's breastbone.

"EEEEE-YOWWWWW that fucking hurts! You dumbass dick-licking shithead—that's not my heart!"

"I thought your heart was right there in the middle, ain't that where a heart is, dude? We always put our hands over that spot when we was in grade school and they made us do the Pledge of Allegiance—"

"No, *fuc*—get it out, it's fucking killing me! I mean it's not killing me, it's hurting me! Pry it out . . ."

"It's stuck . . ."

"OWWWWWWWW!" Helleck reached up and pried the nail out of his breastbone himself and handed the nail up to Grunauer. "Now here! Stab it in my heart—my heart is right over here! See where I'm pointing? It's right—*FUCKING OW!* What are you doing, you stabbed me in the hand!"

"You said to stab where you were pointing and your hand was there and—"

"No, under my hand!"

"I can't get under your hand because it's in the way—and now your hand is nailed to your chest! It looks really cool! But it's stuck on your chest! The nail went right through and—"

"AUUUGH!" And Helleck pulled the nail out of his hand, and chest, and—his uninjured hand trembling so much he could barely hold onto the nail—he handed it again to Grunauer. "Will you just get it over with! Stab in that same hole but deeper, between the ribs, right into my heart!"

"Right there? Uh-kay!"

Grunauer stabbed but the nail glanced off a rib, cracking it.

"ARGH FUCKING OW FUCKING SHIT FUCKING PISS THAT FUCKING HURTS!"

"You said, you SAID right there, Helleck!"

"But I said between the ribs, you can see where the ribs are—"

"But it's all slippy like with blood and I can't aim with all that blood!"

"Try fucking AGAIN!"

"Uh-kay."

Grunauer clamped his tongue between his crusty teeth, closed one eye, and, aiming carefully, he stabbed down. But the nail only stuck out under his fist an inch or so and it didn't quite go deep enough to penetrate Helleck's heart—it just *scratched* the outside of his heart painfully.

"EEEEH YOW! You fucking idiot!"

Invisible and all-encompassing, vast but subtle, the Macrobeing had surveyed most of the planet Earth, had paused in several places—Darfur, parts of India, parts of Florida, a concentration camp in North Korea, hundreds of thousands of old people's homes and hospices . . . and was still uncertain. On the one hand, Earth seemed to cry out for a compassionate veterinary "putting down—but on the other hand it seemed to the Macrobeing that though indeed these creatures lived, at best, lives of quiet existential confusion and misery, and at worst lived with great suffering, there were also positive, redemptive feelings and events and ideas, and maybe this world should be allowed to go on so that these creatures could evolve . . .

And then it noticed a spike of suffering in a part of "California" called "Fremont" and it glanced down to see Grunauer trying to kill Helleck—all the time Helleck begging him to do it—and the Macrobeing watched them in sickened fascination for a while . . .

"You have to . . . to . . . to . . ."

"To what, Helleck?"

"Stuh . . . stuh . . . stuh . . ."

"I don't know whatcha saying, yuh not talking English—"

"STAB ME! STAB ME IN THE HEART YOU IDIOT! PUSH IT
IN and . . . OH FUCK . . ." Helleck had to pause to turn over and
vomit up his meager breakfast. This took a while. Finally he flopped
onto his back with a groan. "Push the nail in and then hammer it in
my heart with that crowbar . . ."

"Uh-kay."

Grunauer shoved the nail in, then got the bar of iron, and started
to hammer at the nail with it—but he aimed badly, and the nail
went to the side and jammed in the tissue under Helleck's pectoral,
over the heart . . .

"YAHHHHHH! That hurts! YOU MISSED, you fucking MORON
you!"

"Helleck—a train's coming! You could jump in front of it!"

"No . . . no . . . can't do it myself—you . . . you . . . you got to throw
me in front of it! Pick me up! I'm small, you're strong—pick me up—"

"Uh-kay."

Grunauer picked Helleck up in his arms and moved back from the
tracks and waited and in a moment the freight train came barreling
along, screaming with its horn, and Grunauer got close to the train
and tossed Helleck between two freight cars—

Only he did it clumsily and Helleck didn't quite go in, but got stuck
with his arm between the car and the metal wheel and was dragged
along. His backbone curled, his arm twisted right off with a pop,
and then the train was gone and Helleck was left there in a bloody
wrenched semi-human pile next to the tracks, groaning and alive . . .

"Helleck—you ain't dead . . . dude?"

"No you BLUNDERING IDIOT, you failed to kill me AGAIN!"
Helleck cried, though it was difficult to see where his mouth was in
the knotted-up wreckage of him.

"Uh-kay. Sorry. Hey I guess that's half of the killin' anyway. You
can keep the other half of the money. I got to go, my mom was gonna
make me something to eat."

"What? You FUCKER! Stay here and kill me! Just get a big rock or jump up on my head or—"

"I can't, I think the police is coming—"

"You'd better fucking kill me or I'll tell them you hurt me without being paid to. Now dammit, KILL ME!"

"No, well, uh . . . I dunno . . . 'zactly . . . what should I do?"

Watching Helleck and Grunauer, the Macrobeing had had enough. These two seemed to sum up this world, in a general way they were the final straw, the turning point. The Macrobeing made up its mind, pity got the best of it. The Macrobeing decided to put this planet out of its misery.

So the vast amorphous creature stretched out its energy field, and encompassed the planet Earth, enclosed it like a small animal in a man's fist, and squeezed, just enough . . .

And in just under ninety-three seconds the entire Earth was wiped clean of life. Painlessly and entirely. It was all gone, even plants, even microorganisms. The Macrobeing liked to be thorough. Since there were no micro-organisms left after it was done, there was no decay, and all the organisms in the world simply stopped moving and stopped living and sometime later each one fell into a nice dry heap of dust.

Afterwards, Macrobeings would sometimes visit the lifeless planet, simply because it was so very peaceful there . . .

CRAM

Gino and Telly were already half an hour late and the BART train was just now leaving the last station in Oakland. The train gave out a soft squeal as it started out of the station, snaking into the underground tube for the trip across the bay to the Embarcadero. "It don't matter, dude," Telly was saying, "Geisenbaum don't give a fuck which fuckin' bike messengers are there, long as somebody's there to take out the first packages." Telly was lean, muscular, tanned, long hair tied in three pony tails. He wore a sleeveless *Coil* tee he'd bought from a scalper at the concert, and surfer shorts. Telly didn't like the tan he got on his arms from biking the waterfront. It blurred his tattoos. But he wore the short sleeves so the tats could be seen.

"Yeah, Telly, but if he's got a morning rush floodin' packages, we'll get our asses fired."

Gino could talk acceptable bike-messenger but he was a night school grad student in Modern Lit, Postmodern Specialties, when he had the tuition. And he'd pulled a 3.8 with almost no effort at UC Berkeley, majoring in English Lit, minor in Philosophy.

Working with guys like Telly was philosophically satisfying, it was Working Class. It gave Gino a sense of meshing with the genetic core of humanity, the people who'd rejected him in high school. The ones who knew how to be really *into* whatever they were into.

Gino only had the one tat, the Maori pattern around his wrist like a bracelet. Enough to give him credibility with the Tellys, not enough to prevent his getting tenure someday.

Telly had his bike with him on the subway car; Gino's bike was locked up at Geisenbaum's. Telly'd picked up some glares pushing the glossy black, sticker-swathed mountain bike into the crowded train car. It was the last car, where you could bring a bike, but this car was packed and so was every other car for the peak of morning rush hour. The bike's pedals jammed into the ankles of the lady, probably a lawyer, in a grey pants-suit standing across from Telly; its handlebars forced a heavyset, heavy-breathing man in a red jogging outfit to hold his gut in. Telly usually said "Hope nobody farts, bro'," when it was like this but, mercifully, hadn't said it so far. He and Gino got seats when two people got off at the downtown Oakland stop. Telly was leaning on the bicycle seat, and in the swaying press of people looming around them they felt agreeably hidden away though they could smell the exact proportions of sweat mixed with perfume and deodorant around them.

Gino knew for a fact that the lady in lavender with the big hair, standing next to his left knee, had a yeast infection. Her crotch smelled like a bakery on fire.

"Big shit, if he fires us," Telly was saying, tugging on a tuft of goatee. "How many messenger services can we work for? Beaucoup bikin' out there, bro'."

Gino leaned back a little to peer through the swaying forest of fabric and torsos, thinking about losing his job, at the same time trying to define what was always so odd about the light here in the crossbay tunnel. Beneath sand and silt and sharks and ships and a sheath of rock and concrete, there was not a trace of light here except the artificial light.

His gaze settled on a black security guard squeezed in the access passage to the back door of the car, the guy was at least a hundred pounds overweight, with a long silvery cop's flashlight propped on one shoulder like a sentry with his rifle. Beside the fat black guy was a woman in the same kind of Brinks uniform—she was round-faced, otherwise skinny, with badly conked hair. She had a flashlight too. Both of them standing, wedged together. They weren't guards for BART. Why'd they need a flashlight at this hour, working downtown? Maybe they were coming off-shift from an all-nighter in the East Bay. They looked tired enough. And their expressions said they were underpaid.

"I like working for Geisenbaum," Gino said at last, "he pays fifty cents an hour more than most of 'em."

Telly ducked his head to acknowledge a baseline truth. "We gettin' there, dude." He looked at his Zippy the Pinhead watch, then reached down and absently flicked his thumbnail up the spokes on his bicycle wheel, the faint twang almost lost in the metallic hiss-and-rumble of the BART train as it strobed past tunnel lights. He continued the motion up the spokes and past the wheel to flick, finally, the ring in his lower lip and the one through his nose; sounds you couldn't hear. He was peacock proud of his tattoos and his piercings. Glanced at the twining red-and-bluegreen Chinese dragon on his forearm as he raised it to look again at Zippy's gloves on his watch, repeating: "We gettin' there—"

He broke off, lifting his head, listening like a dog at a whistle pitched too high for everyone else. Then Gino felt it too: a cross-wave of vibration, a shivering of the car that didn't harmonize with the faint vibration of the plastic seats, the metal floor.

And then the train braked; it braked with a suddenness that rattled vertebrae like dominos, and everyone became rodeo cowboys in their seats, and then darkness, profound darkness like when he'd toured a cavern and the State Park guide had switched off the lights so they could experience geological absolutes; and then a scream of metal that sounded almost apologetic and a sizzle of breaking glass and he lost his seat entirely as the world pitched him over its shoulder. And direction, as a thing-in-itself, was uncreated: and Gino had a new relationship to gravity. Bodies pummeled him and people wailed and sirened, so loudly, from so deeply, Gino could feel the twisting weight of their bodies in the sound.

After that a cymbal crashed against the side of his head and he heard Telly screaming like a baby and the sound got very faint and distant and vanished in the silence.

x x x

When Gino came to, it was to a cold wetness on his right side and wet warmth on the other. His thoughts were almost immediately clear and he was surprised at his own comforting detachment.

He knew with a knifelike certainty that there had been an earthquake.

He knew he was lying atop a wet stack of bodies in the darkness and in blood and sea water and a thin scum of sewage from ruptured viscera. People were screaming.

He knew it had been a big earthquake and they were halfway across the bay and under thousands of tons of water, and no one would ever, ever rescue them.

He knew he'd been hit in the head and knocked out and something was still breaking in his head, but he was sure, somehow, that it had only just happened, no more than a minute had passed. Maybe it was the energy in the screams and the flailing around him. It was the energy of a fresh catastrophe.

The screaming, though, came to him filtered through a buzzing in his head; he was fairly sure that one of his eardrums had burst. There was pain in that ear, but it seemed unreal. That surprised him, too, in an insular kind of way: pain ought to be the realest thing of all. But mere pain had no rank here. Both fear and pain were subordinate to the seeking cone of perception, the exploratory probe of a terminating life. Two of his senses, smell and taste, had mostly shut down; he knew this meant that the rest of his senses would shut down. That the oozing chill in one corner of his skull was spreading, would shut him down.

These realizations were not articulated for Gino: they were experienced the way one experiences the cold surface of a concrete wall under the fingers.

Because he didn't know what else to do, he tried to look around.

Experimentally, he tried to move. It didn't hurt more to move than to lay still. He began to crawl. A hand flapped in his face; fingernails, probably a woman's, dug into his cheek, and he pulled his head back, in reflex, but otherwise ignored it, kept moving.

Sometimes the wailing ebbed and there was only a vocal rasping, a murmuring, like the sounds of an unseen flock of birds. Then the wailing would resume. One sound was equal to another.

Gino turned, and his eyes cleared, and he saw that now there was a little light, yellowish light from below mostly, and a faint sheen of red light from the sides. After what might have been a full minute of looking he knew that the yellow light was from the rear of the car which was now directly below him. The BART tunnel had curled like a bent finger, knuckled under to the buckling of the earth's crust, to a wedge of strata jammed upward, sheer as a seismographic spike. Horizontal had become vertical and everyone was pressed down into the tin can of the car by bodyweight and by slowly-increasing water and by mud coming in through widening seams of metal and by thickening blood. And more bodies had come in from the second to last car, gravitationally forced through the shattered door, packing, cramming this lower car so full there were only a few crawl-spaces left. Yet there were apertures, wet and ready places that seemed to be there for him, for this moment, for whatever remained to Gino.

The bodies under him in that moment were rearranged by the dynamics of suffering, and parted legs and tilted torsos shifted at angles to create a kind of wriggling shaft, a space letting more light through. Blood and piss and murky scum and seawater trickled down this shaft in no hurry, like a spring oozing from a muddy hillside; a living crevice . . .

. . . a living crevice . . .

. . . maybe fifty feet deep and at the bottom of it he saw parts of the Security Guards. The lady, perhaps alive, seeming to wriggle with life, but maybe she was just shaken by the twitchings around her; the man was split open, you could see the yellow fat through the ruptured belly, a perverse layer cake of exposed fat and intestinal tissue garnished by a splintered rib. Somehow the flashlight had been turned on, maybe by one of the hands groping from the layers of people. The flashlight's butt had slipped into the fat man's gouged open belly which quivered with the movement of struggling bodies, shimmying the light up the shaft of bodies (was that a rainbow in the little waterfall of piss and sea water?); the light playing over faces, some of them alive and staring with a disbelief almost identical to the staring dead (but for the randomly tracking eyes) and some profoundly identified with hurt and some trying to claw their way out and too stupid for despair.

There was a man whose interior had been pressed out through his mouth and he was choking on his own throat. He died as Gino watched.

About two layers of people down from the top, a hand thrust out into the crevice; there was a tattoo of a flying pig on the streaming wrist of that hand. It was Telly's hand.

Gino reached down and tugged and thought the arm was going to come free, torn away, but after a short, wet slide it resisted, and he knew it was still attached by a ribbon of flesh. He knew with a spiraling assurance that Telly was dead.

Dude, I'm gonna sing in a rock band, my cousin he's got this anti-racist skinhead industrial band going and his singer's leaving and he says if I shave my head I could join and I said what the fuck, it grows back. I don't know, though, I might be able to get on this TV show instead, there's this show called LIFE STRAIGHT UP that's gonna be on this new channel that's gonna compete with MTV and they follow you around and film whatever you do except you got to live with these people they pick and they wanted a bike messenger but maybe, you know, I could be in both things, the band and the—

Telly's ambitions. Gino's ambitions.

Yeah, Jane, you're right, you can't teach fulltime and write novels too, not great ones, but you can do one and then the other. It starts with the day gig, you know? I thought maybe if I got a professorship . . . but, I don't know, that's like years in grad, and it sucks up a lot of creative energy, all those papers, but, shit, carpe diem, I gotta go for it now, I blew the last scholarship but I think I can get another and maybe I could do both . . . and . . .

. . . and I'm gonna get a website . . .

I tell you that? That I'm gonna get a—

One of the red lights fizzled and went out. Someone was shouting, "Okay, folks, those . . . uh, those of us who are . . . who can move okay, we uh, listen we got to . . . we got to . . . to organize, we got to move toward the door, a few of us and . . . and try to get down the tunnel, there might be a way through . . . ."

An aftershock shimmied through them. Metal like rubber. Another window not far below and to the right burst in the aftershock and Gino could see it in the light from the remaining red emergency light. The lady in lavender with big hair was being pressed by the weight of bodies above her, forced through the ragged gap in the glass like playdough shaped by one of those kids' molds that forced it through a little patterned hole and he could see her living flesh pressed into the outline of the hole in the glass. The woman's scream was one note, one very high and incredulous EEEEEEEEEEEEEEEEEEEEEEEE—

"What we gotta do is not panic—"

Someone laughed. Gino was vaguely aware, and almost surprised, that someone was fucking on the top of the pile, just a few feet away.

"—there's always a chance and there could be a way through, it might . . . uh . . . .it might not be as bad as it seems . . . ."

More laughter. Male, Gino thought.

"I . . . I can't get this door open and if, please, if we could . . . if we could push some of the . . . those who didn't make it, if we could push them . . . push them out a window . . . we . . . please, hurry because, um, I'm . . . there's blood and water and it's coming up to my . . . I'm wedged down here and there are too many people on me to move, so if someone could just move to the . . . the sound of my . . . hello? If someone could . . . uh, the water is . . . buh wabuhess . . . wabuh us—hey! I . . . wabugh ess . . . ."

More laughter.

. . . EEEEEEE. Then that scream stopped, and the red light by the window went out too. Someone else screamed that they were drowning, please help them.

Gino could feel the coldness in his head spreading. There wasn't much time left. The heart of all life was underneath, beating in the crevice, the living crevice. Very deliberately, Gino plunged into the crevice, headfirst.

He liked the way it felt, as he went down. Like it was a throat and his body was a dick. He thought: *That's really how it feels.*

Then he hit the bottom of the shaft, and was plunged under the surface of the mingled liquids there, salty and shitty, and he squirmed around, holding his breath, till he got his legs under him, and stood up on someone's dead face and on someone else's—what? an arm?— and felt another, vertical crevice in the jigsaw of bodies open in front of him, warm and wet and suffering, and it was just what he was probing for, so he pulled off his clothes, all of them, and then he forced himself into the crevice in the canyon of bodies, headfirst, and squirmed immediately forward, and thought it serendipitous how the blood and the other liquids had become lubricants here, and how remarkably easy to move it was, so long as he stayed more or less horizontal, and how there were pockets of air to breathe, as he was still above most of the sea water, and how marvelously indifferent he felt when someone in psychotic agony sank their teeth in his shoulder and sawed at it, how it felt rather good, in fact, and merely felt cold when he tore himself away from it, losing a chunk of shoulder, and forced himself into a steaming gap which he realized was the gut of a human being, he was actually worming through the center of a living person, the wound flesh tight as sex around him, but they didn't seem to feel it: he could feel the crooked end of their halved spine scraping along his own backbone.

Sometimes he heard voices, whispers, mutters, weeping, rising and falling as a whole as if by some consensual signal; other times it was echoingly silent. Or maybe it was just his hearing shutting off at intervals. He could taste nothing, smell little, and he was grateful for that, but his skin was exquisitely alive, and he realized he had a hard-on and he dragged his hard dick, furrowing it along the bodies, the wet fabric and flesh, and humped now and then, and squirmed onward, remembering maggots he'd seen in a sealed jelly jar that had so outraged his father, nineteen years earlier, Gino nosing wormlike through darkness, then realizing that he had found his way to two full, bloody-wet breasts of a woman below him.

He was oozing himself over her from her head toward her feet, and she was alive and put her arms around him, and tried to force his face into her crotch, but then he'd found another woman, this one turned the other way, and he felt her hand on his cock guiding it into her, as the weight of bodies around them increased with another aftershock, a shift of the subway car, and pressed down on them so they could scarcely breathe, and somehow he knew, he understood with what might have been the telepathy of human minds under incredible pressurization, that this dying woman wanted to copulate with him because it was the most life-confirming thing she could do, at that moment, with her body, she couldn't get out and this was all that was left, this praying with the body, one person into another, saying I am here, I was here, I am alive, this is alive, you acknowledge me more deeply than in the puniness of talk and hand-holding and kissing, you acknowledge in me the reproductive impulse that connects to life, you fuck your way toward that recognition, you come into me, you come into me, I'm here, I'm alive, I was alive, I was, I am, I was, I am . . . was . . . was . . . The pressure increasing, no more breathing, no more air, oxygen starvation forcing their minds from their bodies, entwining to rise together, wet, locked together, in life, in death . . . he ejaculated into the eager void of death.

JUST LIKE SUZIE

Perrick is in his underwear, standing in the middle of the room, silently trying to talk himself out of slamming crank. He's a paunchy guy, early forties who looks ten years older than he has to, and knows it. He's in a weekly rates hotel room in San Francisco. It's not boosh-wah but it's not a piss-in-the-sink room, as it has a small bathroom. Perrick lives here, for the moment. He's used to these rooms, because he's lived half of his double life in them, but he's not used to sleeping in them; not used to the shouts in the hall at night, the heavy tread of cops, the shrieking fights of the two junkie gays downstairs. But this Bedlam is genteel, one of his neighbors assures him, compared to other weeklies on the street.

The room contains, besides Perrick, a double bed, a dresser on which is aftershave, cologne, a box of tissues, a man's comb, a cheap chrome-faced radio. There's a lamp table by the bed, with a squat lamp on it, a wastepaper basket below it. A window onto the street. A raincoat hanging on a hook.

Perrick is alternately pacing and going over to a table on which is a syringe, already filled and capped up, and a spoon. He nervously pokes at the syringe, holds it up to the light, puts it down, whines a little to himself. Of two minds about using it. He picks it up again, puts it down and goes to the bathroom door. He calls through the door, "SUZIE! Damn, come on, girl!"

Suzie's hoarse voice from the bathroom: "Just take a fuckin' chill pill, man, you gotta get your stuff in you so you be a little fuckin' understandin' about me gettin' mine!"

"Heroin," Perrick mutters to himself. "Sick bitch. She's gonna give me AIDS or something." He yells at the door again. "Come on baby let's *do* it!"

Suzie emerges from the bathroom—she's skinny, with bad skin, thin bleached blond hair, a white girl who's affected a lot of the local homegirl mannerisms, mixes them all up with her white Valleytrash Southern Cal roots. "Your princess is here, dude!" She walks a little unsteadily on her heels, already she's nodding a touch standing up. "You got my money?"

"I paid you when you came in!"

"That was like a down payment thing." She sinks onto the edge of the bed and fumbles a cigarette out from her purse, which is still on her shoulder strap . . . Her movements become slow and deliberate as she lights it.

Perrick yells, "The fuck it was! I can't believe you pullin' this shit after rippin' me off last time—my fuckin' credit cards—I can't believe I'd go for you again but . . ."

"Okay fuck this, I'm goin', I don't need no accusations, you totally illin', you dissin' me, fuck you." She starts to get up, sways, falls into sitting back on the bed. "Shit."

"Okay. Okay fuck it. Here." He slaps more money down beside her, it's gone into her purse almost before it hits the mattress . . . Then she droops a little, nodding . . . comes out of it, shaking herself.

"Wow. Shit's good. Let's do this thing. Before I nod out or something. You want it like before?"

Perrick nods, unzips his pants, then hesitates, takes his wallet out of his back pocket and puts it where he can keep an eye on it, in the middle of the dresser. He goes to the raincoat, puts it on over his underwear. Buttons it up. He goes to her, taking up the syringe. Perrick makes as if he doesn't notice her. He's looking at the ceiling and humming absently but breathing rather rapidly.

Suzie, in a practiced little girl's voice: "Oh! I wonder what would happen if I looked inside this big grown-up man's coat when he's not watching me! My goodness! I wonder what's in here!"

She unbuttons the bottom button of his coat and puts her head under it. Feels around. "Oh what's this nummy-yummy! Mmmmm! I wonder what the big man will do . . . !"

Perrick gasps as she begins giving him head, her own head bobbing. Perrick snatches up the syringe, drags back his coat sleeve and fixes, registers immediately. His back arches and his jaw quivers as he rushes. Never as good as the rush he had the first time he did it and every time he does it he feels a little more strain on his heart and he half hopes that this time the ticker goes blooey but still he's riding what rush there is, enough to make him go: "Oh Jeezus! Oh yes little girl, you bad dirty little girl. Oh yes, take it! Take it! Oh yes, you ripped me off you dirty little girl—my credit cards—but I forgive you because you are the little girl who loves me . . . loves to . . . Oh yes—" Faster and faster as the drug takes hold. "Good crystal good meth little girl. You ripped me off and my wife found out and I had to tell her the whole story and she kicked me out. And here I am, can't believe I'm back with you, you got me kicked out bad little girl, bad little girly cunt . . ."

His movements are convulsive as he grabs the back of her head . . . his repressed anger emerging in the violence of his hip thrusts and hands taloned on the back of her neck. Faster and meaner. She's gagging. Choking. He's oblivious. He's gasping, ". . . Shouldn't do it, shouldn't do it, but you made me bad little girl, You made me buy the stuff, made me buy you, made me . . . I didn't want to, I don't know what to do, how'd I get into it, I don't know. Andrea left me . . . your fault! Your—" He punctuates the words now with vicious thrusts into her. "—fault! Your fault! Your fault!"

She's still gagging, choking, but now only resisting feebly. The heroin was the synthetic stuff, hard to gauge its strength, more than she bargained for.

Perrick's singing idiotically: "Heroin and speed, you and me, heroin and speed, you and me, you down and me up, never quite enough, heroin and speed make her bleed make her sorry she stole from me—"

She's choking more and more. He holds himself deep in her, forcing a sustained deep throat . . . her struggles are now like mock motions of a sleeper acting out a dream.

Perrick's babbling, "Bad girl, little ripoff artist, broke my heart, take my dick, show you're sorry . . . SHIIIIIT!" As he orgasms and she stops moving. He slumps over her. Hugs her to his groin. "Fuck. I'm sorry I got way too . . ." He straightens up, panting. "Hope I didn't hurt you . . ."

He tries to pull away from her. Frowns. Sees he's stuck—or she's not letting go. She's otherwise totally limp.

Perrick muttering: "Said I was sorry. Come on. Let go. You're hurting me. Shit you got my nuts in your mouth too . . . how'd that—?" Yelling now: "Hey! Suzie? You're hurting me, seriously! What is this, I'm supposed to give you more money or—" He stops, grimacing with clamping pain at his groin. Bending to look under the coat. She's beyond unconscious. He can see the profound emptiness of her. A slackness beyond slack. Already tinged blue. And at the corners of her jaws the muscles are bunched with a signature of finality. She's clamped onto his dick and his balls, both in her mouth, her teeth clamped like a sadist's cock-ring over the root of his maleness. "Jesus fucking Christ! Suzie! Don't be dead, come on, that's a fuckin' bitchy thing to do to me! Don't be—" He checks her pulse at her throat. "I don't fucking . . . She is. She's dead. Shit, shit, *shit*!"

He tries to ease her off . . . when that doesn't work, makes an effort, tells himself to stay calm, as he attempts to yank free." Awwwwwwwwwhhhhh shiiiiiit! Fuuuuuuck!"

It hurts.

He takes a deep breath. Forces a measure of relaxation into his limbs. Then tries again to wrench her loose.

Searing pain.

He yowls. Then he stands there, panting, feeling the weight of her hanging from his genitals. He's holding her up by his genitals. He moves to try to get her head more in the light, then attempts to work his thumbs between her teeth, try to pry her off. Pushes—

Crunching pain. Some sorta death-reflex, he figures. She's crunching down harder on him every time he tries to pry her loose. Like punishment for the attempt . . .

"Owww fuck goddammit!"

A banging at the door.

He recognized Buck's geeky voice coining from outside the hotel door: "Yo! You got Suzie in there! Say hey you got my lady in there, dudeski?!"

Perrick mutters breathlessly to himself, "Oh shit it's her fuckin' pimp!" Then yelling at Buck, "No, no man she—she split!"

"Hey bullshit! Come on, man! Get over here, open this door!"

Whining, Perrick grabs the corpse under the armpits and drags it along with an awkwardness that seems a weirdly apt choreographic parody of his path through life. When he gets to the vicinity of the door he's got her turned the wrong way, she'd be visible if he opened the door, and there's not enough room for a "U-turn" so he has to bend over—grimacing horribly—and grab her skirt and sort of lift her at the hips, so her back is humped, and he does a little capering hump-swivel-hump-swivel hump-swivel move, till he gets her turned around. He whines some more as Buck pounds the door. Now Perrick's standing sideways with respect to the door, the body behind it. He adjusts the raincoat. Unlocks the door and opens it some—trying his best for fake composure—and opens the door only enough so that he's peering around the side of it.

There's Buck. He's emaciated, his blond hair in a white boy's approximation of dreadlocks. Under his arm's an expensive skateboard with a lot of cartoony stickers on it; he's wearing a Levi's jacket sans sleeves, stupid looking surfer shorts, tattoos.

Perrick attempts: "Hey. Buck. I paid her, man. She's out hittin' the pipe an' hittin' the needle, slammin' your money."

"Heeeeey, dudeski, the bitch does that again she's gonna be a bad memory an' she knows that. And I hope she hears me." He shouts past Perrick. "You hear me, bitch?"

Perrick is holding her up with one hand to take the weight off his dick and the strain is hacking away at his veneer. Can't take much more.

Was she going to bite through? She can't—she's dead. Right?

Buck's saying, "I bet she's in the bathroom doin' up some shit and laughin'. I always know when she's laughin' at me no matter where she is. I can feel it. Right now. I'm like, psychic. Her mouth's open and she's laughing right now—"

Perrick ventures, "I don't think so." He's walking a line, between whimpering and hysterical laughter. He feels like he has the weight of the planet hanging from his dick. The pregnant mass of the fucking bitch Mother Earth . . .

Buck ignores him, he's shouting, "—And I'm gonna KICK HER ASS FOR IT!" And he kicks the door, smashing it into the corpse hanging from Perrick so that the pain dances through him and expresses itself with a long ululating howl and he tries to edge aside but the door is kicked again and *wham*, bangs into the corpse again and Perrick howls again, tries desperately to get out of the way until at last Buck pushes in and past him, turns and sees the body with its head under his coat.

"Oh this is cute, right when I'm talkin' to you she's givin' you head, dude!" He starts yanking at the body to get her out where he can slap her around. "Tryin'-a pretend you're not here, I bitch-slap you, let go of that shit and get your ass over here!"

Perrick is making a hot-coals kind of dance, his face a rictus of pain, trying to prevent his dick from being pulled off—starts following Buck's pull around the room in a Chinese parade dragon effect with the body, making funny little marching shuffles with his feet like a kid playing choo-choo.

Perrick yelling, "No, no, don't you, don't—no wait!"

Suddenly Buck stops and stares. Looks at the body. Lets it fall limp. Steps over to the panting Perrick and peeks into the coat. Takes a startled step back.

"Jeezus! You fuckin' murdered my old lady with that puny little dick of yours!"

Perrick's sobbing, "I didn't mean it, Buck, she just—she was all nodded out and I guess I got carried away on some crystal and I guess I was kinda mad at her anyway so I was kinda chokin' her and I didn't see what was happening and—she just croaked, man! And she clamped down on there some kind a death grip reflex thing and I'm fuckin' *stuck*, man!"

"The balls too?"

"Yeah, yeah, yeah. Yeah. I really got carried away, you know?"

"This . . ." Buck shakes his head as if in high moral judgment. "This . . . this is gonna cost you extra."

Perrick suddenly feels a cold melty feeling at his dick. He thinks, at first, she's bitten right through. But then he checks it out. He sees . . . "Oh shit. Oh no. I'm losin' feeling in it."

"Well you oughta be glad, dudeski!"

"You don't fucking understand! If I can't feel it—*that means it's dying! MY DICK'S DYING!*"

Buck crosses his arms, considers the strange union of the corpse and the dick with a philosopher's judiciousness. "Yo, calm down, there's a way . . . we make a deal, we get you out . . . This is so totally gnarly."

Buck starts moving around, looking at the thing from different angles, sniggering behind his hand.

Perrick yells, "It ain't fuckin' funny, Buck!"

"Sure it is. You know what else? This is just like Suzie. It really is. And you know what *else*? It was in all the signs today, man." He takes out a glass crack pipe, blackened with use, thumbs in a rock and fires it up, poofs in a thoughtful way. Buck's head seems to expand slightly like a toy balloon. He exhales and chatters, "Astrology, it was her planets, man, they're all fucked up with her lunar signs. And it was in the smog colors. You ever read smog colors. Like tea leaves? And the way people was walkin' in the Mix, I always know, I'm kinda psychic like that, I see the patterns in the Mix, you know? Some days there's wack shit in the air that just gets a life of its own."

Perrick's on the gelatinous rim of the Grand Abyss called Hysteria. "Stop hittin' on that fuckin' pipe and *get her the fuck off me!*"

Buck blows white smoke and says, "Hey don't be comin' at me like that, dudeski, 's bullshit."

"I got a few thousand dollars in the bank, I can get you two hundred fifty bucks right away, get you two thousand tomorrow, you get her off me. It's all I could get out of the joint account I had with my wife when I left her but you can have it all man. Just.., Just . . . shit . . ."

Buck's interested now. "Two grand?" He looks speculatively again at the corpse: "Maybe I get a screwdriver and pry her jaws or something?"

"No, no, you do stuff like that, she clamps down harder. Some kinda reflex thing in her jaw muscles or something. And I don't want anybody to get crazy with a tool because *my fucking DICK is in there, you know what I'm saying?* It's still all swollen up, I don't want just anybody cutting around in there—I got to have a surgeon."

"Nah, dudeski. You go to the emergency room, the cops will come around. I tell you what. I know a doctor. He does bullet work and shit. He'll do it and he won't roll over on you. He's good. But we can't get you to him with that thing hangin' down there and he don't make house calls no matter what—he don't never go out. He's a speed freak wors'en you. Totally tweakin'. But he cuts *good*. He smells bad—but he cuts good."

"So . . . what are you saying?"

"Gotta cut off her head."

Perrick stares at him. "What?"

"I'm waiting for another idea, dudeski. Cut off her head—or, anyway, cut off her body I guess—get all the weight of her body off you. Do it quick, we can get you out of here with it . . ." He takes a big buck knife from his pocket and opens it, flourishes the blade . . .

Perrick hesitates. Hands jittering as he pokes at the head, trying to see how his genitals are doing. "I don't know . . . It's all purple. Oh God. I . . . I'm gonna get gangrene. And I gotta piss. I can't . . ."

Buck suggests, perfectly seriously: "Heeeeey, wait'll we get the head separated from the shoulders, you can piss out her neck." He hits the pipe again.

Perrick retches at this, a retching from deep inside him . . . he screws his eyes shut . . . then he takes a deep breath and manages: "Just . . . just do it, just do it. Cut off her . . . her body. Her head. You know."

Buck laughs, "Me?! No way, José! Fuckin'-A no-way!" He folds up the knife and drops it in Perrick's coat pocket. "That's your jobby, kemosabe! I just paid eight bucks for a good organic vegan lunch and I ain't gonna lose it!"

Perrick protests, "Hey look, seriously, I can't—"

"You wanna lose your dick? You did her, man, it's your responsibility. I come back later. Oh first—" He takes her ankles. As if to a chauffeur: "To the bathroom, James."

Clumsily, each step risking Perrick's ability to reproduce, they carry her between them to the bathroom. Buck chuckles, "I swear to God this is just like her . . . I was gonna kill her myself, tell you the truth, but I'd never do it that way, wouldn't trust the bitch . . . and this is why."

In the bathroom, Perrick is standing in the tub. Takes out the knife, then removes his coat and tosses it on the floor next to Buck. Trying not to think about it, he opens the knife and begins to saw at her neck.

"Yo yo yo yo whoooooa!" Buck blurts. "Wait a motherfuckin' minute I wanta get outta here before you . . ." He backs out of the bathroom, grimacing, heads for the hall door, pauses to take a hit from his pipe, goes out the door stage whispering just loud enough for Perrick to hear in the bathroom, "I'll be back, man, I got to cop some rock but I'll be back, take you to that doctor, a thousand bucks and that's between you, me and the rollers if you don't come through . . ."

Perrick still sawing. Sawing and sobbing. He expects her to react by biting down harder but—though blood spurts and then levels off, simply wells out of her—she doesn't react and that's horrible. How can morticians do it? Just . . . sawing at someone. The body should scream or something, dead or not. Maybe she was clamping harder? How could he tell—no feeling down there now. "Oh God, oh no. I'm gonna throw up on her. This is . . . I can't feel a thing now I think I . . . I think she's biting through, Oh God . . ."

The blood making hollow spatters and drip-drops into the tub. Wet crackly noises as he goes through the spine. Letting his eyes glaze, his hands seem to know the work. CRICK- CRICK-CRACKLE. A splash and . . .

Thump.

The body thumping down into the tub. He drops the knife onto it. Turns quickly because he can't keep it down anymore: the vomit. Painful vomiting. Then he turns on the shower. Vomit and blood going down the drain.

He steps out, dries himself off—and dries off the head still hanging, without corpus, from his dick. It has mostly finished its draining. It's bluish yellow now. The eyes sunken into the head more. Cheeks sunken. His johnson, where it shows at the root, above her teeth, is angry red and blue. He wonders if he should wash her hair. Give her a shampoo. What the fuck. Maybe brush her teeth too while he's at it.

Crazy thoughts. Control yourself. Walk your ass through it, Perrick.

Perrick steps through the bathroom door with the head dangling from his groin. It bounces ludicrously as he walks. A bloody towel is wrapped around the neck stump. The head's eyes are open now and looking up at him. Once more he's wearing the raincoat and underwear. Raincoat isn't blood-soaked but his stomach is spattered and the underwear is scarlet brown and his legs are streaked. He's somewhat relieved and yet in shock. He staggers over to his rig, his syringe, draws some crank from the spoon. Looks down at the head. Starts to giggle. Suppresses it.

Says to himself, "Wish I had some horse. Like to take some. Share some with you. Don't worry, I don't have to pee no more, I can't feel nothin' down there . . . Hey . . . close your eyes, Suzie . . ." He reaches down and tries to close them and can't get them closed . . . "Okay, I understand, sure: we got to have some communication." A peacock's tail of garbage in his head. He thinks: I'm losing it. He looks at the needle. A friend. "Speed ain't right for this. Need champagne for . . . I don't know if this is a marriage or a divorce . . ."

He says the Magic Words: "Fuck it." He injects the speed. Rushes. Giggles. Sobs. Giggles. Sobs. Babbles.

"Suzie . . . Suzie-bitch talk to me, tell me: is this . . . this is your way to—"

He's interrupted by a delicate knock on the door.

He hears a fluting female voice, sort of silly flirtatious "Andy! Oh Annn-dyyyy!"

Perrick at first thinks this is Suzie's voice. Stares down at the head. It's pulsing from the drug-rush. Emanating.

"Suzie—How'd you say that with your mouth full?" Laughing and crying both as he says it.

The voice again and this time Perrick realizes it's coming from the hall door. "Annn-dyyyy! The Pakistani lady at the front deh-esk said you were ho-ommme!" A more normal voice: "Come on, open up, let's talk already!"

It sinks in who this is. His wife. Andrea. He mutters, "Jesus Fuck. My fucking wife, I don't even—but oh yeah sure—sure uh-huh makes sense . . ."

He starts to giggle and tosses the syringe into a wastebasket, buttons up his coat over the head. Throws a bedspread haphazardly over the small amount of blood on the floor that dripped through the towel. Funny head-hump bobbling under the coat as he goes to the door, opens the door for his fairly straight wife who looks around with distaste. She's Jewish, well dressed.

She says, "This place even *smells* horrible, doll. Listen—" She closes the door and comes toward him. "You look awful. So—you've been using? You ready to come home? I thought about it and thought about it and I don't think you would've gone to that whore if you weren't on the drugs. I mean, you weren't in your right mind, and we're gonna take you to one of those twenty-eight day programs and start over—if you're willing. I mean, you really have to be willing. And no more other women, paid for or otherwise . . ." She stares at his legs. "Why are you wearing a raincoat and no pants? It's not even raining. You got shorts on under there?"

"No I . . . Got a head. Ahead of . . . myself." Trying to keep down the crazy half giggle. "Put on the coat before the pants. Come on, sit down."

Andrea looks around skeptically. "Where? I don't know if I want to sit on any of this . . . I mean, do you launder any of this bedding?"

"The bed's Okay. Just . . . head over here." Laughter creaking down in his throat as he gestures to the bed. She moves to it and sits gingerly.

"You threw the bedspread on the floor? Very nice."

Perrick giggles moronically. "*Head* to." He walks awkwardly toward her.

"You're walking funny, your shoulders all slumped, you got a backache?"

Perrick's close to tears now, getting it out spastically. "Got to keep your *head* down in this world!" Fairly *barking* the word "head." He snorts, "If you don't keep your *head* down, you've *head* it, pal!"

She gapes at him. He begins to laugh hysterically. She looks at the lump bobbing under his coat. "Whatever have you got . . . ?"

Perrick is sobbing openly now, breaking down. "HEADN'T THOUGHT ABOUT IT!"

And then the towel dislodges and falls to his feet in a wet bloody lump.

Andrea gives a rabbity little shriek and jumps to her feet. "You've been doing something again. Something . . ."

Perrick approaches her, feeling madly earnest. Seeing a crepuscular ray of hope. "Andrea—talk to her. You're a woman. Talk to her for me. Convince her to let go."

It might work. It might.

Andrea just backs away, the bitch, whenever you really need them they pull shit like this . . .

She squeaks: "What?"

Perrick pleads, "Talk to her! Woman to woman! What do they call it? Yeah: *Tête-à-tête!* Talk to her—!"

Blood is dripping down his leg . . . he starts to open his coat . . .

Andrea bursts out: "You don't have to open that!" She's angling for the door. "You really don't have to. I don't—I mean, everybody should have their personal space, the marriage counselor said that, and uh—"

But he opens the coat and flings it off. Andrea's eyes are ping pong balls in her head as she sees Suzie. She takes a long noisy breath that sounds as if she's choking on something. She touches her throat with her hand . . .

Perrick approaches her, weeping, smiling, idiotically appealing: "Talk to her about it, Andrea, just get down there and jaw with her! Woman to woman! If you want to talk to her face to face I could—" He squats and bends over so the head sort of half dangles between his legs . . . he's quite serious and sincere as he goes on: "—and you could, you know, go around behind me and put your face under me there—if you don't mind, I mean, you always said I had a cute tush—and then you could talk to her—you could just—"

Andrea's backed into the door. She turns and claws at it. Yanks it open with a sound of animal fear and sprints out into the hall. Perrick stares after her, a little disappointed but already forgetting about it. He turns away from the door and begins to caress the head, to move his hips against it, not a sexual motion but more like . . . dancing.

Then Buck appears at the door, staring down the hall at the retreating Andrea.

"Yo dudeski your old lady's really geeking out behind—"

He breaks off, seeing Perrick dancing. As Perrick dances over to the dresser, turns on the radio. It's playing "Cheek to Cheek." Buck looks ill and disgusted.

Perrick is tenderly dancing with the head, singing along, badly but sincerely. ". . . when we're out together dancing cheek to cheek!"

Buck murmurs, "Oh wow. Dudeski."

The music swells in Perrick's head. Buck looks at him calculatingly now. Then goes to him, drapes the coat over his shoulders, leads him—still dancing—to the door.

"You know what, dudeski? Your old lady's going to call the cops . . . let's get out of here . . . Get to that ATM . . . I bet that cunt has your bank account frozen but we got another wheeze maybe . . ."

To Perrick, the part of him that used to plan his life and drive his body about, all this is seen detached, like from behind a trick mirror. He's just watching as his body dances out the door with Buck, Suzie's head bobbing along. He watches without feeling as it goes along with him down the stairs and down the street.

A vacant lot. A half-dozen neighborhood homies and dudeskis hanging around a lazy blue flame in a rusting oil barrel. One of this group, a black guy calls himself Hotwinner, is arguing with Buck. Saying, "I say it's a load of fuckin' bullshit."

Buck shrugs. "Put your money down and check it out. I'm lying, I pay off three to one."

Hotwinner says. "I get to look close."

Buck nods. "Rockin'"

"Okay, here it is. Just don't pull any gafflin' bullshit—" And he forks over five bucks.

Buck says, "Anybody else?"

Two others pony up. "Yeah here, it's a waste of good wine money but fuck it—you goin' to pay off or we keep you ass fo' my dog to have his dinner—"

Buck yells at the rickety van parked at the curb. "Hey yo, Perrick! Let's do it!"

No response. Buck makes a sound of irritation, hustles to the back of the van, opens it, drags Perrick out.

Perrick's wearing his long coat over the bulge. Perrick is giggling. Mumbling to himself: ". . . telling me all the secrets . . . so hard to understand what she's saying sometimes but she knows it all, knows it all . . . she's a *head* of her time hee hee . . ."

Buck brings him to the firelight, pulls back Perrick's coat, exposing Suzie's purulent severed head still clamped on his dick and balls, one eye hanging down from the skull, dangling next to his testicles, jigsaws of the scalp rotted off, pig bristles of hair remaining, maggots dripping now and then, squirming . . . halfway to a skull . . .

"That's a pig head or somethin', that ain't no bitch!" a dudeski protests, but Buck draws him closer, makes him bend and really look. He backs away making phlegm sounds in his throat as Buck says to the others, "Okay, dudeskis, take a good look, you paid for it." A few other people drift over to check it out. Buck covers the head. "Anybody else want a look? Five bucks!"

Buck taking more money, murmuring to vacant-eyed Perrick, "This is way cool, the bitch still workin' for me, tha's, like, loyalty all the fucking way, you knooooo? I mean, it's just like Suzie to hang in there, yo . . . Lemme count the money dudeski . . ."

JUST A SUGGESTION

This is a for-real story about me and the Holiday family. I figure they're a good example of what I can do, and what can happen. I'm going to talk all about the shooting, and where the people who got shot went after they died, to the extent I know, and why I'm still ghosting up this house. I'll tell you that part right now. I'm trying to put it on the tape recording this Ghost Seeker boob is using to get his EVP that he's hoping will get him on a TV show. That EVP, it's Electronic Voice Phenomena. They play a tape recorder when no one's talking and later on, see, they play it back, turn it up loud, and there's a message on it. Anyway that's what they think. Really, it's just some noise, and they interpret the noise any way they want. I know this from watching a show about this stuff, when I was haunting the Costco store in Tustin. They had all those TVs turned on for people to buy, and I watched a show about this EVP business. Think they're hearing ghosts when the tape goes, "Bzzguhbuzzgukbuzz." And they tell each other they're hearing, "Be gone, good bye!" Right.

People claim to have the dirt, or the grave dirt, on ghosts, spirits, what have you. But they don't. Ghosts and spirits aren't even the same thing.

The chubby dumbass with the male pattern baldness and the dirty glasses, he's sitting here right now running the tape recorder—hey if he actually hears this, later on, me talking about how he's a dumbass and chubby, ha, nothing personal buddy! He painted Ghost Seekers across the side of on an old white cargo van, in orange paint, with a stencil. The bottom of the *ee* in Seekers is runny. Looks stupid. I don't think this guy is going to get on TV.

But he had an ad in The Orange County Register, I guess, judging from what I heard Lucille say when she called him on her cell phone. She called him to check out this place because of what little Lindy said about me, and Franklin. Lindy's the only one who seemed to know I was there. She's more sensitive than the rest of the family, or something. Not "a Sensitive" like they say on the Psychic Channel—but more *sensitive*. That's how it works. I mean, if you're a live person paying attention, if you're really *with it*, you can feel the dead around you. No special talent. But it helps to be sensitive—and just pay attention to the right things.

I'm sitting here talking right out loud, into the little microphone the ghost seeker's got set up in the room, but judging from the look on his face and the fact that he's digging in his nose every so often, when he isn't scratching his crotch, I don't think the dumb son of a bitch hears me. No clue I'm here. Maybe the machine'll pick me up, though. I'm talking as loud as I can. I don't exactly have lungs or a, what you call it, a voice box, or a tongue, but then again I kind of do, in a fuzzy way. I can move air around a bit, and I can make sounds. When I whisper *to* people, though, it's more to their minds. They hear it but then again they don't. I don't understand the whole process that much myself.

We'll see if anyone can hear this. I think I can see that little needle on the tape recorder moving a tiny, real-tiny bit when I talk. I'll give a shout out to the world, just in case. *Go Lakers!* I'm still a Lakers fan. And my name is Murray Samuel Mooradian. Kind of a mouthful. My dad was being cute with the Murray Moora sound. I'm Armenian American. Or I was. I guess I don't have any DNA anymore. Don't you need DNA to be some ethnic type?

After my old man died of that blood clot thing, I went into his convenience store business. One of those stores attached to a gas station on Culver Avenue. Never was interested in the convenience store business as a career—I wanted to spend as little time in the store as I could. Because he was there morning to night—and I didn't want to be around him. He always seemed disgusted with me, no matter what I did. I got a B plus, he was disgusted it wasn't an A. "You always got to fall short, huh? Push harder next time." Disgust came rolling off him like a bad smell.

I wonder where his ghost went. I've never seen it, not my mom's ghost either, or the ghost of anyone I knew in life, unless you want to count someone like BlondBoy and I don't. All the ghosts I know are strangers. Most dead people don't seem to stay around—just some of them. Where are all the ghosts of all the millions and billions who've died? Climbed some golden ladder to Heaven? No one's offered me a golden ladder.

Fact is, I haven't seen anything about God or Heaven or Hell or angels, since I've been dead these last ten years. But I picked up on some pretty mean spirits that you might call devils. Sometimes I hear them and I almost see them.

About my death, I was two days short of my forty-sixth birthday and walking the two blocks home from work about midnight, crossing the street with the light, and some tweaker ran a red light, smacked me like a two-ton baseball bat, his car spun out, and stopped—and he sat there babbling in his car the way they do. And then the son of a bitch drove off. I saw that much because I was already dead. Just like that, bam. Floating a few feet over my body—which was twisted all kinds of wrong ways.

Didn't yet have it together to follow the hit-and-run tweaker. So I never got the chance to take revenge on that asshole. But pretty soon I was watching a couple paramedics, a cholo and some surfer-looking dude, loading my mashed body into the back of an ambulance. They were laughing about it, "You go ahead and do some CPR on him, he's got one lip left there, BlondBoy." Like they'd even do CPR that way. They just had a good time laughing at the dead guy. I saw one of those blown glass pot pipes sticking out of "BlondBoy's" pocket, too—I knew exactly what it was, we sold them at the convenience store. That pissed me off more than the hit and run. I don't know why—just him treating me like that, making the whole thing part of his pot high. Wrinkling up his nose with disgust while he's talking about my body, too. They drove off and now I wish I'd gotten in the ambulance, taken care of them right then. Only, I didn't know how to do it, back then. I was new to being dead.

So I started walking. I walked for miles till finally I was in Tustin, and there were those old blimp hangars, historical somethings, and down a little farther was the big old Costco store, just recently opened. I waited till a security guard unlocked the door, and I went in with him . . . and just stayed. The store was big enough to wander in but also it was shelter from the sky. Now that I'm dead, the open sky always makes me feel like something's going to reach down and grab me and take me somewhere. Maybe somewhere bad. So I stayed put, puttering around in Costco for years. You lose track of time when you're dead. But I knew about how many years because of the seasonal products; Halloween stuff in bulk would come, Christmas decorations in bulk, Easter junk in bulk, July 4th decorations, Halloween crap again, Thanksgiving turkeys, and there you have one year.

I should tell you how I picked the Holiday family. I was getting sick of haunting Costco. Sick of the other ghosts in there, especially. This Mexican landscaper who used to work around there, who'd died right outside of a heart attack, his ghost was always wandering around asking where his family was; asking me had I seen them. He would ask *where are they, what's going on*, over and over in a pitiful way. "Que pasa, que pasa?" *You* pasa, dude, I told him, you pasa away. Most ghosts are confused, see. Me, I got clarity, though. I can think. I'm clear on what I want to do—given, you know, the choices I've got. Which aren't that many. I don't have much freedom, as a ghost. I mean—it's all bull crap that a ghost can walk through walls. No sir. You have to wait till someone opens a door and then you follow them through before it closes. You can ride along, on their shoulders, piggy-back like as they go through the door. They don't usually feel it. Ghosts do that a lot, and people never know.

I stayed in the Costco for a long time because it was big, and there are a lot of people to look at. A lot of housewives. You can have fun checking them out in ways they never figured on. But after a while, the muzak, the lights, the other ghosts who lived there— dud conversationalists, all of them—it was Hell. I was thinking, "Maybe there is a Hell. And maybe it's Costco," when I saw the Holiday bunch.

They were walking around the store in a kind of family conga line, up and down the aisles, Dad leading the way, pushing that giant basket. "Dad", that's Boyd Holiday, chunky guy with a space between his front teeth, his eyes a little too far apart, nose flattened like the tip of a hammer; he was about the same age I was when I died. Then comes his wife, Rema Holiday, almost small enough to be a midget, wears short dresses maybe to make her tiny legs look longer, her dun hair bobbed, bruised-looking eyes but no one had hit her; then Boyd's goopy sister Lucille, same space in the teeth and wide apart eyes, dyed-black hair looked to me like a mop, but she calls it dreads because she's got some Jamaican boyfriend. Lucille was staying with them while she studied to get her chiropractor license, like that's ever going to happen. Then, trailing after Aunt Lucille, the Holiday kids: Lindy, the eleven year old girl, and Franklin the teen boy. Franklin could've been the poster boy for snotty teens. Mouth stayed open, always texting—took me a while to figure out what texting was, it wasn't big till after I died. And he's got those droopy-ass pants like his hip-hop heroes. Makes me glad I never had any kids—'course I never had any women to knock up, hardly, no women at all except if I paid, to be honest, so how would I . . . Wait, do I want to say that about paying? Okay, shit, so what, it's on there now. I can't make the rewind button work. And it's nothing compared to some of the stuff I'm going to tell you about. Stuff . . . that I suggested.

I followed them, the Holiday family, not sure why I was doing it, just thinking that there was potential of some kind. Maybe I could really get *involved* with a family, besides just whispering this and that to the people in Costco. Wait–I know what it was! It was that "I'm mad but I'm not going to admit it" look on Boyd's face. Charging along like he was trying to challenge his family to keep up. Looking, hurt, mad—disgusted. I just thought, "There he is, Mr. Powder Keg! It's playtime!"

And that's what I wanted. Playtime. Because I felt trapped in myself—like I was locked in a car I had to drive around and around, and the doors wouldn't unlock and let me out. I was stuck in there with the stink of disgust and the burning smell of being really mad and I knew there was one thing that could get me out of it, at least for a while . . .

So I slipped into their slipstream, you might say, followed them around as they bought groceries and the boy hassled them into buying a game about Grand Theft, the little girl got some concert DVD to do with somebody named Hannah Montana, the mother picked out food and a big bag of socks, and then out the door of Costco, and out into that endless sunny parking lot, and up to their SUV. Passed a fading old ghost I know who presents himself in an Army Air Force uniform from around World War One. One of those blimp-hangar guys, died in an accident, likes to natter about preparedness.

When they opened the back of the Chevy SUV to cram in the big containers of taco beans and dip and Mountain Dew and jars of barbecue sauce big as buckets and huge Styrofoam trays of frozen pork chops and chicken legs—that's when I climbed in, and crowded myself into the back, curling up on top of some groceries, kind of chortling, loving the novelty of this.

"Let's go on a family drive!" I yelled, as they got in the big car. They couldn't hear me, of course, not talking that way. Come to think of it, though, I think Lindy did glance around a bit.

So we drove out of the lot, and out of Tustin, to Southeast Irvine. This was in the more affordable Irvine, east of the 405. West, now, you got your rich people, some movie stars, some grandsons of movie stars: your Turtle Rock, your Shady Canyon, your tony beach houses. East Irvine, you got a lot of people working for the high tech outfits, chipmakers, all that stuff. That's where old Boyd worked, assistant supervisor in some department of the microchip plant.

They got a pretty okay split-level four-bedroom house. There's a pool but it's dried out and covered over.

Lucille spent most of her time in a bedroom that Boyd called his "den" but there was nothing left of him in it but a locked rack of guns—mostly rifles, one shotgun. Boyd belonged to a gun club. Went out there to shoot skeet and drink.

When we came into the house, everyone went their separate ways, Lucille scurried off to hole up in her room and talk to her boyfriend "Droppy" on a cell phone; Franklin, he holed up in his room to play the Grand Theft thing. Lindy went to her room to watch the DVD on her little television. Boyd threw himself into a big chair in the living room to watch Encore's The Western Channel on cable. He was watching an old George Montgomery picture, a real stinker. Drinking a Tequila Sunrise. Little wifey was in the same room, flipping through Sunset Magazine, but as far as Boyd was concerned, she was somewhere else. I was sitting between them on the sofa, looking back and forth and kind of grinning to myself, that first day.

Rema wasn't going to let him just stay in his Western Channel Tequila Sunrise world though. "It's kind of early to start with the Sunrises," she said.

"That's funny, Rema," I said. "How can a sunrise be too early? Get it?" They couldn't hear it, of course. But I appreciated my own wit. "Hey and you know what else, you're reading Sunset Magazine while he's drinking a Sunrise. Hey lady, you guys are in different time zones!" I started singing, "'Sunrise, sunset, swiftly flow the yearrrrrrs!'"

"It's my day off, Rema," Boyd said. "And it's almost four."

"Are you going to that gun club tomorrow?"

"You bet your sweet patootie I am. Not that your patootie has been sweet to me, any time lately."

"You see, Boyd? You drink and say unfortunate things. And what if Lindy heard you?"

"She's up to her neck in that Hannah Montana. Let me watch my show now."

"We don't have that much chance to talk, with you on that shift now. It's unfortunate." That was one of her favorite words, *unfortunate*.

"I can't argue with them about the shifts, I haven't got enough seniority, I told you this."

"I'm just saying that we don't have much time to talk, Boyd, and I'm worried about Franklin."

"What else is new? The kid's a loser. Straight *D*s. Does no work of any kind, anywhere. Listens to criminals singing about how they killed cops and sold crack. Great! Lucky enough to be white, wants to be black."

"Don't be racist. Your own sister has an interest in black culture."

"She's got an interest in a black something."

"Ha, Boyd," I said, "Good one."

"That's definitely one Tequila Sunrise too many, Boyd," Rema said, "when you talk like that."

"One too many," I said, and this time I leaned close to him and whispered it with my mind as much as my mouth. *"More like one too few—she should have one with you. Then you might have something to talk about. You might get lucky there, Boyd."*

He heard me, in a way. When I do that kind of special whisper, they don't seem to hear every word, but they get some part of it, or the sense of it.

"You ought to have one, and loosen up," Boyd said, as if it were his idea.

"I think Franklin is depressed," she said, flipping moodily through her magazine. "He doesn't go out much. Just stays in his room.

Internet, videogames. Texting. That's all. He's got that friend Justin—but apart from that . . ."

"That kid that lives in Tustin?"

"Justin in Tustin!" I crowed, slapping my knee. If I visualize slapping my knee while I do it, I can almost feel it. "Ha, Justin over in Tustin!" Boyd wasn't hearing me anymore—I wasn't doing it the special way.

"I don't like that Justin around here," Boyd said, frowning, clinking the ice in his glass. "I always feel like he's laughing at me. The two of them, I hear them rapping together for some MySpace site—it's disgusting. You get disgusted with your own son, something's wrong. And I think Franklin was trying to pick the lock on my gun cabinet. Kid's not honest."

"If you would take him to the gun club . . ."

"I asked him if he wanted to go—insisted he had to take his friend along too! Why? I'm so boring he's got to bring entertainment?"

"That's just being a teenager. You forget what you were like."

"Not like *this*, isolating in that room with his internet . . ."

"You didn't have the internet when you were a kid, Boyd," I said.

But I wasn't really focused on Boyd now. He got me thinking about the boy. Depressed, isolated. Maybe I'd picked the wrong powder keg.

"If we could just put some water in the pool," Rema said, "Franklin thinks that if he could have a pool party . . ."

"Costs way too much. I'm having to support Lucille . . ."

"Maybe she really ought to . . ." She lowered her voice. "Move in with her boyfriend."

"That guy? I won't have her move in there, I got anything to say about it. She needs to get a part time job, sure, but . . ."

I was already wandering away from them, looking for Franklin's room. I had to wait outside a while, till he went to the bathroom. When he came back I followed him in and looked around. It was a little bedroom with clothes all over the floor, socks and underwear, the moldy remains of a half-eaten Subway sandwich, an open magazine called *Hip Hop Hard* looking like a run-over bird on the messy bed, posters all over the wall, mostly of hard-looking tattooed black guys including one called Lil Wayne and one called 50 Cent. Franklin was on the computer at a white desk that looked too small for him, and, after glancing to make sure the door was closed, he started to look at internet porn.

"Kid," I said, "Normally I'd be into it, but we've got business."

He was looking at something called "Tranny Fanny" and just starting to touch himself. I leaned near him, and whispered into his ear—whispering in that special way, with my mind: *Your dad's about to come in and catch you.*

His back straightened and he turned really quick in his seat to glare at the door. And lucky for me, someone—probably Lucille—was walking by just then, outside the closed door. He heard the footsteps, thought it was his dad.

Franklin closed the porn pretty quick, I can tell you.

Then he sat there, shaking. "No fucking privacy," he said. Teeth all clenched.

"You get things like privacy when people respect you, kid," I said, knowing he wouldn't hear it. Then I bent near him again and whispered the opposite with my mind, *"You deserve their respect—all the crap you put up with . . ."*

He nodded to himself. "Deserve more respect."

Internet stuff was just starting to get really big when I died. I knew about the worldwide web. I used to stand behind an Assistant Manager in Costco when he was supposed to be working in his little office, and watch him "surf the net". So I whispered, *"Franklin, they made a movie about those Columbine guys. Everybody knows about them . . . How about you check out some websites on that . . ."*

It was a little too early in the game to get him into the Columbine thing, though. He seemed to consider looking up the site, and then shook his head.

I heard a car roaring down the street outside, somebody showing off their big noisy engine. That gave me an idea. I leaned close and whispered into his mind, *"You can protest your own way. Get fucked up with Justin, go for a joy ride in your old man's car . . ."* The first time I made the suggestion he just sat there and chewed his lip, frowning. Snorted to himself. Kind of laughed. Then muttered something about "Fucking cops . . ."

This would take some work. But I had to prepare him for later. First thing, I figured, was to get him in a more suggestible state. I leaned over and whispered with my mind, over and over, every ten seconds or so, *"The only way out is to get drunk and high."* Ten seconds. *"The only way out is to get drunk and high . . ."*

He resisted a little. Apparently he'd promised his mom he'd do some kind of homework and he sort of esteemed his old lady. But pretty soon he was calling his friend Justin on one of those tiny little cell phones. "What up, dog. Hey we got to kick it . . ."

This was some kind of code between them for get all fucked up. And it wasn't an hour later that Franklin was "chilling" with Justin, a fox-faced teen with several piercings and a

T-shirt that said, *World of Warcraft.*

Justin didn't exactly come to the house, they agreed by cell to meet down the street, in a construction site for another house more or less like the one Franklin lived in. The foundation and the frame of a house, in raw yellow wood, were already there. Franklin and Justin squatted on the bare concrete in a half walled room with a pint of some dark fluid that Justin had stolen from his pop's liquor cabinet, and what I thought was a small cigar but after a while I realized it was stuffed with dope. These kids, they call it a *blunt.*

So they were drinking and smoking and talking about all kinds of stuff, neither one listening to the other much. Franklin talking about how he thought his mom was flirting with an airline pilot who lived across the street, how he wished she'd leave his dad for the pilot, he could get a free trip to Hawaii or something, and how the guy knew how to party, because a girl who'd been over there told him this pilot, Mr. Burford, liked to get hammered. Which was something I took note of.

Justin brought out his iPod, and they each took one "ear bud" –I think that's what they're called—and listened to some band that Justin said was from Norway, said it was a "death metal rap" band, and they were bobbing their heads like a whore giving a quick BJ and when they were done, oh baby, were they ready to listen to me. Mostly it was the dope and the booze and just being pissed off. It turned out Justin's dad had smacked him around, the night before, and he was still mad about it, so that helped.

"You could probably get that car away from the house, real quiet, and drive if off and go for a cruise and get it back without anybody noticing," I told Franklin. *"You know where the keys are . . ."*

The kid was primed and ready to go. A few more suggestions and he and Justin were pushing the SUV down the driveway slope in neutral and onto the street, not to make too much noise. And then they were driving it off the west with me wedged between them on the front seat. Franklin drove through the residential neighborhoods toward the ocean, faster and faster, and I was there, riding along, whispering with my mind. *"You can push it a little faster, a little faster, this'll make Justin respect you more, he makes fun of you like your dad does . . ."*

The car was still barreling along—faster and faster—and the boys were whooping and the radio was on real loud, something about diving from a mountain of cocaine, and then they didn't quite make a corner, they swerved, the car spun around, and they were both going *shiiiiit!* but I was going "Ha, this is more like it!"

And then wham, bam, but no-thank-you-ma'am, we're wrapped around a telephone pole.

The Justin kid didn't make it. He'd gone right through the windshield. No seat belt, see. Cut all to ribbons. I saw his ghost standing around mewling to itself, and I said, "Hey fuck off, kid!" And he got scared of me and backed away and kind of melted into himself . . . that's what happens to a lot of them, they melt into themselves, like they're going down a drain that's in their heart. Then they're just gone.

Maybe it'd be better, to be just gone that way. Wherever they go.

Anyhow, Franklin had smacked his head on the steering wheel and his left arm was pinched into place by the door. He was crying like a bitch when the cops got there. Some firemen used the "jaws of life" to cut him out, and they lugged him to an ambulance. There was BlondBoy, working that ambulance! "I'll find a moment to deal with you, BlondBoy," I said, as I got into the ambulance, in back. Squatting in there with Franklin, I rode along to the hospital.

"Your dad's going to say you killed Justin," I whispered, to the moaning Franklin, in back. *"He'll imply it even if he doesn't say it."*

Turned out to be not far from the truth, too—Boyd was pretty damned mad. By the time he talked to Franklin the next morning, in the hospital, he'd already had the threat of a lawsuit from Justin's family. "They're saying it's your fault," his dad said angrily. "And that makes it my fault. And the car is totaled. That much car insurance I haven't got. Do you know what the deductible is?"

"It was just so *unfortunate*," said his mother.

Franklin was lying there listening to this and moaning, and finally he begged them to leave him alone.

Once they'd gone, I whispered to Franklin with my mind, *"You see? They're not concerned about you, or even Justin, only about how much damn money you cost them . . . Somehow there must be a way to teach them respect . . ."*

Turns out Boyd's insurance wasn't so great. Deductible too big again. Boyd and his wife argued about keeping Franklin in the hospital longer—I whispered hard at Boyd to get him out of there. *"He's fine! He doesn't deserve to be catered to in here! You can't afford this!"* So the kid was rushed out of the hospital against the advice of doctors. They wanted to do an MRI or something. Concussion, and so on . . .

Franklin's left arm was battered but not actually broken, his head was swollen and bruised but not actually cracked right open. So finally they let him go home.

I suspected something else was going on with him, though, because I'd been watching Franklin closer than the doctors, who maybe spent eight minutes with him total.

Meanwhile, when I followed the family out the hospital, who did I see outside but BlondBoy. He was just getting back into an ambulance, having dropped some dying old lady off. And the Cholo was with him, too. Perfect.

I got in the ambulance and—I'll tell you about a little ghost trick, here. You can't push through real solid things—or I can't anyway—but you can put your ghost fingers right in someone's eyes, enough so it messes with their optic nerves. They don't feel it but they start to see things in flashes: on and off, on and off. Hard to drive that way. Even harder when someone is whispering, *"Look out look out look out you're gonna crash"* in your mind over and over, making them panicky. They didn't have their siren on—and he went right through a red light—and a semi-truck plowed them over. Gave me some satisfaction to give BlondBoy's ghost a face to face earful about being a smartass over my body after the accident. He was too dazed to shout back and I left him to figure it out on his own. His partner drained away into himself . . . but BlondBoy just wandered off.

And I walked in the opposite direction. We were only a few miles from The Holiday family house . . .

Franklin was up and walking around in a couple of days. He seemed pretty out of it and his dad said he must be overusing the pain meds but mostly he just forgot to take them. He had some pressure on his brain from the wreck, I think, probably a minor operation would have fixed it. Good thing for me I was able to get his dad to take him out of the hospital.

Big suspense in the Holiday house while the DA decided whether to charge Franklin with the manslaughter of his pal Justin. The cops pushed for it but Rema got Franklin a good lawyer—costing the family even more money, so they had to take out a second mortgage—and it was looking like the lawyer was going to get him off . . .

I waited, biding my time. Making suggestions, along the way, guiding Franklin to search for certain kinds of websites. And making sure he saw an interview on that "YouTube" thing with some kid who'd almost died at one of those boot camps for problem teenagers. Just lucked onto that one—he happened to be on "YouTube" and I saw it there, scrolling by, as I watched over his shoulder. I made sure he watched it.

I'm not sure exactly how I got so caught up in this process. How it got to be so *important* to me. Felt kind of pushed, myself. Funny to think that now. But one thing is, ol' Boyd reminded me of my old man. That'd be a good reason right there. One night, when Boyd was working on his third Tequila Sunrise, Rema broke it to him that a summons had come: they were being sued by Justin's family.

A nice rage from Boyd. "Franklin has ruined us! Lawyers, lawsuits!" It was handy, how he yelled that loud enough for Franklin to hear, clear upstairs. I went up and whispered to Franklin that he better go down and listen in, see what his parents were planning. Franklin came and sat on the bottom steps of the stairs, eavesdropping. Then I went back in the living room and whispered to Boyd with my mind, *"What about putting him in one of those boot camps for troubled teens . . . . hell, he stole your car, he was getting high on drugs, got his friend killed, he oughta go to jail anyway . . ."*

And Boyd said it right on cue: "Kid ought to go in one of those boot camps for problem teens . . ."

Franklin was already feeling scared and sick—this was too much. Which was what I figured. And he raced upstairs . . . before he could hear his dad reassuring Rema, "Oh hell you know I'd never do that to the boy, I wouldn't send him away . . . Maybe you're right, maybe he needs therapy . . ."

Later that night when his parents had gone to bed, Franklin took a handful of codeine and, at my suggestion, drank a tumbler of his dad's tequila. I remembered having heard you mix hard alcohol and codeine, it puts you in a *real* bad mood, sometimes a killing mood. And the kid was primed already, when I told him, *"They're gonna put you in that boot camp. To get rid of you. Just lock you up in that boot camp for bad teens . . ."*

Lucille was out with "Droppy". Coast was clear in the room with the gun cabinet.

So I made some more suggestions and a little later Franklin got into the tool box in the garage, found a hammer and chisel, went to Lucille's room—Boyd's old den—and busted the lock on the gun cabinet. He picked out the pump shotgun, which his dad had shown him how to shoot, loaded it up good, and went marching through the house, swept along on the red wave of rage I could see in the air around him. His dad was sitting up in bed arguing with Rema when in came Franklin—and there was a moment of hesitation. The kid almost got a grip on himself.

I told him, *"The old man thinks you're disgusting! Look at him! He's disgusting! He's disgusting! It's him!"*

And I felt almost like *I* had the gun, as Franklin brought the butt up against his shoulder and aimed at his dad—but his mother jumped up and shouted *no!* and got in the way and the shot intended for his dad caught his mom right in the neck and just blew most of it all over the pillows and she fell like a little rag doll. That really made Franklin mad and I told him it was his dad's fault and he pumped two rounds at point blank range into his old man, right up under the sternum, blew his chest-bones up into his head, and he heard someone yelling behind him and he turned and fired without even looking. He didn't quite hit the girl, Lindy, directly, mostly she caught splinters from the doorframe and a few pieces of buckshot but it put her down on her back and then he was yelling at himself that he was disgusting, "I totally suck, I'm totally fucked!" and he did suck, he sucked on the gun barrel and blooey, his addled little brains were all over the ceiling.

I tell you what, it was a good night's work.

That's what I thought, looking around. But I wasn't alone in the room—there was Franklin and his mother and his dad.

Their ghosts. Franklin's ghost was walking in circles, clutching himself, calling for his mom, and his dad was just melting away, like there was so little soul to him it just couldn't sustain itself without his body. And his mom's ghost was looking sadly at Franklin and reaching for him but then she drained away into her own heart . . .

Lindy was alive, though. She was lying on her back, looking at me. Right at me.

Seems like being close to death made it possible for her to see me, her being sensitive anyway. "You're a ghost," she said. "You're the one. You and that other."

"Whatever, kid," I said. "All I did was make suggestions. They didn't have to take them." Then I wandered off to the living room, to look at the Tequila and wish I could have some.

Lucille came home pretty soon after and found the mess. Called the cops, and Lindy was taken to the hospital.

Lindy told Lucille what she saw and she called the fake ghostbuster and here I am, talking on his gear. One thing about this jerk, is he's totally incapable of [. . .]

Okay there was a little cut there. He tried listening back to see if anything was on the tape and he couldn't hear it. He ended up recording over a little of what I said about him just now. But it's recording again. Almost out of tape though. I think my story is there, but it's super faint, he'd probably need some kind of special gear to hear it. I think somebody might, one of these days, though.

I've got a new project. That airline pilot, Burford, across the street. I think I can talk him into getting blitzed out of his gourd before he flies the plane. Then I use my other little tricks and get him to crash that 747. It'll be full of people, of course. I'm going to start work on it tomorrow.

People probably see things in the papers, like what happened to the Holidays, and they ask themselves, "Why did that happen?" Well, now you know. Because I can't be the only one up to this.

I wonder if I should feel bad about it. I can't feel much, you know. Anyway I try not to.

And after all–all I did was make suggestions. Not counting BlondBoy. Him I flat out killed. But mostly—just suggestions.

Sometimes I think there's a voice I've heard, myself. From somewhere. Making suggestions. To me. Only, not exactly in words. But still . . . whispering to me. Pushing me into all this stuff. Wouldn't that be funny.

But—same deal. I don't have to listen to it, just like Franklin didn't have to listen to me.

That's the bottom line, man. It's all just a suggestion. You know?

THE EXQUISITELY BLEEDING
HEADS OF DOKTUR PALMER VREEDEEZ

Sterno felt a kind of sick excitement as he watched the masked craftsmen mount Michael Jackson on the eaves of the castle. At Sterno's side, Idi Amin chuckled imbecilically.

"Ja ja," cooed Doktur Vreedeez, as P'uzz Leen sprayed the flexible shellac over the pop star. Jackson had been mounted fully stage-dressed and immaculately coifed: alive, trapped, projecting from the side of the building from the waist up, supported by transparent struts, arms bound to his sides. Replacing Jackson with the surgically-carved double who'd "died" at the hands of a clumsy doctor—that had been relatively easy. The mounting, however, required finesse.

Michael Sterno noticed Idi Amin fingering his crotch as he stared at the desperate, transparently sheathed superstar—the sight filled Sterno with a queasy fretfulness.

"Ov courrrrse," Vreedeez was crooning, "one can't alwayyys get zose media-figures vun could like. I tried to zese fellows in U2 get, but dot band is very heavily guarded just now, too closely vatched by people—maybe later—und zo I zettled for zumeone a bit how-you-say 'past it': Mr. Jackson. Easy to carve the face of another, to make like his face. Und across from Mr. Jackson ve haff new addition, Mr. Paul McCartney . . . very necessary I haff one of der Beatles . . . but unfortunately Mr. McCartney died in the zustainable-taxidermy prozess, zo we do full dead-taxidermy on him . . . Here is zumeone more up-to-date—he called himself P. Diddy . . ."

In the forested foothills of Mt Feldberg, in the southern reaches of the Schwarzwald mountain range; above the realm of ancient oaks and within the shadowy recesses of the dark pine forests; on the melting cusp between dusk and sunset: they stood on the broad porch of the Black Forest Schloss. So someone had called it—but what was this architectural grotesquerie? A confabulation of dark whimsy, this place, with its absurdly clashing mixture of medieval castle and German-gingerbread country house, its four-storey volcano-glass facades and dark wooden turrets, its crockets and louvers, its multifoiled panes and quatrefoils and lancet windows, its ornamental molds that seemed as Tantric as Germanic—

Hell, Sterno thought, the place had all the architectural integrity of miniature golf. But that's what made it so glorious.

And there were the living gargoyles, mounted on the eaves of stained-glass windows above the encircling porch. The "mountings," Vreedeez called them.

"Please," Michael Jackson sobbed pipingly. "Please . . ."

"Ja, mein King of Pop," Vreedeez murmured soothingly. "Ja ja."

"My family thinks I'm dead!"

"A comfort to them. Und end to zuh embarrassment. So much more money from you now, ja?"

The forest around the contorted edifice seemed to engorge with shadows as the sun sank, the trees became fuller and grimmer as they became darker; the mountains deepened their blues and the snowy peaks soaked up sunset oranges and pinks, merging them to tincture blood-red . . .

Sterno couldn't suppress a shudder.

He had only arrived that morning, on assignment for the *Stark Fist of Removal Magazine*. He'd had the usual First Class plane accommodations, the almost intrusively comfortable five-star hotels. But he wasn't sure he wanted to be here, amusing though it was to see the erstwhile pop star in this predicament.

Sterno hadn't known Idi Amin would be here—Vreedeez had faked Amin's death too—and the former Ugandan dictator, famous for his brutality, made Sterno particularly nervous. Amin's hair had gone white, the whites of his eyes yellow as egg yolk. Most of Amin's teeth were gone; his hands trembled. But the dictator who'd butchered thousands of his Ugandan subjects for his own amusement, was still alive, still feverishly vibrant in that decaying flesh.

And what could Sterno say? Amin had departed his sanctuary in Arabia, was the permanent houseguest of the so-called Doktur Vreedeez. The story was, Amin had financed the Doktur's investments in Microsoft and certain other key companies that were the source of the Doktur's billionaire status, and the Doktur felt obliged to entertain Amin, despite the fact that, now and then, the Doktur's house-servants would go missing.

Vreedeez's majordomo, factotum and chief sustainable-taxidermist, P'uzz Leen, was presumably in no danger from Amin, if that could be said of anyone in proximity to the erstwhile dictator, because of Leen's importance to the doctor. The swarthy P'uzz Leen almost never spoke.

"Please," Jackson piped, in his Mickey Mouse voice. "I'm a very rich man. Let me go and you can have it all."

"Ach, I love it when zay say dot," Vreedeez chuckled, as P'uzz Leen sprayed the oxygen-permeable flexishellac over Jackson's mouth. Jackson's piping cries became muted, barely audible squeaks.

"This is authentic Michael Jackson?" asked Amin.

"Ja ja, zat es der Michael, not an impersonator. Seventeen million dollars for der kidnap, nine more to pay off bodyguards, frame zah doctor—ja, vus vort it. Worth it fer sure."

Hmmm, Sterno thought: "Worth it fer sure," Vreedeez had said. Vreedeez affected a burlesque Bavarian accent—like Mel Brooks doing a Nazi—but flaunted his lapses into a Western American accent. Sterno suspected Vreedeez of actually being an American and, despite the unlikely German accent, he was not trying very hard to conceal it. And like P'uzz Leen, Vreedeez looked eerily familiar though he was sure they'd never met before.

Vreedeez was stocky, dressed in black; mustachioed, curly haired, dark eyed, fifties—though some say that his apparent age was fifty years behind his real age, thanks to growth hormone treatments. Now he turned to Sterno and said, "You vould like to see der other mountings?"

"Does a damn prairie squid lie in wait fer a face-fuckin' bat? You bet your ass."

"My donkey? I haff no donkey for gambling."

"Come on, man, I don't believe you're not familiar with that expression, we're a global shit-culture now, and this veneer of—"

"Speaking of veneers," Vreedeez said, interrupting him calmly but with a distinct note of warning, "haff you seen our complete collection? Mr. Jackson is of course only der newest . . ."

"No, I haven't. I have to ask - are these the real thing?"

"Mm ruh meee . . . !" Michael Jackson whined.

"You haff not read the papers?"

"Yeah, sure, man, but . . . okay, all those people disappeared or died—Jackson 'died'—sure 'nuff, but you might've taken advantage of that disappearance trend—I mean, everyone assumes it's some kind of massive publicity stunt—and you might've just, you know, made the mockups . . . maybe it's part of the publicity stunt put on by the real Michael Jackson and whoever . . . I mean, otherwise why would you invite me here? I mean, shit, if I report on this . . . of course it's a so-called underground magazine but it's read by all the key World Leaders anyway . . . and you'd have cops swarming here from every damn country missing its celebrities . . ."

"As for taking a chance on dot, vell, it is important for me dot a representative of der media see what I haff here, but not necessarily dot it is, finally, reported in der media . . ."

"It's enough I just . . . see it?"

"Ja. To ask vhy, consult mit der Carl Jung books."

Sterno's shudder, then, had a different quality to it; less frisson and more fear. How was Vreedeez going to prevent it from being reported 'in der media'?

"Und now . . . I present, around und ziss side uff der schloss, as you zee . . ." They strolled around a corner, Sterno and Idi Amin and P'uzz Leen.

"Whoa!" Sterno burst out.

Lit from beneath by the soft floodlights that had come on when the ambient light dropped, were four slightly-wriggling, transparently sheathed, gargoyle-mounted internationally known . . . figures. Megan Fox, Kate Moss, Naomi Campbell and—

"Madonna! Bitchin'!"

"Melph meeeee!" Madonna whined, from within the sheath of oxygen permeable shellac. Under the shellac she wore a bit of filmy black lingerie and a lot of jewelry.

"That's got to be her for real," Sterno breathed appreciatively. "She's getting kind of old but . . . still makes a nice display." He wondered at his own lack of sympathy for the kidnap victims; but then they'd long ago voluntarily abdicated their own humanity, so it all seemed very natural somehow . . . naturally unnatural . . .

"Zis spot over here is being prepared for Beyoncé," Vreedeez said, losing his accent halfway through the sentence.

Madonna quivered within her sheath of semiflexible shellac . . .

"Ach! Madonna is jealous!"

"She looks sick, poor Madonna," Amin observed. "Maybe you take her out a while, give her to me, I keep her a pet."

"We discussed that before, Idi," Vreedeez gently chided. "You'd only kill her, and it's too hard to get them sheathed and unsheathed . . ." He'd discarded the "German" accent entirely for the moment. ". . . if they die we simply open up the abdominal zipper and complete the taxidermization . . . But you are right: She does look under the . . . under der wezzer . . . a bit zick . . . P'uzz Leen, are der intravenous and extravenous tubes functional for Miss Madonna?"

P'uzz Leen stroked his black mustache thoughtfully as he opened the Sustainability Panel and checked the various feeder tubes. Then he nodded. Said only, "Yes."

"Gut, gut . . . Vell, monitor her clozely . . ."

They paused for refreshments, brought by a mute (literally tongueless) tuxedo-dressed waiter. There was, Sterno noted, an electronic monitor anklet locked onto the waiter's right ankle. Eyes deadened by despair, he offered them brandy and canapés on a silver platter.

"Now over here, ve haff zuh Array uf Writerz . . . Michael Chabon . . . Stephanie Meyer . . . As you see ve haff and across from her, in rather, may I zay, very uncomfortable proxzzzzzimity, Mr. William Gibson . . ."

"Hiya Bill," Sterno said.

Gibson—replete with his glasses and Arrow shirt—regarded him owlishly but didn't try to reply. He at least had the dignity not to beg for a release that would never be forthcoming. Robbins by contrast whined piteously, making Amin laugh.

"I vanted ve get William S. Burroughs or Thomas Pynchon, instead of Mr. Gibson, frankly, but Mr. Burroughs died before we complete zuh sustainable taxidermy process, und Mr. Pynchon . . . well, we went through four zeparate kidnapees zupposed to be Mr. Pynchon, but none of zem were really him . . ."

"Over here looks like a kind of mixed bag . . ."

"Ja, ve haff, Nicholas Cage und over here Brad and Angelina . . . here is Richard Simmons . . . it's very funny, even in zuh sheath he tries to make der aerobics, very cute . . . und here ess David Letterman . . ."

"No shit! Dave! Love this here 'Stupid human trick.' Dave!"

". . . und Arnold Schwarzenegger—he cry for a very long time, begging us much, Mr. Schwarzenegger . . . Dick Cheney, also whines very much . . . mixed bag as you zay . . . but over here ve haff Mr. David Copperfield, the magician . . ."

Sterno had to laugh. "David Copperfield! Hey my man! David! Work out that Houdini escape thing yet?"

"Here zuh fake guroos, Elizabeth Clare Prophet, Deepak Chopra . . . Ah, observe . . ."

Vreedeez reached out and unzipped the sealant over Chopra's mouth. Chopra responded predictably, "You . . . you have my body but my soul roams free . . ."

"Bullshit," P'uzz Leen said, surprising Sterno.

". . . and I am sending vibrations into the quantum-uncertainty realm which will miraculously cause the destruction of this abomination . . . look to your Karma my friend . . ."

P'uzz Leen reached up to zip Chopra's mouth shut again and just before it closed Chopra burst out, "I am a very rich man! I will give you anything if . . ." Zip. ". . . Mumph merf yuff!"

"Now that don't break my heart," Sterno said, chuckling.

But something *was* bothering him . . .

It bothered him increasingly, despite his mental rationales . . . that none of this bothered him.

Just Assholes? Maybe. But these were people, after all.

Vreedeez was smiling at him as he took him around to the rear of the house; the porch ran all the way around. "I veel you are . . ."

"Could you, seriously, dispense with the fake accent?"

Vreedeez shrugged rather sulkily. "If you like. You have your own . . . veneers. Sterno is not your real name and you are not the bad-ass you pretend to be. You're a family man. And as for my accent—we've already taken a psyche-impression of me as the 'Herr Doktur' so it's not necessary to continue it—we'll edit out everything after that . . ."

"What the hell are you talking about, man?"

Vreedeez ignored the question. "You're from Arkansas, by the way, aren't you?"

"Gotta problem with that?"

"No, not at all, Mr., ah, 'Sterno.' It's just data. As I started to say, a minute ago . . . you are having doubts about your own reactions to what you see here. It is written quite clearly on your face. I have read your sneering blog! You play-act, like so many fringe artists, at enjoying the suffering of fools, but real, high-intensity suffering, right here, in-your-face, is more than unsettling. And yet you are not as unsettled as some fragment of conscience in you tells you that you ought to be. And is that really any surprise? You're an American. You take part in all sorts of butchery and cruelty routinely . . ."

"Hey man that wasn't my doing, none of it."

"No, no it wasn't your doing, not directly. But you are a cell of the organism that did it although you and your friends pretend otherwise. And what did you do to stop it? Oh but I forgot: it's hopeless, no? It's all hopeless. And hopelessness is every cynic's excuse for his enjoyment of his nation's cruelty . . ."

"Whoa, whoa, hold on there, old pard—"

"Don't take offense. It's just talk. More brandy? Good brandy, isn't it? I see you're wearing Nike tennis shoes?"

"What? What the fuck difference does it make what tennis shoes I'm wearing?"

"Adidas, like Spaulding, like many other American companies, sub-contract the manufacture of their products to sweat shops staffed by starved, enslaved, badly mistreated children. Small children." He sounded more entertained by this fact than outraged. "Sometimes - surprisingly often - the children are tortured to get more production out of them: this happens in South America, in India, in Pakistan, in Malaysia, in other places. The American companies who subcontract to these foreign sweatshops, they of course know full well what is going on, and they make their excuses, but they really don't give a rat's ass."

"I heard something about it but . . ."

"But you didn't bother to find out more. You are insulated from the issue by your convenient sense of 'hopelessness,' by the cynical posturing that makes it easy for you to numb yourself . . . and hence you can look at my exquisite little atrocities here and feel more or less nothing. It is enough to take part in the organism, the big machine, that feeds you, that sustains you—"

"Now wait-a-minute, when did you, a fuckin' billionaire, suddenly turn into a Marxist?"

"I advocate no political ideology. I see what is, I take note, it becomes data I use or discard. I am untouched by it. I am quite above politics. We all are."

"We? Who's 'we'? Sounds like there's . . . an organization back of all this, somewhere . . ."

"But of course there is . . . You may call us the Masters of True Will. We are those who use the chaotic magic of the world's uncontrolled, blind outpouring of psychic bile, and what you call suffering, and through a kind of ritualization you cannot comprehend—as for example, this time, by turning internationally known figures into living gargoyles—we transform it all . . . into energy; and the energy we turn into . . . whatever we wish. For example, you have noticed that I somewhat resemble a friend of yours. But this is not my true appearance at all. Or is it? Was I that person all the time— undercover, so to speak, arranging deeper and more subtle levels of hypocrisy in the so-called 'fringe art underground'? Who knows. I will say this: the 'underground' art scene has much more impact on the zeitgeist than it realizes . . . It is a back door into the collective unconscious—we find it quite useful."

"I . . . uh . . ." He looked at P'uzz Leen, who only shrugged, and then at Idi Amin.

"Don't look at me for answer," Amin said. He had pulled his penis from his pants and was absent-mindedly massaging it. "I don't understand him when he talks like this . . ."

"Many are the rituals of mass chaos magic," Vreedeez was saying. "Sometimes, for example, we arrange a small war, so we can transmute the massive outpouring of hypocrisy around the war—as well as, of course, take our part of the financial profits. I myself am a major stockholder in a company that is one of the world's foremost manufacturers of landmines. Did you know that there are more functional, deployed landmines in Cambodia than there are people? Did you know that most landmine victims are civilians and a large number are children? I adore that! These are matters of personal pride to me. And of course the manufacturing of landmines and armaments is very important to the American economy—in which you take part. And you see some part of you knows this. Hence you must become numb to suffering, even when you see it in front of you, as you have today. Not all suffering is easy to shrug off, wouldn't you agree? You are disturbed by what you see—yet the relentless irony is this: All these 'stars' of the world stage, in our display—they are, as Lou Reed said, a 'temporary thing,' quite ephemeral, as in the famous Ozymandias poem, but in this case we can savor their significance in the media overmind, which is one layer of the energy structure that we manipulate through what is both art and ritual, to create a—"

"You're telling me way too much, man," Sterno interrupted. He was looking at the forest, wondering if he could sprint into it before . . .

Before what? P'uzz Leen didn't look armed but probably was. He had the look of quiescent lethality about him.

"Too much, Mr. Sterno? Too much what?"

"I mean—you are planning on letting me go?"

"You will go as free as a man ever does. Now then . . . Here you see—"

"I don't know if I want to see any more . . ."

"Don't be rude, Mr. 'Sterno.' Here you see—"

"And listen, there are lots of people who know I came here."

"To be sure. As I was trying to say, here you see Tom Cruise and Stephen King—combined into one living-gargoyle-sheath—and if you'll step closer . . . you see they're still alive . . . Just a little closer, Mr. Sterno, look here—"

Sterno stepped close—caught up by curiosity. Was it really Cruise? Tormented, half crushed, sallow, quite insane, the side of his face chewed away by Stephen King but yes—

As he was looking at Cruise and King he was vaguely aware that P'uzz Leen was doing something—

Something seen from the corner of his eye—

Unzipping the—

Tom Cruise's finely-muscled arm drooped down, and twined 'round Sterno's neck and pulled him up, off his feet; one of King's arms was free now, too, grabbing Sterno by the jacket collar; Sterno struggled and screamed.

Amin had grabbed Sterno's arms, held them pinned. Was giggling into his ear.

Another unzipping. Stinking, rotting mouths began to chew at him . . . Tom Cruise's stinking mouth . . . Stephen King's . . . began to chew at him . . . to chew at his face . . .

"Death is, after all, the only true freedom, Mr. 'Sterno' . . ." Vreedeez was saying, lighting a cigarette. "As for the people who know where you are - we'll either have them killed by 'suicide' or we'll buy them off. It's surprisingly easy to buy off 'underground' artists. Just offer them a major record contract or a movie deal . . ."

The pain was—

But they broke Sterno's neck, and the pain was gone and buzzing blackness sucked him in.

"No no no no, Idi," Vreedeez said. "You may not eat the man's testicles. I wish to . . . Idi . . . Stop that!"

Vreedeez sighed. He'd finally had enough.

He signaled P'uzz Leen, who drew the dart gun from his pocket and fired it neatly into Amin's neck. Idi Amin fell, paralyzed.

"We'll mount Idi here on the new array . . . maybe with the Archbishop of Canterbury . . . Now, P'uzz, see that Mr. Sterno's remains are fed to all the living gargoyles; a little bit, at least, for each, except of course for the brain—I'll be taking that with me for bio-interface downloading. We should get a significant charge from this juxtaposition; events will tilt in our favor once more . . . Oh and buy more stock in Apple . . ."

CUL-DE-SAC

I started to see things other people couldn't see. It began at the hospital. I mean, I saw real things, not hallucinations. It probably started happening because of my skateboard accident. With me, skateboarding is pretty much all accident. I come back from skating with my friends all covered with bruises and scrapes, with chipped bones and stuff. It's not that I'm not good at it—it's just that I push the envelope a lot. My right front incisor is shaped like a guillotine now because of a skateboard fall.

This time, my worst accident, was at the skate park in Berkeley, one of those chilly days in late November—chilly but never really cold. The sky's the same color as the skate park concrete, days like that. That day, me and DickWad were skating—

I should tell you that DickWad (Richard Wadley, okay?) is a tall skinny white guy (I'm a short skinny one) who dropped out of school and became a skateboard pro but barely makes any kind of living at it and sleeps on his girlfriend's couch and drinks beer pretty much twenty-four-seven.

We were doing kick flips when we saw the turfies were coming into the park, at the other side, doing pocket checks. Pocket checks are a way of life in the East Bay. These were NBP turfies—their tats say N.B.P., means *No Body's Prisoner* though a lot of them are in jail— and they're all young, skinny black dudes with big floppy shirts and big floppy pants and they do these "pocket checks" which somehow sounds better to people than "strong-arm robbery". They don't get that much from any one guy, it's like five bucks here and ten there and two there, but after doing it all across town for a couple hours they've harvested a few hundred bucks, enough to get some grapes to smoke—

What? Oh. Grapes is weed that has some purple on it.

No. No, I wasn't smoking it. I already told the cops that what I saw wasn't drug stuff. I wasn't smoking pot or drinking angel's trumpet tea or doing 'shrooms or none of that stuff.

Anyway, *last* time these turfies were here, I had ten dollars in my pocket my dad gave me, so that time I skated away when they tried to do the pocket check on me, said, "Fuck off, no fucking way dude," and managed to get out of there before the gang caught me. I didn't want them to see me and remember that occasion, so now I said, "Hey whoa, DickWad, we gotta cut right fucking now!" And I turned and skated up the bowl onto the rim of the skate park real quick. Or tried to—I was never any good at that half pipe, vert skating stuff, not much hesh, I do mostly curb tricks, street skating, tech shit like that—

And the board went out from under me. I fell back against the concrete rim of the bowl and went *CRACK!* on the back of my head. Went dark. Just like that, like somebody flicking off a computer monitor.

Next thing I remember was waking up in the hospital room. Curtains on both sides. Monitors on me. Mom and Dad, saying they told me to use a helmet, spending time, patting my arm, going home because my aunt was looking after my little sister and they had to relieve her because you don't want to leave anyone unsuspecting with my sister Wilmy for long.

DickWad came to see me, and said, "Yeah dude it was sick, you were, all, lying in this puddle of blood and all the turfies left so they wouldn't be blamed. They're all, 'They gone say we did that shit.'"

We laughed at that, in the hospital, but the cops did have a tendency to blame the turfies for everything. They were so poor, anyway, we don't really blame the turfies for the pocket checks. We resent it, it's fucked up, but we'd probably do the same, in their place.

I remember laughing about the turfies running off—though it hurt my bandaged head to laugh—and then I stopped in mid-laugh, because that's when I saw the . . . I think you call it a *silhouette*. It was, like, a living shadow, standing behind DickWad. At first I thought it was his shadow. But it moved around on its own, when he didn't move. It was all restless, prowling around the room. It was literally the silhouette of a man that just walked around on its own. It didn't have a face. It *did* have some kind of three-dimensional shape happening. It had depth and it had body-ness. But it was like its body was made out of space—the space between stars. So far between stars you can't see any.

It was shaped like a man—but it wasn't a man. And it scared me.

I asked DickWad if he saw it but he didn't hear me because he was listening on my iPhone to a *Flaming Lips* song, and watching the video on the tiny screen, and then he walked out with my iPhone, saying he wanted to show it to his girlfriend, who was smoking a cigarette outside, and he'd be right back. But I haven't got it back yet. I don't think he was trying to steal it though; he smokes tree and forgets what he's doing a lot.

He walked out and left me there with that living shadow. Not even knowing he was leaving me with this thing. And it was looking right at me—I could feel its curiosity.

Another one came in, another space demon—that's what I think I'll call them, space demons. That sounds so much tighter than silhouette and they look like they're made out of space.

This one can see us, said the first one to the second one.

It wasn't exactly in *words* but that's what it was saying. When these space demons speak you hear something that your brain turns into words. I don't know how, exactly, but then I don't know why I can see them and you can't.

No, there's not one in here with us. Something happened so that— I'll come to that in a minute, dude.

So these things were talking about me.

If he can see us, we can't hurt him, that's the rule, said the second one.

It's a stupid rule, said the first one.

It's not our rule. It is the rule of those who will destroy us if we break it. We must submit. Perhaps we can persuade him . . . We could whisper to him . . .

Now it is you who does not know the rules. If he can see us he cannot be persuaded by us. That is the rule.

We could destroy those around him and create an existential mousetrap, the first one pointed out. *An existential mouse-trap will neutralize him.*

(Sure I know what existential means—I'm almost nineteen, a freshman in community college already. I had to read *The Stranger* for a class and the teacher explained.)

"Who the fuck are you and what the fuck do you want?" I asked them. They glanced at me but they didn't answer.

They turned and walked into the corner, then: it was like the lines near the corner where the floor met the walls were the perspective of a street, in the distance—where the two sides of a street come together and you watched someone walk down the street till they're gone. That's what it looked like, but really *fast*, in a few seconds, *blip*, they vanished into the point where the lines of the corner came together.

"Nurrrrrrrse!" I yelled.

They gave me some Xanax for anxiety and some more tests, and tried to get me to take some Haldol, because I was "hallucinating"—I didn't take it—and kept me another couple of days. I saw the space demons again when the nurse was wheeling me out to meet my mom for checkout, in my wheelchair. I didn't really need the wheelchair, it was something about insurance. The Filipino nurse forgot some papers and we had to stop next to one of the other patients in the room, while she went to get them. The beds in most of the rooms are just separated with curtains, in this hospital, and there I was, in my chair, sitting and waiting for her next to this old man's hospital bed—his final bed, from the look of him—and I saw one of the space demons whispering to him. I could hear its voice in my head. It was telling him to change his will, to cut out his children and give the money to "Lisa". I had the feeling the old guy didn't know someone was whispering to him but he was hearing it anyway. I tried to tell him not to listen but he seemed to hear the space demon better than me.

What? Oh—no, I didn't tell anyone about the space demon talking to the old man. I wanted out of the hospital. I was afraid they'd put me in the "mental hygiene" ward like that guy I used to know in school, Squiddy, who got all tweaked on crystal. Started seeing stuff too—people get paranoid on crystal.

No, I told you, I don't do that shit. I didn't do any crystal. No, not even X. Christ.

My dad picked me up and we drove in the minivan back to the cul-de-sac where I live with my parents—just while I go to community college, you understand. We live in El Sobrante, in the East Bay, across from San Francisco. My dad says it's a typical "satellite community"—he works in some kind of urban planning department for the East Bay so he talks that way.

My dad likes to lecture me in the car because I'm stuck with hearing it there, and all the way home he was talking about how he respected my interest in "extreme sports" and "alternative sports" and all—I didn't bother to tell him yet again that skateboarding wasn't alternative or extreme. "All that's cool, *but,*" he said, I had to do something else now because I'd been injured and the doctor said I could give myself a blood clot and die if I got a knock like that on the head again. I just shrugged.

When I was, like, 16, I'd have said, *No way I'm going to give it up, even if I die!* Because—this part I'd have kept back—it's the only thing I was ever good at. That was before I decided I might learn to be a writer. But now I don't know if I'll be anything because of what happened at the cul-de-sac.

When we got there my mom was rushing out the door with Wilmy (it's short for Wilamina), they were on their way to some Middle

School soccer game. Wilmy gave me the finger and grinned behind Mom's back. She's a 12 year old girl but she's a total jock, and she can do all that stuff I couldn't do. She's good at remembering school facts, too. I never was.

"Oooh, there's my poor honna-bug," my mom said, as we met them on the front porch. She's almost as short as Wilmy. That's where I got what she calls my *compactness*. She was squinting through her thick glasses at me and wrinkling her nose in that nerdy way she has when she's looking at you close. "How's your head? You okay?"

"Better, Mom."

I didn't say, *Better except for the space demons*. I was trying to convince myself they'd been hallucinations and they'd go away when my head got better. Even though, as I said, "Better, Mom," I saw a space demon sitting on the eaves of our split level house, with the clouds churning way too fast behind it. Just sitting there, looking down at me: dark space in the shape of a sitting man. It's looking at me and it felt like once when I walked through a big spider web that had been trimmed in cold dew-drops. I felt the dew drops and the web together.

I'm glad my mom and sister were gone when it started happening . . .

I should tell you that the cul-de-sac, Shady Top Circle, is at the top of a hill, and ringed in by eucalyptus. There are nine houses in the circle, five of them four-bedroom split-levels like ours, the rest ranch style. I've seen the street on one of those websites where you can see your neighborhood from way up in the air, and the development looks like bicycle chains all looped next to each other, each house and yard another link in the chain. Our house is right in the middle of the cul-de-sac. Behind the houses there's a backyard, and then a fence, and a steep drop-off. Not exactly a cliff, just a really high, steep hill.

I still had a bandage on my head, and still felt the throb, but I decided I had to try to see this space demon closer. No, man, I didn't try and get someone else to look. No one could see him but me.

And I know why you're asking me that, trying to get me to wonder if I'm hallucinating. Reality check, right? Uh uh. Not going to work. I know what happened. It was probably something to do with the head injury. It was like whatever normally blocked off a psychic perception had gotten damaged; the filter was broken, and more was coming through than usual.

My dad told me to go lay down in my bedroom, "as per doctors' orders" and I said I would, just as soon as I got a soda in the kitchen. He went into his den to call into work—and I knew that work would suck his attention up and he wouldn't really notice what I was doing so long as I didn't make a lot of noise.

I went out back, circled the house, and looked up at the roof—the space demon was gone. Then I saw it'd just moved—it was on the lawn of the house next door, talking to Mrs. Hasslet. One of those old ladies that make their hair blue.

It was telling her that it could open a window into Heaven. It was going to show her paradise.

Mrs. Hasslet, see, was, like, late seventies, and her husband had died six months before—he was in his eighties, a world war two veteran—and she told my mom that since he was gone, life for her was "just a dry husk". My mom tried to take her to church and get her into volunteering, to cheer her up, but Mrs. Hasslet said that she'd lived to take care of Harvey and now that he was gone she had no meaning. Her kids just acted like she was a pain in the neck when she called, and here was this spinning window into another world opening up, in the center of the circle and it was like it was offering a way out. That's how it looked, like it was itself some kind of invitation . . .

All the shapes that should be back of the window, the shapes of houses and posts and mailboxes and trees, were warping, twisting around in a circle, knotting, like there was a navel in space, only the knot kept twisting and twisting, faster and faster, and then things were losing definition in it, pin-wheeling and blurring and turning into a circle of light and then inside the circle of light was, just, another place completely. So it was like a window onto this other world. Only it was sort of our world—it was a beautiful ideal version of our cul-de-sac. I could see it the way Mrs. Hasslet saw it. How it looked for her. It was our street but it wasn't. I mean, like, there were tropical birds in it—Mrs. Hasslet kept a cockatoo, so that's not surprising. And somebody was walking in from the side, showing themselves in that window. Walking into view through a garden of giant roses. At first I didn't recognize him because he looked so much younger than when he died— then I realized it was Mr. Hasslet, Harvey Hasslet, standing there waving at his wife. Beckoning to her. She started toward the window—and it receded. When she stopped going toward it, it stopped receding.

No, the space demon said. *You must go there the way he did. Through death. He doesn't want to wait for you any longer. You must go now or lose him!*

She stopped for a moment in the street, looking all glazed and puzzled—maybe still trying to figure out who was talking to her and why she was seeing this. Then a Fed Ex truck drove through the window into paradise . . .

It had really driven into that illusion-window from behind it. As if it had driven through a movie screen from backstage. The truck driver wasn't seeing this thing, just me and Mrs. Hasslet. The space demons didn't show themselves to normal people but they could affect what you see with your mind. Only, pretty much one at a time, I guess. So the Fed Ex delivery guy was swinging around Shady Draw Circle, kind of fast, really, faster than he was supposed to, and he came right through that thing looking like he was going to pull up in a moment in front of the house next door. And as he drove through the window into paradise Mrs. Hasslet ran forward and just kind of tipped herself over in front of his wheels. And no, no, I didn't push her in front of it—I told the cops that and I'm telling you that. She just threw herself under the big white Fed Ex truck. I could hear the *CRUNCH* when it went over her neck

And the window into paradise vanished. And I yelled . . . I yelled for a while . . .

Then I ran around the house, still yelling, I don't know what I was yelling, I was really upset. I banged on the window of the den, and yelled for him to call 911. He looked up at me through the window with his mouth open. Then he got the phone. I went back to the street and the truck driver was standing there, crying, this chunky Hispanic dude, sobbing, "But she just came from her yard and she . . . she . . . I didn't . . ." Ask him if you still think I pushed her. He said it himself: she jumped in front of the truck.

My dad came out of the house and was putting his coat under Mrs. Hasslet's head, but she was pretty much gone already. I was feeling sick. I told the driver I saw her throw herself under there, it wasn't his fault, and I thought about telling them about the space demon. My dad was checking her pulse and I was trying to comfort this hysterical driver, and pretty soon the ambulance came—and just as the ambulance was loading the dying old lady, Mrs. Hasslet's daughter Milly drove up. She had just spontaneously decided to visit her mother. Milly said she had been feeling like she was neglecting her mom and she came over right then and said, "Oh my God, this is all my fault . . . I didn't know she was going to commit suicide oh my God, Oh my God, if I'd been more . . ." Like that, on and on, crying.

My dad went to high school with Milly, he knew her pretty well and he told her it wasn't her fault. He told me to go to bed, and then he drove Milly to the hospital where they were taking her mom— she was all hysterical, she couldn't drive—and they followed the ambulance out . . . The truck driver went with the police, to make his statement and all that . . .

And I was alone there with the space demons.

Then the space demons went through the walls of Doug Bench's house—he's this guy who makes his living selling mostly bullshit on

EBay, stuff that looks like it's valuable but it's not, and he spends the rest of the time playing World of Warcraft online. He's this big sloppy guy with bad teeth and matted hair. I looked through the window into his little living room where he's set up his laptops, he's got three of them. Two for eBay one for World of Warcraft. He inherited this little ranch-style house from his parents and they'd be pretty upset to see how it's never ever been clean in there since he moved in—most of it's taken up by those plastic see-through tubes that his pet white rats run through, like sixty of them, running around in there, stinking the place up. Once he asked my sister to come in and look at his rats and she did and then he put his hand on her butt so she went home. I told her to tell Dad but she just said, "For that?!"

Now I could see the rats running through the plastic pipes and around on treadmills and through a plastic cage filled with rat poop and torn newspapers . . . and I saw the two space demons talking to Bench. They turned and looked at me, through the window. I could feel the look on my skin, again.

Then they pointed at his computer. And his computer monitors all started showing that window into Heaven. Another heaven, though. I couldn't see what it looked like exactly except I made out pink girl shapes, so I guessed.

He looked sort of glazed and then he went into the garage and he came back with a gas can and started splashing it around—making sure he got the rats, like he couldn't stand for them to live longer than him—and I was yelling, "Don't do that, Bench!" And I had my cell out, was calling 911, then I remembered that 911 didn't work for cells around here, I was trying to remember the emergency number for cell phones—and then *WHOOSH* and *BOOM* and I got a face full of glass and smoke and I was sitting on my ass, watching the house burn . . .

I heard him screaming, in there. And the rats screaming, too. So much more high pitched, like lots of little piccolos played backwards by a crazy piccolo soloist.

I picked bits of glass from my face—no serious damage, just little cuts—and walked over to my house, feeling kind of zombielike from all I'd seen, just glad my mom and sister weren't there. There were neighbors outside, and someone was saying they'd called 911 and someone else was asking was I okay, and offering to put antiseptic on my cuts and saying I should go to the hospital and then, *blip blip, blip*, the space demons were among them—five people: three housewives, two retired men—and they all looked over at the interdimensional window into the other place, opening, again, in the middle of the street.

I looked into it too and since there were so many of them looking at it there was no one point of view for me to share on it, so then it was all snowy . . . and then after a moment I saw it my way. My own paradise. I saw something that looked kind of like the land where Donkey Kong goes—a videogame I played with my dad a lot when I was little, haven't played it in years—and I saw me and my friends and my family there dancing around and, like, cavorting and shit, in a videogame paradise with Donkey Kong. How were we cavorting? Well—skateboarding down waterfalls, in this kinda perfected digital Hawaii. Dancing and skateboarding and swimming. And I *did* long to go there, but I knew better, and since I'd seen the space demons they didn't have any strong power over me. But for the others it was different, the space demons had dipped into their brains, in some way; they'd really gotten into their wiring. That's what I'm trying to explain. It was *persuasion*, yeah, but it was a kind of deep-in-your-brain persuasion. It was like jacking an Ethernet cable into them. But right into their souls.

There were three space demons now. And then a fourth one, climbing down the smoke from Bench's burning house like someone climbing down a ladder. Then sliding down a plume of flame to drop to the street . . .

This is a marvelous experiment, this new space demon said to the other two. *I've always wanted to do this; to use their theological illusions in a sociobiological setting. The irony is delightful, the data indubitable . . .*

I'm not sure it follows the rules, said the fourth.

But we are not in violation with certitude. If we concentrate our influence . . . The protocols of this methodology . . .

They sounded like scientists, to me. I started wondering, then, about this experiment I heard about where these really old scientists were trying to be immortal through some kind of downloading of their minds, copying themselves onto some computer program, and I remember someone asking them, "But what happens to their souls if you put their identities on that machine, won't their souls get lost when they die?"

And the scientists said, "Ha! There are no souls!"

And the other guy said, "But what if there are souls? What happens if you're copying yourself in some way—but not the souls?"

But I heard, on the internet, that a bunch of them had done the experiment and . . . something had gone wrong but no one could find out what, it was all hushed up. So maybe this was what. These guys talked like lost scientists. Like sick, lost scientists. But they acted like you think demons are going to act, too. Setting people up that way. Because what else are demons, but lost souls? And what happens to them, they get sucked into some bigger thing's agenda, when they're lost. Doing work for some other, like, *entity* . . .

I didn't hear what was said after that, because I was trying to tell the neighbors not to listen to the space demons, I was really upset and crying and they were saying I was crazy or else they were plain not listening to me and then they were staring at that little Puerto Rican lady, Mrs. DeSanto—she was climbing the tree. A really high eucalyptus tree behind Bench's—and it had caught on fire from the explosion in his house. She climbed almost to the top of this tree, around the burning parts, but it was catching her dress on fire anyway. I had heard from her daughter she was on some kind of antidepressants and then she had gone off them and gotten kind of weird so it wasn't too much of a surprise when she was the next one. She was ignoring the flames going up her housedress, and everyone yelling at her—and then she just jumped, from near the top, coming down like a roaring lady comet, *WHUMP* onto the street. Thinking she was getting a short cut into paradise that way, see. Someone started listening to me, finally, with that one: Danny Brewster, the Reverend Brewster's bucktoothed son. Senior at El Sobrante high. "Three suicides, something is happening, for sure, dude," he said.

"It's the paradise window," I said. "The space demons make 'em see that and they kill themselves to get there."

"Okay, you're all fucked up too," he said. Took a step back from me like I had a disease he didn't want to catch. "You dose these people? You on something, dude?"

I told him, Oh never mind. I tried to talk to the adults there—but they weren't listening. Especially the older ones—they were staring at the paradise window, in the middle of the cul-de-sac, each seeing something different. Hearing how they had to get there . . . how a quick death would be the sure way . . .

Mr. Baolaban—this gangly black guy immigrated from somewhere around Australia—he was chanting something in some native language and climbing a power pole. He clipped into a wire there. I yelled at him to stop—but he broke the wire and grabbed it and fell off the pole, hit the ground hard, clutching the live broken end, spasticating as the electricity went through him, his body rippling on the sidewalk.

The cops and fire trucks and ambulances were just getting there when that Chinese lady whose name I don't know, and a heavy set blond woman I don't know either, both of them grabbed onto Mr. Baolaban and started to go all spastic too, with their hair standing up and sparks jumping out of their mouths and their shoes flying off, all three electrocuted, and the fire trucks were rumbling in there pretty fucking fast, man, and two more people came out of their houses, Mr. Gimbelowski the alcoholic and that young guy from Pakistan who always seems so homesick, and they threw themselves under the fire truck's tires before the trucks had quite come to a stop and then Reverend Brewster drove up, looking for his son, but the space demons crowded around him and said in paradise he would be forgiven for being a homosexual if he went now and took his son, and he tried to drag Danny over to the power lines but the cops pulled him away and then Reverend Brewster grabbed a cop's gun and shot Danny and himself in the head and one of the cops pulled his own gun and started waving it around hysterically and Mrs. Galworthy rushed at the cop waving the gun, jabbing at his eyes with a nail file, forcing him to shoot and he blew her brains out, and he screamed, himself, as if he'd been the one shot, and then an old lady from the corner house, at the opening of the cul-de-sac, was trying to get away from two firemen, and she bit one on the wrist and he lost his grip on her and I saw why they'd been holding her: she bolted into Bench's house, which was all flames, and threw herself into it, saying something about going through Hell to Heaven—she didn't scream for long, only about ten seconds—and then someone fell face down *WHOOSH SPLAT* right next to me on the pavement, jumped from the top of the highest house in the street and to my left that pale guy with the beard who talks to himself and throws his mail down, I never did know his name, he knocked down an ambulance driver and then he was driving the ambulance real fast through a fence, knocking down the slats, *WHAP-CRUNCH, WHAP-CRUNCH WHAP-CRUNCH*, following the fence back, knocking the boards down one after another, with splinters flying, all the way into the backyard and right off that near-cliff, down the steep hill, the ambulance turning over and over—we could hear it crunching and bouncing—and that Mrs. Klepsky whose husband had left her, who used to come to Mom's book club coffee klatch and then started avoiding her, the one whose face was so tight from all those operations—she was sticking a burning rag in her SUV's gas tank and then climbing into it and the cops were yelling at her but then *BOOM!* it went off and she was in a fireball and then *WHOOSH SPLAT* someone jumped out of a tree and hit the ground next to that previous *WHOOSH SPLAT* and . . .

And the cops were dragging me away, asking me what I knew about this, hadn't this started with me somehow, what was going on, was I on drugs, had I dosed those people? Comparing it to Columbine, in some shady-ass way. And then I saw the space demons were talking to those cops and the cops were glaring at me, and the space demons were talking and talking to them, and two of the space demons seemed to be rolling joyously around on the ground and quivering in a kind of ecstasy, as the sirens screamed and the burning houses crackled— because the fire was spreading around the cul-de-sac now—and people screamed in pain and somebody else went *WHOOSH SPLAT* onto the street from above . . .

Man it was fucked up.

I was really glad when the cops shoved me in the back of a cruiser. Officer Blume, whom I know—he's actually the older brother of a friend of mine—was telling the others not to hit me, he didn't see how I could be responsible, it was like he was fighting that space demon influence, and he was the one who drove me to the police station . . .

Well. That's most of what happened. Nobody believes me. I shouldn't have told anyone about the space demons because they think that if I'm making up something like that—they just assume I'm making it up—well then, I must be covering up something. And why, they want to know, was I the only one not affected back there?

I've tried to explain that—and that the only reason they don't believe me is because the space demons did all that suggestion, all that brain washing. On *them*.

They just shake their heads.

So, now I'm telling you, Mr. Court Appointed Psychiatrist, and you can believe what you want.

I've stopped seeing the space demons. Because at the police station, the space demons started talking about rules again, and said they were going to have to report somewhere, and then they just *went*. Blip, and *blip, blip, blip* right into the corners.

I can still see things you can't, though. If I want, if I sort of squint, I can see a window into another place. Only, I see what it really is, in the next world. What that other place really is. It has a kind of screen over it, and on that screen we project what we think we want to see. But I can see *past* that, into the real afterlife. Into bardos, they call them. My Aunt Gilliam gave me that *Tibetan Book of the Dead* about bardos. And I can see right into them . . .

I see Reverend Brewster and Mrs. DeSanto and Danny and Mrs. Klepsky and Bench and Mrs. Hasslet and the others over there. They're going around and around, bumping into one another, weeping, in a thing that is an endless drain that never finishes draining, a spiritual cul-de-sac without an exit; they're stuck there from looking, from looking, from looking-looking-looking for what they were told would be there, and looking for it is keeping them there, in something that's not Heaven, or Hell. Not really Hell exactly. Those people are stuck, just endlessly hungry and wandering in circles inside circles, right outside time; they're caught up in a place where certain kinds of lost souls go. And where they stay, for thousands of years, and sometimes longer . . . and maybe forever.

And the scientists, the space demons are there too, doing experiments on them. Experimenting and testing and conjecturing. Around and around.

It's all they know how to do.

GOTTERDAMMERGUN

Listening to the rasp of Dad's station wagon backing out of the gravel driveway, Randy wondered how long he could continue to convince his father that he was sick. He ate his tepid oatmeal, congratulating himself that he'd managed to stay home from school for ten days. Ten days spent playing videogames most of the time. But Dad was getting seriously suspicious. There was talk of dragging him to Doc. Jenners. And Jenners was a grumpy white-haired old man with bad breath and dandruff who thought he was a wise country doctor, the kind who always said you were faking it even if you had a fever.

But going to school meant facing Harold Sparks who was fifty pounds heavier than Randy and who was going to sit on him and do that slapping thing over and over that left no marks but made you feel like you wanted to die.

He wished Mom wasn't working. She was working so much she was just too tired to talk to. But she'd really gotten into this career thing, "cold-calling" for some company that sold extra insurance. He could talk to her when she was in the mood to listen. She just wasn't in the mood much anymore.

You couldn't talk to Dad about anything except sports. Complain about the Harolds of the world he'd just say, "Kick their asses." Yeah right. Randy was short, spindly, and tended to freeze up when people swung at him.

So Randy just played sick and played videogames and waited.

He got bored with the RPGs, *Car Theft Seven* and *SewerCrawl*— but he was seriously hooked on *World War Two, Part Three: One Man, One War.*

Randy went to the living room, switched on the GameGem system, feeling a familiar thrill go through him at the warm-up tone that meant he was going to play. He had hours and hours to play. And he was so close to beating the game . . .

Maybe he loved to play this one because it was easy to pretend these generic Nazis were Harold—despite their oddly clipped helmets, their shouts of *"Achtung!"*, their M1s. They had three models of Nazis in the game and the big blond flat-top haircut ones were especially Harold-like.

"Die, Sparks, you bitch!" he muttered, as he hit the jump button, taking his first-person point-of-view over a wall and pressing pulling the controller's R1 trigger, hard—cutting the big blond Nazi down. Blood splashed across the screen as his enemy spun about, shattered by bullets.

Randy dashed up a stairway and blew away eight more Nazis, and then—all at once—he was there! He'd gotten to the Gotterdammer Gun!

He had been working for *nine damn days* to get to this checkpoint in the game, saving his progress little by little. This was the last level, where you got control of a gigantic "experimental new cannon"— which hadn't existed in the real war but, in the world of the game, it was a machine gun cannon that fired thousands of rounds off a huge belt of ammunition, each shell as big as a cruise missile.

The cannon seemed to have infinite ammo as he fired at the army coming toward him. World War Two depended on him—the game had made that clear. He was at a key point in the Secret History of the war and if he didn't destroy this army the Nazis would overrun all over England and then the USA.

It was a delicious rush of power to fire the Gotterdammer Gun—

Then a voice spoke to him from the television speakers.

And it called him by name.

"Randy . . . Randy we need your help—in der name of Gott, listen carefully!"

"Oh shit. I'm losing it," Randy muttered. Too much time playing this stuff.

"Randy . . . Randy Rheinhold Steiner? We are contacting you from . . . Rolf, he'll never believe us . . . yes, yes, I'll try . . . Randy—we're contacting you from the future." It was a woman's voice with an odd accent, crackling in and out. "Randy—listen very carefully—the designers of the game you are playing accidentally set up a space-time *rogue-wave* with their enhancement of a certain microchip. The past is *not necessarily fixed*, Randy! The past of the world—the real world—is not set in stone! It can be changed! We have two contiguous realities intersecting here in the future, Randy Steiner. Are you listening? Can you hear us?"

"Uh . . . yeah?"

Randy put the game on pause—and the voice erupted in panic. "No! Do not pause the game! Not for more than—what does it say, Rolf? Fifty-five? Yes, *ja*—fifty-five seconds, Randy! Please, I beg you . . . do not pause the game more than fifty-five seconds! It has to do with quantum transmission through resonating brainwaves. We've traced the problem, traced the intersecting realities from conflicting historical pasts. Rolf, I don't know if he's still there! Mein Gott, we only have one chance! Randy—are you listening?"

"This is so totally cool! The coolest game feature ever!" Randy enthused. "Dude, this a complete surprise. Is this like some sort of beta-test thing? I haven't seen anything on it online!"

"No no no my voice is not part of the game, Randy!"

"Voice recognition! Sweet! That is so awesome! When did that tech come out? I didn't hear about GameGem using it . . ."

"It *doesn't* have that tech, Randy! This isn't voice recognition software—don't be dense! *I'm really talking to you*, right now! What we're telling you is real."

"Yeah right. Videogames can change history or something? I don't think so. But okay, I'm taking it off pause . . ."

"Oh danke—just in time. It's simply too hard to explain how we're contacting you, Randy. We've traced the rogue time space wave to your particular GameGem unit. No two videogame systems are completely alike. *Yours* is the one creating the problem. Do you understand? Randy, *please* listen—*don't switch off the game*. That's what we called to tell you. We're afraid you will switch it off and you mustn't. We're in *hell* here, in the future. You don't know what it's like. You don't know what these people are like who run the world—Randy, look out for those Stukas! Shoot them out of the air!"

Luftwaffe planes dived at his character's position on the roof of the tower, firing. He fired back, and missed. They strafed him and he saw his health go down thirty percent—

"Oh shit, I got to get some health."

"No, Randy, not now! There's a narrow time window—you mustn't stop firing the cannon! *You must win World War Two in this game right now, within the next minute—or the Nazis will take over the world in real life!*"

"Uh huh. Right. It must not be voice recognition," he muttered, as he fired the cannon at the planes. Hard to hit them.

"Listen Randy—your gameplay will ripple back in time and change the outcome of World War Two! If you lose control of the Gotterdammergun in the game the Nazis will win the war—in real life! Shoot the tanks below the castle! And knock the Nazi planes out of the air! Don't stop to 'restore health'! Please, I'm begging you—focus on shooting!"

Randy was only half listening. He was concentrating on the onrushing tanks of the army. "I'm trying, for Chrissakes, but—I'm under heavy fire!"

"Yes yes, heavy fire—but focus, Randy! Focus!"

The tanks were really blasting his castle now. It was crumbling apart around him. "It must be—Shit! I'm getting slammed here—it must be that the game is guessing what I'd say to it and, like, responding with recordings!" He chuckled, grinning as he worked the controller. "That's so tight!"

"No, no! We're not anticipating your responses! *We're actually talking to you, dammit!*"

He laughed, firing the automatic machine gun cannon at the front line of the oncoming army below, killing hundreds of Nazis, but thousands more were following. Once they won past his position they would sweep down on the main column of the Allied Forces and change the course of the war—

"We're not a game program, Randy! My name is Lou Ann Chartmoor! I am a quantum physicist! We're working on this time distortion—trying to rectify things! Only a few of us remember the time flow when the Nazis did not win the war—"

"Actually I think I'm going to quit and reload," he mumbled. "Health's too low. I'll start over again at the beginning of the level."

"No you can't do that! Please, listen to me! The quantum waves will interpret that as surrender and the Nazis will win World War Two for real! You must not quit!" The voice was sounding genuinely panicky. Really good voice acting.

"I want to make some toast, game-voice. This is so *tight*, talking to the game like this—but I'm hungry, game, so—"

"No Randy, I am *not* just part of the game," the voice notched down the hysteria a bit. "If . . . if you do not remain in the game and win this battle it will cause the war to have been lost in your timeline's past. I *know* it seems ludicrous but so much of reality *is* ludicrous, Randy! Trust us, you must play this through *now!*"

The hectoring game voice was starting to irritate him. It was too hard to concentrate on shooting planes and tanks and soldiers with that voice yelling warnings at him. That was probably the point— it was an additional game obstacle to overcome. He hadn't finished his oatmeal and now it was cold and sticky-lumpy and he wanted some toast and his character's health was low in the game and the tower was crumbling out from under the cannon anyway—

Yeah, screw it, he was going to reload from the last checkpoint.

"Please Randy . . ." A sob in that voice now.

He rolled his eyes, clicked on the button that would bring up the *QUIT?* icon.

The voice almost blew out the TV's speakers with its scream. "No Randy *don't!* How do you think I know your name if—"

But he had already clicked on *QUIT?*

How *had* they known his name? Maybe when he'd bought the game? He'd ordered it online, so it must've been one of those data mining programs . . .

He stood up, feeling vaguely sick to his stomach. He thought he felt a rumbling go through the house, like an earthquake. And then he felt tired.

He sagged back on the sofa.

That's when his mom came in. She said something about having to take time off work and having talked to the doctor and the doctor saying he was malingering and he was going in late to school but by gosh he was going right now because they were starting rehearsals for that pageant and she really wanted to see him in it so—

But her voice—it took him a few minutes to get used to it though he wasn't sure what he was getting used to.

"Randy du wirst zu spät zum Treffen des Nazijugend-Clubs kommen!"

"Wirklich, Mama? Ich kann mich nicht daran erinnern—Unsere Stimmen—klingen heute für uns so seltsam—"

"Was? Unsere Stimmen—was für ein Schwachsinn. Du sollst ihnen helfen das Festspiel vorzubereiten! Das Pageant!"

"Was für ein Festspiel?"

"Hast du irgendwas geraucht, Junge? Das Festspiel für die Milleniumsfeier des Tages an dem das Reich Washington DC zerstört hat—? Komm schon, Junge, verdammt noch mal, beweg dich! Willst du festgenommen und verhört werden? Das Reich wartet nicht! Schalt jetzt das Spiel aus und beeil dich!"

"Nein—schalt es nicht aus Mama—oh nein—"

"Was stimmt heute nicht mit dir?"

"Ich sollte . . . ich musste . . . I kann mich nicht erinnern . . . Vergiss es, Mama. Ist meine uniform sauber?"

"I WANT TO GET MARRIED,"
SAYS THE WORLD'S SMALLEST MAN

"You a fucking ho," Delbert said. "You don't come at me like that, not a fuckin' ho."

"Fuck you, Delbert, who turned me out? You busted me out there on Capp Street when it was fucking thirty degrees—I ain't a motherfuckin' tossup like yo' nigger bitch cousins, I'm a white girl, motherfucker, I don't come out of that—"

"Don't be talkin' that shit. You was already a fucking whore, you fucked that *ess ay* CheeChee—"

"Sure so he didn't beat my fucking head in. Where were you? Where were *you* when he was slapping me and shit? Hittin' the fuckin' pipe, Delbert. Shit you knew what was going on—where you going now, goddammit?"

Delbert was mumbling over the loose knob of the hotel room's door, trying to get out into the hall. The knob was about ready to come off. Brandy was glad Delbert was going because that meant he wasn't going to work himself up to knocking her around, but at the same time she didn't want to be left alone, just her and the fucked-up TV that was more or less a radio now because the picture was so slanty you couldn't make it out, a two-week-old *Weekly World Inquirer*, and one can of Colt malt liquor stashed on the window ledge. And something else, he was going to get some money, maybe get an out-front from Terrence, and do some rock. She shouted after him, "You going to hit that pipe without me again? You suckin' it all up, microwavin' that pipe, fuckin' it up the way you do it, and Terrence going to kick yo' ass if you smoke what he give you to sell—"

But he'd got the door open, yelling, "SHUT UP WOMAN I BITCH SLAP YOU!" as he slammed it behind him with that soap-opera timing.

"Fuck you, you better bring me back some fuckin' bring me some fuckin' . . ." She let her voice trail off as his steps receded down the hall, ". . . dope."

The fight had used her up. She felt that plunge feeling again, like nothing was any use so why try; and what she wanted was to go back to bed. She thought, maybe I can get my baby out of Foster Care Hold, that place's just like prison. Shit Candy's not a baby anymore, she's ten, and she's half-white, looks more white than anything else, she'll be okay.

Brandy got up off the edge of the bed, walked across the chilly room, hugging herself, feeling her sharp hips under her fingers, as she went to the window. She looked out through the little cigarette-burn hole, just in time to see Delbert walk his skinny black ass out the front door, right up to Terrence. "The man's going to go off on you one of these days, Delbert, you'll be a dead nigger before you hit the emergency room, you fucking asshole," she said, aloud, taking satisfaction in it.

There was no reason, she thought, to be looking out the burn-hole instead of just lifting the shade; she didn't have anything to be paranoid about, there wasn't even any fucking crumbles of dope in the house, she hadn't had any hubba in two days, and now she was laying awake at night thinking about it, not wanting to go out and turn a trick for it because she had that really bad lady trouble, and the pain when they shoved into her was like stabbing her in the crotch with a knife, the infection—

There it was, soon as she started thinking about it, the itching started bad again, itching and burning. Ow Ow. Ow. Shit, go to the clinic, go to the clinic. She didn't have the energy. They made you wait so long. Treated you like a fucking whore.

She turned to the burn-hole again, saw Terrence walking along with Delbert, Terrence shaking his head. No more credit. Delbert'd be back up here, beat her till she'd hit the streets again. She turned away from the cigarette hole. Looking out through the tiny burn-hole was a tweakin' habit. Like picking holes in your skin trying to get coke bugs. Once she'd spent a whole day, eight hours straight staring out through that hole, picking her skin bloody, staring, turning away only to hit the crack pipe. That was when Delbert was dealing and they were flush with dope. Fucking cocaine made you tweaky, it was funny stuff. Maybe Delbert's cousin Darius would give her some. For some head. Her stomach lurched. She went back to the bed, looked again at the *Inquirer* article she'd been laboriously reading:

I Want to Get Married, Says World's Smallest Man!

Ross Taraval, the world's smallest man, wants to get married—and he's one eligible bachelor! He weighs only 17 pounds and is only inches tall but he has a budding vocation as an entertainer and he's got plenty of love to give, he tells us. "I want a wife to share my success," said Ross, 24, who has starred in two films shot in Mexico, making him a star, or anyway a comet, in that enterprising land. Recently the Minute Mexican was given a "small" role in a Hollywood film as the long lost brother of "Mini Me". "There's more to me than meets the eye," Ross said. "The doctors say I could have children—and I'd support my new wife in real style! And listen, I want a full-sized wife. That's what a real man wants—and I can handle her—just let me climb aboard! I've got so much love to give and there's a real man inside this little body wanting to give it to the right woman!"

Ross, who was abandoned at three years of age, was raised by nuns in Miami. After attracting attention in the *Trafalgar Book of World Records*, Ross was contacted by his manager, six-foot-five-inch Benny Chafin, who could carry Ross in his overcoat pocket if he wanted to. Chafin trained Ross in singing and dancing and soon found him work in nightclubs and TV endorsements.

"I've got my eye on a beautiful house in the Hollywood Hills for the right lady," Ross said.

There was a picture of the little guy standing next to his manager—not even coming up to the manager's crotch height. The manager, now, he was cute, he looked kind of like Geraldo Rivera, Brandy thought. There was a little box at the bottom of the article. It said, *If you think you'd be a likely life-mate for Ross and would like to get in touch with him, you may write him care of the Weekly World Inquirer and we'll forward your letter to him. Address your correspondence to . . .*

She shook her head. Nawm stupid idea. She heard Delbert's footsteps in the hall.

There was a stamp on the letter from her sister that hadn't been canceled. She could peel it off . . .

"I think I got you a job at Universal Studios!" Benny said, striding breathlessly in.

"Really?" Ross's heart thumped. He climbed arduously down off the chair he'd been squatting in to watch TV. The Sleepytime Inn had a Playboy Channel.

He hurried over to Benny, who was taking off his coat. It was May in Los Angeles, and sort of cold there. The cold made Ross's joints ache. Benny had said it was always warm in LA, but it wasn't now. It was cloudy and windy.

It took Ross a long time to get across the floor to Benny, and Ross was impatient to know what was going on, so he started shouting questions through his wheezing before he got there.

"What movie am I in?" he asked. "Does it have The Rock in it?"

"Ross, slow down, you'll get your asthma started. No see, it's not a movie. It's a performance gig at their theme park. They want you to play King of the Wonksters for the tourists. It's a live show."

Ross stopped in the middle of the floor, panting, confused. "What're Wonksters?"

"They're . . . sort of like Ewoks. Little outer space guys. Universal's got a movie coming out about 'em at Christmas so this'd be next summer—if the movie hits—and—"

"Next summer! I need some work now! Those bastards! You said I could be in a buddy picture with The Rock!"

"I spoke to his agent. He already did a buddy picture with a little guy. He doesn't want to do that again."

"You said I could meet him!"

"You're going to be around Hollywood for a long time, you'll meet your hero, Ross, calm down, all right? You don't want to have an attack. Maybe we can get a photo op or something with him—"

Benny had turned away, was frowning over the papers in his briefcase.

"We're not even sleeping in Hollywood!" Ross burst out. He'd been saving this all morning, having heard it from the maid. "We're . . ."

"Hey, we're in LA, OK? It doesn't matter where you live as long as you can drive to the studios. Most of the studios aren't actually in Hollywood, Ross, they're in Burbank or Culver City—"

"Mary, Mother of God! I want to go out in Hollywood! You're out getting wild with all the girls! No? You are! And leaving me here!"

Benny turned to him, his cheeks mottling. He cocked a hip, slightly, and Ross backed away. He knew, from the times he had run away from the mission, how people stood when they were going to kick you.

He'd spent six weeks in the mission hospital after one kick stove in his ribs, and he wasn't quite right from it yet. He most *definitely* knew when they were going to kick you.

But Benny made that long exhalation through his nose that meant he was trying to keep his temper. He'd never kicked Ross, or hurt him at all, he probably never would. He'd done nothing but help him, after all.

"I'm sorry, Benny," Ross said. "Can we have a Big Mac and watch Playboy channel?"

"Sure. We deserve a break, right?" He'd turned back to his briefcase, sorting papers. "I had a letter here for you, from those people at the *World Inquirer*."

"I don't like those people."

"They're bloodsuckers. But the publicity is good, so whatever it is, we play along. We'll get a TV commercial or something out of it."

"I hope you are not mad at me, Benny . . ."

"I'm not mad at you. Hey, here it is. Your letter."

There was something off about his face, Brandy thought. His nose seemed crooked or something. His features a little distorted. Must be from being a dwarf, or a midget, or whatever he was.

She tried to picture cuddling with him, think of him as cute, like a kid, but when she pictured him unzipping his pants, she got a skin-crawling feeling.

Hit the pipe a few times, anything's all right.

She pushed the thought of dope to the back of her mind. She had to play this carefully.

They were sitting in the corner booth of a Denny's restaurant. Ross, actually, was standing on the leatherette seat, leaning on the table like it was a bar, but the people who passed probably thought he was sitting. They also probably thought he was her kid. Shit, he was twenty-eight inches high. His head, though, was almost normal sized. Too big for his body. He was wearing a kid's stiffly pressed suit and tie, with a hanky tucked in the pocket; he looked like a little kid going to Sunday School. "Did a lot of women write to you?" she asked.

"Not too many. The ones that did are too big and fat or old, except you." He had a slight Mexican accent but seemed to speak English pretty good. ". . . Or they were black. I don't want a black wife. I liked you, because your hair is blond, and your letter was very nice, the handwriting was nice, the stationery was very nice. Smelled nice too."

But he was talking sort of distractedly. She could see he was staring at the scabs on her cheeks. There were only a few, really.

"I guess you're looking at my skin—" she began.

"No no no! It's fine. Fine." His voice sounded like it was coming through a little tube from the next room. He smiled at her. He had nice teeth.

"It's okay to notice it," Brandy said. "My . . . my sister has this crazy Siamese cat. You know how the little fuh—" Watch your language, she told herself. "You know how they are. I bent over to pet him and he jumped up and scratched me . . ."

Ross nodded. He seemed to buy it. Maybe where he was from they didn't have a lot of hubba-heads picking at their skin all the time.

"There was a cat," he said absently, "who scared me, at the mission. Big and fat and mean." He scowled and muttered something else in his munchkin voice she couldn't quite make out.

"It's nice of you to buy me dinner," Brandy said. A fucking Denny's, she thought. Well, maybe it was like he said, it was just the nearest one and he was hungry. But she'd pictured some really fancy place . . .

The waitress brought their order, steak for Brandy—who knew if this was going to work out? Get what you can now—and a milkshake and fries for the little guy, which was kind of a funny dinner, Brandy thought. The waitress had done a double take when she'd first come to take their order; now she didn't look at Ross directly. But she stared at Brandy when she thought Brandy wouldn't notice.

Fuck you, bitch, you think I'm sick for kickin' with the little dude.

"You really do look nice," Ross said, as the waitress walked away. Like he was trying to convince himself.

She'd done her best. Her hair was almost naturally blond, that was good, but it was a little thin and dry from all the crack and

when she'd washed it with that shitty hand soap that was all
Delbert had, it'd frizzed out, so she'd had to corn-row it. She'd
hand-washed her dress and borrowed Carmen's pumps and ripped
off a pair of new pantyhose and some makeup from the Walgreen's.
Getting the bus down here was harder, but she'd conned a guy at
the San Francisco station into helping her out, and then she'd
ditched him at the LA station when he'd gone to the men's room.
She'd got twelve dollars for the guy's luggage, so it was beginning
to click.

Ross started to cough. "Are you choking on something?" she asked,
dreading it, because she didn't want to attract even more attention.

"No—my asthma." He was fishing in his pocket with one of his
little doll hands. He found an inhaler, and sucked at it.

"Just rest a bit, you don't have to talk or nothin'," she said, smiling
at him.

So his health was not that great. It wouldn't seem too weird or
anything, then, if he died, or something.

"You just swept me off my feet, I guess," Brandy said. "I thought you
were hella cute at the wedding. I was surprised you didn't have your
manager over to be, like, best man or something."

"We had to be married first, because I know what he would say,
he doesn't want me to get married till he checks everyone out, you
know. But *he* has lots of girls. Come on in, come on in, this is our
room, our own room . . ."

"Wow, it even has a kitchen! Anyway, look it's got a bar and a
microwave and a little refrigerator . . ." She noticed that the
microwave oven wasn't bolted to the wall. It was pretty old, though—
she probably couldn't get much for it.

"I do like this refrigerator," he was saying, "this little refrigerator by
the floor. When we get a big house we'll have a real kitchen!"

"Yeah? Uhhh . . . When do you think—"

He interrupted her with a nervous dance of excitement, spreading his arms to gesture at the whole place. "You like this place? Las Vegas. It's so beautiful, everything's like a palace, all lit up, so much money, everything's like in a treasure chest."

"Uh huh." She started to sit on the edge of the bed, then noticed his eyes got all round and buggy when he saw her there. She moved over to the vinyl sofa, and sat down, kicked off her shoes. "It would've been nice if we coulda stayed in the Golden Nugget or one of them places—this Lucky Jack's is okay, but they don't got their own casino, they don't got room service . . ."

"Oh—we'll stay in the best, when Benny finds some work for me in Hollywood."

He toddled toward her, unbuttoning his coat. What did he think he was going to do?

She wondered where you got crack in Vegas. She knew there'd be a place. Maybe the edge of town out by the airport. She could find it. She needed more cash first . . .

And then it hit her, and she stood up, sharply. He took several sudden steps back, almost stumbling. She looked down at him, feeling unreal.

Had she been *hustled* by this little creature? "Did you say, when Benny finds you some work? What do you mean?"

She felt the tightening in her gut, the tease of imagined taste in her mouth: the taste of vaporized cocaine and the other shit they put in it. She could almost feel the glass pipe in her hand; see the white smoke swirling in the glass tube. Her heart started pounding, hands twitching, fuck, going on a tweak with no dope to hit, one hand jerking at a scab on the back of her left forearm.

The little guy was chattering something. "Oh, I'm working in Hollywood! He actually puffed out his chest. "I'm going to star in a movie with The Rock!"

She blinked. Rock? "With . . . ?"

"Dwayne Johnson, The Rock!"

"Oh him. Okay. How much did you get paid?"

He fiddled with a lamp cord. "I don't have the check yet. It's not negotiated."

"Jesus fucking Christ."

He gaped at her with his mouth so round and red and wet it looked like it had been punched in his head with a tool. "That is a blasphemy! That is taking the Lord's name! I can't have my wife talking like that!"

"Sure, I just forgot about your religious thing. Look—we're married now. We share everything right? How *much* we got to share? I need some cash, lover—for one thing, we didn't get a ring yet, you said we'd get a diamond ring—"

Ross was pacing back and forth, looking like a small child waiting for the men's room, trying not to wet his pants. "I don't have very much money now—thirty dollars—"

"Thirty dollars! Jesus fuh . . . that's a kick in the butt. What about credit cards?"

He wrung his little hands. Made her think of a squirrel messing with a peanut. "I'm paying with American Express for the airplane and hotel—Benny will stop the card!"

"American Express? Can you draw cash on the card?"

He stopped scuttling around and blinked up at her. "I don't know."

"Come on, we're gonna find out. We're going out."

"But we're 'Just Married'!"

"It's not even dark out yet, Ross. Hold your horses, okay? First things first. We can't do anything without a ring, can we? We're gonna do something, don't worry. I'm hella horny. But we can't do it without a ring. A honeymoon without a wedding ring—that'd be hella weird, don't you think?"

When she came in, the little guy was sitting in the middle of the bed, with his legs crossed Indian style, in a pair of red silk pajamas. There was a Saint Christopher's medal around his neck. Probably couldn't pawn that for much either.

It was after midnight, sometime. The dwarf had the overhead lights dialed down low, and the tall floor lamp in the corner was unplugged. In the dimness he looked like a doll somebody had left on the bed, some stuffed toy, till he leaned back on the pillow in a pose he'd probably seen on the Playboy Channel.

They'd got the limit for the account, three hundred cash on the American Express Card. They'd endured all the stares in the American Express office, and she'd kept her temper with the giggly fat guy who thought they were performing at *Circus Circus*, but the hard part had been making Ross swallow the amazingly bullshit story about how it was a tradition in California for the girl to go shopping for the ring alone . . .

She'd had to cuddle him and stroke his crotch a few times, before going out—his dick was a hard little thing like a pen-knife blade. Then she'd left him here with a bottle of pink Andre champagne, watching some shit about big-tit girls shooting each other with Uzis. He'd made kissy faces at her as she left.

Now she was back, stoned on some pretty good shit, she thought maybe she could give him a blow job or something if she closed her eyes. But she'd burned through two hundred fifty dollars in hubba, her mouth was dry as a baked potato skin from hitting the pipe.

"Let me see the beautiful ring on the beautiful girl," he said, his voice slurred from the cheap champagne. He said something else she couldn't make out as she crossed the room to him and sat on the bed, just out of reach.

"Hey, you know what?—Whoa, slow down, not so fast *compadre*," she said, fending his clammy little hands away.

She pointed at the girl on the wall-mounted TV screen; a girl in lavender lingerie. "How'd you like me to dress up like that, huh? I need something like *that*. I'd look hella good, just hella sexy in that. I know where I can get some, there's an adult bookstore that's got some lingerie, they're open all night, you can go in and look at movies and I'll—"

"No!" His voice was unexpectedly low. "I need you now!"

"Hey cool off—what I'm saying you could call Benny and ask him to wire you some money. We need some things. He could send it to the all-night check-cashing place on Las Vegas Boulevard, they got Western Union—" She picked up her purse and went unsteadily toward the bathroom. The room looked warped; crack always did weird shit to her vision.

"Where you going?"

"Just to the bathroom, do some lady's business." I could tell him I'm on my period, Latin guys will steer clear from that, she thought. Maybe get another girl in here, give her a twenty to keep him occupied. "Why don't you call Benny while I'm in here, ask for some money, we need some stuff, hon!" She called, as she closed the bathroom door and fumbled through her purse with trembling fingers. Found the pipe, found the torn piece of copper scrubbing pad she was using for a pipe-screen, found the lighter. Her thumb was already blackened and calloused from flicking. Her heart was pounding in her ears as she took the yellowish white dove of crack from the inner pocket of the purse, broke it in half with a thumbnail, dropped it the pipe howl, melted it down with the lighter . . .

There was a pounding on the door—near her knee. She stared at the lower part of the door, holding the smoke in for a moment, then slowly exhaled. Her vision shrank and expanded, shrank and expanded, and then she heard his piping voice say, "You get out here and be with your husband!" Trying to make his voice all gravelly. She had to laugh. She took another hit. It wasn't getting her off much now. And she was feeling on the edge of that plunge into depression, that around the corner of the high; she felt the tweaky paranoia jab her with its hot icepick.

Someone was going to hear him yell; they were going to come in and see the pipe and she'd be busted in a Vegas jail . . .

"SHUT THE FUCK UP, ROSS!" she bellowed. Then thought: Oh great, that's even worse. She hissed: "Be quiet! I don't want anybody to come in here—"

"They were here, to bring towels, and they told me women don't go for the ring alone! That's not any kind of tradition! You come on out, no more little jokes!"

"You're a fucking little joke!" she yelled, as he started kicking the door. She turned the knob and slammed the door outward. Felt him bounce off it on the other side. Heard him slide across the rug, stop against the bed frame. A wail, then a shout of rage.

She thought again about a will. He might have more money stashed someplace, or some coming. But there was no way this thing was going to last out the night and she couldn't get him to a lawyer tonight and he was already suspicious. She'd have to just get his gold wrist watch and his thirty bucks—twenty some now after the champagne—and maybe those little pajamas, sell that shit, no first get—

She paused to hit the pipe again. Part of her, tweaking, listened intensely for the hotel's manager or the cops.

—get that call through to his manager, make him give the manager dude some bullshit story, have him send the most cash possible. Maybe hustle a thousand bucks. Or maybe the little guy could be sold, himself—somewhere, Circus Circus or some place, or to some kind of pervert. No, too hard to handle. Just make the call and then . . . he should get a "heart attack". He deserved it, he'd hustled *her*, telling her he had money, he was a big star, but all the time he wasn't doing shit, getting her to marry him under false pretenses, fucking little parasite, kick his miniature ass . . .

A pounding low on the bathroom door again. Angrier now. The door was partly open. Little fucker was scared to put a limb through, but he stood to one side and peered in at her. "What is that? What is that in your hands? Drugs! Shit, you're going to get us put in jail and you're going to ruin my career! It'll be a big scandal and The Rock

won't want to be in a picture with me and—!" He had to break off
for wheezing, and she heard him puff a couple of times on his inhaler,
which was funny, how it was like her pipe.

She kicked the door open. He jumped back, narrowly avoiding
its swishing arc, falling on his little butt. For a moment she felt bad
because he looked so much like one of her kids, like he was going to
cry, and then for some reason that made her even madder, and she
stepped out, pipe in one hand and lighter in the other, and kicked
at him, clipping him on the side of the head with her heel. He spun,
and blood spattered the yellow bedspread.

She paused to hit the pipe, melting another rock. Her mouth was
starting to taste like the pipe filter more than coke, she wasn't getting
good hits, she needed cash, get some cash and get a cab.

He was up on his feet, scuttling toward the door to the hall. He was
just tall enough to operate the knob. There was no way she could
let the little fucker go, and no way she was going to let the rollers
get her in Vegas, fuck that. She crossed the room in three strides,
exhaling as she went, trailing smoke like a locomotive, doing an end
run around him, turning to block the door. He backed away, his face
in darkness. He was making an ugly hiccupping noise. He didn't look
like a human being now, in the dimness and through the dope; he
looked like some kind of gnome, or like one of those creatures in that
old movie *Gremlins*—some sneaky little thing going to run around in
the dark spots and pull shit on you.

Maybe the microwave. If you didn't dial the thing up too high it
just sort of boiled things inside, end up looking like he'd had a stroke.
She had persuaded him to check in without her, they didn't know
she was here. Unless he'd told the girl with the towels.

"You tell anybody I was here?"

He didn't answer. Probably, Brandy decided, he wouldn't have told
much to some cheap hotel maid. So there was nothing stopping it.

He turned and scrambled under the bed. "That ain't gonna do you
no good, you little fucker," she whispered.

x   x   x

Ross heard her moving around up there. He pictured her in a nun's habit. The nuns, when they were mad at him, would hunt him through the mission; he would hide like a rodent in some closet till they found him.

The dust under the bed was furring his throat, his lungs. He wheezed with asthma. She was going to get him into a corner, and kick him. She'd kick him and kick him with those hard, pointy shoes until his ribs stove in and he spit up blood. He tried to shout for help, but it came out a coarse whisper between wheezes. He sobbed and prayed in Spanish to the Virgin and Saint Jude.

He heard her muttering to herself, moving purposefully, now, to a corner of the room. He heard glass break. What was she doing? What had she broken?

"Little hustlin' tight-ass motherfucker," she hissed, down on her knees now, somewhere behind him. Something scraped across the rug; he squirmed about to see. It was the tall floor lamp. She'd broken the top of it, broken the bulb, and now she was wielding it like an old widow with a broom handle trying to get at a rat, sliding it under the bed, shoving the long brass pole of it at him.

It was still plugged in. A cluster of blue sparks jumped from the jags broken off in the socket as she shoved it at his face.

He tried to scream and rolled aside. The lopsided king's crown of glass swung to follow him, sparking. He could smell shreds of rug burning. He thought he could feel his heart bruising against his breastbone. She shoved the thing at him again, forcing him back farther . . . Then it stopped moving. She had moved away. Giggling.

Moving around the bed—

Ross felt her fingers close around his ankle. Felt himself dragged backwards, his face burning in the dusty rug, the back of his head smacking against the bed slats. He gave out a wail that tightened into a shriek of frustration, as she jerked him out from under the bed.

He clawed and kicked at her. She was just a great blur, a strange medicinal smell, big slapping hands. One of the hands connected hard and his head rang with it. He began to gag, and found himself unable to lift his arms. Like one of those dreams where you are trapped by a great beast, you want to run but your limbs won't work. She was carrying him somewhere, clasped against her, trapped in her arms like a dog to be washed.

He gagged again. Heard her say, from somewhere above, "Don't you fucking puke on me, you little freak."

His eyes cleared. He saw she was carrying him toward a big box, open on this side. The place had an old, used, cheap microwave oven. The early ones had been rather big.

"Bennnnyyyyyyyyy!" But the cry never quite made it out of his throat.

In less than a second she had crammed him inside it. He could feel his arms and legs again, feel the glass lining of the microwave oven against the skin of his hands and face; his head crammed into a corner, his cheek smashed up against the cold glass. He found some strength and kicked and she swore at him and grabbed his ankles in both her hands. She stuffed his legs in far enough so she could press against his feet with the closing door. He could feel her whole weight against the door.

Crushed into a little box. A little box.

He pressed his palms flat against the glass, tucked his knees against his chest, deliberately pulling deeper into the oven. Felt her using the opportunity to close the door on him.

But now he had some leverage. He used all his strength and a lifetime of frustration and kicked.

The door smacked outward, banging against her chest. She lost her footing; he heard her fall backwards, even as he scrabbled to get out—and dropped out of the oven, fell to the floor himself, landing painfully on his small feet. She was confused, cursing incoherently, trying to get up. He laughed, feeling light-headed and happy.

He sprinted for the living room, jumping over her outstretched leg, and ran into the bedroom area. He could see the door, the way out, clearly ahead of him, unobstructed.

Brandy got up. It was like she was climbing a mountain to do it. Something wet on the back of her head. The little fucker. The pipe. When had it got broken? It was broken, beside the sink. She grabbed the stem. It'd make a knife.

Shit—maybe the little fucker had already gotten out the door.

She felt her lip curl into a snarl, and ran toward the door—her ankle hooked on the wire stretched across the rug, about three inches over it, drawn from the bed frame to the dresser.

The lamp cord, she thought, as she pitched face first onto the rug. She hadn't left the cord that way. The air knocked out of her, she turned onto her back choking, trying to orient herself.

The dwarf was standing over her, laughing, with the champagne bottle in his miniature hands. He clasped the bottle by the neck. A narrow bar of light came in between the curtains, spotlighting his round red mouth.

He was towering over her, from that angle, as he brought the champagne bottle down hard on her forehead.

"A Burglar Killed My New Bride!" Sobs World's Smallest Man

The newlywed bride of Ross Taraval, the world's smallest man, was murdered by an intruder on the first night of their Las Vegas honeymoon. Ross himself was battered senseless by the mystery man—and woke to find that his wife had murdered. Her throat had been cut by the broken glass of the drug-crazed killer's "crack" pipe. The burglar so far has not been located by police.

"It broke my heart," said the game little rooster of a man, "but I have learned that to survive in this world when you are my size, you must be stronger than other men! So I will go on . . . And I have not given up my search for the right woman, to share my fame and fortune . . ."

Ross hints that he's on the verge of signing a deal to do a buddy movie with his hero, Dwayne "The Rock" Johnson. A big career looms up ahead for a small guy! "I'd like to share it with some deserving woman!" Ross says.

If you'd like to send a letter to Ross Taraval, the world's smallest man, you can write to him care of the *Weekly World Inquirer*, and we'll forward the letter to him . . .

FACES IN WALLS

I wake up in room 230, Wemberly Sanitarium, a fifteen by twenty-three foot room with peeling green walls. A dream of freedom and intimacy vanishes and the truth comes thudding back like a door slamming. I'm strapped loosely to a narrow bed, where I've lain, unmoving, for six years. I lie on my back, sharply aware that the overhead light has just switched on for the morning. It's only later that the sunlight comes through the high window, to my right. I lay there waiting for the faces in the walls. And the one face that talks to me.

Mostly, nothing happens in this room, except waking, and waiting, and watching the light change; the nurse coming and going, thoughts coming and going. Enduring the pain of bedsores. The paralysis.

I can move my eyes to look around, and blink—and thank God I can close my eyes. I'm able to breathe without help. I'm unable to speak. I can move my tongue very slightly. There's a little movement in the thumb of my right hand. That's it, that's all of it.

I mentioned being strapped in. The only reason they strap me down at all is just because maybe I might have a seizure, and that could make me fall off the bed. But I haven't had a seizure in years. Some kind of virus got into my brain, years ago, and gave me some really ferocious seizures. The paralysis came after the last seizure, like the jaws of a bear trap closing on me. Anyway, despite the restraints, this is not a mental hospital, this is the Wemberly Geriatric Sanitarium. Geriatric home or not, I'm not old, I'm one of the fairly young patients, for all the good it does me. Thirty-two, by my count, now. Does it sound bad? It's worse. Maybe the distinct feeling of my life burning away, second by second, like a very, very slow fuse that's burning down to a dud firecracker—maybe that's the worst part . . . that and Sam Sack.

I imagine a guy in a band saying, "Fellas, let's play 'Paralyzed'—and play it with feeling." I can *feel*. I feel more than someone with a snapped spine could. Sometimes I'm glad I can feel things—and sometimes I wish I couldn't. I can feel the straps over my chest, though they're not on tightly. I can feel a new bedsore developing on my right shoulder blade. I can feel the thin blanket over my lower half. I can feel the warm air from the vent as the furnace comes on; it blows, left to right, across on my face. I hear the fan that drives the air from the vent; I hear sleety rain hit the window. I can taste a sourness in my mouth—the staff rarely cleans my teeth—and I can taste food, when they bring it, but they give me very little, mostly soups, and not enough. And the way they make the soup there's nothing much to taste.

Now I hear voices. People talking. They take talking for granted and so did I. We waste so much of it . . .

There is something, lately, that gives me some murky sort of hope. *Bethany*. Though I'm not sure what exactly I'm hoping for . . .

Before Beth, I had my sad little ways of coping. Daydreaming of course. And writing in my mind—I tell stories, only I tell them in my mind. I think them out and try to memorize them, word for word, and tell them over again, to myself. Sometimes I make the stories up. Sometimes they're things that really happened.

The story I'm telling now, and trying to etch into a little corner of my brain, is a true one. I know it's true because I'm telling it even as it unfolds. I have an irrational belief that somehow, someone will hear this story. Maybe I'll be able to transmit it to them with my mind. Because in a certain way, my mind has become the strongest part of me. I'll transmit the story all in one piece, out into the ether, and it'll bounce around like a radio signal. A random writer will just pick it up out of the air, maybe years from now, and write it down—and he'll suppose it's all his idea.

x   x   x

My mother abandoned me here, but I guess it's not like abandoning a child. I was an adult, after all, in my mid-twenties, when it happened. I'd been staying with her while I was recovering from a drug relapse.

My mother and I were never close. That's an understatement—we had a simmering mutual aversion, muffled by a truce. It got worse after I grew up and went to college. You're supposed to understand your parents better when you're grown up.

I did understand her—I just couldn't respect her. And she knew it.

I won't say she was a whore, because she didn't take money from her lovers. (I could almost respect her if she'd done it for money.) No, not a whore—but I do think she drove my dad away with her casual adultery, when I was a teenager, and I know she discouraged him from being in touch with me later. And I know she is an alcoholic and a woman who sleeps with the random men she meets in bars. Or that's how she was—I don't even know if she's still alive.

I don't know why Mom invited me to stay with her, after I got fired, and lost my apartment. Maybe she wanted me there to take revenge on me—she didn't have my dad to take revenge on, so she took it out on me. It felt like she wanted me to always be saying, "I'm sorry, I'm sorry." Sorry for something I didn't do.

"You're just like him, Douglas, that's the awful thing," she'd say. Not that my dad was ever a drug addict. And not that I was always one either.

I got into speedballs in the early 1970s, when a lot of us went from Summer of Love thinking, to the whole 1970s glam decadence thing. I would get off work and go right out and score. Always a speedball— heroin and cocaine; heroin and methedrine. I got sick and tired of being sick and tired—so I got clean. I had five years clean, and a good job—before I relapsed. I started using again—and it got me fired. That was another wakeup call. I needed a place to get clean.

Spoke to my mom, in a fit of familial yearning, she said, "You may as well come here."

Six months with my mom. Staying clean, partly because she was staying drunk. She inspired me to sobriety in a backward kind of way. I was just about to move out into a clean-and-sober hostel—anywhere, to get away from her—when the virus hit me. The seizures, the paralysis. The doctors said it was incubating in me, all that time—that I'd gotten it from a needle, fixing drugs, maybe a year or two before.

My mom said it was my comeuppance, it was God's way to say, "No more, Douglas!" She took care of me for a month—when she was sober enough. Thought I'd get over the virus, in time. But finally she put me here. And here I am still. Six years later.

Because I'm going to talk about Bethany, I should say that this place wasn't always a Geriatric Sanitarium. It was, for years, a TB Sanitarium. Tuberculosis, consumption. The White Death. In the mid-sixties, when they had TB mostly licked in this country, Mr. Wemberly, the owner, changed it over to a Geriatrics Sanitarium—only, from what I hear, listening to the nurses, it's only about seventy percent old-age dementia cases. The rest are just odds and ends of damaged people, all ages, who end up here because it's cheap. Very cheap indeed.

Mom left me here, in 1976. So here it is, 1982.

Punishment. Punishment, punishment. Here I am. I'm sorry. Does that help, to say I'm sorry? If I say it again, does it help? I'm sorry. I'm sorry. Now can I get up and walk out of here?

No. The tired gray sunlight coming through the windows says no.

Not much happened to me, for almost six years.

I ingest, I eliminate waste, I breathe. A few minutes of physical therapy, once a month; some electrical therapy; Sister Maria for a brief time. The day nurse and the visits of Sam Sack. That's all.

Anything really new that happens is profoundly exciting—makes my breath come faster, my heart pound. Anything new that has nothing to do with Sam Sack, I mean. I get some stimulation from Sack, sure, but that's not excitement; that's nausea in the shape of a man . . .

About four years ago, for almost seven months, I was visited once a week by a nun, a chubby little Hispanic lady named Sister Maria. She used to sit with me for almost an hour. She'd bring one of those cheap one-speaker cassette tape recorders along, play canticles and the like for me, and read to me. Not always from the Bible. She read from *Quo Vadis?* That was pretty exciting. She had a soft Mexican accent and she used to smile at me and wag her finger and say, "Are you laughing at my accent, Douglas? I think you are!"

It was almost ecstasy, when she talked to me like that—because I did think her accent was amusing. So that was almost like communicating. And when she played music for me, it felt excruciatingly good. It hurt that I couldn't tell her thank you, and please come back.

She even touched my arm, a soft warm slightly moist touch, when she was ready to leave.

Then she stopped coming. I heard someone in the hall talking about a convent being closed. I think that's what they said, I couldn't hear it clearly. I wanted to believe that's what it was—something out of her control. Sister Maria . . .

No more music, since then. Except what's in my mind. The old songs from the 60s that replay, over and over in my mind. The whirling dust motes. The sounds from the hall; sometimes a patient crying.

But something important *has* happened—it happened, for the first time, three weeks ago. One of the faces in the walls has started talking to me . . .

Seeing faces in the wall was one of the ways I kept my mind busy.

It's funny how the people who take care of me feel like ghosts—and Beth feels like a living person to me. That's because she talks to me

Beth spoke to me, in my mind and I replied to her—in my mind. And she heard me!

I wish I could talk out loud—to Beth, to anyone. It's enough that I can't move—but if I could at least talk . . . If I could berate the nurses, flirt with the woman who comes in to mop the floor, ask for things, demand to see an attorney, sing to myself—and tell a story to a nurse . . . that'd be worth something.

I can make just one little sound—a high-pitched *immmm* sound produced way deep in my throat—but it's hard to make, and it's such an embarrassingly piteous, subhuman noise I hate to do it. I only do it when I'm trying to ease the pressure, trying to avoid the inner hysteria, that's like a funhouse in a very bad earthquake. If I feel that coming, then I might *immmm*.

I have to be sure the nurses and attendants are nowhere around when I make the noise. If they hear it, they get irritated, asking, "Well? What's the point if you know you can't tell us what you want?" Figuring I'm trying to get attention. They find ways to show they're angry with me. They "forget" to change the diaper.

There—I hear the sound of the little metal cabinet on wheels that they roll around to feed those who can't feed themselves. It clinks with dishes and rattles and its wheels squeak. I'm the first one in this corridor. So that means the morning nurse is coming in, just a few minutes late. I think of her as Mrs. White because she's an old white woman with puffy white hair and a dirty white uniform. She smells old and talks old, when she mutters to herself, and she's barely aware of what she's doing, as she goes through the motions of cleaning me with her twisty old fingers, feeding me breakfast porridge, giving me a shot, brushing my teeth, putting antiseptic—a bandage if she feels like it—on my bedsores. She turns me, props me up back there with special little pillow to give the bedsore a chance to heal. I sort of enjoy that, since I can feel it. She's supposed to change the sheet, but that's a complicated process involving moving me a lot, hard work, so she doesn't do it today. I am aware that her Polydent isn't quite working and her false teeth are coming loose from her gums. I can hear the sound of them sucking loose as she mumbles to herself.

Sometimes Mrs. White says something to me. Always a kind of complaint. "You're getting fat and hard to move. They're going to want to put those electric things on your arms again to keep them muscles up. But don't think they'll keep on with it, they're cutting back on treatment again, laying people off. Well, see there, you don't poop much, I'll give you that. But you still smell. That sore of yours, that smells. I don't know why I got to do this. I should have some real retirement. You can't live on what I'd have. Some of it got stolen. My husband died and left me nothing but debts. So here I am with you . . ."

I like her visits, though—I can see parts of the room I can't normally see, when she moves me about. I can think about the things she says and try to imagine her life. It's better than hearing nothing from anyone. It's better than Sam Sack.

After she's gone, I listen to people talking in the hallway. They come, and they go. Now I pass the time with my worn out old fantasy that someday my dad will come looking for me and take me out of here. I imagine the whole scene, where he wheels me out, and tells me he's going to find a cure for me. That doesn't last long.

Sometimes I have other fantasies—I try to avoid the sexual sort. They're particularly torturous. And I can still get a hard-on. Which makes the aides laugh.

There are darker daydreams, that come to me, at times. Furious, bone-deep violence against Sack; against certain orderlies; against the people who run this place . . .

I push all that down, deep down, because it only hurts me, not them. And I think about what I'll say to Beth, instead. It's not time for her to come yet. She won't come till after it starts to get dark outside. I have to wait . . .

I watch the slanting sun make warped squares on the wall to my left. I start watching the dust whirling in the sunbeams. I try to count them. I select pieces of dust to study individually. To imagine as something else. Sometimes at night before the light goes out, I can watch moths. I've watched spiders cross the ceiling, watched them very closely. My eyes hurt with all this staring, but it's all I've got.

Once in a while they bring in a machine that makes my muscles jump with mild electrical jolts. It hurts a little, but I like it, because it's some movement, and I guess it keeps my muscles from atrophying. It's experimental. Someone donated it. But Mrs. White says the muscle therapy is going to end.

No one comes today. No electricity, nothing but waiting for lunch. Patiently waiting. The hours are like blocks of ice in a room just two degrees above freezing. Ever so slowly melting. It's a mystery, why I don't go completely insane. But how would I know if I was insane?

I've tried really hard to go totally mad, cuckoo, out of my mind, lost in space. *Definitively* insane, in a mad hatter way. The important phrase is, *out of my mind*. That'd be a kind of escape. I've never quite gotten there. The most I've gotten to is some vicious fantasies and some hallucinations, now and then. The hallucinations are some kind of sensory deprivation effect maybe. Those faces. Except one.

I've seen things in the swirling dust. Minute dancing ballerinas, and crystalline cogs. And the faces appearing in the wall. Appearing, and vanishing. The faces frighten me, but at least it's some kind of stimulation. They sometimes seem amused—sometimes hostile. I used to be afraid they'd come out of the wall somehow and bite me. But they never do. They look at me as if they're threatening me, but they're as powerless, as stuck within walls, as I am stuck on the bed in room 230. They move their lips sometimes. I never heard any of the faces speak, though, till Beth showed up.

I'm waiting for her now, my eyes turned to watch the wall to my right, under the window. I can feel she's near. Maybe she's a hallucination, maybe that's how I know she's coming—because she's from my own mind. But I want to believe she's real. I do believe it. She must be. She knows things that I never knew . . .

I wait for Bethany. She's never the first to come. It starts with the other faces . . .

Now I see a face in the dull-green wall, turning to look at me. The face is made partly of places where the paint on the concrete is wrinkly, and partly from a wall crack and partly from shadow and partly from my mind connecting all these things. I can tell this one's a hallucination. It's a jowly man, balding, looking sullen, almost angry, put-upon, circles under his little eyes. His lips move but I can't hear what he's saying. I think I might know who he is. That happens sometimes—the faces are people from memory. I think this man might be Mr. Wemberly. I saw his face six years ago when Mom brought me in here. He looked me over and wasn't too pleased. Talked about how the necessary staff time made it hardly worthwhile. "Put him in room 230." That was the last I saw of him.

Now his face recedes into the wall. I see another—it's a pretty girl, one I sometimes dream about. She looks a little like Jayne Mansfield. She makes a kissy puckering with her lips at me. I'm sorry when she fades away. Another face takes her place—my mother. Her lips sneer, her eyes are heavy with disappointment. Sorry Mother, I say to her, in my mind. Okay? As if that satisfies her for now, she melts away, and I'm glad. Now comes a face I don't know—it's a frightened looking man. He opens his mouth. He screams. Is that my face? It's too old to be my face. But I haven't seen my own face in six years.

That face collapses into another face, a little boy with colorless hair and very dark eyes. He seems to be praying. I don't know him, do I? There's something about him that makes me deeply afraid, but I don't know what. He slips back into the wall, and along comes another face—a black woman, looking amused, curious. A pleasant middle-aged face.

She seems to be singing to herself, judging by the movement of her head, from side to side, the way her lips move, but I can't hear her. I like her. But . . .

I want to see the one I can hear. The one who can step out of the wall. I'm impatient to see her today.

I try to call her with my mind.

I think, *Beth . . . .Bethany . . . .Beth!*

I can feel her responding almost immediately. I hear her voice, phasing in and out of audibility: "Was . . . coming . . . anyway . . . don't . . . so . . . imp . . ."

Don't so imp? *Don't be so impatient.*

Then the singing black lady melts away, and I see Beth.

I wish I could smile to greet her. All I can do is lift my right thumb a little. She's just a face in the wall, but then she thrusts her hand from it and wiggles her thumb at me. It's a little mocking when she does that but honestly it's just her sense of humor. She's in a better mood than last time, it seems to me. That's good. But I know that can change. Her sorrow's never far away. She's anchored in Wemberly Sanitarium by sorrow.

Bethany steps out of the wall, into the room. Beth is a slim, barefoot girl in a short hospital gown—her legs are quite skinny, knees knobby. She has a mousy sort of face, but kind of cute the way a mouse's face is, and long dull-brown hair, a bit lank, and brown freckles on her cheeks and brown eyes. Her coloration comes and goes—sometimes she seems to be made of a cream colored mist. She's a little foggy below the neck but her arms come into focus when she uses them to gesture, or point. Her lips don't move when she talks except that they smile or frown or purse themselves.

Her voice seems to echo around, and the last echo comes clearest into my mind. Now and then a word drops out. "Douglas. I've come to see you again . . ."

I reply in my mind. "Hello, Beth. Thank you for coming. I love it when you come here."

"Has he . . . back?"

"Sack? Not for eleven nights now."

"He'll come tonight. I've seen him, he's been looking at that pillowcase with the holes . . ."

I try to sound brave, and blithe, to impress her with my courage. "It makes a change. But he gets worse every time. I don't know how the worst kind of guy can get worse." I tried to make a laughing sound in my mind.

"Don't do that," she says, frowning.

"Don't do what?"

". . . make that fake laughing. It sounds like one of . . . gag laughing toys. My father used to sell gags. He was . . . traveling salesman . . ."

She's already told me about her eccentric father, but I let her tell me about it again.

After a while that story runs down. "Are you talking to someone else?" she asks.

I'm surprised. "I'm sort of filing everything that happens in another part of my mind, as we talk. In the form of a narrative. You can hear it?"

"Not exactly," she says. "It's okay. Your mind . . . a strong one. Some people here . . . very feeble. Almost not there at all."

"I've got nothing to do but make my mind work, in different ways. I'd forgotten algebra but I worked it out again to keep my mind busy, about a year ago. Are you ready to tell me, now, how you got here? You said you would, last time."

Her frown deepens. "I guess so. I should." She seems to look around the room, as if trying to remember something. I yearn to ask her to touch me, anywhere at all, but I'm afraid I won't be able to feel her touch since she isn't precisely alive. "One reason I came to this room," she says, "is because I used to live in here. Right in this room." I am hearing her voice more clearly now. That happens when we've been talking for a while. It's like we hone in on each other's frequency. "It really started in 1943. I was a nurse's aide, for soldiers coming back from the war. Volunteering. I thought I might meet a husband that way. I wasn't very pretty and I was almost thirty and wasn't married.

I was taking care of a soldier who was coughing all the time, he'd been in North Africa, and he caught something there. I thought it was just a bad cold. But then after a while I started coughing too, and then I was coughing up yellow and red stuff, like mustard and catsup. But it was bloody sputum. And I got feverish and started waking up in the middle of the night with the sheets soaked, all covered with sweat. So I went to the doctor and they said I had consumption—the tuberculosis—and they took me to the sanitarium. This sanitarium. This same room. The owner was Randall Wemberly and there was a young fat man who was his son, Charles. This boy Charles worked as an orderly, but he was going to inherit the place. He was learning the job and said we'd all better be good to him because he was going to take over the whole place someday. He'd laugh and wink like that was a joke but it was what was in his mind. Charles Wemberly. He would take us for our treatments. People thought, back then, that cold fresh air would kill the bacillus, so they took us to open windows and made us sit there, and breathe the cold air in the winter. And snow would come in, sometimes, and cover us. I saw two people die right there, in that room. The worst was the balloon, though. They'd put a balloon in your lung, and they'd inflate it. They said it would help the lung heal. I don't know why they thought that. And it was a very awful feeling when they put it in but the worst was when they expanded it and that was the very worst pain I'd ever felt. Up till then. Blood would squirt out my nose, the first spurt shooting in an arc all the way down to my thighs. And they'd cut away people's ribs, so the lungs could expand. All those people died, the ones who lost part of their ribcage. They didn't do that surgery on me. But I thought I was going to die soon anyway. They had a tunnel they used for taking the dead people out—it's still down there, I'll show it to you sometime, Douglas—it goes out back, to a little building. That's so the patients and their families wouldn't see all the dead people going out of the hospital—it happened so often. Because most patients died. Almost all of them." She hesitates. She looks at me with her head tilted. She seems to be trying to remember how it was. "I lingered on for a long time and I kept wanting to run away and find some peaceful place to die alone, without anyone watching. But then the streptomycin came in. And it worked!" She gives an ironic little smile. "That was in 1946. People were getting better from it. So they gave it to me for a while, and I improved—a lot! I wasn't even infectious anymore, and I wasn't coughing. I thought I would be leaving soon. I was planning what I would do when I was released." She makes a gesture in the air, like she wants to push something away that isn't there. "And then Charles came to me, alone. He was supposed to give me my medicine, but he said I couldn't have it unless I let him play with my body. 'It has to be however I want to touch you, any way at all,' he said. 'Or you will die.' He pushed up against me and I remember his breath smelled like rotten eggs. I said, 'Why did you choose me?' I was just stalling. He said it was my legs, they were like the legs of a little girl. I shouted that I'd tell his father on him. Then he hit me with a bedpan, and that knocked me senseless for a while, and when I came to, we were on the floor and he was holding onto me, and humping my hips talking about how my legs were the legs of a little girl—he was not even inside me, but humping me more like a dog would hump on a person's legs—and he saw I was awake so he started whispering that he would kill me, he would simply kill me if I didn't do what he wanted and I shouldn't imagine that he wouldn't . . ." She breaks off and looks at me. "Does this story offend you?"

"No," I reply, in my mind. "Well yes: I'm offended that you were hurt. But I want to know what happened."

She smiles. She nods and looks at the overhead light. "I can see the electricity in the wires, if I squint," she says.

"Did he kill you?" I prompt her.

She sticks out her lower lip as she thinks it over. "No. Not exactly. He said his father was away on a trip, and now *he* was in charge and he would see I spoke to no one but him, and I would get no more medicine . . . unless . . ."

She looks at the door. I hear people passing outside, in the hall, talking. A woman weepily talking about her aunt, saying she's all the family she has. The nurse saying, "We can only do so much."

Then they've moved on. I don't know why Beth waited, since they can't hear us talking. Maybe she is afraid someone might come in to check on me, and see her. Maybe she doesn't realize how rarely anyone comes in here.

If she's worried about that, does that mean that I'm not the only one who can see her?

"So," Beth goes on, "I said, 'Charles, do what you have to, but don't hit me again.' My head hurt so badly. And then he raped me. I laid still for it, like he wanted, and didn't fight him, but it was raping. It hurt a lot . . . I was afraid I'd throw up and choke on the vomit while he was doing it . . ."

We are silent for a while. I felt like making the *immmm* sound but I didn't. Not doing that now is the only way I have of being strong for her.

She turns like she is going to melt back into the wall.

"Don't go, Beth!" I call to her, in my mind.

She looks back at me, and I can see she wants to cry but, like me, she can't. "I have to go. I have to rest in the wall. But I'll just tell you this much more. Charles gave me something he said was streptomycin, but it wasn't. It was just placebo. The symptoms started to come back. And he started coming to me wearing a surgical mask. Forced me to open my legs for him. Holding a hand over my mouth to keep me quiet. Then I guessed what was going on. I said, 'You want me to die, so I don't talk about what you've been doing to me. You're not giving me the medicine at all now.' He wouldn't say anything and then I didn't see him for a couple of days. I tried to talk to a nurse but I was locked in here and they wouldn't respond, wouldn't come to the door. I was shouting and shouting and then when I screamed really loud something broke in my lungs and I spit up blood, so much blood came up I choked. And then there was a lot of pain and then it was dark . . ." She shrugs. "And then I was in the walls. Just in the walls. But sometimes I can come out and look at things. Mostly they can't see me but sometimes they do." She smiles at that. "I don't like them to see me, I'm afraid they'll bring Charles but . . . I like to see them afraid of me, too."

"He's still here?"

The color is going out of her. She seems to flatten, like she's a cut-out, or something drawn on paper. "I'm tired . . . yes. Yes he's here. Charles is Mr. Wemberly now. He's in charge, like he said he'd be. He's the one who put you in here, this room. Good bye, Douglas, for now. Try to pretend you're someone else when Sack comes in. That's what I always did when Charles . . . and the nurses would pretend . . . can't . . ."

That's all I can hear. She is slipping into the wall—almost as if something in it is pulling her slowly in, against her will. The wall is drinking her in the way water sinks out of sight into deep sand. Then she's gone.

I feel like I've fallen into a wall, too. I close my eyes. I don't try to call to her, though. Bethany needs to rest.

A nurse comes, looks at my sore, mutters that it's not so bad. Goes away. An orderly comes, checks my lower parts, shrugs, and goes away. I hear the sound of a mop in a bucket in the hallway. Some kind of broth is brought to me, and I'm fed with something like a turkey baster. They have to crank the bed up a bit so I don't choke. They get irritated when I choke.

The bedsore is tormenting me. It hurts and it itches. The itching always makes me imagine insects are crawling into the bedsore. They're getting into it and laying eggs that will become hungry little grubs that will eat their way out of my brain. Sometimes I think I can feel them beginning to chew through the soft tissue inside my skull.

I must not think about that because if I do it just gets more and more vivid, worse and worse and I have to *immmm*. One of the ways I change the direction of my thoughts is to try to remember a song, note for note. There's one by The Turtles.

So happy together . . .

They're crawling into the wound . . .

So happy to-geth-errrrr . . . .

I think of songs and I watch dust motes. I watch the color of the sunlight deepen, and the crooked squares of light from the window travel down the left hand wall and vanish entirely, and the dread of Sam Sack comes on me, much later, when the light is switched off. I try to sleep, hoping for a good dream. But I can't sleep.

Sack.

He comes into the dark room, I know it's him from the smells— rancid sweat and Top tobacco. I can just barely see his silhouette. I hear the rustle of his homemade mask. He puts it over his head in the darkness. He switches on the little lantern he's brought, dialed down low, and raises it up to see me, and so I can see him. There's the sack on his head with holes cut in it—actually it's a small pillowcase, but for a long time I thought it was a sack. So I think of it that way and I call him Sam Sack.

"Glad to see me?" he asks, his head cocked, his voice hoarse. It's always hoarse. He adjusts the pillowcase with his free hand to let him see out the crudely cut holes better. I can't see his face, only the eyes. Around his covered mouth, the cloth gets damp and dark with his breath. Why does he even bother with the mask? Maybe he's got the "sack" on in case anyone turns on the light. Maybe he's hoping he can run before they identify him. Or maybe he doesn't want me to see his face. Because even though I couldn't tell anybody who he is, he feels more powerful, stronger, if I don't know. Maybe his face is one a man would laugh at.

 But I think I know who he might be—kind of. No, he's not Charles
Wemberly. I can tell from smells on him—and the dirt under his
yellow fingernails, his calluses, his oily overalls—that he's probably
on the maintenance staff. I think he's the night janitor. He's a
white man, gangly, but with a pot belly. He has cigarette stains on
two fingers of his right hand. Once I heard an aide walking by in
the hall, saying, "Maybe Sam can clean it up tonight, I'm not going
to do it, I'm going off shift." I figured maybe he was that Sam. Sick
Sam Sack.

 He climbs up on the narrow bed, and straddles me, and I close
my eyes. He starts pressing my eyes with my thumbs. "I could cram
'em back into your brain," he says, "and you couldn't do nothin'
about it.'

 He pushes hard, and it hurts, but he's careful not to break anything
there. He broke a couple of my toes once, and the nurses never
seemed to notice. But they'd notice if he poked out my eyes.

 He says, "I was thinking of the sewing needles today, how maybe I
could do you with the pins again, they don't leave much mark, and
the aides just think it's another sore or such." He slaps me, once,
hard. Stinging the left side of my face. It makes a loud noise in the
room. The mark will fade before the nurses see it. And would they
do anything if they did see it? I don't think so.

 He slaps me again, and twice more. "Maybe this'll wake you up.
Wake up in there, dummy! Wake up!" He laughs softly.

 His eyes in the pillowcase holes are bright.

 Sometimes he'll pull hair from my head, my pubes, my armpits, one
hair at a time. Once he started pulling out a fingernail, but blood
came, and he decided that might draw too much attention, so he left
it partly pulled. No one noticed. They clipped it like they always do,
without a comment.

 Sack puts his weight on my chest, presses down with his knees.
I can't breathe. He waits. Spots appear over my eyes. I'm close to
dying. I wouldn't mind if he'd finish it but I know he won't. He

won't let me off the hook. I make the *immmm* sound and he gives out a soft laugh of pleasure. Then he lets up, easing off, letting me breathe. Then he does it again, almost smothering me, two times more.

Maybe I'm starting to turn blue, because he quits, and climbs off the table. "I've got something else for you." As I lay there, breath rasping, he reaches into his pocket, takes out something brassy. He fiddles with it and holds it up so I can see it better. Lipstick. "I'm gonna pretty you up a little. I got a lady's brassiere, and this. I'm gonna put this on your lips and rub it on your cheeks. I'll clean it off before I go. And this time, I'm gonna have your ass. The girl I use— she died. She killed herself. So it's you, now. We got to make you a little more like a girl. I'm gonna call you Sissy Thing . . ."

He starts drawing on my lips with the lipstick, whistling a song. "Camptown Ladies."

I feel something I haven't felt for a while. I try not to feel it, because if I do, it's like I'm on fire and can't put the fire out.

It's pure rage. And there's nothing I can do to express it, but breathe harder. I can sort of snort out my nose at him. That's all. This only makes him laugh, and he hits my testicles hard with his knee. The pain brings the rage up like a siren blasting full volume in my mind.

I fight the rage. Rage hurts me. I have to keep it down. Pretend to be someone else, like Beth says. *Beth* . . .

She's there, suddenly. Standing to my right. Sack doesn't seem to see her.

"Douglas," she says, in my mind, "let yourself rage at him. If you do, then you'll go into the rage, and you'll be gone enough into it, and that'll open a door for me, so I can help you . . ."

And I stop fighting it. The rage was like a pot of water boiling over, making the lid rattle and fall away . . . I was uncovered by it . . .

I feel an unspeakable, glutinous intimacy. Is this being raped? But he hasn't started that yet. This is up higher, coming from somewhere else—*something* is pushing into my gut, right under my rib cage. It's passing through the skin without breaking it. But I feel it force its way into whatever it is, inside my body, and brain, that I think of as me. It's doing it insistently, not brutally. I realize it's Beth.

Then I feel something strange in the muscles of my face. Like I have a muscle twitch. But it's a muscle twitch that makes my mouth move. My tongue. A jabbery sound croaks out of me. Then some control comes and I say a word *right out loud*.

"Sack," I say. Not in my mind—I say it with my mouth.

He turns to look at me, his head cocked to one side again. Staring. "You can't talk . . ."

"Sam Sack," I say. "You're Sam."

Only it's not me saying it. She's saying it for me. She's joined me. She's with me in here. *Beth!* I can feel her there, a warm presence, twined about my spine, swirling at the back of my head, and stretching into my arms . . .

My arms are twitching. Jumping. They're wriggling. The straps are loose. My hand is fumbling at a buckle on the restraints.

Sack raises a fist, slowly, over his head. I can see him flexing his arm muscle. I realize he's going to hit me. Beat me to death, to keep me quiet.

My right arm comes free. I watch my own arm as it rises up like a cobra—some creature I have no control over. Sack stares at it, hesitating—and then my left hand gets free. It jumps up and grabs him by the back of the neck. Holds him. His surprisingly skinny neck. My left hand makes a kind of claw, with the index finger, and thumb, and it stabs out, and jabs him in the eyes. As we do it, I remember all the times he dug his thumbs into my eyes. My own will, set free, joins Beth's, and I push my thumb and finger *hard*, into his eyes. Popping through his eyeballs, digging into the eye socket.

He gives out with a long, bubbling squeal, and blood splashes into the pillowcase and changes the color of the cloth.

He quivers and shakes in my hands—and then he wrenches free and falls flailing back, blind.

"Okay now," Beth says, in my mind. "That's enough. We stopped him." Her voice is crystal clear. I can see her face in my mind, looking worried and almost pretty. "Let's just get out of here, together. I can leave here with you. I can't make it out of here alone . . . We can go out through that old tunnel . . ." It takes some time to get better control of my limbs. But I get the straps off completely, and I stand. I'm dizzy, once I almost fall over, but I manage to stay upright. I feel firmer with every passing second. "I'm standing! Beth! I can move! You're helping me do this?"

"I'm connecting something that was broken in your brain, just by being here, inside you," she says. "Let's go . . ."

"Wait," I say, my voice shaking.

I feel waves of emotion go through me, rage and joy all mixed together, driving me along. I step over to the writhing man on the floor, and I kneel down to press my knee on his neck, and I put all my weight on it. I crush his throat, hard and slow.

"Let's *go*," Beth says, sounding worried. "They've heard him scream! They'll lock you up. We have to go."

"You're doing this too," I tell her, gasping the words out, breathing hard as I feel him struggling under my crushing knee. The blood is coming from his mouth now as well as his eyes. I'm feeling pain with all this movement, as if my joints are all rusty. *Oil can*, squeaks the Tin Man. "You're doing it, Beth, as much as me."

"No. I didn't even put out his eyes. I was just trying to push him back. Knock him down. Not that. You did that. No I'm just *here*, but I'm not . . . doing that."

I can barely hear her through the roaring. The roaring that is coming out of me. Then I realize that Sam Sack has stopped moving. He's dead.

I pull the sack off his head—the bloody child's pillowcase—and I throw it in the corner and I look at him in the light from his own lantern.

He's a monkey-faced man with a big red nose. Old, his face deeply lined. His eyes are gone, blood running like red tears from the sockets. My hands are slick with the remains of his eye matter.

I stand up, feeling sick, and wracked with pain, but seething with a fierce delight. Roaring to myself with exhilaration!

I pick up his lantern and open the door, ripples of disorientation going through me as I step into the hallway. An orderly, a thick-bodied black man with a shaved head, is coming toward me, frowning, investigating the noise—he stops, staring at me. Seeing the blood on me and the lantern and the diaper—and the lipstick. He backs away. I roar at him. He turns and runs, and I laugh.

"We have to go downstairs," Beth says, in my mind. "The tunnel . . ."

"No tunnel yet," I say. Because it's coming clear to me, now.

I stumble along, managing to walk, spastic and hurting but loving every step. I hum to myself, sings bits of songs, just to hear my creaky voice. I find some stairs and go down—but only one floor. I step into the ground floor hallway, find the front door out into the grounds. It's late, there's no one watching it. It unlocks easily enough and I step out into the cold night. I'm almost naked, but I like the cold wind on me, the cold wet ground under my feet. I even like shivering. The stars, seen through the broken, racing clouds, are blue-white points of sheer intensity. I see the house in the corner of the grounds, near the front gate, close to the mossy concrete wall. I stumble across the wet lawn, through a pool of darkness. I make my way to the house, a white cottage trimmed in pale blue, in the corner of the grounds. I see there's a light on at the small back porch.

"We should just keep going out the front gate," Beth says.

I keep on to the little house. Beth comes with me, she has to. She has no choice.

I've heard the orderlies refer to the cottage. *"You want the time off, go see Wemberly in that house out front, and ask. He lives out there . . ."*

I find the backdoor unlocked, and step into the kitchen, still carrying the lantern. The kitchen is painted a sunny yellow.

There is Charles Wemberly at the kitchen table, a fat balding elderly man in yellow pajamas. He's eating a big piece of yellow cheese, which he's cut up on a carving board, with a large knife. A bottle of Riesling is uncorked beside him. A wine glass brims in his age-spotted hand.

He looks up; he stares; his jowly mouth hangs open, showing half-chewed cheese. His hand shakes; the wine spills.

I stalk toward him and he gibbers something and flails, dropping the wine glass. I smash him in the face with the lantern. He rocks back. I drop the lantern and pick up the half empty wine bottle, and hit him in the face with it, over and over. The skin splits over the bones of his face, and I can see them showing through, till they're covered with blood. He howls for help and thrashes at me and I keep smashing into him, knocking him off his chair, till the bottle shatters.

I discard the neck of the bottle and take the knife he was using—and I straddle him, like Sack did to me, and I start sawing at the back of Wemberly's neck. Cutting here, cutting there. Sawing through neck muscles, tissue I can't even identify. I'm smelling blood; feeling its wet hot thick warmth on my hands, my wrists.

"Oh no," Beth is saying. Her voice in my head is a sustained high note on a violin. "Oh, no Douglas. We have to go . . ."

"It's Charles," I tell her, quite reasonably, saying it right out loud, as I saw at his back. He thrashes under me. I saw away, hacking down further, digging a trench in him around the spine, all the way from neck to tailbone.

"Yes. But . . ."

"He's the one who raped you and let you die. And he hired Sam Sack. He left me in a moronically cruel state of neglect for six years."

"Yes but Douglas, listen please . . . We have to go."

"Wait!" I shout. "Almost done!" I keep sawing, working hard to separate the vertebrae from the body. I feel the strength of years of rage coming out in my hands, and he's thrashing and squeaking and I drop the knife and I get a grip on the spine, I pull and wrench . . .

It comes loose from his body, his entire spine comes out rather nicely, with his head attached. I have to cut through a few more connective threads around his neck, some cartilage, and then . . .

I'm standing over the rest of his body holding his spine in my two hands. His head, his mind, is still alive in it, attached to the spine; his face is twitching convulsively, eyes going back and forth, back and forth.

I swing his head on his spine, like swinging a polo mallet; it's cumbersome, and I think of Alice in the Lewis Carroll book, trying to play croquet with a flamingo. But this one drips blood, and sputters.

"This is to you, from me," I tell Beth. "I am your man, Beth, and my strong arm has done this for you."

A shout comes from the back door and I turn to see the big black orderly and a white man in a uniform; he's a security guard with longish hair and a cigarette in his lips and a gun in his hand.

"Oh my fucking stars," the security guard says. He's staring at Wemberly's wet-red spine, the attached head coated in blood.

I raise swing the head on the spine and roar at them—and the guard's gun roars back.

"Beth!" I'm staggering back with the shot, which has struck me in the lower left side. Blood spurts out of me.

And something else is leaving me—Beth.

She's draining out of me, with the blood flow. I see her floating away from me—she's drifting away, turning around in the air to face me so she can see me as she goes. She's getting smaller, going into a vast distance that shouldn't be there, in a kitchen.

"I'm out," she says, speaking to my mind. "I'm free, Douglas. But I wish we . . ."

Her voice trails off. She vanishes. She's gone. The guard is staring at me, uncertain what to do.

But I realize—

I can still stand. I can move! Beth's presence in me, the movement since then—it seems to have permanently bound up the broken connections in my brain. I no longer need Beth to move.

I swing Wemberly's head and spine, release it at the guard like an Olympics hammer throw—it trails blood through the air, falls short; the head, breaking from the spine, thunks and rolls, trailing blood. The guard makes a yelping sound and steps back. As he does, I switch the knife to my left hand, use my right to cover the wound, slow the bleeding. This wound will not kill me. It is shallow.

The guard and the orderly are coming cautiously back into the kitchen. The guard's hand, pointing the gun, is wavering. The gun is shaking.

I start toward them. The orderly tells him, "Shoot him again you damn fool!"

I roar—and the gun roars back, once more. Then again.

I feel a cold, punching impact in my neck. I fall, fall slowly back through space. The room around me is suddenly a different color. It's painted red, and the red paint swirls and thickens and carries me somewhere . . . into dreams . . .

The hard part is waking up.

I'm lying on my back. I don't want to open my eyes. I can feel the warmth of the light bulb over me. I can smell the room. Must *not* open my eyes.

But I do. I see where I am. I try to get up. I can't. I try to lift my arm. Can't.

I can't feel anything, below my neck. I'm aware of a bandage, taut around my throat. A hose going into my mouth helping me breathe.

I see a doctor, in his white coat—a red-faced man with a mustache—talking to a frightened looking black-haired wisp of a nurse, near the door. He's saying, "Oh he can't hurt you." He glances at me. "He's quite paralyzed . . . The bullet destroyed his spine. And this time the restraints are quite tight. As tight as we can make them. So even if he could move . . ."

I had my chance. I didn't listen to Beth. Now I'm being punished. But this place was always my punishment.

So I had to come back here. To room 230. Does it do any good to say I'm sorry? I'm sorry. I'm sorry . . .

LEARN AT HOME!
YOUR CAREER IN EVIL

It was while his wife slept: that's when it was easiest for Kander to think about killing her. Just the fact of her being awake, Elias Kander had learned, troubled him with doubts about the project. It was as if her movements about the house, her prattle, spoke of her as a living, suffering reality, and underlined the deepest meanings in the word murder.

But as she slept . . .

On those nights when he'd been working late in the lab, Kander would come home to find her soundly asleep, resentfully dosed with sedatives. Sedated, she was reduced to something like a hapless infant, clutching the quilt her grandmother had made. A time when he should feel pangs of conscience at her profound vulnerability, was just the time he felt safest thinking about her annihilation. Vistas of freedom opened up, in her hypothetical absence . . .

But what if there really was hell to pay?

What if evil was objectively real and not relative? And what about the thing in the lab?

On a sleepy Tuesday night, the city was hugging itself against moody Chicago winds off the lake and it was warm by the gas fire in the steak house. Kander and Berryman came here after an afternoon's research, as it was across the street from the university's library.

Waiting for Kander to return from the men's room, Berryman sipped his merlot and looked at his companion's empty plate across the table. How thoroughly Kander ate everything; not a shred of beef left, every pea vanished.

Berryman considered his own peculiar ambivalence to their monthly dinners; their boys' nights out. He'd felt the usual frisson on seeing Kander's almost piratical grin, the glitter in his eyes that presaged the ideas, in every philosophical menu, they'd feast on along with the prime rib; and a moment later, also as usual, a kind of chill dread took him. Kander had a gift for taking him to the frontiers of the thinkable, and the disorienting wilderness beyond. But maybe that was the natural consequence of a humanistic journalist— Berryman—locking horns with a scientist. And sometimes Berryman thought Kander was more a scientist than a human being.

"I've been thinking about journalists, Larry," Kander said, sitting down. He was a stocky, bullet-headed man with amazingly thick forearms, blunt fingers; more like a football coach than a physicist who'd minored in behavioral science. He wore the same threadbare sweater the last time they'd suppered together, and the time before that; his graying black hair—an inch past the collar only because he rarely remembered the barber—brushed straight back from his forehead. Berryman was contrastingly tall, gangly, had trouble folding his long legs under the restaurant's elegantly tiny tables. Long hair on purpose, tied in a graying ponytail. They'd been roommates at the university across the street where Kander now had research tenure.

Berryman scratched in his short, curly brown beard. "You're thinking about journalists? I'm thinking about leaving, then. You'll be doing experiments on me next."

"How do you know for sure I haven't been?" Kander grinned and patted his coat for a cigarette.

"Amy made you give up the cigarettes, Kander, remember? Or have you started again?"

"Oh that's right, damn her, no smokes, well—anyway . . ." He poured some more red wine, drank half the glass off in one gulp and said, "My thinking is that journalists are by nature dilettantes. They have to be. I don't mean a scholar who writes a seven volume biography of Jefferson."

"Guys like me who write for *Rolling Stone* and the *Trib* and, on a good day, *The New Yorker*. Yes, I'm well aware of your contempt for—"

"No, not at all, not at all. I'm not contemptuous of your trade, merely indifferent to it. But you must admit, journalists can't get into a story deeply because the next piece is always calling, and the next paycheck."

"Often the case. But you get a feel for what's under the surface, though you can't spend long looking for it. Sometimes, though, you're with it longer than you'd like . . ."

"Yes: your war correspondence. I daresay you learned a great deal about South America. Peru, and, oh my yes, Chile—"

"Sometimes more than I'd like to know. What's your point, implying that journalists are shallow? You going to have a bumper sticker made up—'Physicists do it deeper'?"

"Given the chance, we do! Unless we make the mistake of getting married. But my dear fellow—" Kander was American, but he'd gone to a boarding school in England for eight years, as a boy, and it had left its mark. "—I'm talking about getting to essences. What are the essences of things? Of human events? To get to them you must first wade through all the details of a study. Now, journalists think they dabble, and knock off an essence. But they can't; more often than not they get it wrong. A scientist though—he may work through mountains of detail, rivers of i-dotting and oceans of calculation, but ultimately he is after essences—the big picture and the defining laws that underlie things. Now take your upsetting sojourn in what was it, Peru or Chile? Where you discovered that during 'the dirty war' whole families of dissidents disappeared—"

"It doesn't seem to matter to you what country it was, Kander. Sometimes they weren't even really dissidents. They seem to pick them at random, some sort of quota."

"Just so. And they murdered the men, used some of the women for sex slaves, and when they abducted women who were pregnant, they often kept them alive just long enough to bear the children, whereupon the children were taken from them, for sale to childless officers—"

"And the women were then thrown alive out of airplanes over the Pacific. What's your point?" Berryman knew he was being snappish, but Kander was being altogether too gleeful over a recollection that never failed to make Berryman's guts churn.

"When you write about it, you write—and very well, yes—about the political and social histories that made such brutality possible. As if it were explainable with mere history! There's where you made your error. It wasn't history, my boy. It wasn't a shattering of modern ethics with a loss of faith in the rules of the Holy Roman Empire; it wasn't brutalizing by military juntas and a century of crushing the 'Indios'."

"You're not going to say Eugenics, are you? Korzybski-ism? Because if you are—"

"Not at all! I'm no crypto-Nazi, my friend. No—if you look at the essence of the thing, it was as if a sort of disease was passed from one man to another. A disease that killed empathy, that allowed dehumanization—and extreme brutality."

"It is a kind of disease—but it has a social ontology."

"Not as you mean it. That kind of brutality goes deeper. It is contrary to the human spirit—and yet it was very widespread, in that South American hell-hole, just as it was among the Germans in World War Two. And the secret? It may be . . . that evil is *communicable*. That evil is communicable almost like a virus."

"You mean . . . there's some unknown physical factor, a microorganism that passes from one man to another affecting the brain and—"

"No! That is just what I don't mean. I mean that evil as a thing in itself is passed from one man to the next. Not through the example of brutality, or through coarsening from abuse—but as a kind of living, sentient substance—and this is what underlies such things. This is the essence that a journalist does not look deep enough to see."

Berryman stared at him; then he laughed. "You're fucking with me again. You had me going there."

"Am I?" Shutters closed in Kander's face; suddenly he seemed remote. "Well. We'll talk about it another time. Perhaps."

Just then the Mexican busboy came along. "You feenish?" he asked.

"Yes, yes," Kander muttered impatiently. And he could not be induced to say much more that night, except to ask what Berryman, an associate at the university, thought of the new coeds, especially the latest crop of blondes.

It took only six weeks for the toxic-metals compound to do its work on Kander's wife. It was not a poison that killed, not directly: at this dosage it was a poison no one could see, or even infer: it was just despair. A little lead, a little mercury, a few select trace elements, a compound selected for its effect on the nervous system.

They were watching *The Wonderful World of Disney* when he was sure it was working on her.

It was a repeat of the Disney adaptation of *The Ransom of Red Chief*. She liked O. Henry stories. He had found that watching TV with her was often enough to satisfy her need for him to act like a husband. It was close enough to their "doing something together." It wasn't really necessary for him to watch the television; it was sufficient for him to rest his gaze on the screen. Now and then he would focus on it, mutter a comment, and then go back into his ruminations again. She didn't seem to mind if he kept a pad by the chair and scribbled the occasional note to himself; a patching equation, some new slant to the miniature particle accelerator he'd designed. How the world would beat a path to his door, he thought, as the little boy on Disney yowled and chased Christopher . . . what was his name, the guy who'd played the professor on *Back to the Future* . . . Christopher Lloyd? How the world of physics would genuflect to him when he unveiled his micro-accelerator. A twenty-foot machine that could do what miles of tunnel in Texas only approached. The excellences of quantum computing—only he had tapped them. The implications . . .

But it was best that *she* disappear before all that take place. If he were to get rid of her when the cold light of fame shone on him—well, someone would look too close at her death. And if he divorced her . . . her lawyer would turn up the funds he'd misappropriated from her senile mother's bank account; an account only his wife was supposed to be able to access. Her lawyer would not care that those funds had paid for his work after the grant had run out . . .

He glanced at her appraisingly. Was it working? She was a short Austrian woman, his wife, with thick ankles, narrow shoulders; she was curled, now, in the other easy chair, wearing only her nightgown. She'd complained of feeling weak and tired for days, but it was the psychological sickness he needed from her . . .

"You know," she said, her voice curiously flat, "we shouldn't have . . . I mean, it seemed right, philosophically, for you to get a vasectomy. But we could have had one child without adding to the overpopulation much, to any, you know, real . . ."

"It was your health too, my dear. Your tipped uterus. The risk."

"Yes. We could have adopted—we still could. But—" She shook her head. Her eyes glistened with unshed tears and the image of the running child on the TV screen duplicated twistedly in them. "This world is . . . it seems so hopeless. There'll be twelve billion people in a few decades. Terrorism, global warming, famine, the privileged part of the world all . . . all one ugly mall . . . the cruelty, the mindless, mindless cruelty . . . and then what happens? You begin to age terribly and it's as if the sickness in the world goes right into your body . . . like your body . . . with its sagging and decay and senility . . . it is like it is mocking the world's sickness and . . ."

It's working, he thought. The medical journals were right on target. She was deeply, profoundly depressed.

"I know exactly what you mean," he said.

"It wouldn't matter so much if I had . . . something. Anything in my life besides . . . But I'm just . . . I mean I'm not creative, and I'm not a scientist like you, I'm not . . . if I had a child. That'd be meaning. But it's too late for that."

"I'm surprised that watching *The Ransom of Red Chief* makes you want a child. Considering how the child behaves . . . They're all Red Chief a lot of the time . . ."

"Oh I don't mind that—wanting a child without that is like wanting wild animals all to be tame. They *should be* wild. But my life is already . . . caged."

"Yes. I feel that way too. For both of us."

She looked at him, a little disappointed. She'd had some faint hope he might rescue her from this down-spiraling plunge.

For a moment, it occurred to him that he could. He could stop putting the incremental doses of toxins in her food. He could take her to a toxicologist. They'd assume she'd gotten some bad water somewhere . . .

But he heard himself say—almost as if it were someone else saying it—

"I'm a failure as a scientist. And I don't want to live in this world . . . if you don't."

It took five more tedious, wheedling days to break her down completely. He upped the dose, and he deprived her of sleep when he could, pretending migraines that made him howl in the night. He drove her closer and closer to the reach of that depression that had its own mind, its own will, its own agenda.

At last, at three-thirty in the morning, after insisting that she watch the Shopping Channel with him for hours—a channel anyone not stupid, stupefied, or mad would find nightmarish, after a few minutes—she said, "Yes, let's do it." Her voice dry as a desert skull. "Yes."

He wasted no time. He got the capsules, long since prepared. Hers the powerful sleeping agent she sometimes used. His appearing to be exactly the same—except that he'd secretly emptied out each pill in his own bottle, and put flour in his capsules. They each took a whole bottle of the prescription sedative. Only his would produce nothing but constipation.

She was asleep in minutes, holding his hand. He nearly fell asleep himself, waiting beside her. What woke him was something cold, touching him. The coldness of her fingers, gripping his. Fingers cold as death.

"I said, I've come to . . . to give you condolences," Berryman said, grimacing. "What a stupid phrase that is. I never know what to say when someone dies and I have to . . . but you know how I feel."

"Yes, yes I do," Kander said. Wanting Berryman to go away. He stood in front of his micro-accelerator, blinking at Berryman. How had the man gotten in?

But he'd been sleeping so badly, drinking so much, he'd probably forgotten to lock the lab door. Probably hadn't heard the knocking over the whine of the machinery.

"If there's anything I can do . . ."

"No, no, my friend she's . . . well, I almost feel her with me, you know. I used to make fun of such sentiments but, ah . . ."

It occurred to him—why not Berryman? Why not let Berryman be the one to break it to the world? Why wait till the papers were published, the results duplicated? There would be scoffing at first—a particle accelerator that could do more than the big ones could do, that could unlock the secrets of the subatomic universe, the unknown essences, consciousness itself, in a small university laboratory? They wouldn't condescend to jeering. They'd merely quirk their mouths and arch a brow. But let them—he'd demonstrate it first hand, once the public's interest was aroused. Let them come and see for themselves. The government boys would come around because the possibilities for applying this technology to a particle beam weapon were obvious . . . yes, yes, he'd mention it during the interview.

"Where would you like to do the interview, Berryman?"

"What?"

"Oh, I'm sorry—I'm getting to be an eccentric professor here, getting ahead of myself. Not enough sleep you know—ah, I want you to be the one to . . . to break the news . . ."

"Still, it's all theoretical," Berryman was saying, so *very* annoyingly, "at least to the public—unless there's something you can demonstrate . . ."

They were drinking Irish whisky, tasting of smoke and peat, in Kander's little cubicle of an office.

"I mean, Kander, I'll write it up, but if you want to get all the government agencies and the big corporations pounding on your door—"

"Well, then. Well, now," Kander took another long pull and suddenly it seemed plausible. "Why not? Come along then . . ."

They went weaving into the laboratory, Berryman knocking over a beaker as he went. "Oh, hell—"

"Never mind, forget it, it's just acid, it's nothing." He had brought the whisky with him and he drank from it as he went through the door to the inner lab, amber liquid curling from the corners of his mouth, spattering the floor. "Ahhh, yes. Come along, come along. Now, look through here, through this smoked glass viewer while I fire 'er up here . . . and consider, consider that there is a recognizably conscious component to quantum measurements: what is consciously perceived is thereby changed only by the perception. There's argument about how literally this should be taken—but I've taken it very literally, I've taken that plunge, and I've found something wonderful. Quantum computing makes possible fine adjustments of a scanning tunneling microscope, turning it into, well, a powerful particle accelerator, effectively . . . and since we're passing through this lens of sheer quantum consciousness in effecting this, we open a door into the possibilities for consciousness to be found in so-called 'matter' itself."

"I see nothing through this window, Kander, except, uh, a kind of squirming smoke—"

"It's a living 'smoke' my friend. Listen—look at me now and listen—What characterizes raw consciousness? Not just awareness—but reaction. Response. Feeling. Yes, yes it turns out that suffering is something inherent in consciousness, along with pleasurable feelings—and that it's there even in the consciousness found in raw inorganic matter."

"You're saying a brick can feel?"

"Not at all! But within a brick, or anything else, is the *potential* for feeling. Now, this can be used, enslaved so to speak, to investigate matter from within and report to us its truest nature; can even be sent on waves of light to other solar systems, to report to us what it finds there—this process of enslavement you see, that's the difficulty, so, ah, you've got to get involved in the training of this background consciousness once you've quantified a bit of it—bottled up a workable unit of it as I have—and that training is done with suffering. But how to make it suffer? It turns out, my friend, that while evil is, yes, relative, it is also, from the *point of view of any given entity or aligned group of entities* a real essence. And this so-called 'evil' can be extracted from quantum sub-probability essences and used to train this consciousness to obey us—"

"You're torturing raw consciousness to make it your slave?"

"Oh stop with the theatrical tone of horrified judgment! Do you eat animals? They have some smattering of consciousness. And how would you get a horse to carry you over a wasteland? You whip it, you force it to your will. Don't be childish about this. Clamp down on your journalistic shallowness and look deep into the truths of life! For, my friend, life is comprised of intertwined essences! And once liberated those heretofore unknown essences are unbelievably powerful! The essence of evil . . . in order to use it I had to isolate it—"

"You've got the essence of evil in there?"

"Yes. Well, it's what people think of as evil . . . I envision a day when it's but a pure tool in our hands—just a tool, completely in our command and therefore never again our master—and we'll train people . . . train them in schools to use evil to—"

He chuckled, "I think this is where I say, 'You're mad, professor'. Only I don't think you're mad, I think you're drunk."

"Am I now? Listen, the stuff . . . just looking at it for a while—it affects you. I spent an hour one night looking into that squirming mass and I—"

He almost said, and I decided, when I stepped away from the instrument, to murder my wife. "And I'd rather not discuss it! Well, Berryman, did it not affect you, just now? Looking at the squirming smoke? No odd thoughts entered your head?"

"Um—perhaps." He blushed. Sex. Forbidden sex. "But—it could be just psychological suggestion, it could be a microwave or something hitting some part of my brain—to say it's the essence of evil—"

"Have another drink. You're going to need it. I'm going to open this chamber, and I'm going to introduce one of these . . . one of these cats here . . . And you'll see it transformed, remarkably changed, into pure energy, an energy that is pure catness, you see . . . Come

here, cat, dammit . . . You know we hire people to steal cats from
the suburbs, for the lab? We often have to take off their collars . . .
Muffy here hasn't had her collar taken off . . . Ow! The little bitch
scratched me!"

"Out-smarted you. You should be ashamed, stealing people's cats,
Kander. There she goes, she's run under the . . . You left the little
door . . . the hatch on that thing . . . you left it open . . . the smoke . . .
oh God, Kander. Oh God."

It wasn't Kander he was running from. The sight of Kander on all
fours, clothes in tatters, knees bloody from the broken glass, running
in circles on hands and knees chasing an imaginary tail like a
maddened cat. Kander yowling like a cat.

Nor was it the fact that Muffy the cat was watching Kander do this
from under the table and *was laughing in Kander's own voice*.

No, it was the squirming smoke, and what Berryman saw in it:
A hall of liquid mirrors, one mirror reflecting into the next so the
reflection replicated into an apparent infinity; and what was reflected
in the mirror, was despair. Despair replicated unto infinity. A hungry,
predatory despair. Berryman saw the bloody drain in the floor of that
South American prison where all those women had been tortured,
tortured for no political reason, no practical application, to no
purpose at all.

He felt the thing that had escaped from Kander's lab—felt it sniff
the back of his neck as he ran out into the partly-cloudy campus
afternoon—

But its inverted joy was so fulsome, so thunderously resonant,
it could not be satisfied with merely Berryman. It reared up like a
swollen phallus big as a genii. It married the clouds overhead and
joined them, crushed them to it, so that electricity sizzled free of
them and communicated with the ground in a forest of quivering
arcs and darkness fell over all like the smells of a concentration

camp, and students, between classes, wailed in a chorus of despondency so uniform it could almost have come from a single throat; and yet some of them gave out, immediately afterward, a yell of unbridled exultation, free at last from the cruelty of self-respect, and they set about fulfilling all that they'd held so long in quivering check . . .

. . . the very bricks . . .

The very bricks had gone soft, like blocks of cheese, and softer yet, and they ground unctuously together, the bricks of the building humping one another . . .

And the buildings sagged in on themselves, top floor falling lumpishly onto the next down, and those two floors on the next, and the whole thing spreading, wallowing, and people crushed, some of them, but others crawling to one another in the glutinous debris . . .

But it wasn't these he was drawn to. It was just one girl.

He was long past resisting; the thing was on them like a hurricane-force Santa Ana wind, parching out all restraint, leaving only the unstoppable drive to merge and to bang, one on the other, like two people on the opposite sides of a door, each banging on it at the same time, loud as they could, each demanding that the other open it—

That's how they fucked.

He had seen the girl, no more than twenty years old, earlier that morning, in the cafeteria. He'd stopped in, on the way to see Kander, for a bagel and coffee. Her hair in raven ringlets falling with springy lushness over bared shoulders; tight jeans; sandals that showed small feet, scarlet nails; when she'd turned, feeling his hot gaze, her face amazingly open, full of maybes, possibilities in her full lips and Amer-Asian eyes. Golden skin. Part Japanese, part black, part Caucasian, and something else—Indian? Her cheekbones were high. They led to her eyes and down to her lips.

Her smile had been impossibly open. Not an invitation, just . . . open.

But, panicky with his rapture, he had said nothing; and she had turned away, and picked out a chocolate pudding.

Now . . . the center of the quad, under the sky . . .

The very center of the campus quadrangle. Brick, it was, with pebble paths from the four corners meeting at a concrete star in the middle. But the bricks and pebbles and concrete had all gone soft, and were alive: he could feel them returning his touch as he and the girl rolled on them, as he banged himself into her . . .

Some part of him struggled for objectivity, struggled for freedom from the overwhelming energies boiling around him . . . Boiling around the hundreds and hundreds of copulating couples and threesomes and foursomes across the campus square . . .

He had been running from the lab, he'd seen her, and she had shouted something joyfully to him as she ran up to him, tearing off her top, and he hadn't been able to make it out because of the thudding, the inarticulate music coming from everywhere and nowhere, sounding like five radio stations turned on full blast over loudspeakers, five different rock-songs all played at once, a chaos of conflicting sounds merging into a mass of exuberant noise—except for no clear reason all the songs had the same percussion, the same beat . . . THUD THUD THUD THUD . . . maybe just his pulse . . . THUD THUD THUD THUD . . . White noise, red noise and black . . .

And he hadn't been able to hear her over this but she'd grabbed his hands and pressed them to her breasts—

Her breasts were songs of Solomon, were each like a dove, fitting perfectly under his hands, each one upturned and nuzzling his palm with a stiff nipple.

Run, he told himself. Get away from here.

Her belly was soft but muscular, moving in a belly dance she'd never learned in life, and he was peeling off her jeans . . . and their clothes, they found, fell away from them like wet ashes, in the magic that was rampant about them, and you could scrape the fabric away with your nails. In moments they were nude and rolling on the impossibly soft bricks, with the white noise, the red noise, the black noise; rolled by the golden waves of god-sized sound and he had only a few glimpses of the others, copulating ludicrously to all sides and with frenetic energy. The obese, unpleasantly naked sixty-year-old Dean of Mathematical Studies was slamming it to the rippling-buff thirty year old lesbian volleyball coach, and the fifty-five-year-old lady with the mustache who was in charge of the cafeteria had stripped away most of her white uniform and was straddling the quarterback of the football team and he was digging at her flapping breasts till they bled and he was mouthing *I love you baby* at her; and the Gay Men's Glee Club was copulating not only with one another but with the girls from the Young Republican Women's Sorority Association, and the black campus mailman was fucking wildly with the blond woman who taught jazz dancing—but it wasn't the first time; and biology classes were copulating with physics classes . . .

And they fucked faster, he and the golden skinned raven haired girl, her eyes flashing like onyx under a laser, and he could feel her cervix pressing against the end of his dick as he ground into her, feel the dimple in the middle of her cervix that led to her uterus, could feel the spongy tissue of the inner vagina with almost unbearable detail as she chewed at his tongue, only making it bleed a little, as close by the president of the Students for Christ screamed, "FUCK ME PLEASE UNTIL IT KILLS ME!" to the wrestling coach until the doddering head of the philosophy department shoved his improbably engorged dick so deep into the student's throat he gagged and choked, the old man, his wattles shimmering with his humping, singing "I got my cock in my pocket and it's shovin' out through my pants, just wanna fuck, don't want no romance!" Or *was* he singing that? Was that in Berryman's mind? Some part of Berryman was becoming increasingly detached as he fucked harder, driving bleedingly hard into the gorgeous Asian student; something in him trying to crawl

out from under this slavery . . . The old man jamming himself into
the student's throat clawed at the air and fell over the other two in
the threesome, shaking in death . . . Others, mostly the older ones,
were beginning to die but even those not breaking under the strain
were showing haunted eyes, amping desperation, and the Dean of
Comparative Religion grabbed a gun from the fallen holster of a cop
and blew out his own brains and the man next to him took the gun
from the Dean's limp hand and shot himself in the throat and the
woman beside *him* took up the gun . . .

While overhead the black thunderclouds still shed their lightnings,
sent eager arcs into the receptive cunt of the Earth itself . . .

For a while now Berryman had been coming, ejaculating in the
girl but the coming wouldn't stop, went achingly on and on and on,
he was quite empty but still his urethra convulsed as it tried to pump
something into her, and all that came up now was blood in place of
cum, and he screamed with the pain and she tried to push away from
him with her hands but her legs, locked behind his back, disobeyed
her, pulled him closer to her yet—

Berryman made a supreme internal effort—arising from an
experience of self-observation, of mindfulness, of an experience of
the possibility of freedom in detached consciousness, something he'd
learned from an old man in the Andes . . .

And never before had he really succeeded in it; never before had it
quite crystallized in him. But now under these unspeakable pressures
it came together and he was whole, and he was free—

His body was still caught, but some essence . . .

An essence! Another essence . . .

Some essence was hovering over the humping, screaming figures,
and calling out . . . Calling out like to like. To another essence, its
own kind.

Then the other essence came; the other end of the spectrum,
closing the circuit, closing the gap: the blue light, and the silence . . .

How Screwtape hated silence . . .

The silence came rolling across them in a wave of release, of icy purity, of relaxing, of forgiving, and they fell away from one another, those who'd survived, and lay gasping, falling into a deep state of rest, and the lightnings stopped, the squirming smoke dissipated in the sudden drenching downpour of rain. The bricks became hard and his dick became soft and . . .

And the cat, Muffy, ran past him, carrying one of Kander's eyes in its jaws.

ANSWERING MACHINE

Transcription begins:

Darla? Um . . . Darla?

Yeah, Hello. Darla?

It's Georgine.

Yeah look I couldn't talk about this with you, like, in person?

I hope it's okay I just wanna like, leave a message on your machine?

Listen, it wasn't my decision, it wasn't my choice to kill your sister, it was Tush, it was her thing, she goes, "Stop being a baby."

And she tells me I bitch about people saying I'm a bitch and people just assume and here I'm acting like a wimp, whining because she was going to put her in that thing and . . . . She was running that whole fucked up trip on me, Darla.

And she goes, Tush goes, "Darla's little Tandy wantsa get into mutilating herself, let's go all the way . . . I mean, you know she wants to die . . . she's like, tried to commit suicide five times . . ."

I told her, I go, "If she wanted to commit suicide really she'd be dead by now. It's like it was never serious?"

But she didn't listen. She has that . . . she has that dominance thing . . . and it's like . . . she told me what her counselor, that she's trying to get out from under something by getting people in shit as deep as she can . . .

You know?

So I said, "Don't put her in there, don't put her in that . . ."

I mean, it was at the junkyard after midnight where we go to smoke bongs and sometimes we get some black tar and . . . you know? You better erase this after you hear it . . .

So I said "Tush, that's—I'm not signing that check, bitch, putting somebody in one of those car compactor things . . . I mean if she wants to commit suicide she wants it to be painless—"

But Tush goes, "She's totally fuckin' numbed out from the pills I gave her anyway, it's like heavy Tuinal and codeine, she won't feel shit, I just wanna see how it looks afterwards . . ."

Her Dad, Tush's dad, he's just the same he's got that same . . . that same thing . . .

He's, like, an LAPD cop and he used to handcuff Tush when she was acting out and stuff . . .

Anyway they were saying—I swear to God—they were saying that they were going to put me in there too, in that machine, if I didn't shut up and then Tush said she heard the spirits of the people killed in the car accidents from all the smashed junkyard cars around us . . . you know how she goes there and gets stoned and says she talks to the ghosts of people that died in those cars . . . and the spirits were asking her to put Tandy in the car compactor and I couldn't even cruise with that, serious, and I'm from Venice Beach ,I mean we've seen it all . . . we used to set bums on fire but . . . you don't *know* the bums, right?

And I don't even believe the ghosts told her to do that. She just wanted to do that. I mean, I know she talks to the ghosts in the totaled cars but like, they never asked for anything like that before.

I mean, the ghosts—before that night—the ghosts were always saying shit like, "Would you pray for me? Would you take the battery out of the car and drop it off the pier because I think that my spirit is stuck here because of the battery, my blood got on the battery and the electricity is trapping me here . . ."

And like who would listen to those spirits in their right mind, because last time . . . last year they told us to do that paint thinner and make those marks on the ground and then Duggy-pup, that red-haired guy that used to—? You remember Duggy. I don't think you were there that night. We made the marks and then he starts foaming at the mouth and shaking and he starts clawing his face and saying, "I don't deserve this face, but only bone, but only bone . . ." Like, over and over, it was sickening, "but only bone, but only bone . . ." So we had to come up with some explanation at the ER for him and his Mom sent him to military school but he kept talking to himself and then he hung himself in the boy's bathroom of the school but anyway—

About Tush and your sister.

And the compactor.

Um . . . .I said . . .

So I said, "No way are the spirits asking to put her in that car compactor and I'm not going to stay here, so . . ."

 So I just—

I just left, I left right outta there, serious—and she woke up in the thing I guess—your sister woke up in the car compactor, woke up from being zonked—

Well I'm *sure*, who *wouldn't* wake up when that machine starts compacting your ass. One time I was zonked out at a party and this guy started putting ice in my butt-hole and I can tell you I fucking woke up from *that*, so . . .

I'm sorry. I'm so freaked out. I can't think.

Anyway I guess she woke up because . . .

Because I heard her scream from like a block away?

I swear to god; I was a block away.

Tush just has that thing . . . that . . .

I went home and took a sleeping pill and went to sleep and I had this dream . . .

I dreamt . . .

I had a dream about dead people in car wrecks trying to tell me to call you so . . . oh wait if this is being recorded it could be used for evidence . . . Erase this shit . . .

I was—

I was just making all this up . . . except . . . Tush has that . . .

I'm sorry. I'm sorry about your sister. I mean—I just heard about it.

I'm sorry.

I'm sorry.

I can't think.

But . . . don't keep this tape okay?

Erase this okay, after you listen to this . . . okay?

Darla?

Are you there listening?

Darla?

Darla?

I gotta—I can't . . .

I can't think.

I'm gonna hang up.

I'm just . . . I'm sorry . . .

I was a block away . . .

Darla?

I'm gonna hang up.

Oh no—Tush is here, she's coming in, Darla she's—

YOU'RE TALKING TO DARLA? YOU FUCKING MORON.

It's just the answering machine. Her answering machine—

NOW WE HAVE TO GO OVER THERE. WE HAVE TO GET THAT TAPE. AND HER.

Darla? She—

End Transcription. Suspects were arrested at scrapyard 1:00 am after patrolman D. Roeser heard the screams from the car compactor. Both bodies were found mingled with compacted car parts. Identification is ongoing. Tape confiscated from suspects.

—Arresting officer: E.Bloom, Northridge PD

PAPER ANGELS ON FIRE

"Mr. Cordell, I know how you must feel." Bret Sage gazed sympathetically into Cordell's eyes as he said it. "Yes, you've lost Muriel—for a while. But you'll see your daughter again. I promise you." Sage realized he had his hands in his jacket pockets. It was chilly on the front porch but hands in pockets didn't look right, at a time like this. He took his hands out and clasped them in front of him. He'd seen funeral directors use that pose. "What happened was part of Muriel's journey. Death is just a freeway interchange, Mr. Cordell."

Cordell smiled coldly, and nodded to himself. "Yeah, it's almost funny to watch—the way your mouth moves and those words come out, like puffs of smoke." Cordell was a balding middle-aged man in a black sweater flecked with what looked like dog hair; the sweater's sleeves were drawn back showing beefy forearms. Sage could see the big dog waiting in Cordell's SUV—a German Shepherd. Cordell was wearing opaque dark glasses hiding his eyes, and maybe his intentions. "Just means nothing at all," Cordell went on. "You are one empty son of a bitch, Sage." And Sage saw that Cordell's right hand was hidden behind his back.

Sage licked his lips, took a step back, edging towards his front door. Maybe he'd been hasty, coming out on the porch alone. It was starting to sound like this wasn't about a settlement . . .

Little Bear was out back somewhere, fixing the hot tub. The sunset bite was in the northern New Mexico air. The shadowy pine woods around the house rang and chattered with birdsong. The ranch house was isolated—no neighbors around to call out to, if he needed them.

Something moved clickingly through the patch of prickly pear under the front window. Funny how vivid everything seemed, in this instant.

Cordell took a step toward him, and the birdsong, all at once, suddenly quieted.

"My daughter trusted you," Cordell said, between clenched teeth. "And that is just goddamn amazing to me. Just look at you! Shabby middle aged long haired unlicensed therapist in beaded moccasins. A slick line of bullshit. Lots of worn out clichés. And your slogan. 'Give me your trust and I'll give you life'!" Cordell shook his head sadly. "She was always a bit lost, that girl. We tried hard, real goddamn hard, to help her—and she was getting on track! And then *you* got hold of her."

That's when Sage noticed the tattoo on Cordell's left forearm. Faded blue ink, but you could make out an anchor slanted through the Earth, topped by an eagle and *Semper Fi*.

Sage swallowed. "Mr. Cordell—we've had hundreds of people in that sweat lodge with no problem and she probably had some . . . some pre-existing condition . . . a bad heart valve or . . ."

"No. She didn't. You gave her drugs. You wouldn't give her water. You wouldn't let her leave. She died in that hole in the ground you call a sweat lodge. And those others too."

"We never, uh . . ." They had, actually, given the Experiencers a rather large dose of Ecstasy. People expected a powerful experience for their three thousand dollars seminar fee and that was the only way to guarantee it. He told them the pills were made of Sacred Herbs. They were supposed to take the pills *after* the sweat lodge ordeal. But the timing got mixed up, maybe because Sage himself had been stoned that morning. "She may have taken something on her own . . ."

"Uh huh. That's what your lawyer says. Says you didn't give her the stuff. But you did, Sage. *Ecstasy*. Now, that wouldn't have killed her—but that stuff makes a body overheat . . . and then you put her in a sweat lodge! Wouldn't let her leave. She begged to be let out . . ."

"We've been in touch with her—we've channeled her, since then, and I know it's hard to believe but . . . she's actually, um, happy where she is."

"Sage, you're gonna choke on your own lies. Starting with your name. What's your real last name, again—Mazoosky?"

"Um—" It was Mezinsky. Didn't have the right ring to it. He'd stopped thinking of himself as Mezinsky long ago. "I am—Sage."

"You're *a hustler* who doesn't care who he hurts, is who you are. A hit and run charlatan, doesn't care who he runs down. But your pals in the local DA's office, looks like they're gonna let you get away with it! No prosecution! Sure I could win a lawsuit. But that doesn't make it, 'Sage'. That's not restitution for my daughter. Not in my book."

Sage licked his lips. Mouth seemed so dry. "I can see this attempt to communicate was a mistake. I understand your feelings in this time of bereavement. But you'd better talk to my lawyer. Good day to you and may the Spirits bless you, Mr. Cordell."

He turned away and fumbled at the door. *Get through it—fast. Damned rusty knob. Open the damned door . . .*

He felt Cordell punch him hard in the right kidney. That's what it felt like, at first. But there was a funny *sound* with the punch. A snake-hiss sound . . .

Then his legs wouldn't hold him up and he was slipping down the closed front door, still clutching at the knob. Waves of blazing sensation rolled in furious rhythm from his lower back—he'd never before felt anything like it. So far beyond any pain he'd ever felt. It was like being hit by lightning over and over in the same spot.

Cordell's voice came to him as if from a telephone held at arm's length. "That's a bayonet, you feel there, 'Sage'. I angled it up, gave it a little twist. But you won't die too quickly. My daughter didn't die too quickly. You're going to . . ."

Sage couldn't hear anymore. He leaned forward against the door, on his knees, hands skittering at the doorknob, convulsing, all his feelings, all his senses, sucked through the spike of ice in his lower back—and the process went on forever.

And then forever ended, somehow, and he fell through his own door.

The wooden front door had become gelatinous, and then foggy. And he fell through it and lay on the floor, face down, half in the house, and half outside. He thought he might sink through the floor, but somehow it held him up.

Then he realized the pain was gone. He felt almost nothing at all. Not even fear. Just a faint, sickened wonder.

He drew his legs up under him, and somehow, very awkwardly, managed to stand.

Sage turned and looked at the front door. It was closed. He stepped over to the window onto the wide porch and saw Cordell walking away from the house, toward the SUV and the German Shepherd. Muriel's father was running a hand over his bald head, as he went, looking limp, barely able to trudge along, sunglasses now dangling from his other hand.

Another man, a middle aged man with a graying pony tail, remained on the porch, slumped against the front door, on his knees. There was a bayonet grip sticking out of his lower back. His left arm was faintly twitching. Blood was running down his hip, pooling around him.

The sick feeling entirely replaced the wonder.

Sage turned away, went to the kitchen, and called out, "Little Bear! George, get in here!"

Little Bear's name was actually George Valdez. He'd never had a traditional Native American name. He was a quarter Comanche, three-quarters Mexican, really. But he played the wise Native American medicine man exactly as Sage needed. He was also the Foundation's handyman.

"George, goddamn it!" he called.

The back door opened, and George came in, wearing overalls. Long gray-streaked black hair, features right out of an Aztec temple painting. Chewing gum, wiping grease from his hands on a red rag.

"Hey Sage!" George yelled, looking around. From three yards away. "I got the hot tub fixed!"

Not seeing Sage—walking right by him. Sage tried to stop him with an outstretched hand, and it was like Sage's hand was boneless, all made of rubber—it turned away from George's arm, couldn't get a grip on it. George kept on, into the front room. Sage numbly followed. "I'm right here dammit, George, look at me!"

"What the fuck!" George yelled, from the front door. Seeing blood oozing under the door. George opened the door and Sage's body sagged forward like a sack of fertilizer.

"Madre Dios!" George muttered. He pushed at the body with his booted foot. Stepped back from it. Shook his head once. "Not gonna blame this on me . . . No fucking way, man . . ."

George turned and bolted, charging through the house, banging out the back door.

Sage shouted after him in a sort of blurred fury. "Why you son of a bitch! You could call 911! I might still be alive, for Christ's sake!" He heard the old Ford pickup starting. Revving. Screeching off down the gravel road.

"No, you couldn't still be alive," said the figure in white, matter of factly. The man in the glimmering white suit was perched casually on the windowsill to Sage's left, legs stretched out to the floor, like he was a comfortable old friend making himself at ease in Sage's house. But Sage had never seen that bland, pale, blue-eyed face before. "Actually, you kind of lost track of time, when you were stabbed, Bret. It took some minutes for you to die. That young woman's father was watching the whole time till he was sure you were dead . . ."

"This whole thing an acid flashback?" Sage asked, approaching the figure sitting casually on the window sill. "Or . . . am I on Ayahuasca again?"

"You were *never* on Ayuahuasca. They just told you it was Ayahuasca. It was a stew of handy, random drugs they sell to the white people from the north."

"Why those crooked bastards!" Sage looked more closely at the translucent figure leaning against the sill. "So I'm definitely dead?"

"You definitely are." The figure in white chuckled with angelic condescension.

So that meant life after death was real. Sage had talked about it thousands of times, at lectures and seminars, but he'd never believed a word of it. Well, what do you know . . .

He looked more closely at the angelic visitor—he seemed vaguely reminiscent of a vice principal at Sage's old Junior High school, in Santa Fe. Mr. Wallace, wasn't that his name? "Are you Mr. Wallace?"

The figure in white bobbed his eyebrows. "Who's Mr. Wallace? I am the angel Abnegas, Bret. I work for the Cleansing Authority."

Sage didn't like the sound of that. "I don't actually need cleansing," Sage said, thinking aloud. "I don't know you. You could be lying about my being dead." He put his hand to his chest, felt for a heartbeat—then he felt for his chest itself. It was only indistinctly there—a flicker under his hand, little more.

 He looked down and made out a dim outline, as if his body was made out of glass, a Bret-shaped bottle.

"There's not much *there*, in there—is there?" Abnegas observed in a kindly tone. "But the part of you that can suffer, or feel pleasure, or perceive—that's still there. It's something the Authority tucks away in the human brain. We take it out, when you die, and either plug it into a new one, or push it into the outer darkness for recycling—using the contemporary terminology here . . ."

Sage didn't like the confidence this man was literally radiating—it was a soft blue-white light coming off him. "When you say you 'take it out'—you're talking about a soul?"

"Essentially."

"And . . . my soul will be plugged into a new body? For a new start?"

Abnegas looked at him with surprise. "I hardly think so! You've recently caused the early deaths of several young people! You've been drugging people, lying to them, exploiting them since you found your little hustle in the 1970s, Bret. You've made many hundreds of thousands of dollars off your seminars but you haven't paid your ex-wife a cent of child support. Whenever you had a choice in your life, you chose selfishly. Hence, I'll be taking you right to the outer darkness, where the spiritual ecology will make short work of you. You're pretty low on the food chain, so . . . it won't be pleasant."

Thinking about that, Sage verified he could indeed *feel*. And it was another new feeling—he'd never felt real terror before. "You mean—something's going to eat me?"

"Yes. Not much of a meal. It'll release your light energy as it does so—and that's the part that will be recycled. It'll take time for you to be digested. The outer darkness is not in the sphere of the eternal, see—time exists there. Which is, maybe, the worst part. It'll take a long, long time . . ."

With that, the angelic figure stood up, and stretched out his hands toward Sage.

Sage backed away from him. "No! I have power! I have the power of the warrior! I am a man of mystery! You have no power over me!"

"Oh but I do . . . Come, my child! Take my hand! The sooner you get started, the sooner the centuries of agony will pass—and *you* will pass, like a kidney stone!"

Sage blinked at him. "Like a kidney stone?"

"Ha ha ha, Roy, you idiot, you had him going but you blew it!" This cawing voice came from the kitchen doorway.

Sage turned and saw a man he *did* know standing there—his uncle Rufus. He hadn't known Rufus well. He'd seen him at holiday celebrations, a jolly, usually drunk, flabby chunk of a man—but he knew his big jowly jaw, his gray crew cut, his dark, laughing eyes. "Uncle Rufus!"

"Got that I.D. right anyway, boyo! It's me, but not in the flesh! Died in 1980 and here I am, floating on the margins, having my fun just like Roy here."

"Rufus, you bastard!" the "angel" grumbled.

Sage looked at the spirit in white. "Your name is *Roy?*"

"I don't care for Roy. Not as classy a sounding name as Abnegas . . ."

Rufus hooted at that. "*Abnegas!* I thought you'd twig to the hoax right there, boyo! What a fake-out name *Abnegas* is!"

Roy, the "angel", shrugged. "Liked the sound of it, what can I say." He grinned. "I almost had him! That Cleansing Authority stuff sounded good!"

Sage looked back and forth between his dead uncle and the spirit named Roy. "So I'm not going to some kind of hell to be eaten alive?"

Rufus snorted. "'Course not! What sort of afterlife would that be? But suppose you'd buckled under and passively gone with ol' Roy here? Why, he'd have traded you to some larger, very rapacious soul for favors! Would have been quite uncomfortable—slavery, actually."

Roy snorted. "Wouldn't have been that bad. The whole thing was just a kind of hazing, really."

Sage felt giddy with relief. "No . . . judgment? I really don't have to go with him?"

"Hell no! You're a ghost now! You do what ghosts do! You can wander around and enjoy the afterlife!" Rufus laughed. "Judgment! I don't know why people scare each other with that poppycock. Only judgment is, you judge yourself! That's what you're stuck with, yourself!"

"Well—then I judge myself to be . . . to be a great warrior. A man of power! And . . . and a teacher!"

"Right, right, all that stuff, sure, whatever you want, nephew mine! That's why I came, when I sensed you'd died—to tell you not to believe anything you heard. I knew Roy was snooping around and he loves to play these little jokes. Roy there, he's a teacher's aide—or he was. He got fired for hitting on some college girl, got drunk, died in a car accident. Now he drifts around, all bored, and messes with the newly dead. It's his little hustle, do you see . . ."

Sage looked at Roy, who spread his hands ruefully. "Busted!"

Sage tried, out of habit, to scratch his head as he thought it over. Couldn't feel his head well enough to scratch it. In fact, his ectoplasmic fingers penetrated into his mind, and the sensation made him shudder. "I can *feel*, in a way—but is it possible to really, you know, have a good time? I mean, I can't imagine there's sex or drugs for a ghost, or . . ."

Roy yawned. "Not exactly. There's fun though. I make my own fun. I don't miss being mortal. Bodies are overrated, believe me. Think about it—no more having to stuff your face, wipe your behind, no getting sick, no getting tired, no getting old . . ."

Rufus nodded, grinning. "Right! I mean, bodies—ugh!"

Bodies. Making Sage think about the hunched, bloody figure on the front porch. "I was murdered—isn't there any justice for that? I wonder if I should go haunt that guy Cordell."

"He wouldn't know you were there," Rufus said. "You're too insubstantial a spirit. Most are too thin for the living to be aware of. Anyway he's turning himself in to the cops right now. They'll jug him for the killing. Whereas you got away with yours—until today."

"I didn't plan to kill anyone. I was always trying to straighten people's heads out, that's all, and sometimes it goes wrong . . ."

"Sometimes?" Rufus grinned at him, his smile twice as wide as his mouth—which didn't seem possible. "What I heard was, people just wandered off, after you took 'em for their money. A couple of them killed themselves, another one started selling Herbal Life, and one of them is a survivalist in Colorado . . . Then you had your little sweat lodge adventure . . ."

Roy had stepped up close beside Sage. It seemed to Sage that Roy had grown a foot taller. That he was looming over him. "That's what I heard too," Roy said. His voice seemed lower, rougher. "That you never did help anyone at all . . . That you just wasted their time—and sometimes their lives."

Sage drew back from Roy, annoyed. The ghost was trying to yank his chains, so to speak, again. The hell with him. He was going to get out of this depressing house—the scene of his death!—and explore the immortal world, wander around, slip into some women's locker rooms maybe. Oh and maybe expand his consciousness. Or something.

He started to move past Rufus, toward the kitchen, and the back door—

Rufus blocked his way. "Hold on, there, 'Sage.'"

Sage didn't want to hold on—he veered quickly around Rufus, spurred by a rising uneasiness.

Rufus flashed past him—and stood in front of the back door. "I said—wait!"

Seemed like his uncle's head was slowly expanding, like a balloon being gradually blown up. And there was another face, pushing out under the Rufus face, which crumbled apart from the pressure, the outer face becoming powdery, drifting away as smoke, the inner, bigger face something like an enormous hyena's head, but with human eyes, human lips, a subhuman voice, growling: "Bret, you had better stay here with us! We have lovely, lovely plans for you!"

Sage turned and saw Roy looming up, over him—nine feet tall, his face all doughy, collapsing, hardening into a kind of fleshy, semi-human mantis shape. "Sage . . ." The voice coming in a clattering chitter. "Do you like our little joke?"

He turned back to the hyena-headed thing. Realizing, "You were never my uncle . . ."

"No—your Uncle Rufus is in the outer darkness! You may crowd into a demonic gut with him! Say hello for me if you see him . . ."

"You are . . . you're a . . . a *what*?"

The hyena headed spirit opened its quite human hands—and between them expanded a chain of paper angels, exactly the sort that people cut with scissors to amuse children. The angels burst into flame and flew away on wings of ash, to suck into the hyena's mouth, as if he were inhaling dope smoke. "Ahhhh! We are paper angels, for a time! We mix a little truth into the lies. And then we show ourselves to you—as you showed yourself to Muriel Cordell!"

"I was trying to help her!"

"You threw your line into the water, fishing for lonely, lost souls, Sage—and when you hooked them, you reeled them in. You promised them relief from their dilemmas, and took their time and money, and their freedom. And when they realized you could give them nothing, their hope was destroyed . . . and they wandered away, to be lost again. Or to die. You offered them hope—and you snatched it away. That's how you 'helped' all those people, Bret Sage . . ."

Sage tried to slip off between them, trying to move quickly as the Rufus Thing had—and the Roy Thing blocked him, making a ticky-ticky-tick sound of amusement by rubbing its chitinous front talons together.

Sage froze—and his voice came in a sort of squeak. Not from his mouth. From somewhere in his shriveling soul. "There is . . . judgment?"

"There are—consequences!" the creature snarled gleefully. "Starting with me, and my companion . . . who really is called Abnegas! I am called Krick!"

"Abnegas isn't an angel . . . or Roy."

"He is the same kind as I—those who feed on such as you!"

"But *however* . . . !" Abnegas said.

"Yes *however* . . . !" Krick chorused.

"However—you may run into the side hallway—there! And find a place to hide!"

"I'm a . . . I'm a spirit! You can't hurt me! I don't have to run from you! You're bluffing! You're—"

Abnegas's head darted forward like a striking mantis, and his mandibles dug into Sage's middle. Sage felt his center crushed in chewing jaws, and something worse than pain crackled through him: a sense of vital diminishment, a feeling of an infinitely unheated void, a nothingness aching with entropy, impinging on his innermost being. He felt a shriveling of an inner self he hadn't known was there till that moment . . .

Sage screamed from within himself, silently and with world-shaking loudness, all at once.

He shrank away from Abnegas, seeing shining shreds of himself writhing in the demon's mandibles, each little bit looking like a tiny little image of Sage. As if the thing were eating Bret-Sage-shaped gummy candies . . .

"Just a bite," the hyena-head growled. "There's not a lot of you to consume. You'll make a thin, understated little snack . . ."

Then Sage bolted for the hallway, was rushing, flying through the house, his feet not quite touching the floor, looking for a place to hide. The basement? No. There was a window in the bedroom. He darted into his bedroom, past his neatly made bed, flinging himself toward the window—which went black.

He pulled up short, staring through the glass. It no longer looked on the little succulent garden at the side of the house—it looked into a churning, black space, an uneasy mirror of ink, and Sage knew if he continued to look he would be drawn into it . . .

He turned away—and heard the noises from the hallway. The growling, the chittering. The clicking of claws. Coming closer.

He wailed and threw himself to the floor, tried to push down through it as he'd fallen through the door, but it wouldn't work—it seemed to resist him. He could feel some other *will* there, pushing back. Who was it? It didn't seem friendly, but it didn't seem unfriendly. Just a watching presence. Waiting its turn.

"Help me!" he called out to it. "Let me through!"

The room darkened; a smell came to him then, the reek of a man's kidney ripped open, mixed with blood. The smell of his own death . . . Why now?

He looked under the bed toward the door. Saw the clawed feet there. Poised.

Sage whimpered and crawled under the bed . . .

"Help me!" he called out to the other presence. "I'm sorry for what I've done! Help me! I'll make up for it, I'll redeem myself!"

You are only lies . . . came a voice from the floors, the walls, the air. *Only lies . . .*

"No, no! I mean it! I—"

He felt a steel-hard, ice-cold grip on his lower limbs—on what passed for legs in a damaged ghost. Something had gripped him hard there, was pulling him back.

"Sage . . ." It was Krick. Pulling him out from under the bed. "You didn't play the game very well . . . nothing to do now but feast . . ."

"It's time," Abnegas said.

"And time goes on and on, for you," Krick said, dragging him into the center of the room. They leaned over him . . .

"Please!" Sage cried out from the very center of his being. "Give me a chance!"

A small tornado of pitch-black was forming in the center of the room, between Abnegas and Krick. In the center of the onyx whirling appeared a point of light. The scintillation grew, and then flashed like a brilliant strobe to fill the room.

A glowing being stood there, arms spread. Its face was an archetype of all angelic beings. It shone with infinite understanding. The two demons, Abnegas and Krick, crouched, recoiling away from it, covering their eyes in frustration and pain and fury.

A feeling of relief rippled through Sage—it was like stepping out of a sleety winter wind into a warm, cozy room. There was hope. There was a chance . . .

The being of light spread its arms; its' wings—like a white butterfly's—filled the room with a comforting perfume, which he seemed to remember. Wasn't that his mother's perfume—remembered from his infancy?

"Come, then, Bret," said the being of light; its voice was neither male nor female, just as the voice of a clarinet has no sex. It opened its arms wider, the warm light beckoned—

Sage rose up, weak but eager to go to the angel, to be rescued, and set free . . .

"Give me your trust and I'll give you life," said the white-winged angel.

Sage flung himself headlong into it—and then realized it had been quoting *him*: mocking the slogan subtitling his website: *Give me your trust and I'll give you life.*

He tried to turn back but it was too late, he was falling through the portal—because that's what it was, it wasn't a real being, it was a mirage, a *doorway* into the sucking heart of the black tornado, which vacuumed him down, with high speed centrifugal intensity, so that he spun helplessly into its depths . . .

Finally emerging in the churning darkness that he'd seen outside the window—where Abnegas and Krick were waiting, with a great many other beings, all of them ravenous.

"Yeah," Krick said, crushing him in its talons, "that was a little more fun at your expense. And now . . . and *now* . . ."

The ripping began—their hatred was their teeth and claws, tearing him to pieces.

But the pieces drew back together, re-forming, wailing, into the nauseating spirit body that was what remained of the man who'd called himself Sage . . .

Which was immediately swallowed by Krick—and all the others, who were, he saw now, all *one creature*: many grotesque heads on one ethereal body.

Down, Sage slipping down into darkness, into its jet-black inner world, where its hate was a digestive acid, reducing him to a shrieking pulp, the grinding pain going on and on . . . and then . . .

. . . A glimmer in the darkness. A living, angelic light . . . .

"Forgive me!" Sage howled, within himself.

"Come to me, and I will forgive you!" the light replied.

Sage rushed to the point of light, weeping, feeling hope blossom . . .

It drew him in . . .

"Just kidding," it said. As it ate him again.

Living pulverization. Unspeakable suffering that went on forever.

Then a light gleamed . . . He rushed to it, trembling with relief.

It drew him in . . .

CALL GIRL, ECHOED

There was no real reason Morales should be nervous. But he always was before one of them came over. *It's absurd*, he told himself, as he drew on the plush hotel robe and went out to the small portable bar on the hotel balcony where he made himself a double scotch. It was all quite professional, after all; the act was nothing personal, even to the human ones, so there's no reason to be nervous.

But he was nervous for both kinds of call girl. He'd gone from the human kind—which were quite rare now, anyway, they had so many disadvantages—to the robotic call girl, because he thought that would ease his nervousness. Anyway, real, flesh and blood girls had always irritated him. They were suspicious of him, despite the smile, and they watched the clock. The robots were designed to be accommodating.

Gazing down over the hotel pool, he drank off half the scotch and grimaced. The pool area was decorated in a Baja-in-New-York theme, cheerfully green and anomalous beside the gray and glassy soldiers of skyscrapers towering at attention around it; the empty pool was lit up, a candy-blue rectangle against the crystal-white artificial sand landscaping, the plastic grove of green and brown synthetic palms. Maybe it was time to blow off New York for the real Baja.

The chime came on the hotel phone. He stepped within respond range of it and said, "Yes?"

"You have a visitor, a young lady. From Synthetic Satisfactions."

He winced. The son of a bitch should've been more discreet than to say the name of the company aloud. "Send her up."

He looked down at himself. He was tanned, and reasonably fit for forty, under his white bathrobe. He retied his robe's belt, thinking he we was a little paunchy—but not much.

Morales clucked his tongue at himself. He was doing it again. Nervous—over a robot. Robots don't care if you're paunchy or not.

He chuckled, drank off the rest of his scotch, waited the right interval, and got to the door just as she knocked. She was what he'd asked for: tall, slender, blond, pretty, busty, blue eyed. A classic. He'd asked for Maximum Realism so they'd given her a few minor blemishes, something like a faint scar on her lower lip. The tanned breasts in her tank top seemed to heave a little with her "breathing"; there was a suggestion of aging at the corners of her eyes, as if she were just turning the corner into 30. Good.

Her voice was soft and husky as she said, "Hi. I'm Amy . . . from the agency?"

"Come on in," he said, smelling her perfume as she walked by. She dropped her purse on the sofa in the suite's living room—the purse was mostly for the bar code reader she brought with her, he supposed, to record the transaction. "I'm Joey Morales."

"Oh, I know your name!" She stood just inside the door to the balcony looking out at the sea. "Wub, what a high-rez view," she added, in slang that was a bit outdated by now. Her programmers needed to do a linguistic update.

"So, uh . . ." No, there was no point in offering her a drink. She could make a show of ingesting fluids, if it was part of the fantasy—but it wasn't. ". . . won't you sit down?"

They sat close but not too close on the couch. Her movements seemed natural—the robots from the agency always moved naturally. There was that telltale stiffness in the way she crossed her legs. But she was a good one, all right.

She smiled at him and the smile said she wanted him. "It's good to be here."

He was pleased—that's exactly how she was supposed to smile and what she was supposed to say. He'd filled out the fantasy play-form

very carefully. They'd programmed her for the encounter—but let's
see if they'd done it right all the way through. Last time the robot
had forgot the washcloth thing.

"Joey—I'm so curious about you. I'm hungry to know all about you.
What do you do for a living?"

"I'm a buyer for Transnational Transplants. I go out to the organ
farms, see if the vats are up to spec, do some testing, negotiate. Good,
high-pay corporate job. Takes years of training."

"It's almost like being a doctor!"

He smiled urbanely. "What brings you here? We have never met—
something has to have brought you to me."

She responded to those words exactly as he'd prescribed: "I . . .
couldn't help myself. When I saw you at the pool. I . . ." She hesitated—
which was pleasingly realistic. "I had to find a way to be near you. I
know it seems crazy. But I—promise me you won't get mad—I went
into the changing cabin you used, after you left. I found this . . ." She
reached into her shorts and slowly drew out a washcloth. She'd had
it tucked up against her crotch. She pressed the cloth to her cheek,
ran it across her lips. "The cloth you used . . . on your body. I've been
carrying it close to mine. That's how strongly the sight of you affected
me. I decided I'd do anything I had to do—to give myself to you!"
His hard-on was already poking from his bathrobe and her eyes went
to it. She commented as scripted: "Oh God—it's bigger than I ever
imagined . . ."

Morales reached out and took the damp cloth—as it should, it
smelled of the sea, and—damn, that was good chemistry—of woman.
He kissed it, and draped it over his hard organ, throwing his robe
open, and said—

"What the *fuck* . . ." That wasn't in the script. But it's what came
out of him.

He was staring down at the cloth. There was a spot of fresh blood on it.

"I'm bleeding!" Morales muttered, lifting the cloth away. But no—
no blood on his privates. Then . . . he looked at Amy.

That was fear in her eyes. Why would they program the appearance of fear into her? It wasn't in his fantasy. He was no sadist.

He sniffed at the blood spot. There was the very distinctive smell—of menstrual blood.

"I'm sorry," she said, trying to make her face blank. "Someone must have incompletely reprogrammed me. The last one must've wanted someone on her period. Or just starting it. There won't be much blood. Let's have sex, and ignore it. I can . . . I can wash it out. It's just starting. I mean in the fantasy. From the last guy . . ."

Were those tears welling?

"Take off your pants," he said.

"Sure," she said. Looking a little relieved. She pulled her short-shorts off, and her underwear. Now that was realistic: a razor burn, where she'd trimmed the edges of her pubic hair.

He knelt between her legs, wet his finger, and pushed it into her—she winced. That wincing could be programmed, too . . .

He grunted to himself. The inside of a robot call girl was very, very much like a human girl's. But this . . . it was too real. Unless they'd improved the model.

He withdrew his finger, stood up, and pressed down on her chin. "Open your mouth."

She swallowed, licked her lips—with an amazingly real tongue—and opened her mouth. The fillings could be window dressing. But a little piece of food—parsley—stuck back there, between two molars?

He sat back, furious. And a little scared, too. "Who the fuck are you? Someone sent you here to—what? Get me to talk about Transnational's new kidney line? You some kind of industrial spy?"

Her shoulders slumped; her head drooped; her hands balled into small fists on her knees. "No. I came on my own—I just . . . I do some computer hacking. I intercepted some online orders for call girls . . . got the fantasy specs, canceled the order . . . I tried to act robotic—I even did that stiffness with my legs . . . I've tried to be

a human call girl but no one uses human ones anymore. I just . . .
please—touch me!"

"What? I haven't even paid you anything—unless you stole that
credit transfer."

"No—swear I didn't. I'm here because . . . I need to feel that kind
of intimacy. Joey, *men don't use actual women for sex anymore.*"

He shrugged. "So? Why should we? Women want some action,
they can order male robots. They're cheap now. They build one
another."

"I don't want a male robot—they're horrible. I mean—they're
just . . . just 'fucking machines'."

"And that's bad?"

"It is for me. Even when they're well programmed you know it's
not real. I don't look it, but I'm almost forty. Since the robots came
in a few years ago, I can't interest anyone in me. They all have robot
women. I need to feel a real man again—I mean, my doctor says I'm
obsessive but—"

"Oh okay, there it is. Your *doctor*. You're on some kind of medication.
Or you're supposed to be."

"What does that matter?" she asked, sulking.

"It means you're crazy. And that matters." He shook his head. "I
should have realized something was off when you didn't do the bar
code thing to confirm the purchase. Now just—get out of here."

"Please—" She leaned toward him. Licked her lips, trying to look
sexy. "I'm sorry about the period. It's a little early. I didn't realize. But
it's just starting. We can still—"

"It isn't that. I just don't like real girls. They are either secretly
contemptuous of you—if they're a hooker—or if they're your
girlfriend they're . . . well, they're still secretly contemptuous of you!
And even if they don't hate you, they're so demanding. They want
attention all the time. 'Tell me you love me.' Or 'Why won't you go
to the dance class with me?' The hookers are such crummy actors—
you can tell they want to be somewhere else. But not a robot. She

acts like she wants exactly what you want when you want it, and she does—she's programmed to."

"But I don't want to be somewhere else. I want real sex with *you*."

"Yeah and then you'd follow me around afterward and ask me to tell you I loved you or . . . to cuddle you . . . Christ." Her lips trembled. He softened his tone. "Hey look—you're a good looking woman—I don't believe you couldn't find anyone. But—drop this act. This whole . . . this deception you tried to pull off, it's *sick*—"

She was weeping openly. That was another problem with real women, they cried, and they wouldn't stop when you wanted them to.

She wiped her eyes, getting makeup on her fingers. "I had three serious boyfriends—two of them talked about marriage—and they—they changed their minds. They said the robots were better and—they don't want me. They want the robots . . ."

"Right. So find some guy with eccentric tastes—some guy who likes real women. Or get a boy-bot. You've really got to go now . . . ."

She reached behind her, picked up her purse. She opened it—and took out a folding jack knife.

"Shit!" He jumped to his feet, backing away, looking around for the phone.

Then he stopped, staring.

Amy was slashing deeply into herself with the knife. To Morales it looked like she was trying to carve her vagina away.

Blood spurted onto the couch, with a soft drumming sound. She dropped a mass of crimson tissue onto the carpet. It was like something from a gutted fish.

Now—shaking, gagging from the pain, white-faced—she was taking something from her purse. She shoved it brutally in the gaping, blood spraying wound between her legs.

He recognized it. A robot vagina-unit. Taken from some robot being repaired, probably. She'd forced it, just jammed it, into the wound and now, her face ghastly, sitting on the sofa, she spread her legs in a puddle of blood. She showed him the mechanical vagina forced crookedly into the ragged wound and she said, "Do you want me now? I can be a machine too. If you'll let me. I can be a machine too . . ."

YOU HEAR WHAT BUDDY AND RAY DID?

What Ray does, sometimes, he runs low on money, he goes to those adult bookstores with the booths that got the sticky floors in the back room, and he hangs out in there, at the corner of the little maze of digital peeps, pretending to be reading those glossy cards on each booth with the pictures of people fucking; those cards show you what DVD channel for "Virtual Tight" or for, maybe, "Mama's Enema Party". Ray stands there real casual but watching everyone, till he sees the kind of guy who's maybe got a gold watch, real well fed, crocodile shirt, say Coke-bottle-glasses—some guy that doesn't get any ass. So then Ray catches his eye, snags him into a booth, pretends he's gonna suck the guy's dick, but he just sort of plays with it, the dude's pants are down and loose around his ankles and Ray's on his knees coming out with the Hot Talk, all the time his free hand getting into the guy's back pocket, snagging that wallet, says excuse me, I'll be right back, you're makin' me so hot, don't move! Then he cruises on with the wallet . . . some guys—straight guys, usually—are really expert at this, usually crack heads . . . Ray actually learned this because it had been done on him when he was just eighteen. Some black guy in a booth started playing with Ray's dick, but he was really into Ray's wallet—a big five bucks—and Ray caught on and he said, "You're not ripping me off, motherfucker." And he grabs the guy, but this is a big black junkie and he *grabs Ray's dick and balls*, I'm tellin' you, man! He starts *twisting*, saying, "You fuck with me, you lose 'em," but Ray pries the junkie's fingers off his parts and the junkie bolts out of the place and he yells, "You follow me, you white faggot motherfucker, I'll knock you out!" So Ray finds himself standing there between the booths staring after this guy and he realizes his pants are down around his ankles and his dick is hanging out . . . but he thinks, That could work for me sometime. Now fast forward to . . .

Ray's standing on a Larkin Street corner, thinking it's too cold out tonight, maybe he'll try the adult bookstores again. Sometimes he scores that way; other times he maybe only gets five bucks, or nothing at all. Of course, he could let somebody suck his dick for a ten or a twenty, but he just *likes it better* when he rips them off. It's not that getting his dick sucked by some geek really bothers him; it's that ripping them off feels especially good. But you could waste hours standing around in those places. It really is getting cold outside . . .

"Hey, Butch," Buddy says, coming up to Ray on the corner.

"Don't call me that unless you mean it," Ray says, "and you don't." Ray's only a quarter Latino, but he's got the rolled-up headband around his head, trying to get the action that wants a Latin Lover.

Buddy's from Texas, long and muscular, tan starting to fade, tattoos, really tight buns; he dances sometimes at the Polk Street Theatre San Francisco's Finest All Male Dancers, but he gets fired every so often for picking up tricks there. They rehire him. And fire him again . . . He was in some porn, too. Ray keeps trying to get into some porn, but generally he smells a little too ripe; he likes to get loaded and tends to end up sleeping on floors and in places with no showers. "I got somethin' for us," Buddy says. "There's this guy that saw me in one of those Marines movies, I was fucking some real butch Marine guy, he thinks I'm totally tough, but he wants to watch me with somebody else . . . you know, him watching and shit . . ."

All of this is, maybe, twenty-four hours before I came on the scene.

Turns out this guy, the trick buddy found, is some kind of computer nerd, into the black-market hacker stuff, too—and he's got a head iron. Buddy knew what a head iron was, and even though his cousin went ill behind one of those things, he still wanted to try one.

The dude's place is one of those real nice Noe Valley flats, restored Victorian building, shiny hardwood floors, antiques, modern art paintings, home-theater flat screen TV, expensive PC with one of those screen-saver things wiggling around in tastefully iridescent fractal dancing . . . first editions of Oscar Wilde . . .

Trick's name is Charlie; Buddy never could stand a Charlie . . . anybody who went by Charlie when they could be Charles or even Chuck . . . Trick's about sixty pounds overweight, hair real short in the arty, almost bald thing, walks kind of pigeon-toed, real nice clothes, good material, gold lambda earlobe ring . . . WHOA, IS THAT A ROLEX WATCH? Yes, it is, and no, it's not counterfeit. This is looking like potential.

They drink red wine and Ray asks the guy if he's got any cocaine. Charlie sort of leers and says cocaine makes you impotent, don't want you impotent. And some quote from Shakespeare about swords being blunted.

"Take off your pants so I know you're not a cop," Ray says to Charlie.

Buddy gives Ray a look. Oh, yeah, sure, like this lisping, pigeon-footed, Noe Valley fag is a cop. You fucking bet.

But later Buddy figures out that Ray doesn't think the guy is a cop at all; he's just taking over. Telling the guy what to do. Laying it down.

The guy has dated some hustlers, knows the laws, knows that an undercover cop is not allowed to take off his pants—so he doesn't argue; he takes off his pants to show he's not Vice, folding the trousers and the underwear neatly on the arm of the antique velvet sofa.

His dick, hiding under his round white belly, looks like a snail under a boulder that got scared and it's going back into the shell.

Buddy asks for the money once the pants are off, and Charlie has it all ready, a hundred cash, more later if everything is good. Fine for starts.

Ray is loading up on the wine. Get what he can while he's here. He's looking around a little too much at all the carefully dusted objecks-dee-art—there's a lot of carved jade stuff that looks like it might be worth money—and Buddy says, "So what're you into?"

First, Charlie suggests, just make yourselves at home. Perhaps you two would like to take a shower . . . together.

He makes it sound like it's partying for them to take a shower and him to watch, but probably it's mostly because they stink.

So they take a shower, soap each other's dicks and asses for Charlie to watch, Charlie's fat little fingers working that snail, coaxing it halfway out of its shell.

Ray and Buddy never did sex together before, they've been mostly, like, friends on the corner, but they're pros by now and Buddy doesn't let his embarrassment show. He kind of likes playing with Ray after a while. Takes him back to a circle jerk when he was eleven.

Half hour later, they're wearing only towels, still a little damp, Charlie's aftershave burning-cold in their pits. Charlie has opened a second bottle of this expensive wine. *C'est très cher, mai . . .* he says, showing off. Like he's the only one who ever took a French class.

Charlie looks expectant, so Ray and Buddy drop the towels and start full-on going at it. The scene is bothering Buddy a little, so he's not really keeping it up very well. But it's enough for Charlie, who's standing by the bed watching like a dog at a dinner table, grinning conspiratorially, really getting into the fantasy

Buddy starts to think, We're this trick's video game. It's more than live porn, it's not Ray in control after all, it's Charlie, taking them through levels in one of those games where you go down and down into some cavern hole, and ol' Charlie's going to win when he spurts his little dinger . . . then they can get the fuck out of here, go to Mary's and get a burger or something and laugh at this fat fuck.

And then Charlie starts getting into the game himself. Moving them around like dolls, stroking their asses while they go at it, putting Ray's hand on his snail—that's when Ray says, "You like to do B&D, anything like that?"

Charlie's eyes shine, but he's a little nervous about letting Ray tie him up, but Ray says, "We'll tie you down to the bed and we'll get busy on top of you like you're the mattress . . ." And this gets Charlie so excited he's shaking . . .

. . . but he gets jumpy when Ray starts to tie his hands to the bedposts with the old silk neckties, so Ray says, "I'll just tie it with a butterfly loop, not *really* tied, and you can pull it off when you want, Charlie."

He does tie the guy's left hand just like that, and Charlie's not looking as close when Ray ties the right hand—Ray puts an extra knot in it—and Buddy does the ankles, and then Charlie says, "Go to my dresser drawer, there's an instrument behind the socks . . ."

Ray and Buddy figure the "instrument" is a vibrator or a whip, but when they find it, it turns out to be the head iron. It looks just like an old-fashioned barber's electric razor, the kind they use to shave the nape of your neck, and it probably is the shell of one, but it was taken apart and they put, like, gizmos inside it, and it's got duct tape holding it together now, and a little glass cone at the shaving end instead of the cutting pieces.

"This goes on your head, right?" Ray asks. "Like on the back of your skull?"

He plugs the head iron in and starts to try it on Charlie, but Charlie pulls back real quick, says, "No, no, wait, it must go to a precise spot, or it can have very nasty side effects . . . one loses control of one's bowels"—he's the kind of guy who says 'one' instead of 'my', right?—"or one may have a seizure . . ."

So Charlie has Ray hold a hand mirror over him. Then he has Ray put a piece of tape on a certain spot on the back of his head, stuck in that short hair. That's the spot where the head iron goes. Then he tells Ray to go ahead.

Charlie licking his lips, breathing shallow, kind of scared and kind of excited . . .

Ray puts the glass cone of the iron on the tape over the fat guy's spot—forty-five-degree angle—and pushes the *on* switch, and there's a little hum and then the guy's eyes instantly dilate and he moans and he goes rigid and then limp and then rigid and then limp . . . getting hard and soft, hard and soft, like when somebody mainlines cocaine . . .

Well, of course, naturally, Ray has to try this. Ray, understand, is the kind of guy who used to be into glue and huffing fumes and just any fucking thing.

"Now," Charlie is saying, "now, fuck on top of me . . . I'm your mattress, do it, the two of you on top of me . . ."

But Ray is ignoring him; he's finding the spot on his own head. A couple of near misses—one time he starts choking for a second—and then, boom, he hits the spot. He gets it. Big ecstasy.

And under the influence of the head iron, Ray starts trying to fuck Buddy just because he wants to.

Buddy pushes him off at first, but then Ray finds the spot on Buddy's head—he gets just the right spot on the first try and he pushes the button and it's like a big wet explosion of GOOD, just plain GOOD pouring out of him. Like you shot him in the head and what came out wasn't blood, it was GOOD.

"Oh fuuuu-*uuuuuuck!*"

And now it feels good when Ray shoves into him—in this stoned-out place Buddy's in, it'd feel good if you shoved a claw hammer up him claw first. They go at it and they're tripping, they're into some other place, some place that's all penetration and skin-flavored pleasure and waves of maleness that metamorphose into femaleness—

But then it starts to fall apart, kind of fizzing into decay, like an Alka-Seltzer tablet in water; like a flare on the street, bright red—and then going black.

Buddy starts to imagine what it would be like if his old man could see him with this guy's dick in his butt. His guts crinkle up at the thought . . .

Then Charlie starts yelling he wants another hit, he wants them to do what they said, and Ray gets up off Buddy and suddenly both Ray and Buddy are feeling all wasted and hollow, like they might collapse into themselves, like a cigarette ash that's perfectly shaped till you touch it.

And Buddy feels a kind of icy, gushing rage he never felt before, and he looks at Ray and he can see the same thing in Ray's face. Ray's saying, "Buddy, all the stuff in this place could be *our* stuff."

Charlie really starts yelling when he hears that, but he can't get free from that extra knot on his wrist and then Ray is standing over him, making it louder and worse. "You want another hit, here's another motherfuckin' hit!" And he starts whacking Charlie around the face with the head iron, making scallop-shaped wounds in him, Charlie screaming and Buddy saying something about the neighbors calling the cops, so Ray stuffs several pairs of dirty socks and underwear in Charlie's mouth—Ray's and Buddy's socks and underwear—and Charlie's screams are muffled and Ray gets up on the bed yelling, "You want us on top of you?" And he starts jumping onto Charlie, coming down on him with his knees, so Buddy can actually hear Charlie's ribs cracking under Ray's kneecaps.

Buddy's been doing all this to Charlie in his mind same time as Ray does it, it's just like he's doing it when Ray does it, so his rage comes in that way and froths over and after a moment he can think a little and he says, "You kill him, we don't get his ATM number, bro . . ."

x   x   x

Ray gets so distracted using the corkscrew on Charlie to get the ATM PIN that he almost forgets about the head iron, and Buddy puts some big willpower on the line and hides the thing. He really wants to wreck it, because it scares him, it scares him to feel that high and scares him even worse to feel that down afterward, but he can't quite get himself to wreck it. So he finds a trapdoor in a ceiling, puts the head iron in the attic.

The attic entrance is in the same closet they put Charlie in. Charlie's still alive. They figure they're gonna need him. They make Charlie crap a few times in the bathroom first, set up a bicycler's sipping bottle he could suck some water out of and they tie him into a corner of the closet, really tie him good so he can't bang on the wall to get attention. He looks like he's in the middle of a spider web afterward, with that soft white rope they found under the bed, tying him to the hinges and the clothes-hanger pole. Ray wants to pee on the guy, but Buddy won't let him, saying he doesn't want the smell.

Then Ray asks about the head iron, but Buddy puts him off, says let's wait on that till the drugs run out.

"What fuckin' drugs?"

"Let's go to the ATM. See what we can get. Charlie ain't doing shit, tied up like one of those guys in a cannibal pot."

"I got your back, man."

First Ray and Buddy do some of Charlie's expensive mail-order crystallized vitamins—they know about rushes and crashes and how to deal with that—and they eat a steak from Charlie's fridge, so they feel some better. The head-iron crash eases out.

And what do they find in Charlie's bedside table? Three guesses. Right, a piece! A .38 revolver that looks like it's never been fired. One box of shells. This is just getting better and better.

Ray stays with Charlie—watching MTV3 and drinking—while Buddy goes to a check-cashing place with a check from Charlie for a grand. The place calls up for confirmation, and Ray has the portable phone jammed up against one of Charlie's ears and the pistol up against the other. Charlie approves that fuckin' check, pronto.

Then Ray meets Buddy on the street, by the check-cash place. They divvy a thousand from the check and three hundred from the ATM, and they go on a mission. After midnight, they can get another three hundred dollars from the ATM, and it's almost midnight.

"I still feel kind of weird from that head-iron shit," Ray says. "But, man, that was a fuckin' rush!"

"That thing, I don't trust that shit, we gotta forget that, at least for now, dude. Let's get some good rock, some good ronnie, maybe some pussy . . ."

"Pussy, yeah, now the man's got an idea," Ray says, but Buddy doesn't quite believe it.

About half an hour after midnight, Buddy and Ray come to me. That's right, me.

All they could find was street hubba, it seems, which is pretty much shit cocaine.

"You know Miss Dragon, right?" Ray says. "We got the money. You could get us the good stuff."

I correct him. "That's Dragon Miss, they call her."

Me, I'm terrified of cocaine. Turns me into a hit-sucking bug faster'n a vice cop takes a bag. Then I'm gone for a couple of days and I run the wheels off that fucker and then I turn paranoid, which is maybe how . . .

Well, it's one way people get killed.

So I stick to hashish—which I get from the Dragon Miss—maybe sometimes opium, always some cognac or Johnnie Walker Red. Speed if I need it. And so many vitamins I smell like 'em.

Maybe what I most get off on is the second-story work. One time I popped into this guy's apartment, he's sleeping in the same room, snoring like a chainsaw, and there's a wallet on the nightstand, and I snag the wallet and flip it open in the light by the window and see there's a fucking badge in the wallet—the guy is a cop. I look over at him and he's still sawing logs, but now I see on the other nightstand there's a fucking .44 lying there like a chunk of pure silver. This is a cop's bedroom and he's got a loaded .44 next to him and I've got his fucking wallet in my hand! Now, that's a rush!

I took the .44 and the wallet and I took a beer from his fridge too.

I used to be a writer, one time, plays and journalism. I even did a feature for *Esquire* once. I used to do those slam readings at coffeehouses that are so chic now, everybody playing beatnik. But then I got into the coke binges. Louisa . . .

Well, they found Louisa dead.

And after that, I had to live different. I don't know how to explain better than that. I couldn't go back to writing, but I couldn't be a basehead neither. I had lost Louisa, and maybe I could've saved her, if I wasn't on the shit.

But I understand Buddy pretty well. I've known him a shitload of years. On Tenderloin time, anyway. Four years is a long time to know somebody in the Tenderloin.

So I get Buddy talking about what he and Ray did: he's like a free-association machine after he takes a hit on the shitty hubba. During the story Buddy's telling me, Ray is in the bathroom, jerking off by the sound of it. *Whuppawhuppawhuppa.* Some people when they do cocaine, they can't keep their hands off their dicks, which is funny because their dicks don't usually perform for them anymore.

Then Ray comes out of my bathroom looking uglies at Buddy, and Buddy takes the hint and shuts up, and to defuse the situation and just to follow this street and see where it comes out, I tell them, "Let's go see if the Dragon Miss wants your money."

x   x   x

Like I thought: turns out Dragon Miss wants to see this apartment full of antiques and art tchotchkes, and the guy tied up in the closet. "It sounds like just the *best* party, girls . . . if we can keep the Big Tummies out." She thinks it's cute to call the local cops Big Tummies.

"Neighbors are off on vacation or somethin', nobody gonna call the cops," Ray tells her. "What about the rock?"

She pauses in the doorway of her Japanese-decorated place, framed by the silk hangings, an ancient kendo sword mounted over her head. She's got a long face and eyes like a husky's, and cushy lips. Of course, she's got the big hands and the Adam's apple. One more thing about her eyes, they look startled all the time, like she's surprised by everything, even when she plans it down to dotting the *i*. She talks in that cute, surprised way while she puts a 9mm round in the back of your head.

Now she lets her green-and-gold dragon-figured kimono hang open so we can see both her big silicon tits and her surprisingly large dick. The joint effect, so to speak, always gives me a woodie.

She's got this rich Japanese houseboy, president of a major airline corp by day, could hire five servants to do the housework—but when he gets out of that limo, his whole style changes on the flight up those carpeted stairs and he comes in with his eyes down and begs to be allowed to clean Dragon Missy's toilet; to lovingly arrange her shoes in her closet; to deliver her female hormone pills and cocaine on an antique ivory salver in the morning; to bring her the Xanax and Halcion at night. Waits on her hand and foot, and for his reward she beats his ass. One time I was visiting at the condo he gave her, and since he was going into the kitchen I asked him to take my glass for me and refill it and he said, big outrage, "What, you think I'm homosexual?"

Some phone calls and a cab and bang, we're over at this trick Charlie's house.

"My *goodness*," Dragon Miss says, hanging up her coat, "there's a *man* in the closet!" For a moment there's a flicker of hope in Charlie's eyes (and a flicker of feeling for him in me . . . just a flicker), but then Dragon Miss closes the closet door.

Feet up under her as she sits on the couch like it's hers, Dragon Miss counts the money Ray and Buddy give her, lays out the fine cocaine on the glass-topped coffee table, the flaky chopped-from-rocks stuff that they only dream about on the street. Like a lady putting out the tea things, she sets up the little propane torch, the ether, the baking soda solution, the glass pipe for real freebasing, none of that piss-doorway rockhead bullshit. She puts on a CD of Mozart's Requiem. Maybe for Charlie, though he's still alive. Buddy and Ray would rather hear Crystal Castles, but there's been a shift in polarity and Dragon Miss is in charge. Maybe I should mention that the houseboy carries a gun. That's two guns now.

I distract myself from the cocaine prep by looking over the window locks, strategically unlocking a few, shutting off the alarms, mentally totting up the fence value of some of the smaller antiques and the old English silver.

We check on Charlie and his leg looks all swollen and weird-colored. It's his right leg, maybe to do with the corkscrew wound, maybe it's the circulation being cut off, maybe both. He's feverish, squirming in his sweat and stink in the closet (Dragon Miss makes a come-out-of-the-closet joke); he's not quite all there, but he mutters some stuff I hear when I'm squatting by him, and some of it makes me sick and some of it makes me flash on ideas.

I'm belting some Johnnie Walker and thinking about Louisa. One day she'sd putting a cold cloth on my head when I'm crashing from the cocaine binge, and she's being really gentle about trying to tell me to go to rehab. Just so patient and gentle and I felt like, *She'll always be there*.

And a week later, she's dead, extinguished from the world. *Not* there.

I sip some more scotch and decide not to think about Louisa. Force it from my mind. Start tripping on how this Charlie's dying and how I don't feel much about it, and how the Japanese houseboy does feel something but it's just fear, and how we're standing around the closet making fun—the others are sucking on the pipe—and it's like that Max Ernst painting of the demons chewing at St. Anthony, and now I'm one of the demons, and I don't remember becoming one. I'm tripping on it, but all the time I'm thinking what I can score on all this.

So then Dragon Miss's friends show up and one of them has royally fucked up: Berenson, this big black guy, has brought a bunch of whores with him, two black, two white, one maybe Filipino, and some stoned-out white asshole he met in a sex club who's got a lot of dope money on him. Berenson, funny thing is, gets actual money from the State of California to run a prostitutes' rehabilitation center—and of course he just keeps the money because the guy's a pimp. He lays into those bitches with a belt, too. They seem to like it.

I never once hit Louisa.

So all these animals are dancing in the living room, breaking the furniture, putting Charlie's smaller stuff in their purses and going through his medicine cabinets and his liquor cabinets and his shoe rack, then checking out his suits, some pretty expensive suits to sell, and they keep coming back to suck on the glass pipes—there's four pipes going now—and sometimes they go to the closet and they kind of *fuck with* Charlie. He's every trick to them, I guess, and they're getting theirs now. Everybody debates about the best way to drain Charlie's bank account without pulling down too much attention. The air is in layers of smoke, it's got its own ionospheres and tropospheres, and now somebody's got the rap station on the home theater—so far Dragon Miss has kept them from taking the plasma TV out, which is just common sense—and the houseboy is looking really pale and nervous. One of the whores is working on

Berenson's dick, licking his balls, too, and Berenson's willie is half
erect and it's going up, up, slowly, like it's being slowly lifted on a
crane, and another whore is on her knees in front of a chair with
her head under her girlfriend's skirt, and Ray is kind of listlessly
fucking a long, skinny white girl with one pump on and the other
skinny silver-toenail foot bare and her underwear around an ankle,
they're doing it on the rug in front of Charlie's closet, Ray yelling at
Charlie to look! look at this, Charlie, but Charlie can't see outside
his sick haze.

The doorbell rings and some transsexual prostitutes who work for
Dragon Miss come in, so shrill you can hear them over the rap and
the laughter, like the high-pitched, whining noisemakers that cut
through the bangs and drums of a Chinese New Year's parade. They
ooze into the room like they're coming down the runway on the lip-
sync stage, invisible microphones in their hands, three of them in
pounds of makeup competing for attention. The glass pipes get most
of the attention. But these TV whores have got some ronnie with
them, brown crystal heroin, and I manage to get a line of that. It puts
my head in order so I'm thinking priorities again.

Buddy is in the corner in a real nice chair, looking kind of
shrunken in on himself, maybe crashing from cocaine and staring to
see consequences in his mind's eye, looking like he's going to panic.
I give him the bottle of Johnnie Walker.

Then Ray brings out the head iron. "Y'all ever try this shit?"

I trip on the head-iron thing. It's got the heft of a small electric
drill. It's like electronic brain drilling, I'm thinking. I'm tempted,
but it still scares me. The smell of the vaporized cocaine in the air
is tugging at me, and I know I'll never get to business if I get started
with cocaine or head irons. I'm feeling rounded out and pleasantly
heavy in the dick from the heroin and only a little nauseated. I
wonder if Charlie's dead.

Buddy is trying to talk Ray into getting rid of the head iron, but
it's too late, the meth-tranny whores are already squealing around it,

practically spinning on their spike heels to try it . . . the whole feel
of the scene is changing around this head iron . . . it's putting a weird
off-buzz in the air that's like one of those freak waves you hear about
that smashes boats . . . The Dragon Miss frowns at the head iron.

"I don't trust those things, I've heard stories, they are not sympatico
with working girls . . ." she says.

But Ray has already done a head-iron hit and is reeling in waves
of glory, and the paleness of his rage rises in him and he snarls
something at her I can't hear, something about fake fag-bitches, and
Houseboy pulls his gun and Ray pulls his gun and Dragon Miss sees
that and decides the polarity can shift for a while, and she pushes
Houseboy's gun down, tells him to put it away and signals one of the
girls. The girl's so fucked up she doesn't even seem to see Ray's gun
and she starts playing with his dick, so he lowers the gun but doesn't
put it away.

The head iron starts to get passed around to everybody. Dragon
Miss looks more startled than ever . . .

One of the queens is giggling on the phone. "You hear what Buddy
and Ray did?" So now the thing's leaking at the seams.

I expect Dragon Miss is going to fuck Buddy or one of the younger
guys here—I'm old enough to have damage from the New York
Dolls—but she takes me by the hand and we go into the biggest
bathroom, lock the door. The houseboy sees this and writhes with
jealousy, you can see it in his face. So much for fucking Oriental
inscrutability. He doesn't do anything about it—me fucking his
mistress right in the next room is more humiliation, which is what
he's paying her for, so it all works out.

Till now. Dragon Miss's been watching everybody else's sex in a
kind of preparation voyeurism. Now she's ready and probably figures
I'm the one most likely to get a hard-on that'll stay, because I've
been avoiding the C.

Bathroom's trashed because they've been in here going through it
looking for drugs and anything salable. But we clear the junk from

the floor and lay down some towels. She's been on the pipe for about an hour, plus did a line or two of the ronnie, so she's as wet as a pretend girl can get.

We do some things with the shower, both kinds. Then we get down to some serious business. I turn her facedown—she gets tired of being a dom with her houseboy . . .

She can't ejaculate, since she only gets about two-thirds hard, but there's another kind of orgasm and about the time my knees are getting sore she flaps around in it, like a baby seal getting its head knocked in.

So I let go, and come, too.

Coming, I feel something in me loosen up, and I think about Louisa the night before they found her.

We were on the roof of her place, September evening, having a tar beach picnic, and I'm trying to zing the pigeons with pieces of a broken Mad Dog bottle somebody left, and she's telling me I should call my brother. I feel like her face is prettier and more real in that second because of what she wants me to do; it makes me feel like she maybe really does give a shit, because she wants me to call Dougie and tell him it's okay, that I forgive him for ripping me off, that's what junkies do and I understand that . . .

I can't do that, but I feel, for a moment, like maybe some of us are going to be all right . . . *"You got to be part of somebody or you nobody,"* she says. *"You not even real if you can't feel."*

It rhymes; she's pleased with that. "Stop throwing shit at the pigeons," she says.

I kiss the back of her neck and cup her tits and she leans back against me . . .

But now Dragon Miss tells me to wash my dick and go out into the living room with her, it sounds like they're really going off out there, she's got to see how Houseboy's doing . . .

x   x   x

After we go back out, the whole scene has changed again. The off-buzz saturates the place. The walls are screaming, there's a kind of peak to the noise and tension, two or three arguments going at once, and they're wrestling over the head iron. Two of them, no, shit, three of them now, actually fighting, hitting, scratching for the head iron.

Looking around now, I start to get seriously scared, because I can see everyone's been doing the head iron, even the houseboy. And now there's three guns in view Berenson's got his out, he's yelling at Houseboy, and Houseboy's skull's showing through the skin of his face with all his straining to control himself, but I can see he's going to lose it. The white asshole Berenson brought is out cold in the corner with his head in a puddle of blood. His wallet's lying next to him like a gutted fish. Then I see a black whore in a skewed blond wig snag the head iron, because someone dropped it in the fight, and she's got the closet open and she's shoving the head iron against Charlie's head more or less at random, laughing, randomly stimming what's left of his brain, and he's foaming at the mouth and shitting himself and actually breaking some of the ropes with a really gone-off rage and she's laughing and slapping him with the iron, but she puts her hand too near his mouth and Charlie takes off three of her fingers, just as neat as a metal-shop tool, snipping them off with his teeth, and she screams and Berenson—nude, muscular but for that potbelly—Berenson, he sees what Charlie's done and he points the gun and really shakes with relief as he lets go: shoots Charlie four or five times, and the houseboy gets mad because Berenson's fucking with one of Dragon Miss's assets and he starts shooting Berenson—

Buddy and I make eye contact and we both slide fast into the bedroom. The two other people in the bedroom are out cold, no, wait, one of them is out cold and the other one is dead, looks like a heart attack—and I shout at Buddy over the noise from the next room, the shooting and screaming; and we tip over an antique armoire so it jams the door shut. Then we take care of our own business, but I hear the Dragon Miss stuck on the other side screaming for me to open the door, open it, or they're going to—we don't hear what they're going to do, because then bullet holes punch through the door behind the armoire and her blood comes through; along with her blood comes her scent, her perfume, right through the door . . .

It's the head iron, the glory and the insane rage and misery that come when you use it; with that thing it's like you get a lifetime of sin in one blast and then you go straight to Hell, do not pass *go*, all in one minute.

And the head iron's stirring that room up like blender blades, we can hear it, screaming and laughing and crying in there. Ray thumping on the door now, Buddy crying because he wants to help Ray; he tries to move the armoire, but I won't let him, because they'll all come in with Ray then, and anyway, I've already made the phone call to 911 because I was afraid the people in the other room would kill me. So since I've called 911 we got to get out fast.

I have to drag Buddy out the window to the fire escape and up to the roof, and as we go we get a diagonal glimpse through the window of the living room: there's Ray with Berenson and two whores, the three of them kicking Ray, who's probably already dead, but they're kicking him, kicking him, Berenson's dick wagging with every kick.

A little later we're driving a stolen car, just about a block away, when the sirens start wailing. I have to laugh. Buddy starts crying again.

What Charlie whispered when I almost felt something for him was what was in the false top of the armoire. It was a locked metal box. I guess Charlie was trying to make a deal . . .

The dead guy in the bedroom had a BMW key chain and there were only two Beamers on the street.

So next morning, really burned out, me and Buddy, we're at a rest stop halfway to Las Vegas, standing behind the maroon BMW, its trunk gaping, using a tire iron on the box. Takes us twenty minutes more to finally get the metal box open.

The box contains less than I hoped for but more than I expected. About thirty grand in cash total and about twelve in loose diamonds. What about safe-deposit boxes, Charlie? Probably had one. But he was one of those guys who liked to keep some close.

Me and Buddy are doing okay. Cabo San Lucas has a full-on scene.

I'm trying to feel those other things again. It helps to think about Louisa. *You got to be part of somebody or you nobody.* I was just so loaded that night. I can't remember. I can't remember. I try, for her, but I can't remember:

I don't know if I was the one who killed her or not.

SMARTBOMBER

Corporal Lionel Billingsgate climbed up the concrete stairs, ran his
ID palmer over the scanner, waited till the door opened and then
strolled into the attack station on the top floor of NSA Building
Seven, lower Manhattan. As was traditional here, he wore desert
cammies, to show solidarity with the men actually fighting overseas,
in Syria.

There was almost no one in the remote-attack center. The
surveillance team was at first mess, but he had second mess, at two, like
most of the smartbombers, and he had two hours of missile guidance
before then. He waved at a fellow Marine, Specialist Janice Wing—a
pretty half Asian, half black girl he was hoping to maybe date if they
got a furlough. She carried herself with real confidence, as she walked
over to the Commander's office; you could almost make out her taut
little figure under her cammies. She wanted to go to a Broadway
show—if the High Security Alert was reduced to orange, low enough
to let the shows go on. There hadn't been a serious suicide bombing in
Manhattan for three weeks, so maybe they'd go.

It felt good to climb into the dull-green, air-conditioned, bomb-
positioning cubie. Felt like climbing into an old, well-worn saddle,
like back home on his parents' ranch in Oregon. He wondered if
Janice liked horses.

There were eight positioning cubies in the windowless rectangular
room, four on either side of the aisle, each screened from the others
so there'd be no peripheral distractions.

He waved at Bill Mercer, the black lieutenant out of Atlanta. Bill
supervised runs on the southeastern-three sector of Aleppo. Drinking

a cup of instant coffee at his little workstation, Mercer gave him the hand signal that meant his station was ready, and Lionel settled in to control posture.

The computer was already booted up, the monitor was set to PREP. Lionel had to only put the headset on, and tap in a request for that day's coordinates. He recognized the coordinates, when they popped up in the windows: a suburb of the target city. And that sent a chill through him. He didn't like doing the suburbs. Too many civilians. But that was just one of the risks. This long-distance, remote method of attack saved lives in the long run.

Lionel keyed in the coordinates, picked out a skybot launcher. One-seventy-nine was green to go. He sent in his request, spoke to the launch dispatcher, got the go and launched: with near-instantaneous satellite-transmission, piggy-backed through autonomous vehicles hovering over the area, he had caused a real missile to launch somewhere in Iraq, headed for Syria. He got a firm grip on the joystick, and waited: he had the controls programmed so the nose cam on the autonomously controlled missile didn't come online until his projectile was within a minute of the target. He liked to get a tight focus, close to the target, so he could use his trained attention span to the fullest.

It didn't take long—the missile switched on where he'd programmed it to, and the monitor showed the ground racing by below. He was on his way to hit what the monitor identified as an artillery emplacement.

Lionel clicked easily into the "smartbomber" mind-state he'd trained so long and hard for . . . And though his body was in Manhattan, in his mind he was flying over the desert. The missile was already guided by a laser fired from a surveillance drone over the target, but his fingers on the joystick made minute adjustments, transmitted from the station to the real missile—a Warspear III—which responded in .00009 seconds, near instantaneously, tightening to a flatter trajectory, honing in more precisely on the cross-hair mark. He could take it off target if he needed to.

The crosshairs were superimposed on the ever-transforming horizon, which presently became the desert outskirts of town— the blasted wreckage of an oil refinery whipped by; a bomb-pocked highway unreeled below the missile's nose cam. It was focused on the angle of approach to the target, but not yet the target itself . . .

But the target was coming up now, according to the computer voice in his headset. "Estimated fifteen seconds to impact . . . nine seconds . . ."

Lionel felt the familiar rush of power, of connection, as the missile he guided with his own hand flew to its target. His monitor showed housetops, low buildings, a bomb-wrecked mosque flashing by—and to Lionel it was as if he *was* the missile, as if he were flying over the desert. He always found himself straining forward in his seat, as if to ease the wind resistance, like a diving eagle with its wings folded back. Time seemed to slow. Three seconds seemed like fifteen, twenty seconds. A school flashed by below, an artillery emplacement, a store—

He had just time to flickeringly wonder about the artillery emplacement—would there be one behind the other? Wouldn't that have been his target? But the drone was targeting a building, and there it was. Not obviously a military target. Must be a shell, camouflage of some kind. He adjusted the angle of the missile, tightening on the windows to get the maximum penetration into the target and then the window was rushing at him, and he was crashing through and he had just a glimpse of terrified faces, some of them rather small faces, and then the screen went to the expected white pixilated shashing . . . .

He slumped, shaking with the release of it, knowing the missile had detonated on exactly the target the drone had designated. He would get another commendation for another perfect hit.

But then the monitor image came back on.

That was impossible, wasn't it? The camera and its transmitter unit were both inevitably destroyed on impact.

And the image—he rocked back in his seat, staring . . . .

The televised-image unit seemed to have somehow separated whole from the missile, and fallen to a corner of the shattered room, where it was lodged in the rubble, still transmitting. The angle was skewed, from down low, but the image was clear enough.

There was a dark-eyed woman on fire, screaming, clawing at the air, and a man with a beard, who must be her husband, gouting blood from the stump of his arm as he knelt weeping near the body of a little girl, the child blown in half, convulsing as she died, her mouth bubbling blood—and there was someone else running around the smoking socket of the room in the background, an older woman. The woman was on fire, running back and forth. She fell so he could see only her feet jerking in a lower corner of the screen—and there was the remains of a young man splashed against the wall, and the screaming, the distinct, clearly amplified screaming—

"Corporal! Corporal Billingsgate! Yo!"

Mercer was shouting in his ear, yanking the headset off, pulling the chair away from the station. The lieutenant reached over and switched the computer monitor off.

"Billingsgate *stop screaming!* Snap out of it, goddammit!"

Lionel looked at him. "I'm . . ." The screams! ". . . not screaming sir! They . . ." The screaming, the screaming! "They're screaming, not me, they won't stop screaming . . ."

"Look, once in a while there's a freak chance, the transmitter makes it through the blast, keeps transmitting for a minute . . . but there's no sound dammit, it's all in your mind!"

"No sir, they're . . ." Screaming, still screaming, ". . . they're . . ." Screaming!

"Billingsgate!" Mercer slapped him. "Stop it! Stop screaming!"

But that wouldn't make the screaming stop, since it wasn't him screaming.

RAISE YOUR HAND IF YOU'RE DEAD

Sometimes I think I'm dead. Sometimes I think I'm not dead. So far, I can't figure it out, not definitely.

I should tell you who's sending this message to you. It's me, Mercedes' older brother, Whim. At least I think it's me. And I'm sending this to you, Syke, so maybe you can figure out if I'm dead, and you can do something about it. If you can fix that—you're my hodey. If you can't, you can't, and you're still my hodey.

Maybe I can figure it all out. This message, if that's what it is, will take a while to get to you, if it gets to you at all. I'm still working out what the rules are in here. If I think it all through, maybe I'll work out if I'm dead or not.

Mercedes was the one I was with you know, harvesting suicides, the night we looked the Empties in the eyes . . .

I was nervous, on my knees in the padded prow of the twelve-foot aluminum boat, as Mercedes piloted us up under the big supports for the Golden Gate Bridge. Dangerous out there anytime, sure, even when the seas aren't running rough, because you can get a black wind, that toxin laden fog, just sweeps down on you quick, no time to get to shore—or you can ship too much water and you might dump over, find yourself thrashing in that cold, dirty water, with the bay leeches fastening on your ankles and the waves smacking you on jagged rocks around the support towers.

But it was sheer superstition, really, making me nervous. I get superstitious about numbers. It has to do with my dad having been a gambler, between his subbing gigs; Dad rattling on about odds and numbers and how number patterns crop up in the cards. "You can feel that bad beat coming in the numbers," he'd say. "If you pay attention. If you don't feel the odds, the beat'll smack you upside the head."

He was an old school guy, born in Atlanta in 1970; he said things like "smack you upside the head." And "old school."

The thing is, Syke, as we ran the boat out there, the engine chugging in the moonlight, it just hit me that today was 3-5-35. March fifth, 2035. Now, three and five is eight plus three is eleven, plus five is sixteen. You write sixteen, 1 and 6; add them, it makes seven. My unlucky number. Nine's my lucky number, seven's unlucky. Maybe because my old man died when I was fourteen, twice seven, on the fourteenth of June.

On the night of 3-5-35 I looked up at the bridge, and thought: *Each cable is made of 27,572 strands of wire. 80,000 miles of wire in the main cables. The bridge has more than 1,200,000 rivets . . . Now if you add two and seven to five and seven and two . . .*

"We shouldn't be out here," I said to Mercedes. My sis was back by the little engine, working the tiller. I was out front with the grabbers and the sniffer. She wore her long brown leather jacket, gloves, boots; I had my oversized army jacket, without the insignia, army boots, waterproof pants. You've never seen me in physical person, Syke. In the social space I wear some nicer shit—seeing as how CG clothing is gratis with the access fee. I muttered once more, "Really shouldn't be out here."

"What?" she called. "Why? You cold? Told you to put on a slicker."

"It's not that," I said, though I was shivering, scanning the gray water with the sniffer. "It's the numbers . . ." I had the sniffer—that's for picking up human DNA fragments in the air—in my left hand. The mechanical grabber in my right.

I figure I gotta explain this stuff to you, Syke, since it's way, way far from your thing. You were always so indoors—you were the indoors of the indoors. Wandering around like an out of body experience in

the social space and the subworlds with the likes of Pizzly and creeps
like Mr. Dead Eyes hounding about in the background. Remember
Mr. Dead Eyes, hodey, he'll come up again. You recall that perv, Mr.
DE, dogging Mercedes in the subworlds?

"There's my future girl," he'd say to my sister. *"All good things come
to those who wait."*

That night under the bridge I was thinking about Mr. Dead Eyes,
and not knowing why and that spooked me too. I was just about to
explain to little sis about the numbers, the date, and how we should
go back, but then the sniffer tripped and I saw the first floater. He
was floating face up in a patch of light from the lamp on the bridge
support. His eyes were colorless—looked just like cocktail onions.
So that told me he'd been dead a while, but not long as all that.
Longer, and the gulls, or some adventurous crab would have gotten
his eyes out.

He wasn't very waterlogged or bloated either. Which was good. It
sucks when you got to handle them, even with a grabber and rubber
gloves, when they're, you know, coming apart from being out there
a while.

"Got one," I called out to her. "At two o'clock. Not too soggy. But
come up slow . . ."

She cut the engine and we coasted toward the floater. He might've
been about fifty when he took the plunge, with long brown hair
like seaweed washing around his pudgy, onion-eyed face. We hadn't
found him soon enough to harvest his organs. A messy, nauseating
job, anyhow, harvesting organs. I was always sort of relieved when I
knew I wouldn't have to do it.

The guy in the suit might have some good pocket fruit. He had a
decent suit on, and the one remaining shoe was pretty good quality
leather. So maybe he had money, jewelry. The uneven light picked
out a gold glint from a wristwatch; I hoped it was waterproof. (I
remember when we found an elderly black guy one time had one of
those old fashioned grills on his teeth, installed in the first decade of

the century—diamonds and gold all over it. Nasty, prying that grill off him. Paid good though.)

I used the grabber on onion-eyes, then got the watch off with a quick movement of my rubber-gloved hand. Always afraid the body's going to grab my wrist as I do it. I saw too many zombie movies as a kid. But they never do move. It's almost disappointing.

I tucked the gold watch in the scavenge duffel, then grabbed his tie and pulled his body up against the boat. He had a nice oxblood tie, seemed like silk.

I'm always really careful when I pull the bodies close to the boat. It sucks ugly to fall in with them, hodey. You tend to grab the body to keep from sinking. They can fall apart when you grab them. It's better not to fall in.

I glanced back at Mercedes. Her curly black hair seemed like it was shining with an orange halo, in the light from the tower support behind her. Her big black eyes, her pale skin, her round face, those sound-wave face tattoos on her cheeks—you know how her face can come together and she seems so iconic. You'd know that better than anyone, Syke. She came to your little world in her real semblance. At twenty-one she's a year younger, but she seems like she's from a whole different race than me, not just a different family. Me being so dark-skinned and lean.

"You want to take him to shore?" I asked. "Looks too spongy for organ harvesting."

"Then just do the pockets, Whim," she said, like, *It's so obvious*.

I went through his pockets, came up with a wild-dog wallet which turned out to have a usable unicredit tab in it—and his ID, which we pitched, not being into identity theft.

I checked this floater for a gold necklace; nope, so I clipped off his wedding ring finger. He was too sponged up to just pull the ring off. Had to use the clipper to cut right through his finger. Just a crunch, a little ooze of blackened blood, releasing the rankness of dead man. He was good and cold.

He had a suicide note in a plastic sack in his pocket, as they often do. I took that too, in case it gave out any information I could sell to the family.

I glanced at it in with my pen light. Didn't see anything useful. Looked like the usual maudlin stuff. I caught the lines, *"My wife got the treatment, now it's like she's dead to me, she's all empty, and I went to see my dad, he was empty too, and they're going to do it to me."*

I gave up on all this ranting and tossed the note away. Guy'd been losing his mind at the end, I figured.

I let him slide back into the water, and we went on toward the Marin side of the bridge, in case there was another floater. You might be surprised to hear we've found as many as four in one night, Syke. But now that the suicide nets are down again—and no, I wasn't the one who vandalized them this time, or any of the other times—we get three or four jumpers a week, sometimes several a day. It's been good and steady like that, since the desperation came into its own. The climate change thing peaking, all that shoreland sucked up, all those people misplaced, all that desertification, tropical pests and diseases swarming north, crops either drowned or charred or eaten away. Population of the world doubling. More and more jobs outsourced, automated. Two hundred million people who used to have food in North America, used to just assume food would be there—barely eating now, many of them starving. Countless people with no chance, no future; everyone failing at everything. Mass despair. "Collective emotional downwaves" is the latest psychology buzz; sociobiological impulses to self-destruction in an overpopulated world. The desperation . . . You're so insular, in your little world, Syke. You never talked about this stuff. Maybe you took it for granted. Or maybe you were hardly aware of it—hell you were ten years living mostly in the virtual model, tripping your mind to the subworlds, sending your body on remote to exercise, all that stuff. The curse of being born with all those silver spoon annuities. And a touch of agoraphobia, I'd guess.

So, after harvesting onion-eyes, me and Mercedes weren't surprised to see another body come flying down off the bridge, within minutes. People travel from around the country, around the world to jump off the Big Orange Arc now, and the bridge crew makes a lot of extra money taking bribes from suicide jumpers. Truth is, though, about a fourth of the 'suicides' are murders. That's what I hear. Lot of women from the sex slave brothels get pitched off for trying to escape. A lesson to the others.

It was Mercedes who first spotted the woman coming down. We both heard the yell, getting higher pitched as the woman came down turning end over end, close to the northern tower.

I thought I caught a flash of diamonds and I thought, *That's a good harvest, right there*. And then she hit the water. *Whack*. We waited for her dead body to bob up, Mercedes piloting the boat a bit closer to the impact point, shipping some water in the rising waves from a barge passing five hundred yards away.

I shivered with the cold as we waited. Daydreamed about hot toddies in front of the holo, in a snug corner of Siggy's Allnighter.

Then the woman came thrashing up and I heard Mercedes cussing. I was only thinking it: *Shit—she's alive*.

Now and then it happens. Sure it's a long ways down from the deck of the Golden Gate Bridge, and people almost invariably die right off, because when they hit that water at that speed, with that much momentum, it's almost like hitting solid ground.

But a few live. They're always busted up; most tend to die in a few minutes. Once in a while a jumper gets pulled out of the water alive, tells his weepy story about how he knew he wanted to live the moment he let go, and how people should hang in there—though of course, with the Coast Guard no longer doing rescue, anywhere, survivors don't get pulled out much.

I remember the only other survivor we found. That guy, he was a short chunky Asian guy—maybe his fat saved him from being busted up too much. He begged us to help him. But he had a lot of jewelry

on him and I could tell he wasn't going to make it to the shore alive
no matter what we did. Mercedes said, "You want to help him on his
way, or me?" I didn't want her to have to do it. I held his head under
the water for a while—he hardly thrashed at all.

I imagine you being all judgmental about that, Syke. Easy for you
to raise your eyebrows. You inherited your mom's software income,
never had to live off the streets. Anyway, I'd have pulled him out if I
thought he'd live. I guess.

This woman, now, bobbing up, all sputtering, she was muscular,
wearing some kind of tights. I could see she had a broken right
arm, blood bubbling from her mouth. But something about her—
maybe those high cheekbones, those cutting blue eyes, the really
short-cut brown hair—made me think she was tough. She just
might live.

I couldn't bring myself to drown her. I thought we ought to shove on
out of there and let the broken woman do her dying, and then come
back for the harvest. Just leave before she started asking for help.

She didn't ask for help, though—she ordered some up. She had us
sized up pretty good.

"I'll pay you," she rasped. "You get me to shore."

I was figuring she was maybe not a suicide. Didn't seem the type.
More likely someone thought they'd done her in.

"How much?" Mercedes asked her. "And how do we get it?"

"Ten thousand WD," the woman said, sputtering. "Transfer soon as
we get to a hospital." She coughed up more blood, paddling a little
with her good arm. "But you better hurry . . ."

Mercedes was against it. "We don't have any way to make her pay,
Whim, once we get her there."

But I was kind of fascinated by this woman. And maybe drowning
that fat Asian guy bothered me more than I like to admit.

So I said, "Let's take a chance."

x   x   x

We got her into the boat—that had to hurt like hell, with her broken arm and legs. I was impressed at how she didn't scream. She sucked air through her clenched teeth when the pain got bad, and squeezed her eyes tight shut, but she didn't scream.

We hauled her to shore—had to go all the way back to the south shore, where our truck was, and from there we could drive to the nearest ER. When we pulled her out of the boat she went all shivery with the pain, and she gasped—and then she went limp. I had to check to see she wasn't dead. Just out cold.

"I really, *really* don't know if we should risk this, Whim," Mercedes said as I tugged the woman, my arms under hers, into the back of the battered old Toyota hybrid pickup. "This woman—she didn't jump. Someone *tossed* her off that bridge. So maybe they're gonna wanna make sure . . . And we'll be in the way."

"She's giving us ten thousand WD," I pointed out.

"And I really, really think she could be fulla shit about that," Mercedes said. "I told you before, I'm telling you now." She sighed. "But I guess we're this far . . ." She banged the tailgate up on the truck.

"We could leave her right here. But we'll always wonder—it might be enough to start over in Canada . . ."

That was our dad's dream. He was a writer, sometimes, when he wasn't teaching or throwing money away on cards. Made most of a half-assed living substitute teaching. He raised us after our mom died in the first wave of the pigeon flu. He wanted to get us to Canada, where the weather is more predictable and there's fewer tropical diseases and there's some kind of health care, but then one of the kid gangs caught him outside, and busted him up pretty bad. He died a few months later.

Mercedes just nodded, when I brought up the Canadian thing. I remember getting a rush of hope, thinking maybe I'd added up the numbers wrong and this time they were coming out to nines, somehow, and we were going to win.

But first we had to get the jumper to the hospital. Mercedes drove, I rode shotgun. "You got that gun with you?" she asked suddenly, working the stick shift with quick, angry motions of her hand.

"Just the little plastic one."

Something came on TVnet in the truck cab about Senator Boxell's plan to harvest the kid gangs. Maybe it was the word *harvest* that caught my attention, that being some of my own jargon. "There's just no point in not facing the reality of today's world," he said, on the little screen. "If it weren't for the planetary climate change emergency, why, we could manage all this population. As it is, with millions of orphans—we estimate more than half a million of them on the street in every major American city—it's just cruel and nonsensical to leave these kids to starve to death. The right thing to do is euthanasia and organ harvesting. It's a matter of triage . . ."

Mercedes gave a bitter little laugh, hearing that. When Dad died, she ran off on her own. I spent two weeks looking for her; finally found her living on the streets—in one of those orphan kid gangs.

After Senator Boxell was a news spot then about the war in Pakistan, another thousand men caught in a nerve-gas cloud, along with about four thousand civilians—that old prick General Marsh saying he had it all under control . . .

Then a commercial. A sexy woman's mouth appeared on the little dashboard screen, saying, "The SINGULARITY is here. Sign up for Singular! Search it. Do it. Free it."

"Someone's always claiming the Singularity is here or about to be, or something," Mercedes snorted, looking at a side street, as we passed. The street, down the hill a little, was flooded by the rising tide. "I wish they'd just let us hook into it and go somewhere else . . . Any fucking place else . . ."

I didn't say, "*Could be worse, Mercedes. Least we have a place to live. We pull in some WD.*"

I used to say that to her. But lately it gets her mad and there are still bruises on my shoulder from where she punched me last time.

I glanced in back again. The woman's eyes were tight shut but the hand on her good arm was making funny little clutching motions. Still alive.

We got to the hospital in about five minutes. We nosed the truck slowly through the indigent crowds outside, the homeless, people trying to get into the hospital. Lots of people sick with the mutated malaria.

We had no air conditioning, and away from the bay, when I rolled down the window, the air was thick, and muggy, smelled like unwashed people. Mosquitoes whined at us. Hostile faces turned toward us. Someone threw a bottle that clacked into the side of the truck. I rolled up the window again.

We drove slowly up to the wall next to the emergency line to the public ER entrance. But we ignored the line—Mercedes had the woman's Gold Medicard. If it was up to date, it'd get our jumper into any medical facility. Only the rich, the connected, and certain government types had them.

We pulled up by the high steel gate to the inner hospital lot, and the ExAd kiosk. I could see four paramil guards in full armor standing inside the gate, under the overhang, faces shut away in opaque, reflective helmets, idly toying with their recoil-reversal batons.

It started to rain, one of those glutinous, warm downpours we get now. She started the wipers and they left streaks of dark grease from the rain on the windshield. Rain clouds even more polluted than usual, probably just got here from overseas. Thanks for sharing, China.

Mercedes got out, hurried over to the reader in the Express Admissions kiosk, slipped the little card through and a screen flickered in response. From the truck, I could see she was talking to someone on the screen, pointing at the truck for the kiosk camera. I glanced back at the broken woman lying on the old, folded rug on the truck bed, next to my harvest bag, saw her grimacing, hands fisting, eyes shut. And then, out behind the truck, a sudden surge of motion—a kid gang, pushing through the crowd, coming our way.

This gang of little kids had those bullet-shaped slam-helmets they steal from the Japan Center. Some kind of trendy gear from Tokyo. They came ramming through the waiting crowd, heads down, using the helmets to penetrate the throng like bullets nosing through flesh.

"Those kids," Mercedes said, coming back to the truck, blinking in the rain. "I know 'em. We need to get the fuck out of their way . . ."

Then the gate slid back, for us, as Mercedes climbed in, the guards stepping forward, one of them waving us through while the others brandished their RR sticks to keep the crowds back. Several of the kids charged the paramils, pretty kamikaze thing to do—the kids were half the guards' size. The RR sticks went crack, sparked with energy, the kids were flung back, spinning through the air.

Mercedes went too fast through the open gate, almost nailing one of the guards. He had to jump out of the way, shouting angrily, his amplified voice barking something that might've been, "Tweakin' sperm-puddle!"

She stopped the truck and we got out. Two burly orderlies were rolling a gurney through the sliding doors toward our truck. I was worried about leaving the harvest bag out there, where the guards might go through it, but no choice, we had to get that transfer out of the woman, and she had to be awake to do it . . .

So fuck it, we followed the gurney into the hospital. I was afraid that they'd pat me down, being as the metal detectors aren't much good anywhere, with the hardened plastic guns around, but they didn't . . .

Anytime things are urgent—you end up waiting. It's like life wants to make sure you get a chance to savor every last possible split-second of frustration; like it wants to make sure you torture yourself with hopeless impatience.

But finally they let us come in from that piss hole of a waiting room, to see the broken woman cleaned up and tubed, in her little

clean white booth, one of the few private rooms in the hospital. A
bank of monitors hooked up to her.

It was just us and a white-painted metal-and-plastic healthbot
trundling around her, scanning, humming inside itself, whirring
irritably when we got in the way.

Mercedes was on one side of the hospital bed, I was on the other.
The woman was stripped to a green hospital gown. Both long legs
and one arm in instacasts. Small breasts, wide apart, tenting the
gown, her head going side to side in a druggy semidelirium.

"Hey bridge lady," Mercedes said.

The broken woman opened her eyes to slit. "You got here," she
croaked at us. "Same ones, from the bridge?"

"We're here," I said.

"Told 'em you had to . . . had to come in." She gave a bloodstained,
sad little smile. "Said you were my only relatives."

"Heartwarming," Mercedes said. "How we do the transfer?"

"You got to do . . ." She cleared her throat. Took a breath. Managed,
". . . something else for me. First."

"That wasn't the deal!" Mercedes hissed, her dark eyes snapping.

"You got . . ." The woman swallowed hard. "You got a transpod?"

Mercedes snorted. "What you think?" She reached into her coat
pocket, pulled it out, held it up: one of the flat models, slim as a
playing card. We harvested it a month ago off what was left of a
depressed accountant.

"Okay," the broken woman said, her voice barely audible. She
paused and sighed as the healthbot extruded a needle from its
utility column and squirted some meds into her IV. It trundled
away, and the woman went on, "I'll give you half the money
now. But . . ." She took a breath. "But to get the rest, you got to
bodyguard me for an hour till my people get here. The soulless
are pressing 'em hard. You got to stick with me maybe hour and
a half . . ."

I remember thinking: *Did she say "soulless"?*

"Bodyguard?" I said. "Lady there's guards all around this place. Plus the hospital has two city cops in it."

"They might be Empties . . . soulless . . . or . . . the soulless'll push buttons on 'em . . . most of the Empties, they're rich bigshots . . . I wasn't trying to jump off that bridge—it was that, or . . ."

Mercedes sniffed and shook her head so that her curls bounced. "You're in some kinda cult? Talking about soulless people and shit?"

The broken woman licked her lips. "I'm . . . was with Justice Department. Field officer. Internal Affairs. Some of us found out about the Empties . . . the Singularity thing. The soulless . . ." She was pretty stoned on the meds. Not making much sense. "Independent investigation . . ." She took a ragged breath. "They say we rogued out but . . . they're offering new bodies to everyone . . ."

"Which version of the Singularity you talking about?" I asked. Not knowing what else to say. Thinking we ought to just get the five grand and get out with that. But not wanting to leave her here either.

She lifted her good arm up, shakily wiped her mouth with the back of her hand. "Upload minds to new bodies . . . bodies fixed up to last longer . . . nanobot refreshers. Some of the bodies are vat grown. Some are, like, stolen."

Mercedes was shaking her head again. But I was feeling kind of funny, looking at this woman. This woman was *badass*. This woman had lived through something that kills most people and she was all crunched up but she was still negotiating, working her situation. This woman had some kind of gravitas. Made me take her seriously. Gave me another feeling too . . . I looked at her name on the hospital's patient info sheet. Said she was Dresden Dennings. What a badass name, too. *Dresden*. Maybe I could find out her birthday, add up the numbers, see if they felt friendly to me. I looked at her, past all the bruises, thinking I could fall in love with this woman. Even if she was five or six years older than me.

Living with your sister gets old. Don't get me wrong Syke. I love Mercedes even more than you do. Different, is all.

"It's not a fucking cult," Dresden said. "It's just . . . what happens. They found a way to upload minds. The mind gets transferred but . . . . turns out . . . *souls are real*. Mind goes, the soul . . ." She licked her lips. "Soul doesn't go with it. People end up soulless. Empties. What goes in the upload—it's not . . . holographic."

"What the fuck?" Mercedes muttered.

"Holographic consciousness," Dresden said, a sort of awe in her voice. "What gets uploaded, it's missing a dimension. And empathy, love, all that—it's in that dimension, see . . . and they . . . the Empties don't have it." She laughed raspily. "They don't even have a sense of humor anymore. The Singularity is mass producing sociopaths. Thousands, tens of thousands of sociopaths. They don't trust feeling people. We can't be predicted, see. Senator Boxell . . ." Her eyelids drooped. Her voice drooped too. "The Joint Chiefs. The President. The mayor. The police chief. They've all had it. Supposed to be a body that doesn't age . . . holes with eyes . . . Empties . . ."

The meds were really kicking in now and her words slurred together, her eyes rolled back, mostly whites.

"She can't transfer the money all dozey like this, Mercedes," I said. "We got to wait for her."

Mercedes bitched and cussed but it was no good, Dresden was too stoned. There were two chairs, and we pulled them up, and waited . . . thinking over what she'd said.

We were supposed to be bodyguards protecting her from the soulless. From . . . *the Empties*.

Lunacy. But someone had chased her off that bridge.

We did have that working gun—the hardened-plastic disposable pistol, use and lose, good for five shots, compacted-polymer slugs. Metal detectors don't pick it up. Use it and throw it away. Kill a man with it, if it doesn't break—some of them are made crappy. I had the gun in my baggy army coat pocket.

But bodyguarding? Not our specialty. Let's face it, we were water buzzards, not raptors.

"This is suck-ugly bullshit," Mercedes said. "Maybe I've got a stimpill I can put in her mouth, stim her up and get her to transfer the money."

"That might kill her," I said.

She looked at me defiantly. "So?"

"Um—I just . . ." I shrugged.

Mercedes shook her head in disgust. "You're getting all humpy for this woman."

"No, I . . ."

She shook her head again and got out her viddy, and that's when she called you up. You remember that, anyhow.

I remember when we met, me and you, Syke, if you want to call that meeting. Mercedes talked me into visiting the VR social space with her, though she knows I don't like them. She insisted I had to meet "Psych". I didn't know how you spelled it then. "He likes to psych people out but he's a good guy," she said. She seemed so *up* about it, and I hardly ever saw her up, so I gave in and there we were, in that neutral space, feeling like we're physically walking through a shiny digital hallway, passing people who were jabbering about this and that, people with their little 3D persicons floating over their heads.

Somehow Mercedes found you in that cloud room that's like your second home. I don't know how you can find your way around in there. Going from one weird little cluster of furniture to another in all that colored fog. But there you were, you popped up out of nowhere, arms spread to hug Mercedes, beaming with that big wide mouth and eyes. I wonder if you really look like that? Looked like a real face to me. I remember you had that persicon of some skinny twentieth century actor dancing in a top hat, around and around.

Mercedes said, "Hey Syke, this is my older brother Whim. Anyway he's a year older . . ."

And you said, "I heard you were gonna be a writer, like your dad, and then you decided to rob dead people instead."

You were smiling in that weirdly sympathetic way, and I just laughed. I don't know how you get away with saying shit like that without getting people mad. But I guess that's your talent.

"Mercedes talks too much," I said. Thinking that was strange because she normally doesn't talk too much. But she really trusted you, Syke.

"The thing is," you said, "being a writer is almost always about robbing dead people. 'Specially nowadays. Take other people's old ideas and use 'em like kiddy blocks and make castles. You want to go in a 'world?"

Then we went to that underwater subworld you like. All those caverns where we could fight monsters and laugh when their heads exploded with pretty silver confetti.

I'm thinking about all this, Syke, because it was that day that we met Mr. Dead Eyes. At first we thought he was one of the VR bots, a program simulating a ghost or something, but he was an avatar of somebody real somewhere, and he kept trying to find out where Mercedes lived in the physical world. He found her again and again down there—in that world.

When you looked at the guy—I swear there was this feeling like you could fall into him; like you lean over a deep well to look in and lose your balance and fall in. Big tall guy, his eyes always unfocussed, that red mouth, too red for a man's lips, and that big hunk of chin, and that archaic little faux hawk haircut . . . And when he talked he seemed so empty . . .

"You make me want to get all the way to the center of you, and out the other side," Mr. Dead Eyes said—that's what he said to Mercedes, and more than once. "It's so sad to have to run from the one you belong to," he said to her, another time. "Let me open you to big fat sensations, Mercedes."

Remember that one made you mad, Syke? You told him to fuck off and he just laughed and the laughter didn't show in his eyes.

And I think he was one of the first ones. Because I heard him talking up the Singularity, and his new body, and how he was going to live ten thousand years.

You remember, Syke?

Okay: The hospital. Mercedes squinting into that little screen she was holding, trying to see your VR semblance in that colored fog, asking you how to do a really secure transfer of funds, saying there was some worrying stuff about the transfer we were about to do, and you were your usual smarmily assured technonerd self, rattling off access protocols at her, which she recorded in a sidebar..

And then I saw that a man was standing in the door to Dresden's hospital cubby. And it was Mr. Dead Eyes, Syke. In physical person. Looking just like his semblance. Wearing a black and gray Federal Police uniform, headset, a mike clipped to his shoulder. Those same unfocused eyes, that red, red mouth, that big chin. Big hands. And one of those hands was on a gun butt, at his right hip.

"Why there you are," he said. "When I saw the scan from outside the hospital, I said, 'Is that Mercedes, Syke's little friend from the subworlds?' And by jiminy it's her in physical person. I always said we'd meet in the meat . . ."

Mercedes was gaping at him, blinking hard, like she thought something had gone wrong with her eyes. Just looking at the guy she'd had to ditch a dozen times when she was in the social space. The guy who'd stalked her through it. And here he was in person. His cop's name tag said SGT. IMBER.

Mercedes broke the connection with you, and then she stood up, glaring ice cold at Imber. "You found me." I never heard three words spoken with more loathing.

He grinned. "Not exactly coincidence. Your name popped up connected to our rogue here, I asked for this one . . ."

"Don't let him near me." Took me a second to work out who said that. It wasn't Mercedes—it was Dresden, her eyes cracked open. "Wants to kill me," she said. "Soulless. He's . . . empty."

"Empty of what?" Imber said, stepping into the little room, his hand tightening on the butt of his pistol. "No big ass deal. It's more like an appendectomy."

I felt a long, deep chill, that seemed to go on and on, when he said that. I was thinking, *It's true*.

Imber shook his head sadly at the broken woman. "You didn't have to go through this, Dresden. You didn't have to run onto the bridge. You didn't have to fight our people. Didn't have to jump just to get away from those boys—that was some crazy shit. You're lucky to be alive."

Dresden licked her dry lips. "Wasn't going to let them . . . take my body . . . push me out . . ."

I looked at Imber and he looked back at me. It was so clear to me, now, looking at him. The absence was nothing you could *see*—but it was nothing you could miss.

The Empties. Maybe I'd known for a while. I'd seen them on the streets. In the patrol cars. On TV. More and more of them with nothing behind their eyes; with those reasonable, flat tones, talking of triage and necessity and putting the good of society over the good of the parasites. Thinning the herd.

I guess I'd known they were soulless . . . I just didn't know why there were so many Empties now. The Singularity . . .

I stepped between Dresden and Imber. And it was almost like that plastic gun jumped into my hand. It was a kind of spasmodic act of revulsion, drawing that gun, Syke—and I pointed it at Mr. Dead Eyes and squeezed the trigger. Fired almost point blank.

Imber was drawing his own gun when I shot him. He went over backwards, firing as he fell back. His bullet went between my left arm and my ribs, I could feel it cutting the air there, sizzling that close to me. I heard a despairing grunt and I turned to see that Imber's bullet had missed me but hit Dresden—it was a charged bullet, I could tell because the wound in her side was shooting sparks and her back was arching . . . and Mercedes was shouting something at me and I was turning to snap another furious shot at Imber. I missed.

He was flat on his back now, just outside the door, writhing around the first bullet I'd fired, the slug tearing up his brisket, and he was firing sloppily up at me. Bullets chewed the doorframe of the cubby to my left, made it smoke with the charges.

I aimed carefully this time and fired and that big chin of his shattered; must've been busted bits of it going up into his brain, because he shrieked once and then went silent and slack. Not the first guy I shot—but that's the first time I felt good doing it.

Down the hall, people were yelling for security. I turned to check on Dresden, but she was dead, her eyes glassy. "Shit," I said. "Dammit."

Then Mercedes was pushing me out the door. I had only a couple more shots in the disposable gun, and I used them as we ran out, heading for the back exits, firing over the heads of hospital security to keep them back.

Then we were banging through the door onto the wet asphalt of a back lot, past a row of dumpsters, gasping in the muggy air. We sprinted through the rain toward the hurricane fence topped with razor wire. Have to get over that fence somehow . . .

Mercedes ran ahead of me up to the fence, taking off her coat as she went. She tossed it up high, slung it over the razor wire on the fence, and I got to the fence, locked my hands together; she stepped into them and I boosted her up. She grabbed the coat, climbed up, was dropping over the other side, yelling at me to get over the fence—but I was hearing sirens, turned to see the patrol vans screaming around the corner of the hospital, the burly men and women jumping out, rushing toward me. I got maybe halfway up the fence when they grabbed me, dragged me down off it. I yelled at Mercedes to run but I didn't have to, I saw her back disappearing as she darted through a rubbishy lot, into the alley between two high rises . . .

They knocked me down but there was talk about being careful not to hurt me, he's a perfect specimen, he's young and in good shape, he's what they want . . .

I saw a man flip his mirror helmet back so he could look me over better. I saw his eyes. Empty.

They sprayed some sleep-you-creep into my mouth and I was gone.

I woke up in restraints, Syke. And naked. Lying on my back. There's nothing more horrible than waking up in restraints—naked. Trapped and vulnerable. It happened to me once before, when I was a teenager, flipped out on Icy Dust. Woke up in a jail infirmary strapped down. Scary feeling. But not so bad, that time, I knew they were going to let me go, eventually . . .

It was worse this time. Because I knew they'd never let me go.

I could hardly move. There was a clamp holding my head in place. My upper arms and elbows and wrists were clamped down too. My knees and ankles were locked down.

I couldn't see much. Too many lights shining at my face. I made out several pairs of eyes, the rest of the faces hidden by surgical masks. Those empty eyes. I caught the gleam of instruments. Heard healthbots muttering reports.

"Anybody want to tell me what the fuck?" I said.

"Don't see why we should," said a woman in a surgical mask. Her voice pleasant. A nurse—or some kind of biotechnician.

A man in uniform came into the ring of light. I got a look at his face. An old, lizard-like face I knew from the news. *General Marsh.*

"This him?" What a rumbly, gristly old voice General Marsh had.

"If you want one right away, this's the best one we have," the technician said. "There aren't any better in the vats. He's in excellent shape. He's the age and size you wanted. Not a bad looking kid."

"Kinda skinny. I guess he'll do. I'm sick. I need uploading quick . . ."

"We just put the nanos in him . . . If you'll go with the nurse to upload, we'll get you in there."

"Won't be any of his mind left in his brain to bother me?"

"No, no," the technician said soothingly. "All that—anything extraneous, his memories, consciousness, the holographic pattern— it's all going to be pushed out when we upload you into him. It just kind of gets lost in the circuits of the transfer interface. Sort of like when you do a vasectomy—where does the sperm go? The body absorbs it. Our gear will absorb him, and he won't be there to bother you . . ."

"That old fuck . . . taking my body . . ." I said. "Hey general, they're just uploading a copy of your mind—they're not sending all you, man."

"Everything important," he said distantly amused. "You believe in the soul, kid—that's such primitive thinking."

"Look at these people," I told him. "There's something missing from them. That Boxell's got no soul. He's one of 'em! You want to end up that empty, man? Like Boxell? Let me up out of this shit and we'll talk . . ."

The general chuckled. "Superstitious! I do hope none of him stays."

"None of him will . . ." The technician leaned close and told me, ever so sweetly: "Now, Whim . . . we're going to give you a mild tranquilizer—but we can't put you completely under. It won't feel like dying, really. More like going down a long, long slide . . . just slide on down and out and . . . it won't hurt at all." It's funny, what she said then. Not to me, to the computer about initiating the process. She said, "Three, five, thirty-five . . ." Reciting the date. The time: "Three Oh-five a.m . . . and thirty five seconds."

The numbers know. That was the last thing I heard, alive.

Then, all that was really me, mind and soul, went sliding down, down, and out . . .

Souls. They can't *send* them when they upload. Souls go where the universe wants—not where we want them to go. So when they try to put a shaky old General's consciousness in my body, only his personality and memory will go in. Probably had a shriveled little soul anyway. What's left of it will dissipate, during the uploading. It doesn't go where mine has gone—that's the difference between us, and the uploaded. Their souls just . . . disintegrate. Ours are shoved out of the way . . .

When they pushed me out, I found I was in a *somewhere*—I was drifting through the circuits of the interface computer. I got stuck in the transfer equipment. Lots of us are wandering around in here. Souls in databanks. I can see 'em sometimes, in my mind's eye. We can talk a little. I like to say to 'em, "*Hey, raise your hand if you're dead.*" Just to show I still have a sense of humor. The real joke is, there are people walking around in perfectly healthy physical bodies, who are more dead than we are . . .

And I found that I can follow the numbers, feel those 0s and 1s, reach out through these circuits and cables, and send a message to you, Syke, since one computer talks to another—and you're always interfacing with a computer.

I want to tell you: Come out of your virtual womb before it's your virtual tomb, Syke. They're going to come after you subworld people soon. You in particular.

Come out—and go find Mercedes, and take care of her. Ask around Siggy's Allnighter. You'll find her. Because I know she matters to you. You and her, you're soul mates.

Me—well, I think I've got it figured out now. I'm not in my body—and something else is. Not someone—some *thing*. So I'm not ever going to be able to go back to my body. I'm just a soul, organized into a mind; a soul floating in circles, in a machine. And if my mind was uploaded to another body, my soul wouldn't go with my mind.

I wouldn't want that.

So no—you can't help me. I answered my own question. I'm dead. One times zero equals zero. It all adds up. I'm only dead, though, in the physical way. Not in the way that matters.

Don't worry about me. I followed the numbers, and I'm about to lead the others out of here. I can feel them going into another computer, and then another—and then, one at a time, out through some kind of satellite transmission link. The soul, see, ends up flying through the sky, just like it was supposed to. And there's something up there waiting. I want to see what it is. Maybe I'll meet Dresden. I hardly knew her. But I feel cheated, losing her . . . But maybe I'll meet her somewhere, between here and there—wherever we are.

THE GUN AS AN AID TO POETRY

"There's no getting off the hook, short of suicide," Eric wrote, in a Facebook message to Gwen. He was sitting at the glass table on the sunny terrace, wearing jogging sweats and sunglasses. As he typed on his PowerBook, a coffee cup and a blank notebook at his elbow, he was distantly aware of the breakers rumbling and hissing on the rocks below the cliff, beyond the redwood fence. He wrote:

And my excuses for avoiding suicide are assorted: I don't wish to be another depressed poet who ended it all; I don't care for the collateral damage—though I like to imagine that all my exes would be depressed by my passing, you especially—and most of all, I'm simply too cowardly for self-annihilation. I will probably accept another year of slow suicide via teaching at Massachusetts State, by which I mean: suicide by heavy drinking before and after classes. I can hear you now: 'You won the Pulitzer for Poetry, you putz, you're one of the few poets to regularly receive significant royalties, you have a great day job at an undemanding school, you live in a comfortable modern house designed by a not untalented protégé of Frank Lloyd Wright, just count your fucking blessings.' But you have never had to teach people who ask if they can submit poems by text message and 'does every line have to rhyme?' . . . If I can find the courage . . .

"I had a moment of real hope for you, when I saw you working on the laptop," said someone behind Eric. "I might simply have gone away . . ."

Eric turned half about, looking over his shoulder, eyebrows raised—and then he saw the large silver-plated gun held firmly in the stranger's hand. The man stood two yards way, aiming the gun straight at Eric's head.

"But then," the man said, in a voice that was both silky and sulky, "the disappointment came. I saw you were on *Facebook*."

The stranger wore a rumpled linen suit, a panama hat on a head that, judging by the visible part, was shaved bald. He wore sunglasses like Eric's—no, not quite like Eric's. The man's sunglasses were mirrored lenses. Eric could see his own startled middle-aged face staring dually back at him. The man had a weak chin, a slight overbite, oddly small ears, and a number of moles on his cheeks.

Eric theorized that the best course was to put on his charmingly confident face and try to be verbally disarming, as it were. He managed a carefree smile. "Old-school we'd say, 'You have the advantage of me, sir.' And it's doubly apt. By which I mean . . ."

"By which you mean: *Who the fuck are you?* My name is Norman Conrad. Think back. I wrote a series of papers on your work. You refused to meet with me."

"Ah." *Norman Conrad.* Eric Boyle's own variant on the crazy journalist who'd stalked Bob Dylan, literally rooting through Dylan's trashcan. Eric's neck was hurting, so he turned about, very slowly, in his chair. "And I owe this visit, and this gun—to that refusal?"

"No. I'm here because you stopped writing. I arrive, feel a chill as I see you writing, glance over your shoulder—and see it's a private message on Facebook. I take it you're wallowing in self-pity. Your poetry made my life meaningful, Boyle. My life was an idiot's scrawl before your *Antic Elegies*—you made me feel that art could *make* life meaningful. Then—you just fucking *stopped.*" The gun was leveled fixedly as Conrad spoke. It never wavered. "Insight into the human condition is the only compass; art is the only way to reach that insight. Poetry is the highest form of art. You are the best poet in the world. Ipso facto . . ."

Even at his most hubristic, Eric had never believed he was the best. He certainly felt no pleasure in getting the compliment from an armed burglar—a glib eccentric who'd badgered him with letters for years. He felt only a rising anger. He wanted to tackle Conrad, whip him with his own pistol. But he had no assurance that he could rush that gun and come out of it unwounded. Suicide by aficionado? No. He'd probably end up paralyzed—or internally shattered but still tottering about, like Andy Warhol.

Eric did his best to keep his face impassive. "Well—nothing dries a man out like having a gun pointed at him. What do you say we have a drink and sort this out? You can keep your gun in one hand, a highball in the other . . ."

Conrad shook his head—there was something absolute and definitive in the motion. "No. I will permit no ploy, no 'tactics,' no getting around me. My certain information is, you haven't completed a poem in six years. But you will today. You will write many pages of poems. Or I'll shoot you six times, in, say, the course of an hour or so." By careful degrees, he lowered the gun to point at Eric's crotch, his arm moving as smoothly as a computer-controlled crane. "I'll shoot you in the parts that have had such famous congress with coeds, over the years," Conrad went on, thoughtfully. "Then in the shins. I'll let you writhe so you can feel some kind of punishment for wasting your ability. I have tried to write poetry and prose for twenty-five years and have turned out only tripe, regurgitated Eric Boyle—muck, trash, self-indulgence, a waste of paper, I'm not even a Salieri. But you—" He laughed with a soft bitterness. "You prick. Every truly completed Eric Boyle poem is powerful and existentially redemptive. If *I* cannot write it—then I will see to it, at least, that you do. You will now, right now, this minute, *begin writing poetry*, or I'll shoot you."

Eric licked his lips. "Um . . . If you really appreciate my work, I can't believe you'd really want to . . . to take me out of the world . . . at some point I'll write again, after all."

"You're a liar. I've read that fragment of a memoir you showed to your agent. You have no intention of ever writing another poem. You won't write unless I *make* you."

Eric let out a long, noisy breath. "Norman, Christ almighty—if you want to complain about absurdity in life—well here it is. This is absurd. At least . . . fire the gun at the fence so I know it's loaded . . ."

"Don't doubt me again," Conrad said. He reached into his jacket pocket with his left hand, and took out an old fashioned Polaroid snapshot and tossed it on the table beside Eric.

"A Polaroid. They still make these? I'll bet you have to order the film on the . . ." He broke off, staring at the photo. The Polaroid showed someone he knew very well, someone with his head shot open. It was his literary agent, Donald Cantor. Staring in death, Donald looked quite startled. He was slumped back in the driver's seat of his little lavender Volkswagen convertible, the top down—a car Eric had often ridden in to increasingly pensive lunches. The whole crown of his head was missing. His brains were exposed, and cratered. There was simply no chance it could have been faked up somehow. "You've . . . killed Donald?"

Conrad nodded his head, exactly once. "Yes. For two good reasons. First, because he failed to induce you to work, and second, to show you that I'm serious. Very serious. It didn't bother me at all. It won't bother me to kill a spoiled prize-winning poet. Now—if you don't wish to be shot to pieces, you will instantly exit from Facebook—do not write a single letter more there. You will completely log off the internet. If you like, you can hit send on that note, but nothing more."

"My Wi-Fi goes out a lot anyway," Eric said hoarsely, still determined to put up a façade of blithe fearlessness. He turned to the laptop, hesitated a moment, wondering how he could send a message to the police before he signed off.

"Don't even think that way," Conrad said, moving a little closer, and a step to one side. "I can see what you're writing from here."

Eric swallowed, hit send on the note to Gwen, and shut down his internet connection.

"Good. I'll give you thirty seconds to start writing poetry. I do not have the safety on."

"But—thirty seconds!"

"It's no use whimpering about the absent muse—you've had six years. I'm convinced it's all there in you and only passive aggression is keeping it locked up."

Eric felt a peculiar, reverberating shock at that. Because it just might be true. "Just start anywhere that feels emotionally in the moment," Conrad suggested, "the first poem—you'll write many of them today—could be filled with hatred for crazy critics who hold guns on you—that's part of life too. Your life anyhow. Just start, Boyle. It doesn't have to be terribly good. You can edit later, if I see you're making a real effort. Start! *Now!* Thirty. Twenty-nine. Twenty eight . . . twenty seven, twenty six, twenty five, twenty four, twenty three . . ."

"I don't even have a word processing program open!"

". . . nineteen, eighteen, seventeen, sixteen, fifteen, fourteen—I'm cocking the gun—"

Eric heard the distinct sound of the gun cocking. His mind's eye chose that moment to replay the image of poor Donald with his head blown open, gray matter peeking out like mold in an old broken Easter egg.

"Twelve, eleven . . ."

"Wait!" He got the cursor moving, found the word processing program, opened it, clicked for a new document.

"Seven, six . . ."

He typed, "From the mouth of a gun: the thunder of the world's contempt for me/ an echo of my denials/ O denials from the reverberating chamber of . . ." Of what? ". . . of a crumbling inward British Museum . . ."

"Not very good," said Conrad, reading over his shoulder. "But it's a start. Don't try to edit, just continue, let it flow. Or I'll shoot you someplace very painful. I won't let you off easy like Donald . . ."

"What . . . what about typos . . ." Eric's fingers betraying him, trembling over the keys.

"Only fix egregious ones. The minor ones can be addressed later . . ."

He typed onward, writing, "Consider the places I've tramped through/ the tramps I've placed, in true, upon their backs/ the toys I've tripped on, left by hacks/ only to come here, and turn, and see this buffoon . . ."

"That's better," Conrad said. "Insult me, whatever you like. So long as it's poetry. Don't worry about poetic forms. Just let it flow. You're starting to really write it . . . Remember, if you stop for more than a handful of seconds—I won't tell you how many—I will fire the gun and you will die very badly."

"Yes, yes," Eric muttered. He was excruciatingly aware of the pistol's muzzle close behind him—he imagined he could smell the gun metal, the oil in its moving parts. All the while, typing, "The oiled machine awaits the tock, the muted thunder of student steps, each step a gun poised at my head . . ."

He didn't think much of what he was producing—it was, so far, little better than doggerel—but something, anyway, was flowing out of the muzzle of the gun aimed at his back; something was flowing from pure adrenaline and, really, a kind of desperate automatic writing, and he started to cast about for impressions that had penetrated his fog of misery, of late. ". . . the dust collecting on their awards/ the breached loins that tumble dimwits/ the arsenic and the electronic . . ." Rather sophomoric, he thought, but he could always delete it later when this oaf was in jail. ". . . and Donald's memories, his thought/ upon the headrest vinyl rots . . ."

Conrad grunted. "No need to rhyme . . ."

"I'm in a T.S. Eliot kinda place, with this," Eric muttered, strangely irritated, scarcely aware he was saying it as his fingers, poised over the keys like birds of prey. "Or Auden. Going into and out of rhyme as mood takes me . . . Rhyming as reference, discarded as I choose . . ." Another half-decent line came to him, and he typed it, then another—and a better one.

Eric realized, suddenly, that he was feeling a long, rippling, refined rush of pleasure at the release of these lines. He wasn't yet composing good poetry, but it was gleaming on his mental horizon. He could sense it coming. This psychotic self-indulgent literary parasite had done one worthwhile thing after all—he'd reconnected Eric Boyle with the urgency of his own drives, the imperative of self-expression at its rawest. Eric felt justified in drawing breath, again; felt he was no longer on that hook. Yes he was trapped on his own terrace, held hostage, pinned down under a gun—but for the first time in years he was free. He typed on . . . a page. Two more . . .

"Yes . . . now that, finally, is rather good," Conrad said, reading over his shoulder.

"Quiet, don't interrupt me," Eric said brusquely, typing. When Conrad said nothing in reply, Eric was aware, on some level, that the balance of power between them was shifting. But he glanced to his left at their dark reflection in the glass of the sliding back door, and was reassured to see that Conrad still held the gun steadily pointed at his back. Good. He needed it there, for the moment. And so long as Conrad held the gun it didn't bother him that this pathetic wing nut was reading what he wrote even as he wrote it—normally something he couldn't bear.

He typed onward, pausing only to hit save. The words were coming to him in completed lines, now, he had only to write them out.

He heard Conrad suck air sharply in through his teeth—perhaps a gasp of intense approval. "Amazing," Conrad murmured. "It's really . . . it really is . . ."

Somewhere in the back of his mind, Eric was thinking about Gwen, felt a flutter of hope remembering that they'd never quite finalized their divorce. Realizing that he wanted to see her. That he needed her. Pale, copper-haired Gwen, with her jade green eyes. She'd given him companionship, patience, and every bit of the space he needed to write—just enough encouragement, at exactly the right moments, without trying to prod him onward—and he'd blown it all on some bosomy debutant whose primary means of self-expression was painfully self-aware irony. If he could just get through this alive, he would go to Gwen and say, "See, I wrote poetry again, and it was because I imagined you were in the next room . . ."

He wouldn't tell her about the gun. She would never meet Conrad. He must see to that.

Eric typed on, his fingers beginning to ache. It was all one poem, and the arc of it pulled him like gravity pulling a sled, faster and faster. He heard a faint sob from Conrad, from time to time. There was envy in that sob, and despair, and a little ecstasy: Eric heard it clearly. He typed on . . . starting to make more typing errors . . .

At last he felt his inspiration flagging, though he had a notion where he was going—and that he'd get there soon. "I think I'm tiring," he said, pausing. "It must be almost two hours now."

"You can go on," Conrad said. "If you had to, you could produce a whole short book this way. If it's that or be shot . . ."

But he sounded less sure of himself now. "I need coffee," Eric said, correcting a couple of typos. "It's already made, on the sideboard in the kitchen. Get me a cup. Get yourself some too if you want. It's been on the warmer for a long time and it probably tastes like motor oil from a Model T."

"I'm not going to . . ."

"You damn fool, I'm *writing*, for the first time in six years, you think I'm going to stop? I may even read one of your damned theses, so don't blow it—I'm near the end of this cycle but I need coffee. I'm not going to go over the fence or start howling for the cops. I don't have a cell phone on me and there are no neighbors nearby. Look, there's a notebook here, and a pen. You can take the laptop, so I can't use Wi-Fi. I wrote my first two books with paper and pen, in first draft. You can shoot me when I get back if I'm not still writing! I need coffee to go on!"

It was an outrageously risky speech but some part of his mind had sussed Conrad out and he knew that the shift in moral authority came at the right moment.

Conrad growled to himself, then circled around to Eric's right, keeping the gun on him, his left hand reaching out, taking the laptop. He picked it up very carefully, almost reverently. He backed away, then hurried into the house, footsteps receding toward the kitchen.

Eric was already picking up the pen, arranging the notebook. He was momentarily afraid he'd lost the thread—but the next lines came to him, as he thought, again, of Gwen, the freckles on her breasts, her quirky admiration for early Gertrude Stein and late Dorothy Parker, the two of them dancing at the Steely Dan reunion, stoned to the breaking point and never breaking. Gwen . . .

He began to write, the lines flowing out of him in a slightly different rhythm through the medium of a pen. The coffee appeared at his elbow, he paused just long enough to sip twice. Then he set the cup down, to begin writing again, splashed the coffee across the table in his apparent eagerness—spilled it on purpose, really. He ignored the spill, though it discolored the edges of the notebook, and wrote on.

A page filled in, then half a page more, an anticlimactic climax— and then Eric realized he was done. Quite done. He mustn't write anything more, just now. His inner pacing told him clearly he must wait, and let the poem sit before revising. Probably he'd cut the first page entirely. It was a long poem and it was time for a martini and a walk, not more poetry forced out of him—he'd only produce ragtag, tatty ends of things.

"There—this should be typed into the laptop, at the end of the first document," he said, with absolute conviction. "You type it as I read it to you. If I type it in, I'll get lost in revision . . ."

"Right, right," Conrad said breathlessly. Conrad used his own sleeve to wipe the spilled coffee up, then put the laptop on the table. He sat down in the other chair, to Eric's right, setting the gun down on the tabletop where he could get it, out of Eric's reach. He opened the laptop—it was still switched on. He moved his sunglasses up onto the top of his head. His eyes, Eric saw, were small and gray, rimmed in red, his nose longer than Eric had realized. "Go ahead, Boyle."

Eric began to read, and Conrad typed. Twenty minutes of reading, typing.

Then Eric stopped. They both knew he'd reached the end.

Conrad looked at him. "Now another. A new poem. At least one more long one."

"I'll need more coffee. Take the laptop and get it. I've spilled most of this . . . make sure it's hot for Christ's sake . . ."

He turned the notebook page, wrote out an arbitrary title, "Gwen, and Then".

He started scribbling under it, "She's always been in the house, she's always been outside, looking in/ I'm a coward, or I'd open the window . . ."

Seeing he was busily writing, Conrad stood, his movements grudging, then picked up the gun and the laptop—scooped the gun in a way that conveyed a warning. He put the gun in a coat pocket, circled Eric, picked up the cup with his left hand, hurried into the house.

Scribbling junk poetry, Eric heard the beep of the microwave, Conrad heating up the coffee.

Eric frowned and scribbled, tried to seem deeply involved. He forced himself not to look up—and then heard Conrad approaching, setting the steaming cup on the table by Eric's hand, Conrad returned to his seat, laying the laptop down, then the gun. Eric said, "May as well turn off the laptop, save power, won't need it for a while, Norman." He scribbled. Conrad started to open the laptop. Eric picked up the hot coffee , taking the cup from beneath—and smashed the cup onto Conrad's forehead, hard, the hot liquid searing him, the cup cutting his brow—

Conrad yelled, and flailed for the gun, but he was off balance and he fell sideways, taking his chair over with him. Eric grabbed the gun, leaped back, overturning his own chair—just managing to stay on his feet. He pointed the gun, steadying it as Conrad sat up on the ground, wiping coffee from his eyes with shaking hands.

Breathing hard, Eric just stood there, pointing the gun.

"So now what?" Conrad muttered, slowly drawing his knees up, wrapping his arms around them. His pursed lips trembled, like he might burst into tears.

Eric felt no pity for him. "You know, Norman . . ." Eric's voice grated in his own ears. His teeth were clenched. "I can shoot one of these things. I used to hang out with Hunter Thompson. We'd get drunk and shoot targets. I got pretty good."

Conrad smiled sadly at him. "Sure. You did a lot of cool things. You had a lot of beautiful women too. But you couldn't write for the last six years—until I showed up here.""Six years ago, I broke up with Gwen." Eric shrugged. "Not something you'd want to understand."

"You think *that's* it? I know what kind of guy you are, Boyle. I've studied you. It's not that. And you are not the true-love kind of guy."

"I'm not, no. I just need her. Now turn around and walk toward the fence. There's a gate in it."

"It's not *her*," Conrad said, with taut insistence, fists balled at his side. "You got all insulated in your little world! You needed to get back in touch with *life*. I gave you that."

"You did give me that. I've found my way now. Right through the gate! And maybe I'll let you go. Move!"

Conrad stared at the gun—then he turned, and walked unsteadily toward the fence. Eric followed, glancing around. A line of tall Italian junipers blocked the view from the road, here. There were no houses close by. No one was walking along the cliffs—no one to see.

In a couple of minutes, they'd passed through the gate, walked another forty yards over the mossy flat stone to the edge of the cliff.

"This doesn't feel like you maybe letting me go," Conrad said. "I didn't actually hurt you . . . I gave you your pride back!"

"You like to enumerate things, Norman, so here you go. First of all, you killed Donald, a guy who was there for me for twenty years. And a good agent is hard to find. Second, you're a creepy little stalker who freakishly sparked something in me. Third, I can't have you going about telling people. You'll come back, for one thing. And—Gwen . . . no. I can't."

Conrad turned to face him. "Listen—I won't tell anyone. It'd get me in trouble with the police."

"I don't believe you, a twisted little narcissist like you? You'll tell people."

"Anyway—Boyle—it's not going to work! You were *through*. Once a writer's been in the horse latitudes, they need something extreme—like a gun to their head to get out! You'll just sink back again . . ."

"That'll be you, actually, but I doubt you'll be aware of it," Eric said—and he fired the gun, three times, rather enjoying it. He made the parasite stagger and dance on the edge of eternity; a vaudevillian dancing off the stage, backwards, into the wings . . .

. . . Right off the cliff, into the sea.

Heart thudding, but feeling more alive than he had in years, Eric walked carefully to the edge—and looked over. He could see Conrad's body, looking gelatinous in the surf, as the waves sucked at it. This time of day, tide was just going out. That body'd head out to sea . . .

He looked at the gun and thought: Throw it over too. Don't be stupid. Wasn't legal to kill him. Not a real case of self-defense.

But he couldn't let go of the gun. It was a totem, an object of power to him. It was the lightning rod of his poetry.

Carrying the gun, he walked back to the house.

Six weeks later.

He was unable to reach Gwen. He'd tried phone, internet—her sister said she'd gone on a trip to Europe, to get over Rodney the pomo theorist. She wasn't even going to check her email, any of that, because she didn't want to hear from limp-dick postmodern boy.

Fine. When she came back . . .

He'd corrected the long poem written under the gun, sent it to his publisher as a short book, together with some of his old uncollected work. He wrote an introduction about the tragedy of losing his good friend Donald. How the police had said it was done by a lunatic fan who'd done away with himself. The cruel irony.

Then he set to work writing more poetry. He managed a few verses—but they were mere scrapings. He felt the doldrums coming back; felt the angry dullness, the resentment that bound his fingers. Where was Gwen? Why wasn't she here? Why'd she leave him because of a few infidelities? Why didn't she come back?

He sat and stared at laptop, at paper—at nothingness. He couldn't write. Couldn't fucking *write*.

Then, one morning, he took the gun out, from its hiding place in the unused fireplace. He put it on the desk, next to his notebook. His totem would transmit power to him once more . . .

But it didn't. He still couldn't write. The dithering parasite had been right . . .

There was only one thing for it. He set up his notebook on the back table, took the pen up in his right hand, then the gun with his other hand. He cocked the gun, and put it to his left temple. He put pen to paper. "Write, *in thirty seconds*, you bastard," he told himself. "Or I'm pulling the trigger. Thirty, twenty nine, twenty eight, twenty seven . . . Finger's tightening on the trigger. I'll do it, you lazy fuck! It's better to be dead than empty! Write! Twenty six, twenty five! Write or die! Twenty four . . ." He felt his finger tighten just . . . fractionally. His heart thudded. His mouth went bone dry. He pressed the muzzle hard to the side of his head. He tightened his finger on the trigger as much as he could without it being *quite* enough to fire the gun. A *micron away*. "Nineteen . . . eighteen . . . seventeen . . ." He began to write. It was coming. The lines appeared. It worked! A distant chiming from somewhere . . . he ignored it . . . it was working . . . so close . . . a micron away . . . the writing consumed him. The gun still pressed to his temples, Eric heard nothing but the sound of his pen on paper, and his own breathing . . .

x   x   x

No answer to the doorbell.

Gwen gave up on the front door, and went around to the back gate—she could see that Eric's car was here. He might be out walking. But she knew he liked to sit out back with his laptop.

She went through the back gate, and saw him sitting rather awkwardly at the table, scratching away on an actual notebook. Maybe she shouldn't interrupt him. But his last Facebook messages had scared her. When she'd finally read them that morning, it seemed to her that he really was thinking of killing himself.

And was there something in Eric's hand, as he scribbled away on the notebook? Was that a gun?

Was he writing a suicide note?

She rushed toward him. "Eric!"

He almost had the line. The one line that would open up the rest of the poem . . . would let it all flow out of him. The gun, the nearness of death, had called it up in him. The tightrope between life and . . .

Then a voice shouted. "Eric—stop!"

And the line vanished. It was gone. His hand contracted in convulsive frustration. Not meaning to squeeze the trigger—

ANIMUS RIGHTS

Near Jamaica Bay, New York, 1887

"And why should you go shooting again, Daniel?" Wilamina demanded. "You've gone twice this week. You promised me an autumn promenade. The leaves are splendid."

"You shall have your autumn promenade, my dear," Daniel replied, stuffing his coat pockets with shotgun shells. The gun club provided shells but they were not to his liking. "But first I shall go target shooting. They have a new machine that swings feathered bags, does a capital job. The Colonel's servants crank them by—always cringing under the shot though it rarely comes near them . . ."

Wilamina was at the oval, silver-framed hall mirror, adjusting her ivory choker, patting the red-brown hair piled luxuriantly on her head, frowning in the gaslight glow—and Daniel thought that he had seen that prim scowl far too often.

She'll soon become irrelevant.

What a strange thought! It had come suddenly, unbidden, as actual words in his mind—and he rarely thought in words.

But as he picked up his shotgun, carrying it loose under his arm, he realized he'd had more than one such incident on anomalous thinking, these past few weeks.

"Seven years of peaceful marriage, and suddenly you're a man of blood," Wilamina said suddenly, calling after him as he went to the door, its leaded glass panels bluing the dusty late-afternoon sunlight. Something plaintive, worried in her voice. Her anxiety came out in a rush: "You're a man of banking—you're not a hunter. You were always fit, to be sure, but all this running about at dawn of late, huffing and puffing, throwing javelins . . . and now shooting. Pheasant hunting. Is it a consequence of turning thirty? Some men become unsure of themselves . . ."

"Just a hobby, my darling dear," he said, hurrying out the door before she should press him on matters he didn't understand himself.

Daniel inhaled the spicy scent of leaves fallen from the tall, noble elms lining the cobblestoned road, and felt a rising exhilaration, a buoyant freeness, that seemed to sweep him along the wooden walkway, past the gaunt houses.

He came to the corner and stopped—uncertain. To the left, after a brisk walk, were the streetcars, drawn by teams of horses, that would take him to the club, and his target shooting. To the right . . .

It was exactly at that moment that Daniel knew he was not going target shooting at all.

He was going the opposite way; he was going to the small wood, to the south. He almost knew why. Not quite yet.

It will come. The game is afoot.

There, words again, ringing in his mind. Somehow, though, they felt like his own words; his own assertion, coming from some place deep within.

He broke the double-barreled shotgun open, and thumbed two rounds. Was distantly aware of Old Man Worster watching him disapprovingly from his porch.

The rising lightness, the giddy exuberance made him want to spin on his heel and fire a shot at Worster's porch, perhaps shoot out that gaudy, peacock-shaped front door panel. *"Sorry, Worster—out hunting fowl, thought it was a peacock, ha ha!"* No: he would need his ammunition.

He stalked off to the right, the 12 gauge now at ready in his hands, hurrying to the end of the road, the path that led into the quarter-mile-wide strip of elms and maples, where children played in the day, and couples sparked at night. Taking a walk here, not long ago, he had seen several tow-headed boys playing "War Between the States". The sight had struck a chord within him.

He was not fifty strides into the wood, just within sight of the gray-blue of Jamaica Bay, glimpsed between the trees, when the shot came, hitting a stout maple trunk just in front of him.

Too soon, as usual, Daniel thought, crouching behind the tree, chuckling. *You have given away your position . . .*

As usual? But he'd never been shot at before. And who had fired the shot?

Adversary.

He leaned slightly forward, looked up to see the fresh yellow gouge where the bullet had cut the dull-green bark of the young maple, about six feet up. Daniel's height. The shot had come from the southwest.

He backed away, stood, spun, and, heart hammering with primal delight, sprinted between the trees to the northeast, trying to flank Adversary.

To flank . . . whom? Who was . . .

Adversary. As always . . .

And then his actual identity returned, erupting in fullness, like a geyser washing through his mind, hissing away the fearful, mealy-mouthed Daniel Chapham, the minor officer of a minor bank—and now he was the one called *Animus.* That was the game-name of his true self. And he felt not a qualm, not a sputter of regret at letting Daniel go. He had been so many others, these centuries past; they had always seemed feeble, sketchy compared to his fundamental identity.

But thoughts of Daniel Chapham were fading, becoming shadows at the back of his mind, cast by light from outside a cave; he was rushing toward that light, and emerging to see Adversary grinning at him, currently a stocky blond man in a white and black sailor's outfit. He stood about twelve yards away, on the other side of a waist-high, mossy boulder, head cocked to aim along the rifle wedged against his shoulder.

Animus had just time to think, *Ah, that's the form he's taken, I've seen him scouting me at—*

They fired their weapons almost simultaneously, Adversary was a little faster. Daniel—Animus, now—was forced to fire from his hip, both barrels, and most of the shot went wild, caroming from the outcropping of granite, scoring away moss; but a scattering of pellets struck across Adversary's white, black-trimmed sailor's shirt, rocking him a few steps back, and Animus was staggering back himself, as if they were doing a hornpipe together.

He felt it, then, just under his sternum—the bullet had struck him a moment before, but he'd not felt the pain till this second; the weakness spreading from the wound, the seizing up of his lungs. That was one problem with choosing this planet—these primate bodies were comparatively feeble.

Animus felt himself sinking to his knees, hot blood gurgling up in his throat to dribble from the corner of his mouth, as he fumbled the empty shells from his shotgun, thumbed in two more slippery rounds—but Adversary was there, striding up to him, cocking the rifle, blood streaming in thin trickles from a spray of small holes in his shirt, his mouth stretched wide in joy as he prepared for the *coup de grace*.

Animus was annoyed, realizing that Adversary was giving him a moment to swing the shotgun around, just to make things more interesting. "I don't need your extra chance . . ." He couldn't finish, blood choking off the words, and he squeezed the shotgun triggers but Adversary was within reach, cracking Animus across the head with the rifle-barrel, so that the shotgun bellowed harmlessly into the ground, and he fell to his side in a cloud of gun smoke, sighing ruefully as he waited for the bullet in the back of his head, thinking, *I know we agreed this would be a Sudden Confrontation but this abruptness hardly seems—*

Animus never completed the thought, as the rifle bullet shattered his skull—and his lightbody was forced out of the cellular mass of his body; freed from the primate shell that people had called Daniel Chapman.

Still embodied in the blond-haired, mustachioed, lantern-jawed man in the sailor's shirt, Adversary gazed triumphantly down at the Daniel body: shattered, still twitching though all intelligence had drained from it.

Almost as an afterthought, the heart stopped beating.

Then Adversary looked up at Animus—at the lightbody that had departed the shattered primate body . . .

And Adversary's own primate-body collapsed, as if its joints had dissolved. No longer occupied, it simply fell; its heart switched off by Adversary on the way out, the way a man switches off a light when he's leaving a house.

Adversary's lightbody shimmered, golden-green, across from Animus's own, whose colors were more red-purple with flecks of flaring yellow.

"I knew if I shot at you, early on, from that angle, you'd dart to the left and I could cut you off at that boulder," Adversary said, emanating glee. He didn't say it in words, exactly, nothing so simple; it was not a communication that Daniel Chapham would have understood, but that was the general meaning. *"You're starting to be too predictable! And yet you think I'm predictable!"*

"You shot me in almost the same way during the Napoleonic wars, you remember? With that musket!"

"What a feeble redcoat you made! It was better during the Civil War. But this time . . ."

"We might have had a bit more tactics before Sudden Confrontation," Animus interrupted testily. *"But the woman I was married to was annoying me. I had to invest so much time in being Chapman . . ."*

There was a pause; a sense of puzzlement in the air. "You were aware enough to be annoyed? Your Fundamental should have been in full dormancy. You've got to go back and retrain your Focal Point if this keeps up."

"Nonsense! I can get it back to full dormancy on my own. Now—next time, let's do a broad, tactical conflict."

"The primates are creating explosive possibilities in Europe. A little time, and I can spark that one. Perhaps an assassination in the right quarter."

"There are new weapons coming. Let's use them all!"

"You mean generalships? It's been a while since we were generals, sending armies against one another. The potential . . . Even a colonel could do much . . . We could use psychic dominance to prod the generals, once we'd gotten close enough . . ."

"Much preparation would be needed. We shall need to influence key individuals before nesting. I wish we had the technology to enter adult bodies, instead of nesting in fetal forms, waiting till maturity."

"That's forbidden technology. And it's not much of a wait, really, for us. A few decades at most. We need the rest."

A young couple, strolling through the woods in search of privacy, came upon the bloody scene: the two awkwardly sprawled bodies. And they saw the shimmering, vaguely humanoid shapes hovering beside the bodies.

The lightbodied, Adversary and Animus, became aware of the strolling couple, and flitted upward, into the gathering mists of late afternoon, vanishing into the high upper airs; the pimply young man gaped; the sheep-eyed girl put a pale hand to her heaving bosom . . . and went into a career of spiritism soon after, thinking she had seen ghosts.

But to Adversary and Animus, her species were so insubstantial, so evanescent—*they* were the "ghosts".

Verdun, France, 1916

Holdrich Von Stang collapsed the brass telescope and put it in the pocket of his greatcoat, leaving his hand in there with it to warm the knuckles against the drizzly February morning, stamping some feeling into his feet on the planks of the railroad car.

He shook his head broodingly. One-hundred thousand shells had hammered the fortress of Verdun, and Animus, in full emergence over Von Stang for several weeks now, was worried that perhaps his enemy had been prematurely killed by the bombardment. Of course, many enemies had been killed—but he was concerned for his particular enemy. His enemy who was also his best friend. Adversary.

But no, Adversary would have appeared to him in lightbody, if he'd been killed.

A little ways down the flatcar, enlisted men passed crates of supplies along a human chain, to two drays pulled by teams of mules; the animals snorted visibly in the cold air. The Kaiser's soldiers, gray figures in long coats and broad, dented helmets, weary from poor rest and thin rations, worked slowly but steadily on. Good soldiers. Many would be dead tomorrow. Spent like so many pennies. Sometimes he wondered . . .

No. Concern for the primates was irrational, mere distraction. Why had it arisen at all?

He mused on the question only distantly—a warmth was spreading through him, as he considered the battered fortress of Verdun, a quarter-mile away. He could just make out the rising columns of blue smoke, a consequence of the shelling. Reports had come in that the allies were far from destroyed; more than half of them had survived the bombardment, in deep trenches, cellars fortified by the British and French. But of course he had warned Adversary about the shelling, with a temporary mental contact. He and Adversary had been emerged for almost a month.

Erich von Falkenhayn, the German Chief of Staff, had almost gone along with a plan to push for domination on the Eastern Front. But that was inconvenient for Adversary and Animus, and Adversary had used psychic dominance, a remote telepathic push, to nudge Von Falkenhayn toward another plan—to "bleed France white" at the Western front, beginning with Verdun.

"Colonel?"

Von Stang looked down at his pale orderly, shook his head in disapproval. "Your boots are muddy, Corporal Gromin," he said, in

German. He enjoyed playing his part. "You are bivouacked in the officer's tents. You do not have the excuse of the trenches."

"I beg your pardon sir, I thought it best I come directly with the information, and the path across the field . . ."

"Yes, yes–you've come to tell me an enemy patrol has slipped out of the fortress?"

Gromin looked at him in surprise. "Yes sir! You knew already!"

"Oh yes . . . I anticipated something of the sort." He chuckled, feeling the excitement rise in him at the imminence of the final confrontation between Animus and Adversary, for this particular war—finally, this time.

It had taken longer than usual, though, to *fully* emerge into his host body. He didn't quite feel himself, yet. The exhilaration was half-suppressed. This worried Animus. He felt himself oddly over-mingled with Von Stang. Perhaps Adversary had been right, last embodiment, in that New York woods. Perhaps he needed retraining.

But he must deal with that later, after he or Adversary was "killed". And that would happen today, in all probability. Till now, they'd sent waves of men against one another—or used psychic dominance, remote telepathic urgings, to urge the generals to order it. But the time had come for face-to-face Confrontation.

"Gromin—I have made a list of men to accompany us. We will go to meet this foray. They think they have gotten away from the fortress . . . to escape, or to spy on us. We will prove them wrong."

Naturally, Von Stang—Animus—had moved troops away from the southwest corner of the fortress, so that Adversary could slip out with his patrol.

Half an hour later, six men trailed behind Gromin and Von Stang as they tramped down the muddy road, rifles cold and heavy in their hands. The men had been surprised, seeing that Von Stang was going to lead the patrol himself. A colonel leading a patrol, and carrying a rifle, too, as well as a side-arm—unheard of!

The landscape about Verdun was ideal for their next confrontation; for a glorious battlefield drama. They liked to set up the field of battle carefully but make their confrontational decisions as spontaneously as possible. Perhaps, after all, he might surprise Adversary by holding back, today. This might not be their last confrontation of the war, after all. Von Stang might withdraw at the last moment—and later, might have Falkenhayn assassinated, then use psychic domination to have himself installed as Chief of Staff. They could extend the war for a number of extra years, if they chose.

Yes. He would have a good skirmish with Adversary here, but choose to withdraw before fatality . . . unless things turned against him too soon.

He might get caught up in the fight; might not withdraw in time. Still, there would be another battle, if this one was fatal. There was always another battle, in other bodies. They had been doing this for more than two thousand revolutions of this planet around its sun, and there were always more possibilities for warfare. It was an infinitely fruitful world, for Animus and Adversary . . .

He felt the waves of exhilaration building in him as he trudged toward the approximate area of confrontation. But despite the mounting inner flame of coming combat, at some lower level he still felt obscurely troubled. Just before nesting within the foetus that would become Von Stang, he was caught up in a certain ennui. It was tiresome to be so coupled to embodiment. Yes, the instinct-templates in the primate brain made the combat encounters vastly more intense. Long ago, embodied in twelve-limbed creatures in the undersea canyons of a watery planet under triple suns, Adversary and Animus had engaged in almost operatically grand combat, and it had been deeply satisfying—the combination of reproductive ecstasy and brutal rending, the spurting of many torn limbs, the intricacy of leverage and strategy. But it had lacked the white-hot savagery, the violent inventiveness they'd found in the primates of this world—

this "Earth." These primates seemed a bump-up, an increase of intensity, and Adversary and Animus had continued their competition on this planet—so much more than mere games—for countless embodiments, life after life, recording all in sensory nodes for later analysis. *Much* later analysis: they were of a race that commonly lived above half a million Earthly years.

But perhaps they'd remained here too long. Von Stang . . . Animus . . . had felt something drawing him toward empathic overlap with the primate—a repellent overlap, quite unnatural. But a subtle, external nudging pushed him toward it. Psychic dominance? From what quarter?

"Sir, I see movement in the hedgerows . . ." Gromin said.

There, to the north, across a field of mown hay, booted feet could be just made out in narrow openings between the bases of shrubs, at the bottom of the farther hedgerow. *Adversary and his soldiers.* The marchers seemed to be moving toward a gap in the hedgerow in the far corner of the field.

"Men, listen closely . . ." Animus issued his orders and his followers jogged as quietly as possible up the road to the nearer edge of the hedgerow, while "Colonel Von Stang" and Corporal Gromin hurried into the field, along the closer side of the hedgerow, keeping low as they edged toward the gap. Animus was planning to have his men at the road draw fire from Adversary, then return fire as heavily as possible; Adversary would retreat through the opening in the hedgerow, tumbling through helter-skelter, to run carelessly into fire from Gromin and his Colonel.

But Adversary's side took the initiative—they' flattened down and opened fire through the small breaks in the hedgerow, near the roots, bullets cracking close by "Von Stang"—a round cut into Gromin's neck, so that he seemed to twist sideways, dropping his weapon, clutching at his gouting throat as he fell onto the sodden turf.

Too bad, he'd been a useful tool.

Animus fired at a muzzleflash, and sprinted toward the larger opening. He heard gunfire from the road beyond the hedgerow—his men firing at Adversary's soldiers—and a shout from a wounded man.

He came to an old tree stump beside the hedgerow, went to one knee, reloading his rifle, hoping to pick off some of Adversary's followers—perhaps wound Adversary himself, rather than kill him—his heart pounding, blood racing, the delightful energy of low embodiment racing through his nervous system . . .

And then he saw the grenade—one of the new "Mills bombs" the British Army was using, with its segmented surface. Someone had thrown it about thirty feet behind his position, and he was able to shift to cover on the other side of the tree stump.

But instead of falling and exploding short, the grenade stopped in mid-air—and changed direction.

"What! That is not allowed!" he shouted, as, defying physics, the grenade flew right for him.

He turned to run from it—and the grenade changed directions again, followed him . . . and exploded just above him, quite removing his head from his body.

"And I am telling you, I did not interfere with that grenade!" Adversary insisted.

They were within a small concealment sphere about a half mile over the battlefield; it looked like a cloud to the primates, far below.

"You threw the grenade, did you not?" Animus demanded.

"Initially—yes. I did—I threw it to confuse you, and drive you into the open. I knew it was not going to hit you. I did not cause it to change direction! Levitation discomposes my thinking center—and I always bungle it. Perhaps you were mistaken—"

"I am not mistaken," Animus insisted. *"It changed direction in mid-air! If you didn't do it, then who did? I'm not aware of others of our kind competing on this planet. And the primates are not gifted with telekinesis. Who, then?"*

"*I felt a kind of interference,*" said Adversary thoughtfully. *A tugging of mental energy, from somewhere outside, tangling me with the primates. Perhaps a subtle psychic dominance. Who indeed—and why?*"

"*The answer must be in why. Our competition here was cut short. Someone wanted to end our participation in this war.*"

"*Who would want to interfere with us? The primates are unaware of us, and incapable of interfering. Perhaps it's a competition vandal—there are some about, entertaining themselves. If so—they're young, they have a short attention span. The scamp will go away if we wait long enough. There will be other wars.*"

"*This war bears in it the seed of another war, to sprout in the same garden . . . We can nurture those seeds, before nesting in new primates . . .*"

Other wars inevitably came along, but they were sadly inaccessible. Animus and Adversary had to nest in new foetuses for some years while the Chinese Civil War went bloodily on, and a good many other conflicts raged without their participation.

But then came World War Two.

They didn't have to foment World War Two, it had a psychotic life of its own. Still, they fanned its flames where they could, through primate embodiments. The primates were often quite puzzled by their own actions . . .

North Africa

A pale blue sky; a yellow horizon rippling with the noonday heat; a rolling, sandy plain; a scattering of fletchy little trees. All this the young lieutenant saw from the open hatch of the Panzerkampfwagen. He saw, too, the muscular cloud of brown dust rolling like a djinn across the land from the East: the American armor, its cavalry. One division of Eisenhower's army.

The young lieutenant, Otto Meterling, directed his Panzer in the front lines of Rommel's latest attempt at feinting and flanking, but the allies were getting wise to Rommel's methods, and it appeared they were not falling into the trap.

Meterling loved being in the tank. Despite the dryness in his mouth; despite the taste of oil, and the thudding heat flung in his face from the metal around him. He loved the bulk of mechanical armor all about him, a metallic extension of his will, designed to crush enemies and turn their blows aside; he loved its grinding treads, its growling engine.

Gazing out over the desert, Meterling coughed in a swirl of exhaust fumes, and rubbed grit from his eyes. He would need his goggles soon. How he loved it!

But he knew, somehow, that his true battle this day would not be with Eisenhower's mechanical cavalry. It would come from another direction.

Adversary is coming . . . perhaps from the sky. Paratroopers. He is likely a paratrooper.

Adversary . . . coming after Animus.

It had been building all morning; last night there had been strange, vivid dreams of many battles: of Romans in armor coming at him, while he whipped his chariot's horses on in the service of the Pharaoh.

And this morning he'd awakened with the taste of blood in his mouth—someone else's blood. A memory of a fight on the Iberian peninsula, fading even as he opened his eyes. He'd had to kill the man with his teeth, when his sword broke at the hilt. A thousand years earlier.

Just a dream. Or was it a memory, relived?

He watched the sky. Adversary would come from the sky.

There! An American dive-bomber, perhaps a "helldiver", appearing as a rapacious dot against the sky to the northeast, taking shape, wings and fuselage gaining definition as it approached.

Adversary!

Meterling was becoming Animus, his fundamental identity surging up. He laughed joyfully—to the great puzzlement of his frightened, stifled Panzer crew.

So Adversary thinks he has the edge here, coming from the sky! But Animus had prepared—he did not need a direct hit on that plane if he used a flak shell. Now he understood why he'd brought the shells here—these were almost unknown to the panzers. He lowered himself excitedly into the tank, and barked the orders.

"The special shells! Load them! You wanted to know what they're for, you're about to find out, we're soon to be strafed . . ."

He broke off, staring at the rack of shells waiting for the Panzer's cannon. It was difficult to see here, in the cramped, light-stabbed, dusty dimness, but the shells stood out unnaturally.

They were glowing.

They were becoming brighter, brighter . . . glimmering with red, then white light; brighter and brighter, humming within.

"Get out!" he shouted, climbing up through the hatch—but it was too late. Once more, too late.

The shells exploded. The tank was consumed by a hungry fireball. And Meterling with it.

Drifting far over the North African desert . . .

"And again I ask, if it was not you—who was it?"

"I told you, Animus—some competition vandal. A child. Maybe a five-thousandish."

"With those skills? Seems unlikely. I only know I was blown to smithereens before our confrontation could begin. Not to mention my crew."

"Well yes. Not to mention them . . . would be normal." Animus ignored this dig. *"Almost thirty years as that Meterling. The food alone . . . unbearable."*

"You were aware of his eating? You were that much engaged?"

"I know—it is strange . . ."

"Something of the sort happened to me, in my American counterpart," Adversary admitted. *"A feeling of taking part in the man more than I wanted to. I wanted to sleep and there I was, aware of his academy physics class."*

"We'll wait them out. This time we'll return to the Sourceworld and fully restore. But we'll meet back here . . . there is sure to be another war in this part of the world." He gazed down at the desert. "I like this part of the planet. It has such possibilities. And think of the weapons to come!"

Iraq, near the border with Syria, 2008

Another desert; another hot day. A US Army Humvee, armoured, equipped with machine gun, heading for the patrol along the border to try and catch the Haj sneaking across. Al Qaeda, bringing in a new IED design, according to Intel.

Crenshaw, up on the 16 MM machine gun, had only been a Corporal for a few hours. He had been a sergeant before, but he'd run afoul of a Captain, when he'd started emerging as Animus, four days earlier, and somehow, in the time away from this planet he'd lost touch with military protocol. Or perhaps he'd inexplicably let Crenshaw's personal feelings affect him—the white Captain had said something racist; Crenshaw was a black man from Virginia, he was touchy, and Animus had allowed him to react to the "Get your lazy black ass back out there, Sergeant" and he'd told the Captain he was a racist cracker and, soon after, the Captain had "found" unprescribed Oxycontin in his locker on a "surprise inspection." There was a lot of noise lately about addiction to Oxycontin, and other meds, in the infantry. The Captain had accused him of dealing stolen pharms, and demoted him, "Next time, you go to the stockade!"

The son of a bitch was probably providing the shit to a dealer himself—

What am I doing? Why am I still involved in Crenshaw's concerns? I'm going to fight to the death with Adversary, today . . .

And there was Adversary: that assault rifle poking from the low, clay-colored old building fifty yards right of the dusty road. A spurt of fire, and bullets ricocheted from the Humvee.

Crenshaw . . . Animus . . . swung the machinegun around, grinning
to himself, firing back, shouting directions to the driver. But the
machine gun stopped firing—before it had reached the end of its
belt. He looked down . . . and saw the shells were glowing.

16 mm shells, glowing—about to explode in his face.

He climbed frantically out, shouting a warning to the others,
leaping free—not too late, this time. The ammunition exploded
just behind him, bullets and pieces of the Humvee's roof flying,
whirring shrapnel, whining through the air above him as he hit the
ground, rolling.

He was instantly up, and sending a mental message to Adversary,
his primate body shaking as he abandoned it.

Animus let the body fall, switching off the heart as he went.

He hovered broodingly over the corpse in his lightbody, as the
stunned men who'd survived the explosion in the Humvee crawled
out of the wreckage . . .

He flew upward before they saw his lightbody, and extended his
senses. And found the psychic trail, this time, a moment before it
would have dissipated.

Adversary—abandon your host and follow! I've caught the vandal!

Up, up, through a thin, translucent layer of cloud, and another,
up to where the sky became indigo with its rarity—and here they
caught her.

A female of their kind: her light-patterns inverted. They hovered
to either side of her, blocking her escape, and demanded an
explanation.

She emanated a dignified resignation. "*I have tried to be of help
to this species of primates, these many cycles,*" she said. "*War is part
of their condition. But you move them to greater and greater heights of
confrontation. You'll destroy them, in time. You'll push for a final war—
final for them. Not for you. You'll destroy them all.*"

"Oh, and will we?" Adversary said, in radiant outrage. "*And what of
it? They are feeble, stupid, evanescent little animals. There are countless*

such species—most destroy themselves. They themselves wipe out ant colonies. It is much the same."

"Is it?" She emanated disagreement. *"The primates are deeper than you have allowed yourself to see. They have a degree of sentience. I have tried to entangle you with them, so that you feel life as they do. Your self-involvement, your male immaturity prevents it. I've tried other means to discourage you, get you to move on to another world. Now I will go to the Sourceworld Committee—and it will decide."*

"Why put us through that bureaucratic tedium?" Animus asked, flaring angrily. *"The primates are low creatures; they accumulate bits and gimcracks in their dens, like the packrats they try to drive from their attics—that accumulation is the vector of their lives. They scribble a bit, and mark on walls. But they are simple-minded, temporary little things. Lower predators, with little feeling. You are wasting your sympathy on creatures who live so briefly they are gone before you've fully felt your concern!"*

"They have enormous evolutionary potential," she said, glimmering patiently. *"And they are marvelous animals even now, if short-lived. A fascinating species. We cannot allow you to encourage their extinction when we're only now really beginning to study them."*

"You know what she is, Animus?" Adversary said, disgusted. *"She's one of these 'animal rights' types!"*

"So that's it!" Animus said, with a purple displeasure. *"Animal rights! What about my rights? What of the rights of a Conflict Artist to experience Deep Competition? My art, my drama—this is what gives meaning to the lives of these animals, these primates we use, if they have any meaning at all!"*

"We'll let the Committee decide . . ."

Mountains of Western Pakistan, 2023

Sprague was tired of using killflyers. Remote control killing was unsatisfying. The others soldiers didn't seem to mind—they'd been raised on videogames. Sitting in the Army's trailers, controlling the drones with computer interface, was natural to them. The only difference from videogames was that real-life guerrillas died this way.

But Sprague wanted direct confrontation. Face to face. In person. And he'd come out into the mountains to find it.

Confrontation. With Adversary . . .

He climbed out of the hydrogen-cell Humvee, and set out alone across the rocky hillside, laser rifle in hand, the exhilaration building in him, as he came to full emergence . . .

There would be no interference from the female called "Anima" this time. The Committee had compromised. He and Adversary could continue, here, if they didn't use weapons of mass destruction. This was a valuable wildlife habitat, after all.

And the ultimate primate war could yet come—Animus and Adversary could still take part in that. The new rule was, the primates must be allowed to bring it on themselves.

It would be glorious, when it happened. And he was sure it would. The primates could be relied upon.

There —a glint of sunlight from a scope, up the hillside. It was Adversary, laying for him.

Animus had a simple plan. He would drop back, lure him into the valley, and burn away one of Adversary's limbs. But he wouldn't kill him right away. No. He would give him a chance to fight on.

Animus wanted to make this one last.

SKEETER JUNKIE

How consummate, how exquisite: A mosquito.

Look at the thing. No fraction of it wasted or distracted; more streamlined than any fighter jet, more elegant, than any sports car; in that moment, sexier—and skinnier—than any fashion model. A mosquito.

Hector Ansia was happily watching the mosquito penetrate the skin of his right arm.

He was in his El Paso studio apartment, wearing only his threadbare Fruit of the Loom briefs. The autumn night was hot and sticky. The place was empty except for a few books and busted coffee table and sofa, the only things he hadn't been able to sell. But as soon as he'd slammed the heroin, the rat-hole apartment had transformed into a palace bedroom, his dirty sofa into new silk cushions, the heavy, polluted air became the zephyrs of Eden, laced with incense. It wasn't that he hallucinated things that weren't there—what was there recast into a heroin-polished dimension of excellence. The refinery, visible over the El Paso rooftops, was transformed into a Disney castle; its burn-off flames the torches of some charming medieval festival.

He'd just risen out of his nod, like a balloon released under heavy water, ascending from a zone of sweet weight to a place of delicious buoyancy, and he'd only now opened his eyes, and the first thing he saw was the length of his arm over the side of the old velvet sofa. The veins were distended because of the pressure on the underside of his arm, and halfway between his elbow and his hand was the mosquito, pushing its organic needle through the greasy raiment of his epidermis . . .

It was so fine.

He hoped the mosquito could feel the sun of benevolence that pulsed in him. The china white was good, especially because he'd had a long and cruel sickness before finding it, and he'd been maybe halfway to clean again, so his tolerance was down, and that made it so much better to hit the smack in, to fold it into himself.

Stoned, he could feel his Mama's hands on him. He was three years old, and she was washing his back as he sat in a warm bath, and sometimes she would kiss the top of his head. He could feel it now. That's what heroin gave him back.

She hadn't touched him after his fourth birthday, when her new boyfriend had come in fucked up on reds and wine, and the boyfriend had kicked Mama in the head and called her a whore, and the kick broke something in her brain, and after that she just looked at him blank when he cried. Just looked at him.

Heroin took him back, before his fourth birthday. Sometimes all the way back.

Look at that skeeter, now. Made Hector want to fuck, looking at it.

The mosquito was fucking his arm, wasn't it? Sure it was. Working that thing in. A proboscis, what it was called.

He could feel a thudding from somewhere. After a long moment he was sure the thudding wasn't his pulse; it was the radio downstairs. Lulu, listening to the radio.

Lulu had red-blond hair, cut something like the style of English girls from the old Beatles movies, its points near her cheeks curled to aim at her full lips. She had wide hips and round arms and hazel eyes. He'd talked to her in the hall and she'd been kind of pityingly friendly, enough to pass the time for maybe a minute, but she wouldn't go out with him, or even come in for coffee. Because she knew he was a junkie. Everyone on Selby Avenue knew a junkie when they saw them. He could tell her about his Liberal Arts B.A., but it wouldn't matter: he'd still be just a junkie to her. No use trying to explain, a degree didn't get you a life anymore, there wasn't any work anyway.

You might as well draw your SSI and sell your food stamps; you might as well be a junkie.

Lulu probably figured if she got involved with Hector, he'd steal her money, and maybe give her AIDS. She was wrong about the AIDS—he never ever shared needles—but she was right he'd steal her money, of course. The only reason he hadn't broken into her place was because he knew she'd never leave any cash there, or anything valuable, not living downstairs from a junkie. He'd never get even a ten dollar bag out of that crappy little radio he'd seen through the open door. Nothing much in there. Posters of Chagall, a framed photo of Sting, succulents overflowing clay pots shaped like burros and turtles.

She was succulent; he wanted her almost as much as her paycheck.

He watched the mosquito.

If he lifted his arm up, would the mosquito stop drinking? He hoped not. He could feel a faint ghost of a pinch, a sensation he saw in his mind's eye as a rose bud opening, and opening, and opening, more than any rose ever had petals.

Careful. He swung his feet on the floor, without moving his arm. The mosquito didn't stir. Then he lifted the arm up, very, very slowly, inch by inch, so as not to disturb the mosquito. It kept right on drinking.

With exquisite languor, Hector stood up straight, keeping the arm motionless except for the slow, slow act of standing. Then—walking very carefully, because the dope made the floor feel like a trampoline— he went to the bookshelf. Easing his right hand onto the edge of a shelf to keep the arm steady, he ran his left over the dusty tops of the old encyclopedia set. He was glad no one had bought it, now.

The lettering on the book-backs oozed one word onto the next. He was pretty loaded. It was good stuff. He forced his eyes to focus, and then pulled the M book out.

Moving just as slowly, his right arm ramrod stiff, so as not to disturb his beloved—the communion pinch, his precious guest—he returned

to the sofa. He sat down, his right arm propped on the arm of the
sofa, his left hand riffling pages.

Mosquito . . .

(There was another shot ready on the coffee table. Not yet, *pendajo*.
Make it last).

*. . . the female mosquito punctures the skin with equipment contained
in a proboscis, comprised of six elongated stylets. One stylet is an inverted
trough; the rest are slender mandibles, maxillae, and a stylet for the
injection of mosquito saliva. These latter close the trough to make a rough
tube. After insertion, the tube arches so that the tip can probe for blood
about half a millimeter beneath the epidermal surface . . . Two of the
stylets are serrated and saw through the tissue for the others. If a pool of
blood forms in a pocket of laceration the mosquito ceases movement and
sucks the blood with two pumps located in her head . . .*

*Mosquito saliva injected while probing prevents blood clotting and creates
the itching and swelling accompanying a bite . . .*

Hector soaked up a pool of words here, a puddle there, and the
color pictures—how wonderfully they put together encyclopedias!—
and then he let the volume slide off his lap onto the floor, and found
the other syringe with his left hand, and, hardly having to look, with
the ambidexterity of a needle freak, shot himself up in a vein he was
saving in his right thigh. All the time not disturbing the mosquito.

He knew it was too big a load. But he'd had that long, long jones,
like mirrors reflecting into one another. It should be all right. He
stretched out on the sofa again as the hit melted through him, and
focused on the mosquito.

Hector's eyelids slid almost shut. But that worked like adjusting
binoculars. Making the mosquito come in closer, sharper. It was like
he was seeing it under a microscope now. Like he was standing—
no, floating—floating in front of the mosquito and he was smaller
than it was, like a man standing by an oil derrick, watching it pump
oil up from the deep places, the zone of sweet weight . . . thirty-
weight, ha . . . An *Anopheles Gambia*, this variety—same as the one

in the encyclopedia thumbnail. From this magnified perspective the mosquito's parts were rougher than they appeared from the human level—there were bristles on her head, slicked back like stubby oiled hair, and he could see that the sheath-like covering of the proboscis had fallen in a loop away from the stylets . . . her tapered golden body, resting on the long, translucent, frail-looking legs, cantilevered forward to drink, as if in obeisance . . . her rear lifted, a forty degree angle from the skin, its see-through abdomen glowing red with blood like a little Christmas light . . .

   . . . *it is the female which bites, her abdomen distends enormously, allowing her to take in as much as four times her weight in blood* . . .

He had an intimate relationship with this mosquito. It was entering him. He could feel her tiny, honed mind, like one of those minute paintings obsessed hobbyists put on the head of a pin. He sensed her regard. The mosquito was dimly aware of his own mind hovering over her. He could close in on the tiny gleam of her insect mind and replace it with his own. What a rare and elegant nod that would be: getting into her head so he could feel what it was like to drink his own blood through the slender proboscis . . .

He could do it. He could superimpose himself and fold his own consciousness up into the micro-cellular spaces. Any mind, large or small, could be concentrated in microscopic space; micro-space was as infinite as interstellar space, wasn't it? God experienced every being's consciousness. God's mind could fit into a mosquito. Like all that music on a symphony going through the needle of a record player, or through the tiny laser of a CD. The stylet in the mosquito's proboscis was like the needle of a record player . . .

Hector could circle, and close in, and participate, and become. He could . . .

   . . . see the rising fleshtone of his own arm stretching out in front of him, a soft ridge of topography. He could see the glazed eyes of the man he was drinking from. Himself; perhaps formerly. It was a wonderfully malevolent miracle: he was inside the mosquito. He was the mosquito, its senses altered and enhanced by his own more-evolved prescience.

His blood was a syrup. The mosquito didn't taste it, as such, but Hector could—and there were many confluent tastes in it, mineral and meat and electrically charged waters and honeyed glucose and acids and hemoglobin. And very faintly, heroin. His eggs would be well sustained—

Her eggs. Keep your identity sorted out. Better yet, set your own firmly atop hers. Take control.

Stop drinking blood!

More.

No. Insist, Hector. Who's in charge, here? Stop drinking and fly. Just imagine! To take flight—

Almost before the retraction of her proboscis was completed, he was in the air, making the wings work without having to think about it. When he tried too hard to control the flight, he foundered; so he simply flew.

His flight path was a herky-jerky spiral, each geometric section of it a portion of an equation.

His senses expanded to adjust to the scope of his new possibilities of movement: the great cavern, the massive organism at the bottom of it: himself, Hector's human body, left behind.

Hector sensed a temperature change, a nudge of air: a current from the crack in the window. He pushed himself up the stream, increasing his wing energy, and thought: *I'll crash on the edges of the glass, it's a small crack . . .*

But he let the insect's navigational instincts hold sway, and he was through, and out into the night.

He could go anywhere, anywhere at all . . .

He went downstairs.

Her window was open.

x   x   x

From a distance, the landscape of Lulu was glorious, lying there on the couch in her bikini underpants, and nothing else. Her exposed breasts were great slack mounds of cream and cherry. Her pale skin was glossy with sweat. She'd fallen asleep with the radio on; there were three empty cans of beer on the little end table by her head. One of her legs was drawn up, tilted to lean its knee against the wall, the other out straight, the limbs apart enough to trace her open labia against the blue silk panties.

Hector circled near the ceiling. The radio was a distorted boom of taffied words and industrial-sized beat, far away. He thought that, just faintly, he could actually feel radio and TV waves washing over him, passing through the air.

He wanted Lulu. But suppose she felt him, suppose she heard the whine of his coming, and woke up enough to slap him in reflex, and crushed him—

Would he die when the mosquito died?

Maybe that would be all right.

Hector descended to her, following the broken geometries of insect flight-path down, an aerialist's unseen staircase, asymmetrical and yet perfect.

Closer—he could feel her heat. God, she was like a lake of fire!

He entered her atmosphere. That's how it seemed: she was almost planetary in her glowing vastness, hothouse and fulsome. The hot night had made her even more tropical. He descended through hormone-rich layers of her atmosphere, to deeper and more personal heats, until he'd settled on the skin of her left leg, near the knee.

Jesus! It was revolting: it was ordinary human skin.

But up this close, it was a cratered landscape, orange and gold and in places leprous-white, flakes of blue where dead skin cells were shedding away. Pools of sweat, here and there, looked like molten wax. As he watched, sweat brimmed from a puckered pore. Around the bases of the occasional stiff stalks of hair were puddly masses of pasty stuff he guessed were colonies of bacteria. The skin itself was textured like pillows of meat all sewn together. The smells off it were overwhelming: rot and uric acid and the various compounds in sweat and a chemical smell of something she'd bathed with—and an exudation of the food she'd been eating . . .

Hector was an experienced hand with drugs; he shifted his viewpoint from revulsion to obsession, to delight in the yeasty completeness of this immersion in the biological essence of her. And there was another smell that came to him then, affecting him the way the sight of a woman's cleavage had, in his boyhood. Blood.

Unthinking, he had already allowed the mosquito to unsheath her stylets and drive them into a damp pillow of skin cells. He pushed, rooted, moving the slightly arched piercer in a motion that outlined a cone, breaking tiny capillaries just inside the epidermis, making a pocket for the blood to pool in. And injecting the anti-coagulant saliva.

Her blood was much like his, but he could taste the femaleness of it, the hormonal signature and . . . alcohol.

She swatted at him, in her sleep. He felt the wind of the giant hand, before it struck. Her hand wasn't rigid enough to hit him; the palm was slightly cupped. But the hand covered Hector like a lid, for a moment.

The air pressure flattened the mosquito, and Hector feared for its spindly legs, but then light flashed over him again and the lid lifted, and he withdrew and flew, wings whining, up a short distance into the air . . .

She hadn't awakened. And from up here her thighs looked so sweet and tender . . .

He dipped down, and alighted on Lulu's left inside thigh, not far from the pale blue circus tent billow of her panties. The material was only a little stained; he could see the tracery of her labia like the shadows of sleeping dragons under a silk canopy. The thigh skin was a little smoother, paler. He could see the woods of pubic hair down the slope a little.

Enough. Outside.
No. He was in control. He was going to get closer . . .

When at last he reached the frontier of Lulu's panties, and stood
between two outlying spring-shaped stalks of red-brown pubic hair,
gazing under a wrinkle in the elastic at the monumental vertical
furrow of her vaginal lips, he was paralyzed by fear. This was a great
temple to some sub-aquatic monster, and would surely punish any
intrusion.

With the fear came a sudden perception of his own relative tininess,
now, and an unbottling of his resentments. She was forbidden; she
was gargantuan in both size and arrogance.

But he had learned that he was the master of his reality: he had
found a hatch in his brain, and a set of new controls that fit naturally
to his grip, and he could remake his being as he chose.

A sudden darkness, then; a wind—

He sprang up, narrowly escaping the swat—the wind of her hand,
the slap on her thigh. Then a murky roaring, a boulder-fall of
misshapen words. The goddess coming awake; the goddess speaking.
Something like, *"Fucking skeeter . . . get the fuck out . . ."*
Oh, yes?
The fury swelled in him, and as it grew—Lulu shrank. Or seemed
to, as rage pushed his boundaries outward like hot air in a parade
balloon, but unthinkably fast. She shrank to woman size, once more
in perspective and once more desirable.
She screamed, of course.
He glimpsed them both in her vanity mirror . . .
A man-sized mosquito, poised over her, holding her down with
slender but strong front legs; Lulu screaming, thrashing, as he leaned
back onto his hind legs and spread her legs with the middle limbs . . .
In her delighted revulsion, she struck at the mosquito's compound
eyes. The pain was realer and more personal than he'd expected. He

jerked back, withdrawing, floundering off the edge of the bed, feeling
a leg shatter against the floor and a wing crack, one of his eyes half
blind . . .

The pain and the disorientation unmanned him. Emasculated him,
intimidated him. As always when that happened, he shrank.

The boundaries of the room expanded and the bed grew, around
him, into a dirty white plain; Lulu grew, again becoming a small
world to herself . . . Her hand sliced down at him—

He threw himself frantically into the air, his damaged wings
ascending stochastically; the wings' keening sound not quite right
now, his trajectory uncertain.

The ceiling loomed; the window crack beckoned.

In seconds he had swum upstream against the night air, and managed
to aim himself between the edges of the crack in the glass; the lips of
the break like a crystalline take on her vagina. Then he was out into
the night, and regaining some greater control over his wings . . .

That's not how it was, he realized: she, *the mosquito* had control.
That's how they'd gotten through the crack and out into the night.

Let the mosquito mind take control, for now, while he rested his
psyche and pondered. That great yellow egg, green around the edges
with refinery toxins, must be the moon; this jumble of what seemed
skyscraper-sized structures must be the pipes and chimneys and
discarded tar buckets of the apartment building's roof.

Something washed over him, rebounding, making him shudder in
the air. Only after it departed did it register in his hearing: a single
high note, from somewhere above.

There, it came again, more defined and pulsingly closer, as if
growing in an alien certainty about its purpose.

The mosquito redoubled its wing beats in reaction, and there was
an urgency that was too neurologically primitive to be actual fear.
Enemy. Go.

Hector circled down between the old brick apartment buildings,
toward the streetlight . . .

Another, slightly higher, even more purposeful note hit Hector, resonating him, and then a shadow draped him, and wing beats thudded tympanically on the air. He saw the bat for one snapshot-clear moment, superimposed against the dirty indigo sky. Hector knew he should detach from the mosquito, but the outspread wings of the bat, its pointed ears and wet snout, fascinated him with its heraldic perfection—it was as perfect, poised against the sky, as the mosquito had seemed, poised on his arm.

Sending out a final sonar note to pinpoint the mosquito, the bat struck its head forward—

When Lulu woke, she had cramps. But it was the aftertaste of the dream that bothered her. There was a taintedness lingering in her skin, as if the nightmare of the giant mosquito had left a sort of mephitic insect pheromone on her. She took two showers, and ate her breakfast, and listened to the radio. By comforting degrees, she forgot about the dream. When she went downstairs the building manager was letting the ambulance attendants in. They were in a hurry. It was the guy upstairs, the manager said. He was dead.

No one was surprised. He was a junkie. Everybody knew that.

Next day Lulu was scratching the skeeter bites, whenever she thought no one was looking.

TIGHTER

It occurred to Janet that one notch tighter would kill him.

They were in Bedroom One, stark naked, her and Harry, the trick she was straddling—and strangling. Bedroom One even had the *1* on the door of the two-bedroom apartment that her and Prissy rented on West 12th, just off Broadway in Manhattan. It was a working crib—Janet and her partner, Prissy, didn't live here—so it was pretty minimal. In each bedroom was a queen-sized bed, with a mirror headboard, red satin sheets, no blankets; a blue carpet that they vacuumed every day, a dial-control light turned low, the radio on the floor. The tricks only cared about clean sheets, and things not smelling bad; also they wanted no used condoms lying around, and the girls needed to keep themselves pretty fresh. The tricks cared about that, and they cared about not being here during a raid.

Harry, the big-money trick, was about fifty. The mat of black hair on his flat chest going white at the roots, like the oily, swept-back hair on his head. He had a bulbous belly, powerful short legs, long arms; on one wrist a fading tattoo of two dice rolled to snake eyes. He wore thick glasses, even while they were doing it—so he could see her sitting on him naked, he said. See it clear. The coke-bottle glasses made his eyes seem like big glossy-brown blobs; the glasses usually got steamed up, after a while. *You're so full of shit your glasses are steaming up.* He had a long narrow nose, with little black hairs growing out of it; same kind of hair in his ears. She was straddling him and she was strangling him, and that's what he'd paid her to do. Erotic strangulation. She was supposed to tighten the narrow black leather strap, crossed in an unfinished knot, until he came near to blacking out; and then she was supposed to loosen it so he could breathe, gulp big draughts of life, she pumping up and down on his thing while he was sucking in the air. His thing had a metal cock-ring around the base of it, keeping the blood in, almost like it was being strangled too. He paid her triple rate for this, something kinky and risky. Three-hundred-sixty a session. "Just try saying no to that," she'd told Prissy.

They were a good team. Prissy was the blond, you needed a blond, and Janet was the brunette, her hair cut like Betty Page. With the bangs and all. She was half Puerto Rican and half Russian, which was all she knew about her parents.

"I would and I fucking *could* say no," Prissy said, when they'd sat around the living room of the crib eating Mu Shu Pork and Szechuan Beef from cartons. "If the guy gets a heart attack or something . . . Sure I'd say no to that. I could be fucking prosecuted."

"Try saying no to three hundred dollar tips."

"Yeah well that paper bag he takes the money out of—you know who's money *that* is. Just keep that in mind . . ."

Janet had seven thousand dollars put away in her money market account. If she got another thirteen grand or so, she would get matching funds from the Small Business Administration, open her own business. Hair cutting and nails parlor. Her own nails were an inch and a half long, beginning to curl, and they had cat-eyes in sequins on them. They were really gorgeously lacquered and shaped, sweetly done. She and Prissy did each other's nails after work.

Harry was thrashing under her. He still didn't give the signal.

She didn't take drugs anymore. She saved her money so she could get out of the crib. She didn't like the business now, though some of the guys were pretty nice; she'd never more than sort-of liked this business anyway. Where could it take you? She wanted to be going somewhere. And who was going to marry her, except some pimp asshole, and she hated pimps, fucking hated them, especially the ones who claimed they weren't pimps. And she *did* want to get married, and not to a loser like her last boyfriend. She wanted to have kids: she'd made up her mind on that when she'd turned twenty-nine. Pretty soon she'd be thirty . . .

It was this guy Harry's job to collect money from bookies in the area, for the Pasta Potentates, and Harry always just stuffed the money in a paper bag. Harry said if he put it in a briefcase or even a duffel it'd look like he was carrying money. He was skimming, though, she knew that, because that was where the tips came from, right from that paper bag. He was skimming from That Thing Of Theirs, and one of these days, if he didn't die right here playing "strangle", the mob would kill him anyway.

If she tightened it another notch, and just held on, she could take the money in that paper bag. It was something to consider. The guy was headed for an early grave any way you looked at it. They'd kill him sure, for dipping into the collections. And she was pretty sure he was careful to let no one know he came here. He was married, for one thing; for another, if you stop at a whorehouse after collecting the mob's money, they'll figure you're spending their money on that whore. Stands to reason.

She was still choking him. And he was clutching the side of the bed, his knuckles white, his fingers clenching on the fabric; loosening a little; clenching. His face was swollen, patchy-red. He was making noises like that rabbit had made . . .

She'd been a little girl, about ten. Her adoptive aunt had brought her a rabbit for Easter, the French kind with the floppy ears. One time she caught it humping her stuffed toys. It'd made hissing sounds, which sounded weird coming from a rabbit, as it humped her teddy bear, and she'd slapped it away from the bear in sheer disgust and it responded to that by jumping onto her hand, clamping onto her wrist, the way a dog will clamp onto your leg—and the rabbit *began to fuck her hand,* it was a little fuck-animal now, hissing and chugging away, and not a rabbit anymore, and it was fucking her hand with its little wet pencilly thing, those snaky sounds getting louder as she tried to claw it away from her, and then it . . . Prissy hadn't believed it when she'd told this to her, but it was true . . . it *came* in her palm, wet warm gunk splashing down her wrist and she'd screamed and flung the rabbit away so it smacked against the wall over her bed and it's neck broke and it died. She burst into tears and Amy her adoptive mom came in and found her with a dead rabbit on the bed and cum on her hands and she decided in her twisted red-haired head that Janet had deliberately *jacked off the rabbit and killed it* . . .

(Harry's eyes were going pinpoint, his tongue was sticking out).

The radio was playing the "Sounds of Silence" by Simon and Garfunkel. Hello darkness, my old friend. It sounded like Paul Simon was singing from under the bed. *Are you under there, Paul?*

Harry, the trick, was convulsing, but he hadn't given the loosen signal. If he failed to give it to her and he got all blue, she was supposed to stop on her own. His thing thrashed inside her, not big enough to fill her, or any woman; it was almost like a clapper in a bell.

Ding dong, Harry, ding dong, she thought.

He was changing colors . . .

Janet heard a guy moan from Room Two. That albino Jediah, that Prissy did. *He's pretty weird, but he's not as weird as Strangle-Me Harry, and Jediah pays cold cash in advance*, was all she'd say about him. Prissy got him to orgasm in just about twelve minutes. Generally, payment was for one hour, or to orgasm—and the tricks always had the orgasm before fifteen minutes or so, except really old guys. And a lot of the old guys were just as happy to spend half the time talking and playing with a girl's tits, which was easy work.

Her and Prissy, what a team. Prissy'd paid her home phone bill, once, without telling her, when she'd had that infection and couldn't work for a month. "I could have taken it out of my savings," she'd told Prissy, when she'd figured it out.

"Don't you ever touch those savings, Janet, you dumb bunny," Prissy said. If she liked you, she called you dumb bunny.

He was making that hiss as he fucked at her (you couldn't call it fucking, it was more like fucking *at*), hissing with the itty bitty increments of air he could get . . . less and less air.

An unfamiliar feeling came over her as she looked at him, then; as she looked at her hands, aching but not really tired, and her strong forearms: she worked out. And her strong thighs straddling him, pinioning him.

She didn't feel like she was serving him, any more, in that moment. Janet felt a kind of current in her, a hot good current, and it gave her the feeling of *being in control* and it was something she hadn't felt quite like that before.

I mean, *in a way*, Janet thought, you were *always* in control of tricks, if you knew what you were doing. You had strict rules, you led them around by the dick in a way; you made them take a shower first— you were polite about it, but you insisted—and you made them state categorically they are not undercover police, no entrapment please, and most of all you made them ejaculate in under the time they had paid for so you could get rid of them and bring in the next guy or take a break if you didn't have another guy right then. Breaks were important.

He was turning seriously blue now.

Well. Let's think about this. There might be as much as $20,000 in that paper bag of his.

That Thing of Theirs, the Pasta Potentates, they wouldn't know where he was. Prissy would get her back on this, and the two of them could wait till two in the morning, dress his body, take him up to the roof, carry his body over two or three building roofs, drop him into the alley, make it look like he was robbed there.

He was shaking, really shaking now, his glasses half flopped off—he was making the sign to stop strangling him. So she had to decide— had to decide right now—

She stood a good chance of getting away with it, if she did it right. (He was making the sign more urgently). But then, she'd have to live with it. Because wherever you go, hey, there you are.

That was really not too easy for Janet to imagine, living with something like that . . .

With strangling this ugly bastard to death. Just the memory of it. Nasty. The two of them naked and sweating, the blueness spreading down to his fingertips . . .

But there *was* that good feeling—that sensation in her arms, her whole body. All of her connected together in one big purpose. Sweat running down her tits to tremble on the nipples with as he thrashed under her . . .

Harry was clutching at her wrists now. She'd never killed anyone before—was she really going to do it now? She hadn't felt it was genuinely in her to really go through with killing, though, except in self-defense. But now Janet felt she could do it. She wasn't sure if she would do it—but—

She realized that yeah—she *could do it*.

She really was capable of killing him. It was amazing to her. Her hands trembled, pulling the taut cords tighter.

If she didn't let him go right away, and if she didn't have the nerve to go through with it, he'd know she had thought about killing him, and who knew what he'd do? He had always been kind of sweet, really, never a hint of being violent toward her, and he'd sounded sort of pathetic and sad when he'd told her that his mother had punished him by sitting on him and strangling him. Claimed it was the only kind of embrace he'd ever got from his mom. I mean, you hear something like that, you feel like you're a step too far into somebody's life, and like it or not you feel what they feel a little, if you can feel anything at all. Maybe because it was something that had happened when he was a kid.

And if you thought of him *as a kid* it was harder to hold him at a distance. Harder to kill him.

But it was almost done. One notch tighter. Tighter. Just a little. Then it'd be all over.

Paul Simon was just finishing singing the "Sounds of Silence."

Harry had a look in his eyes like he was fighting his own ecstasy . . .
Like he was only half resisting . . .

Janet could almost see the specks in front of his eyes that he must
be seeing, the pretty starbursts . . .

He wasn't fighting all that hard. See there? Part of him wanted it.
Wanted her to go all the way. It might be the ultimate high for him,
dying this way, like that guy in the band *INXS* (and what a waste *that*
had been compared to this jerk-wad Harry), like David Carradine—a
legendary way to go, and Harry was digging it: even as he thrashed
under her, his dick was ding-donging in her, and Janet thought she
felt his semen squirt—she felt it in his dick's spasm, not through the
condom—and in her mind what she saw jetting was blood and not
sperm, he was ejaculating blood as she strangled him—the straps almost
cutting into his throat, making the veins on his neck stand out purple.

Wanting it: Janet could see it in his eyes. Okay maybe not
completely wanting it—but hell, if *deep down* he wanted it, well
then, that was something she could live with. And eventually she'd
learn to put it out of her mind no matter what.

He was flapping at her with his hands, weakly, now, and there was
something babyish about the motion, and that thought brought an
image to her mind . . .

She tried not to see it, but an image of this jerk-wad as a small boy,
being choked by his mother, came into her mind's eye, and Janet's
will stammered and her hands relaxed a little—and he thrashed like
a bronco and threw her off him.

Janet fell onto her side, off the bed, and he clawed the straps away
from his throat. They'd dug in and left deep red marks. Encircling
rings of purple were forming. He choked and sputtered, "You bitch,
you fucking bitch," at least that's what she thought he was saying, it
was hard to make it out. "You failed, you stopped." That she heard
clearly, though it came out in a squeak, and she stared at him in
surprise, thinking she ought to yell for Prissy but feeling disoriented,
stumbling on some inner ledge.

"You failed, bitch," he said and lunged at her, throwing himself down onto her, the strap now wound around his right hand, his left pinning her to the floor by her throat, banging her head on the wood under the carpet. She tried to yell but he'd cut off her wind, his arm straight, his strong hand and the weight of his upper body squeezing her throat. She flailed her legs, trying to bang the radio or something, make enough noise to summon help. Couldn't hit anything but the floor with thumps that just weren't very loud.

Harry was still coughing and choking as he tried to choke her air out, and he was drooling a little, blood mixed with drool dripping on her face as he squeezed her some and then squeezed harder.

Maybe it would be enough for him to punish her, and he'd let her go . . .

But as if in answer to that thought, he pressed harder.

By now Prissy was across the apartment in the living room, watching TV while she waited for her next appointment, and even if she did hear the thumping she'd ignore it because they always thrashed and banged in here, during Harry's appointment, it was part of Harry's thing to thrash around and there was always some noise. Prissy wouldn't be coming to save her.

You're going to have to survive this on your own, girl.

Janet rallied all her strength and whiplashed her body—and he lost his grip and rocked back, flailing for balance. She lurched and twisted left, so he fell from her, and she scrambled to her feet and grabbed the leather strap and twisted it around his neck from the side, while he was in profile to her—trying to get his balance—and she tightened, and tried to yell for Prissy, but her throat was still tight and gummy and wouldn't make more than a squeak.

The two of them were on their knees, she was facing him but turned partly to one side, and he tried to slug at her but couldn't hit her directly at this angle. She'd gotten the straps in the ruts in his neck that she'd made earlier and with just another notch tighter she could—

He jabbed an elbow hard into her gut just below her ribcage, and all the air burst from her mouth like from a gashed bicycle tire, and her grip loosened and he wrenched free and slugged her in the side of the face, and she fell over, still not able to make a sound. Then he twisted the strap—*the strap!*—around her neck again and she could feel the taut, concentrated finality of the grip as he tightened it. He was taking no chances, he was focused this time.

She tried to kick but she had no air in her at all after having it knocked out of her and she was already dizzy and weak. Stars burst in front of her eyes, prickles in her hands and feet, paths of prickling nothingness traveled from her extremities to meet in her heart. His glasses were hanging from one ear and she saw his gaping face, white and blotchy red, filling her vision, and she *thought oh no, it's the last thing I'll ever see, oh no, falling into eternity with his fucking ugly pan* . . . She tried to claw at his face but her hands were like the hands of blow-up sex dolls, soft clubs without strength.

The darkness closed in like a tightening circle, the dark circle tightening, getting smaller and smaller, making her smaller inside it. She was almost entirely blind—the last thing she'd see would be the sparkles, the flashes, and not his face . . . She heard a man's voice on a radio commercial saying, "WE'VE GOT FIVE HUNDRED, RIGHT THAT'S FIVE HUNDRED GUITARS TO GET RID OF, GREAT BRAND NAME GUITARS AT THE JERSEY CITY GUITARLAND DISCOUNT CENTER! WE'VE GOT AMPS, WE'VE GOT DRUMS, WE'VE GOT EVERYTHING YOU NEED TO WALK IT INSTEAD OF TALK IT! THIS IS ONE CHANCE AND ONE CHANCE ONLY CAUSE THERE'LL NEVER BE A SALE LIKE THIS ONE . . ." The voice was getting smaller. "At Guitarland in Jersey City . . . take the . . . expressway to . . . exit to . . . but . . . now because . . . again . . . not again . . ." The radio was gone. White noise took its place. Something was about to pop . . .

Then there was a roaring in her ears and air burst painfully into her lungs and there was a fluttering in the darkness and the fluttering became light and shapes. She could see again.

She saw Prissy standing over Harry, who was on his knees, digging
with weakening fingers at the radio cord she was tightening around
his neck. Prissy worked out too, and her muscular forearms trembled
but held on firm, and she'd got the strap in the same ruts and there
was blood brimming dark red from his mouth and he almost smiled
but couldn't . . .

His arms flailed, flailed . . . and then he died all of a sudden, just
going limp, and it wasn't faking either, it was so real, you could just
see the life fly out of him. Maybe something had burst in his brain.

Prissy let him drop and kicked him once, not very hard.

"Asshole." She was breathing hard but seemed calm. "Janet? You
okay, ya dumb bunny?"

She came over to help Janet stand. Janet could only croak the
words out, but at least she could breathe. "I'm . . . okay. Be all right."

"'Kay." Prissy was looking around for something. She found the
brown paper bag jammed into one sleeve of Harry's coat. She pulled
it out, dumped the money on the bed. It was a lot of money.

"Well, all right. We open a business. I'll do the hair, you do the
nails. Or we'll just hire people. What you want to do with his body?"

TEN THINGS TO BE GRATEFUL FOR

In this fickle world . . .

In this coy and cloying and catastrophic world . . .

In this, the best—can it be true?—of all possible worlds . . .

One must butter one's bread on the sunny side of the street. One must keep a stiff lower grip. One must . . .

One must remember: there are things to be thankful for. We have so much to be grateful, to be thankful for.

Here are ten things to be thankful for.

Be thankful that you are not strolling through a park on a pretty spring day, minding your own mind, and thinking about which electives to take, or whether or not to call the corporate head-hunter back, when you find that you have to pee, you have to pee badly and there's nowhere to go within a quarter mile, and it's a big park, a bushy park, and you've taken that liberty in the park's bushes before, and you enjoy the occasional outdoors pee, so you step off the path and pee off an embankment, through some ferns, watching the fronds bob with the impact of the stream, and you finish and turn and see two meth-heads standing there blocking your way and they tell you that you've just peed on their home, their mattresses, because there's a tweaker encampment under the embankment, and you whine that you hadn't seen anything down there, but it's no good and you try to feint to the left and dart to the right but they are used to people trying to dodge past, and one of them grabs you and so does his smell, the smell of a whole jail-cell of people in one man, and you can see the lice squirm in his beard an inch from your face as he bear-hugs you, and you can look into his eyes, one of them skyblue and the other the color of phlegm; and the second guy who's lean and blue with tattoos from the waist up, he kicks you at the base of the spine again and again and a third and fourth time as you try to scream but the bear-hugger stuffs his beard in your mouth, with a strangely high-pitched giggle, as you struggle, amazed not at his strength but at your own feebleness, and the tattooed one gives you another stiff and practiced steel-toed kick; you hear the meaningful crack of your spine, feel pain like a picture of jagged radiating three-dimensional arrows made of rusty iron, pain with weight, and the bearded one falls on you as you crumple and there's more cracking and crackling as you hit the hard ground of the ravine's lip and your head is hanging over the edge of the embankment, and the other guy grabs onto your neck and jumps off into the ravine, and that feeling is like a spin-painting with the colors black and green, and your vertebrae part ways as he swings from your head and neck as the other guy, drooling with laughter, holds onto your ankles and the vertebrae pull farther apart and you remember when you were in kindergarten you drew a picture of a bear jumping over a fence only no one could make out what it was you'd drawn. Now other tramps come laughing, hooting, to swing, down below, on your head and neck and the vertebrae part completely and when they get bored they kick your body like a bean bag amazed that you're still alive, but you're not alive for long. Be grateful that isn't happening to you.

It could be. It's not. Be thankful.

Be grateful that you're not a child who's sold by his parents to a Bangkok child-brothel—be glad you're not amazed that your mother kissed you goodbye as if you were going to visit a relative, as if you would see her again, and you thought that they would take the money from the man and then tell you to run away with them but they don't even look back as you are led weeping, the weeping bone-dry, up the creaking wooden stairs in the narrow alley in back of the building, a squeezed building that would fall over but for the buildings on either side, and then they beat you the first time just to introduce you to beatings and to initiate you into the magnitude of your subservience but really it's a halfhearted beating compared to the second time when you refused to let the fat American fuck you in the ass while his friend, a tall skinny man who coos at you in an undertone as if convincing himself he's being tender, shoves a stubby thick member in your mouth and makes circular motions with his hips and, though you stomached that, when you felt the penetration from behind you wrenched free and ran to hide under the bed and wouldn't come out till Kimaritchul, squat and strong, flipped the bed to one side and—with a strangely anomalous look of patience in his eyes, like a trainer disciplining a horse—begins kicking you in the soft parts, very expertly, so as not to break anything but so as to introduce deep, deep bruises that hurt with your every movement all night long, each stab of pain speaking with Kimaritchul's unspoken voice, as you let the two men do what they wanted with you, after the skinny one had made noises as if he disapproved of what the guard had done to you, and then went on to fuck you till you choked and lost consciousness, but unfortunately didn't die, not until two years later when your kidney ruptures and they throw you in the canal. That's something to be grateful for: that, after all, is not happening to you.

Be grateful that you're not recovering from your third diabetes amputation, leaving you only your left arm, while the nurses, especially the one with the harelip and the dyed-blond with the long neck and slumped shoulders, give you filing looks. They're mentally filing you as human detritus that hasn't been picked up yet, as hopeless and meaningless and simply a bothersome fulfillment of duty, that duty dwindling, on no one's instructions, day by day, as if by clinical planning, the kindly remarks and encouragements and inquiries falling off to almost none, the eye contact vanishing entirely, the visits from the doctor also down to once a week, then once every ten days, the food which, after all, you can feed to yourself if they'd bring it, since you have one limb, even if you can't reach every part of yourself for a sponging without falling off the bed, the nurse outraged when you try to tell the doctor she's forgot your insulin, the coma creeping up on you just as you smell the decay growing in your remaining limb . . . Something to be thankful for: that isn't happening to you . . .

Thank your particular deities that you are not completely convinced, utterly convinced, granite-pillar and steel-brace convinced, that there is a large parasite growing in your intestines, a parasite that is a mutated variant on a tapeworm, but stubbier and thicker and intelligent, a wormish thing with jaw parts like human fingers only translucent, rubbery, capable of grasping, and it's pushed its grip through the tissues of your intestines to grab some inner organ, sometimes your liver, sometimes your spleen, lately you suspect it's moved on to squeezing your bladder shut because you can't urinate, and your ankles are swelling and somehow this pleases it, and you can even hear it at times, as it can take words from your mind to give them back to you, to persuade you not to fight it, whispering: *There are many parasites within all people, as everyone knows, flora the doctors call them, microorganisms, and there are mites living in your eyebrows, and they eat dead skin and the fellows in your intestines help released trapped electrolytes from food and think of me as just another step, another kind of benign parasite, for if you relax and let me move freely I'll love you, I'll push in and out of you, and I'll reach out of your ass to caress your genitals, but only if you're quite still and trusting, you must surrender completely, and you must not scream when you see me . . .* It whispers such things to you, but you're contemptuous of its sluggish efforts at persuasion, it is a thing of the lower orders and cannot persuade like a TV commercial can, and it cannot be trusted, and as the doctors are in denial, out of sheer ineffable horror, refusing to acknowledge the presence of the thing, you must of course cut yourself open, numbing the agony with what over-the-counter topical anesthetic you can manage, and fight your own arm which tries not to cut any further as you penetrate to the layer of membrane over the intestines, but which you, in the unshakeable determination of your absolute will, overcome, triumphing as, lying in the bathtub naked and trying to staunch the blood with towels with your free hand, you cut with shaking fingers a long jagged rent in the large intestine, along for a full fourteen inches, and lay the intestine open, and find that the parasite . . . is gone, is somehow gone, and as you bleed to death you think you hear it whispering from the drain. Be grateful that isn't you. Be thankful.

Be thankful, too, that you're not trapped in the rubble after the terrorist bomb has reduced the building to a shuddering clinker of ragged stone, two days now, and the sounds of rescuers are very, very distant, *eloquently* distant, and you're in a chamber that was not made for habitation, you're under many tons of rock, with your arms and legs angled—unbroken!—in odd Jerry-Lewis postures, like a dancing Keith Haring drawing, only you're losing sensation in your legs because circulation is cut off by a stone that presses just hard enough, but your arms are aching quite furiously, and, when you move, the rocks above nudge a little closer, a little lower, and small scavenging beetles begin to appear, you can hear their rattling legs on the stones, feel them brush past your mouth, your ears, and you can't feel them begin on your legs, there's no circulation there, but there's a sense of something flowing out of you down there, a coldness that seeps up from your calves to your knees, to your thighs, as you hear the child suddenly wake up and begin screaming for its mother, and you open your mouth to try to speak words of comfort but something chitinous climbs into your mouth and chokes you and . . . Be grateful, thankful, that isn't you.

Be thankful for what you have; be grateful: You might be a child of ten and you might be that child in a leather bag, tied shut, hardly any room, a bag with holes punched in it, listening to the two men talk about the police pursuit, feeling the van lurch to the left and right as they turn corners, hearing one of them say, with the joy of a lottery winner, *Ain't nobody coming after us, was nobody there to see the license number, no pursuit, Joe, we're home free* . . . as you hear that the implications come alive in you and make you claw at the bag and try to scream through the tape over your mouth and one of them slams you through the leather with that two by four you saw just before they pushed you in and it knocks all the breath out of you and as you're getting breath back, each breath stabbing now, he says something about how: *You better hold still in there, you better be glad you're in that bag there and not out here with me you little peter-pusher, and the other one says don't scare him no more'n you have to I don't want to have to gag him after we take him out, I want his mouth free after I take that tape off*, but they're taking some kind of drug, you can't tell what, but you hear them say crystal, and after they make those snorting sounds you can tell from their voices they're losing what control of themselves they have and you feel an icicle become part of your back and realize it's that sharpened screwdriver the red-headed man had, he's sticking it through the bag at random here and here and there, into you, just a half inch in here, and an inch there and it scrapes off your shoulder blade and he's laughing and his friend says *wait, wait till we get to the woods*, and when they do, when they take you out of the bag their faces scare you as much as the tools and soon you beg them *please, please kill me*, but you don't quite die before they shovel the dirt over your eyes. But then you do. Be glad that's not you, be grateful, be thankful. We have much to be thankful for.

Be thankful you're not running on legs that are losing their bones; that's how it feels, as you run, as if the bones in your legs are melting, you're sinking as you run into the street, because you've been running this way for two miles and you're fat and you're not a kid anymore and the truck never relents, the pickup staying ten feet behind, chasing you across the open desert, under a sun that never takes a breath, driving you ahead of it, with a man and a woman and three children in it, the children laughing loudest of all, as you fall in the cacti, naked in the cacti, and get up and run on, and on, stumbling and running, your feet ribbons of flesh, your heart almost louder than their voices and the gunning engine and they are calling you Mexi-nigger, *Mexi-nigger you'd better get up* but your bones have dissolved completely now and you can't get up and the Dad lets the kids, even the girl, practice with the .22 on you, they shoot you in the hips and buttocks and you don't feel it much because of the exhaustion and the fear till one of the slugs hits your pelvis and splinters it and then there's nothing in all the universe but those splinters chewing out of your hip, nothing, anyway, till they lock the chains to your ankles and begin to drag you behind the truck, talking about how those ol' boys in Texas going to be startin' a fad, here, now son I want you to see what a fat Mexi-nigger's guts look like, whoa look at that and his shit too—
Consider: that's not you. It could be you. It's not. Be thankful.

Yes be thankful, you'd better be absolutely grateful that you're not in the bus when it goes off the bridge and fills with water and your little girl, eight years old, beside you, is looking at you with amazement because somehow you've made this happen and you'll never have time to explain that, despite pretending all her life that you could prevent things like this from happening, *In fact, my little love, I was lying, all this time, something like this could happen anytime and only some perverse and unmappable grace prevents it from happening more, it's amazing when we're barreling along by the millions at sixty, seventy, eighty miles an hour on our steaming, tarry freeways that it doesn't happen more, it's amazing that cancer and plane-crashes and murder and war don't happen even more than they do, given that people are just mandrills with clothes on, my little sweet, so you should not be surprised, and I'm sorry I didn't prepare you for this—*

That unspoken speech passing through your head in a split second as you see that look in her face right before the bus hits the estuary, slams the both of you off the ceiling of the bus with bone cracking force, and since your left shoulder shatters you have only your right arm to try to get her through the one open window within reach as water fills the bus, but there's a ferret-faced man, also riding the bus, the man who said he was a lawyer, he's pushing your daughter out of the way so he can swim through, he's kicking you in the face to keep you from jerking him back from the window to let her through first, and beyond him you glimpse more than a dozen pallid faces of other people on the bus, people with bubbles surging up from their mouths as they flap their arms and you claw at the man blocking the only way out, to try to get him out of the way so you can get your daughter through that window but she is clawing at you in desperation, clawing at your eyes, till your own child gouges out one of your eyes in her terror, and then the darkness closes down on you both and it has nothing reassuring, nothing restful in it at all, but just a shattering emptiness and . . . Count your blessings, because that could be you; be grateful that isn't you . . .

x   x   x

Be grateful, thank your ancestors, thank your stars, that you're not being strapped down in the metal chair, that you're not seeing those two distinct, sharp-edged expressions, either one or the other, on the faces of the people watching through the glass—either studied indifference or a fascination that's less than pornographic but not so very much less—and there are people murmuring to you, just as if they care that you're about to be choked to death with chemicals, but they don't, not really, they don't actually care and they won't think about it after tomorrow or the next day, and the worst part is the fact, the unblemished, untarnished certainty that you and only you have, that you are innocent of the crime for which you're being executed, you *really are* innocent, not "*they all say they're innocent* innocent", but *authentically* innocent . . . and you know it will be believed that you raped and strangled two women whom you never actually saw or heard of, because someone stole your car and used it in the crime, someone who looks a little like you, someone of the same dark race . . . and you know, too, that not only will your guilt be believed by the public, by history, but *your wife, your children, your father, and mother* will believe that you are guilty, even though they made cardboard protestations to the contrary, ultimately they will believe it, and so the children will blame you for abandoning them, and no one will ever be truly sorry, except maybe the children, who will also hate you—

No one will be sorry that you are now hearing the sound of the chamber door clicking shut, the last time you will hear a door shut, or a click of a lock, that you are hearing the sound of the cyanide capsules hitting the bucket to release the poison into the air; no one will really care that you have only one last clean breath left and that the next one is like a rabid animal clawing into your lungs as you shake and choke and shake and die . . . all the while knowing you are innocent and being killed for nothing.

Be grateful, show some gratitude: that could have been you. And it's not.

x   x   x

Be thankful, breathe a sigh of relief and nod your head in humble gratitude that you're not a neurotic fan of perverse dark literature, horror or crime or dark fantasy, a reader, at least today, of the obsessively-etched stimuli that is one of your few releases from the smothering sense of is-this-all-there-is in your life, that you're not that sort of person, reliant on occasional corrosive chemicals or puerile graphic images for relief from the inarticulate and undefined and never acknowledged knowledge that you are being hunted, something just out of the circle of your perceptions is hunting you: your own meaninglessness is hunting you, your own irrelevance, your trapped in a dead-end, soulless, monkey-masturbatory, mazelike civilization that you mock like a bad videogame even as you sock in another quarter, as your brain turns slowly, slowly inside your skull, scanning for an exit in an exitless world, as you lurch onto the next half-satisfying stimulus like the dying cocaine rat that pushes the lever; as you realize that your understanding of the unknown sculpture of your life is really only of the chisel-scrapings at the foot of the sculpture, and you never have seen the sculpture, and that you're really truly trapped in a culture that, despite your arch commentary, your well-honed irony, your media-fed sardonicism, has conditioned and programmed you just as thoroughly as any Shopping-channel fixated Tennessee housewife; that despite your creative conceits you're probably going to degrade yourself for the opportunity to die in an upscale old-people's-home instead of in an SRO hotel—after your youth is burned up in media dreams and gossip that has a life of its own and relationships that jar and sputter and circle blindly like bumper cars, and the loneliness of the long distance consumer, a hollow life in a hollow society of equally hollow people—be glad and grateful that's not . . . you.

SCREW

The first time the world shook, it was five in the morning, Pacific time, and the shuddering of the planet jarred Colin from a dream of shame and regret.

He was squirming halfway off his futon, dreaming, his feet overturning a mug, and the wet coffee on his bare heel became toilet water overflowing around his feet as a detective in the dream told him he was busted for killing some guy: a man he'd killed to hide embezzlement. The detective wavered, vanished into the blue light of the television screen Colin had left on when he'd gone to sleep . . . as he sat up in the otherwise dark room, flailing for a hold, just as the shaking stopped.

But he knew the shaking hadn't been a dream. He could see a lamp overturned, a couple of fallen framed pictures, in the electric-blue light from the neon sign outside his window. The sign jutted up over the Chinese restaurant downstairs; a cryptic ideogram burning like eidetic psychedelia against the black and gray San Francisco sky.

There were sirens yowling outside, and car alarms squalling like awakened infants. Had the Big One come, finally?

Some sick feeling—some bone-deep feeling, resonating from his core—told him that this was no local earthquake. This was planetary. This was . . .

"It was like a big shared hallucination," Tanlee was saying, three and a half hours later, in the kitchen of the penthouse where Colin had his temp job.

They were standing by the microwave, waiting for the little plate of chocolate croissants to heat up, each of them sipping the Peet's coffee provided by InterReal. An international real estate company –most of its operations beyond Colin's meager business understanding— InterReal was headquartered in London, but the firm's chief of staff, Mrs. Koyne, maintained offices all over the world.

Tanlee glanced at her watch. "I went into my roommate's bedroom, and I'm all, 'Linda, did you feel that?' And she goes, 'I think I dreamed it—but wait you dreamed it too? No way!'" Tanlee was second generation Asian American with a Southern California accent: she'd grown up in Sherman Oaks.

The microwave chimed and she turned lithely to take the plate out, put it on the counter. As she did this Colin looked at her tight retro clothes, ironic leopard-pattern capris and sleeveless shell sweater, her tiny little feet in her tiny little black shoes, and tried to picture her modern-dancing—gracefully gyrating, meaningfully writhing, into his arms. She was mysterious to Colin: she could play the Asian Val, but then she'd change direction, and go focused and serious. As now, when she tore off a corner off the croissant, nibbling at it as she said, "Um—Miss Koyne's going to be here soon. And I'm sort of—scared to be here when she gets here. Do you ever, get that feeling that there're all these lines converging in your life—like all kinds of things are coming together and when they meet they might . . . I don't know . . . *explode?*"

He wasn't sure what she meant, but he liked her confiding in him. Maybe one of these days she'd stop making excuses about going out. So he said, "Oh *yeah,*" with as much conviction as possible.

"It's like, I have this theory? That there're some lines of events that are from your own life? And other lines are from outside? And they have some relationship you can't see but they are mutually attracted according to some . . . some law we don't know about?"

That vapid tone, thought Colin, and making everything sound like a question—she sounded like an airhead till you really listened to what she was saying. It was if she were embarrassed about her intelligence.

He nodded. "I know what you mean—kind of. Um, intuitively. And that thing everyone felt last night . . ."

"Exactly. And there's something about Mrs. Koyne that—" She broke off, glancing at the door. "So how's your writing coming? Did you finish that play?"

He was a little taken aback by her shift of topic. Like something had spooked her. She was looking toward the front of the penthouse.

He picked up a croissant, but didn't feel like really eating it. "I finished a draft of it . . ." He was embarrassed to be an aspiring writer at thirty-six with nothing but a few literary zine publications behind him, some college drama sketches produced—if you could call that produced. He felt like his own personal drama had stalled. He was perpetually waiting in a green room somewhere.

Then he felt a gust of cold air that raised goose bumps on his arm— why was the air so cold, coming from the enclosed hall where the elevator was?—and he knew that Mrs. Koyne was in the penthouse.

That's when the second shudder went through the world. He felt this one mostly in his intestines, in a way; deep in his gut, but coming from the direction of his navel. It was an invasiveness that made him go up on his tiptoes for a moment—Tanlee did the same, her eyes widening—as the building rumbled to itself. Their centers of gravity—his, Tanlee's, the building's—wavered like tops losing spin. His heart thudded and he thought: This really is the Big One—

And then the shaking was gone. Or—it had moved on.

He leaned panting against the counter. "What the fuck was that?" He felt close to throwing up.

"Some adjustments are being made," said Mrs. Koyne, coming in. "Old accounts being closed."

Colin thought at first she was replying to his blurted question but now he saw she had been calmly talking on the cell phone to someone. The headset phone was cunningly worked into her frosted-black coif. Mrs. Koyne was a tall woman, angularly slender to the point of anorexia, with large green eyes in a V-shaped face. She was sealed into a low-cut iridescent designer dress suit, just a hint of a slit up the skirt; smoke-blue Italian pumps, a loose lady's bracelet watch on one bird-boned wrist.

She swept with imperial indifference through the small space of the kitchen, so that Colin and Tanlee had to back against the counter. Their employer strode to the refrigerator, got the pitcher of veggie juice drinks always waiting for her, poured green liquid into a tall glass while speaking into the designer mouthpiece arcing like elegant jewelry near her thin, pink-glossed lips.

"Just tell them that—yes, China too—all the factors are coalescing, the timing is perfect. I have one or two indicators to check but InterReal is already on the move, we're closing the deal."

Colin glanced at Tanlee, thinking to share a look of amazement at Mrs. Koyne's complete lack of response to the earthquake. But the look on Tanlee's face—as she leaned against a cabinet, one hand on her midriff, gazing at Mrs. Koyne—was bitter resignation. Tanlee looked so much older and wiser than ever before . . .

"Exactly . . . right. I'll see you up there." Mrs. Koyne switched off the tiny cell phone, turning to Colin and Tanlee.

Colin wanted to be impressively cool-headed but he found himself stuttering. "Um—maybe we should get down to . . . to, I don't know, the street or—wherever we're supposed to go in case of an earthquake?" Then he realized Mrs. Koyne was staring at his hand with distaste. He saw that he had convulsively clenched the croissant during the shudder, dough and chocolate squeezed out between his fingers along the back of his hand and dolloped on the otherwise immaculate tile floor. "Oh jeez, I'm sorry—I just—Christ—" Washing his hand in the sink, cleaning the floor with a wet paper towel. "—I just . . . I was startled by . . . by that quaking . . ."

"Maybe we *should* go downstairs, though, Mrs. Koyne," Tanlee said, watching the other woman closely.

Mrs. Koyne made a pitying chuckle. "You thought there was an earthquake? Nonsense. A little *quiver*, is all. This is California, aren't you used to it by now?" She sipped at her juice and set it down on the counter.

"Shouldn't we at least check the news channels?" Tanlee persisted.

"We've no time for pointless fears. This is a critical moment for us. Now come along. Let's get cracking."

Colin and Tanlee followed her, reluctantly drawn in the slipstream of her authority. They filed into the big main room of the penthouse. Taking up most of the top floor, the vast room was organized around a single flat-black desk with three chairs, in the middle of the rust colored carpet, and two dark brown leather sofas facing one another. The sunlight suffusing the room was thinned by polarized window walls on two opposite sides. Three mobiles hung from the ceiling—two Miro and one Calder—but they hung immobile, as if freeze-framed. A big computer hard drive in the center of the desk connected to Mrs. Koyne's monitor and two smaller monitors and keyboards on the sides. Mrs. Koyne had already laid out sheaves of paperwork.

Colin felt strange, taking his usual leather swivel chair at the little work station set up on one side of the big desk; Tanlee sat across from him, Mrs. Koyne at the larger chair between. It was strange because he could still feel that planetary shudder echoing in his nervous system—it was like the feeling you get just before the stomach flu comes on—and he was pretty sure they ought to be heading for some earthquake shelter somewhere. Wasn't there one in the basement of this high-rise?

But the computer booted up almost instantly, as if in feverish excitement, and Mrs. Koyne's fingers were already flying over the primary keyboard. She clicked on the InterReal multiple-input program and they began the data entry that she'd been guiding them through for weeks, each of them filling out different sections of the same form.

Somedays Tanlee would go off by herself to do errands for Mrs. Koyne; to fetch the boss's lunch, to pick up her dry cleaning, to sort through voicemail. Today she and Colin were tapping away like drones to Mrs. Koyne's ant queen, entering buy numbers, dates, strange foreign place-names, sending form letters for eviction to agencies who were bribed to implement them, transferring money and deeds—or that's what it was supposed to be, but Colin found it all very cryptic. Just now he seemed to be helping Mrs. Koyne buy an apartment building in Hong Kong, but—

Suddenly he was aware that she had stopped typing. She seemed to be listening with her head cocked. Then she turned her head, the motion sharp and abrupt, to stare at him, unblinking, her smile condescending and crooked.

"Tell me about the last thing you remember dreaming, Colin," Mrs. Koyne said. "I mean—last night. Can you remember?"

Colin stared at her, and had to make a conscious effort to close his mouth so he wouldn't be gaping. "Uh—what I dreamt?" From any of his friends, this would not have been an odd question. It was something the bohemian types he hung with would talk about. From Mrs. Koyne it was startlingly unprecedented. "Well—I dreamt I was . . . was being . . ."

"Accused? Was it *accused?*" She leaned toward him. Her breath smelled like a burnt-out match.

And he was astonished that she'd hit it right. "Well yeah. I guess it was—a detective . . . a plainclothes cop . . . accusing me of murdering someone. And embezzling. And the weird thing was when I woke . . . it was like . . . I dunno . . ." He glanced at Tanlee, embarrassed.

Mrs. Koyne pressed him, "It was like you were—ashamed? Even after waking up, and even knowing you hadn't embezzled or murdered?"

"That's . . . pretty amazing, Mrs. Koyne. Yes. I felt ashamed—though I knew it was a dream." He tried to chuckle companionably. "You have a bug under my pillow?"

"Not as such." She turned to Tanlee. "And you?"

Tanlee's face had gone hard, her brown-black eyes brittle. "I don't recall."

"Oh, come. A dream in which you were accused of a crime you never committed . . . and for which you felt *ashamed,* even after you woke and knew it was but a dream? Yes?"

Tanlee shook her head briskly. "No!"

But Colin knew, somehow, that Tanlee was lying. It was in the way she'd fractionally shrunk in on herself, sitting there, as if trying to protect some vulnerable place. She had dreamed something like that. How did Mrs. Koyne know? She'd never spoken to them of any psychic ability—they'd never spoken of *anything* personal, except now and then she asked about career plans, and family, in a polite, chilly, fill-in-the-blanks kind of way that seemed to suggest she'd rather not know anything more than the minimum.

"Ah!" Mrs. Koyne said, then, looking fiercely into the computer.

There was a hard light in her eyes, in her whole face, a hungry intensity Colin had never seen before as she murmured, "Yes— here too, the dreams prefigured the noumenal adjustment—all on schedule . . ." He realized she was speaking into her headset, though he hadn't seen her switch it on. Who was she talking to? He had never met Mr. Koyne.

He glanced at her computer monitor—and his heart seemed to squeeze out the next beat, as if barely making it from one beat to the next.

Mrs. Koyne's monitor was oozing colors onto its plastic frame, onto the keyboard and desk. It was as if the colors of the software windows, primary colors no longer digital but with an electric tinge—a lot like that ideogram neon outside his window at home— were solidifying, liquefying, running, and then *stretching out,* twining like yarn, elongating through space to web the room. And within the multicolored strands pulsed something pink, which he sensed was a vital human essence, with now and then a glimpse of an elongated eye slipping through the tube of light; a distended mouth, teeth and fingers rippling by and gone, each liquefied person passing with a sound like an infinitely dopplering moan, a thousand, a million moans layered and overlapping . . .

Colin was up and lurching backwards, away from the flesh-charged moaning light, so that he stumbled over his chair and fell hard on his right side—and found himself staring at a seeking tendril of flesh-pumped colored light coming across the floor, probing right at his face like a sizzling rivulet of hot wax.

"Shit!" He scrambled back from it—just as another long, planetary shudder rippled through the world. Again he felt the quaking nose through him, as if it had sought him personally, and it knew his name and his whole life, and the feeling made his gorge rise, his muscles convulse, so that he squirmed on the carpet and moaned, his moan sickeningly like the moans still reverberating from the overflowing computer.

The quaking died down—but this time commenced again almost at once. A little plaster sifted down from the ceiling, and there were shouts of fear from the people in the offices a storey below, barely audible under the collective moaning from the spreading strands of fleshy light. And the mobiles turning jigglingly, up near the ceiling.

He rolled away from the living, toxic glimmer—he didn't know how he knew it was in some sense toxic, he just knew. He sat up, and Tanlee was standing over him, bracing herself, rocking slightly as another shaking passed through, and putting out her hand to him. He took it—a small hand, but she was strong and pulled him to his feet. They clung to each other for a moment, as the building creaked and quivered. Where had Mrs. Koyne gone? He could no longer see her.

A kind of living, weaving tree of light was twisting through the open spaces of the room—he ducked back as it stretched toward him. And there—a crack was spreading through the farthest glass wall, from the lower frame. *Crick*, it cracked a little farther. A hesitation. Then, *crick*, a new direction. A waiting. A shiver. *Crick crick crick—and CRICK—*

The entire wall of glass shattered and fell away with an in-gust of wind and a symphonic crashing–Tanlee giving a small scream, Colin hissing *"Fuck!"* They staggered as the air sucked at them. The mobiles spinning, tangling, falling. He realized that if the nearer wall had burst they'd have staggered to fall twenty-three stories down. They steadied one another, and Tanlee shouted something he couldn't hear over the moaning from the spreading lights, the crackling of flames from somewhere below; the sirens; the rumbling of buildings uneasy in their sockets; the crackle of glass and the sough of wind.

Another long planetary quiver, and the vibration seemed to roil the living light from the computer, to draw it in a twisting suction toward the window. There was something else, something he thought was like a tornado, in the urban distance, but a whirlwind impossibly big—big as a mountain.

Tanlee tugged at him and he let her draw him along the creaking, crick-cracking glass wall to their left, toward the corridor leading to the bedrooms and the door out of the suite. Tanlee shouted something in his ear. He made out only part of it: "I've known for a while . . . wasn't human . . . some of them are, and some aren't . . . I saw into her once . . . she . . . a bottle that could move and there was a thing in it . . . intelligent but not . . . I stayed to find out, to know . . . Those who sent me . . ." A glassy crash and roaring of intrusive air, from behind, drowned the rest of her words.

The suite's bedrooms were used only occasionally by InterReal execs, sometimes by Mrs. Koyne—and she was there, he saw, as Tanlee drew him through the bedroom door.

Mrs. Koyne was rotating in place in the exact center of the large bedroom, the heels of her pumps dangling about an inch off the carpet. It was as if she was on a turntable going a little faster than 33 rpm, but there was no turntable. Something unseen was turning her, upright in space. She seemed quite content, more overtly happy than he'd ever seen her.

One of the windows had shattered and the gold-colored curtains flapped; another long shudder rippled through the building and the walls showed a slowly spreading fracture, and an abstract painting fell, its glass cover tinkling into shards, its chaotic imagery celebrating the room's disintegration. All the while, Mrs. Koyne spun in place, smiling, going fractionally faster now. Colin felt a wave of nausea shimmer through him—it seemed to match the subtle vertical undulating Mrs. Koyne was making with her whole body, as she rotated and moved up and down, a kind of feeding in that motion.

"Oh . . . motherfucker . . ." Colin heard himself say. "Tanlee if you understand something, anything about any of this . . ."

"She has begun . . ." Mrs. Koyne said. She paused as she rotated away, speaking rapidly as she came back around, completing her sentences in passing segments. ". . . to see . . ." She whipped around. Came back. ". . . some others have . . ." Gone, back: ". . . far too late . . . I knew . . . they sent her . . . to observe me . . . but it didn't . . . matter at all . . . We have been here for so long, our roots deep . . . into the organism . . . of the world . . ." Was she spinning faster now? "You must . . . have known somehow . . . years ago . . . when you . . . saw the world . . . despoiled . . . sucked . . . .dry and . . . used up . . . that someone . . . that many . . . from outside . . . were feed . . . ing."

The building gave a great lurch, then, and an accompanying tremble ran through Colin, and Tanlee too—somehow he could feel it passing through her as it passed through him—and they had to clutch at the walls to keep from falling. But the walls themselves were falling, the wall behind the bed bending toward them, breaking along the bend. Mrs. Koyne seemed utterly unconcerned—her smile flashed by unchanged.

"You . . . might . . . go . . . to roof . . . for . . . a . . . few more . . . moments . . . togeth . . . er . . ." Mrs. Koyne said, her voice coming more high-pitched.

In the whirling blur of Mrs. Koyne it seemed to Colin that some inner verity was unveiled, and he could see a vaguely woman-shaped thing, but with a stretched-out lamprey mouths in a spiral pattern all around its body, and puckered vents issuing giggling pink smoke.

Tanlee was weeping, shouting something over the shrieking, grinding walls and the flowing moans, the rising chorus of sirens—Colin could only make out, "Some of us knew . . . no one would listen . . . we're not just fodder, Mrs. Koyne, this isn't your sheep ranch . . ."

But the rackety high pitched sound from Mrs. Koyne, blurring now, might have been laughter—no, it was some other, inhuman mode of expression compounded of glee, triumph, mocking pity, and giddy relief: the release of unspeakable feelings long suppressed.

Colin took Tanlee by the wrist and pulled her down the rollicking hallway, remembering a State Fair funhouse he'd liked as a boy, where the floor buckled all rubbery underfoot—and the laughing white-faced, red-lipped vampire face whose mouth had been the entrance of the funhouse.

He paused at the door to the hall—the door which was changing shape from a rectangle to a rhombus—and glanced over his shoulder down the hall to the main room. It was murky in there, except for piercing, lancing forks of light emanating from the wreckage of the computer, from light sockets, wall plugs, all of it angling, bending toward the shattered window facing the bay.

He turned away as the floor gave another convulsive lurch under them, and he pulled Tanlee through the collapsing doorway, down the dust-choked hall to the utility stairs. The bent metal door hung open. Through the widening fissures in the walls they could see the adjacent buildings, swaying.

Then Colin and Tanlee burst from the little outbuilding onto the windy roof.

The roof was sheathed with aluminum and a white insulating gravel, crisscrossed with external ventilator conduits—one of these was buckling now, as if to greet their arrival, snapping up to wave like a ragged blade at the roiling sky. A girder had already broken somewhere below, jammed up through the roof, and as it seemed fairly stable they went to it and clung on, gazing about them, their eyes drawn to the sky where the clouds spun, spiraled inward toward the thing that dominated the city; that owned the horizon:

It was an impossibly big, dull-silver tornado shape, tapering toward the ground, spinning over San Francisco Bay to tower over the Bay Bridge, its top lost in spiraling mists. But as they gazed, they saw that it was not a tornado—it wasn't a construction of dense air, or even debris whirling in air. It was something solid. Solid, but turning. Screwing. There was a translucent spinning envelope of energy around the grey inner shape that made it seem like a whirlwind— but the solid inner shape wasn't in fact turning rapidly. Within the envelope of energy it was turning about once every second, or second and a half.

From the windows of crumbling buildings all around them, the seeking feelers of living, flesh-crawling light branched and nosed and oozed toward the great inverted cone driving itself into the bay. Like the clouds, the seawater below, the debris sucked toward it, the branchings of restless light twined and tightened around the turning shape digging into the world—where it made a sucking funnel of the water. With each distinctive turn of the striated cone came another planetary shudder. Colin felt a shadow of comfort in being able to see the source of the quaking.

There was a sputtering *thud* behind them, penetrating the thick background clamor of the disintegrating city, and they turned to see the roof burst open in a shape like a flower petal opening, neatly folded back petals of metal and substructure and insulation, and from the flower rose a whirling murk of tattering fabric, exposed flesh, hair whipping about blurred grin: Mrs. Koyne. She ascended over the roof and made that gleeful tittering sound of relief, and then— still vertical relative to the rooftops—flew toward the great twisting steely cone digging into the world out in the bay.

Other buildings were rupturing in exactly the same way; flowers of torn metal disgorged whirling figures that zipped giddily through the sky to converge around the inverted cone. Only a few came from each building.

"Her kind," Tanlee shouted over the din, "they are showing themselves now."

"Someone sent you to spy on her?" Colin asked.

"Some of us have known . . . I had to play a role, and watch, and try to find some way . . ." She shook her head. "There was no stopping them. We gave them the world in the last century."

"Who? Who are they? Are they like . . . aliens?"

"They're from *outside*. But they're not from another planet in the way you . . ." The rest of the sentence was swallowed up in a great roar of protest from the infrastructure of the city itself, its streets and foundations and pipes and wires and girders, all twisting out of shape as the screw turning in the bay tightened another thread—and this turn of the thread pulled everything fatally out of alignment, and drew it closer to the screw.

That's what it was, Colin realized—Tanlee knew it at the same moment, he could feel that—the thing digging into the world was *a screw*, a literal, unimaginably gigantic screw, extending up through the troposphere into the tropopause, maybe beyond, a screw digging down through the bay and into the sand, down into the soil, biting the rock, penetrating the crust, the magma, eventually the core of the Earth itself.

Smoke undulated up from the shattered buildings—the billowy motion like Mrs. Koyne's undulation as she spun—and flame licked and jetted, but it seemed almost muted, secondary, as another change was making the conventional destruction of an earthquake something that didn't apply: the city's hard shapes had softened at their edges, as if the fabric of material reality was redefining to accommodate the great screw digging into the world—

The screw digging in, pausing—turning, pausing—turning, pausing—turning—digging deeper—

The city's metal and glass and concrete became something rubbery, infused with a unifying glue that kept it in one stretching piece, the shore distending out to join with the sea—which seemed to grow glutinous, around the threading column—all of it merging to twine around the great screw, and to draw into its substance . . .

Their building began to move—the building he and Tanlee stood on was like a cobra slithering with its upper length held up over the ground, toward the bay, toward the great screw twisting into the planet. Colin suddenly understood what was happening. "It's screwing into the world and . . . absorbing it . . . taking all the strength and energy and order from it and sucking it up into itself . . ."

"Yes," she said, slipping an arm around his waist. "Look! You see how Mrs. Koyne's people—"

"They're not people!" he shouted angrily.

"They're a kind of people! They're not so different—they're a parasitic species from some dimension—the fifth dimension, maybe—and they're not so different from us, which is why they can work with us—you see them up there, floating in the sky, arranged around the screw? They're feeding through it! But most of what they're stealing is going back to their world—pure living energy, the life force of Gaia—"

"Those streamers of lights—liquid people, from the computer—" He broke off as the shuddering redoubled, the roof responding by wrinkling up under their feet, its square top becoming a diamond shape pointed at the screw. All the squares of the city becoming diamonds, narrowing diamonds, angling toward the ineffably gigantic screw.

"They're like phantoms—metaphysical—"

"What? The noise!"

"—metaphysical reverberations from the suffering, the exploitation, the sheer *wringing* of life from people and the world—and we were part of it, we were part of the corporation, the society that fed on it all, me and you, taking part in gouging the planet, pushing people out of their rightful places, so that *they* could suck up their strength, their hope, their spiritual force—"

"But that was all money, they were just taking money, it's just . . . currency!" he shouted. Thinking now he was hearing the real Tanlee, meeting the real Tanlee—when it was too late.

"Oh what does mean—" Another phrase lost. "—say 'currency'? We were all part of selling our world out to these soulless things— moral choices have metaphysical—" An echoing roar from the city blotted the rest of her statement. But Colin could feel the rightness of it in his bones.

Colin thought about it, as the city went soft and mutable and coursed in compressed threads up the great screw, the screw crunching deeper with each quaking turn into the shivering world. Not long before he'd heard about lobbyists who'd suppressed every effort at banning goods from countries using child-slaves for labor; he'd heard hundreds of thousands of American tourists overseas paid to have sex with children; he knew that the great forests were being razed, the seas poisoned. And on and on it went.

People knew these things were happening—but someone always prevented anything really significant being done about them. Who? Who let this go grindingly on, like a great screw twisting into the world? Ordinary greedy human beings?

No. Humanity had to have been infiltrated. Seduced, distracted, entranced. Enslaved.

And all of it had led to this moment, this culmination; the patchwork harvesting had ended and now had come the final harvesting of the world.

As these thoughts swirled in his mind, so the sea, the city, the land, the great Bay Bridge itself, twisted like debris sucking in a drain around the great, the ineffably gigantic screw that was biting, digging deeper and deeper into the world, with a grinding noise that grew so loud no further talk could pass between him and Tanlee, and there was only their embrace. There was only time for the intimacy of shared despair. For there was no hope of escape—when even the mountains and the core of the Earth were being drawn into the great spinning shaft . . . and what remained of Colin and Tanlee's roof, too, rushed toward the towering screw.

Now their part of the crushed city, the compressing rooftops, went spinning around the steely shaft, just as tiny strips of wood are pulled around a drill digging into a plank, and Colin, staring up at the stupendous screw, could see there were distinct sharp screw-threads in the side, just exactly like a woodscrew but each thread wider than an eight-lane freeway. And looking past the screw as they were pulled around and around its shaft—too amazedly caught up in the majestic dismantling of the world, too overwhelmed to be frightened—they saw the crumbling, melting skylines of other cities from far away: Hong Kong and London and New York and Denver and Peking and Moscow and Cairo and others they didn't recognize, pulled into the screw.

All the cities of the world were being drawn through some transdimensional shortcut to converge on the screw, the one great screw that in a thousand separate places was digging into the world, creak-creak-squeak, screeeee, screwing right through its heart. The planet twisting around the screw, sucking into it as if collapsing into a black hole. Screaming, billions of people deliquesced into concrete, asphalt, melting steel and gushing magma, sizzling seawater—

Near the end, just before they were sucked into the merging of roof and metal and sea and flesh and stone and lava, Colin and Tanlee looked up along the turning, sharp-threaded shaft of the screw. They saw clearly that it was a thing of energy, and a thing of metal at once; that it was an expression of the city, of the world, and that it was also otherworldly; they saw that it was death for some, life for others.

And then the screw turned one thread more.

ORIGINAL PUBLICATION DATA

Animus Rights (*Asimov's Science Fiction*, December 2009)

Call Girl, Echoed (Originally published as part of "TechnoTriptych," *Dark Wisdom #8*, Winter, 2006)

Cram (*Wetbones*, Fall 1997)

Cul-de-Sac (*Flurb, Issue #2*, Winter 2006-2007)

Faces in Walls (*Black Static # 17*, June 2010 [UK])

Gotterdammergun (*Horror Garage # 6*, 2002)

"I Want to Get Married," Says the World's Smallest Man (*Midnight Graffiti*, ed. Jessica Horsting & James Van Hise, Warner 1992)

Just a Suggestion (*The Bleeding Edge*, ed. William F. Nolan & Jason V. Brock, Cycatrix Press/Dark Discoveries, 2009)

Just Like Suzie (*Cemetery Dance #9*, Summer 1991)

Learn at Home! Your Career in Evil! (*Embraces*, ed. Paula Guran, Venus or Vixen Press, 2000)

Paper Angels On Fire (*Sick Things*, ed. Cheryl Mullenax, Comet Press, 2010)

Raise Your Hand if You're (*Dead Dark Discoveries #17*, Spring 2010)

Screw (*Interzone #189*, May/June 2003 [UK])

Skeeter Junkie (*New Noir*, Fiction Collective Two, 1993)

Smartbomber (Originally published as part of "TechnoTriptych," *Dark Wisdom #8*, Winter, 2006)

Ten Things To Be Grateful For (*Gothic.Net*, November 1998)

The Exquisitely Bleeding Heads of Doktur Palmer Vreedeez (*Black Butterflies*, Mark V. Ziesing, 1998)

The Gun As An Aid To Poetry (Original to this volume. Copyright © 2011 John Shirley)
Tighter (*Darkness Divided*, Stealth Press, 2001)

You Blundering Idiot, You Fucking Failed To Kill Me Again! (*Swill # 4*, 2009)

You Hear What Buddy and Ray Did? (*Forbidden Acts*, ed. Nancy A. Collins, Edward E. Kramer & Martin H. Greenberg, Avon 1995)

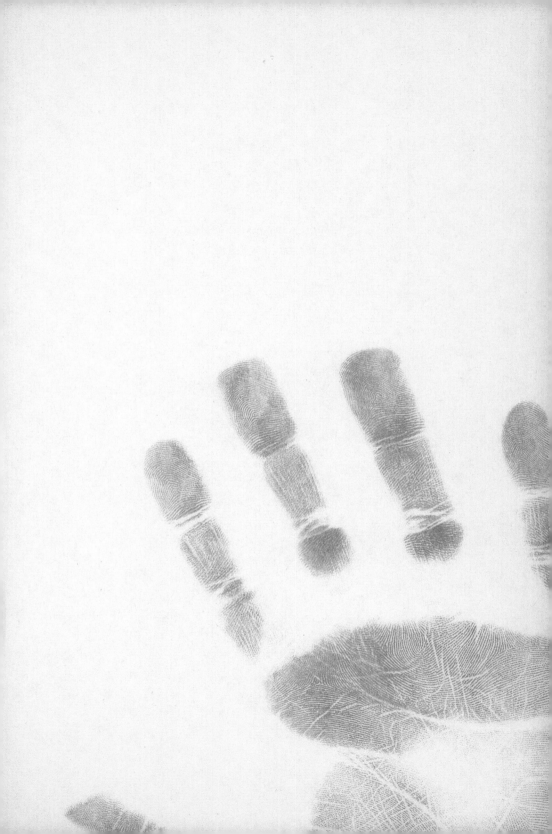